I

Newsmakers #3

ADVANCE ACCLAIM FOR *THE SEPARATISTS*

"Visceral and timely, Wiehl's reportage and storytelling blend beautifully— *The Separatists* is a compelling mystery and exceptional addition to the Newsmakers series."

— KARIN SLAUGHTER, *NEW YORK TIMES* AND #1 INTERNATIONALLY BESTSELLING WRITER

"BREAKING NEWS! Lis Wiehl has written another blockbuster - using her insider's eye to nail the dangerous mix of media and politics. *The Separatists* is bold, timely, thrilling and a simply stunning read."

—LINDA FAIRSTEIN, *NEW YORK TIMES* BESTSELLING AUTHOR

ACCLAIM FOR *THE CANDIDATE*

". . . there is plenty of suspense, exciting twists and complex characters that make it hard to put down."

—*RT BOOK REVIEWS*, 4-STAR REVIEW

"*The Candidate* is a political thrill ride. It's like being thrown into the middle of a presidential campaign, but with some major—and terrifying—twists. Never has the corruption of power been more chillingly portrayed. This book is a spellbinding trip into the heart of darkness. I couldn't put it down."

—RITA COSBY, EMYY-WINNING TV HOST, RADIO HOST, AND BESTSELLING AUTHOR

"Lis Wiehl's latest thriller *The Candidate* opens a number of windows for the reader. Can an ambitious reporter keep her soul while fighting her way to the top of the TV news industry? That intense conflict will keep you turning pages."

—BILL O'REILLY, FOX NEWS ANCHOR

ACCLAIM FOR *THE NEWSMAKERS*

"This book is distinctive, with a terrific plot and an imperfect main character who is spellbinding. Kudos to Lis Wiehl for imaginative, yet absolutely believable in this 'me' world, great writing. Wiehl has distanced herself from the pack with this one."

—*Suspense Magazine*

". . . Wiehl is more than up to the task in crafting a superb page-turner as provocative as it is scary."

—*Providence Journal*

"Wiehl's insider knowledge of the television news industry gives this novel credibility and excitement beyond the everyday tale."

—*RT Book Reviews*, 4-star review

"*The Newsmakers* is sure to grip readers and open their eyes to the intense field that is journalism."

—*CBA Retailers + Resources*

"*The Newsmakers*—introducing a compelling new character in cable-news star Erica Sparks—is a twisty, suspenseful adventure with the ring of authenticity that only an insider could provide. Wiehl and Stuart bring us into the world of major-league broadcasting with verve and thrills."

—William Landay, *New York Times* bestselling author of *Defending Jacob*

"A heart-pounding thrill ride from someone who knows the news business inside out. Lis Wiehl's *The Newsmakers* is not to be missed!"

—Karin Slaughter, author of *Pretty Girls*

"A page-turner from the word 'go'! Completely entertaining! Outrageously readable! This quick-cut action-thriller spotlights television's cutthroat deal-making, unholy alliances, and lust for success. Gotta love Lis! As always, she nails it."

—Hank Phillippi Ryan, Agatha, Anthony, and Mary Higgins Clark award-winning author of *What You See*

"*The Newsmakers* is a stunning debut thriller in a new series by one of my favorite authors. Lis Wiehl casts her insider's eye on the intrigue and drama of high-stakes television journalism. Terrorist attack? Murder of a presidential candidate? A reporter whose own life is at risk? This thrill ride has them all. Wiehl has crafted another bestselling winner with this powerful crime novel."

—LINDA FAIRSTEIN, *NEW YORK TIMES* BESTSELLING AUTHOR

"Lis Wiehl is a seasoned journalist who knows the news business. Here, she's fashioned a tantalizing story that takes full advantage of her insider status. It's a fascinating thriller, which poses a curious question: What happens when reality is not quite good enough? The answer is going to shock you."

—STEVE BERRY, *NEW YORK TIMES* BESTSELLING AUTHOR

"*The Newsmakers* is sensational—taut, troubling, and terrifying. With Erica Sparks, Lis Wiehl has created her most memorable character yet: a reporter who has smarts, drive, heart—and a dark past that threatens to pull her down. Waiting for book two won't be easy."

—KATE WHITE, *NEW YORK TIMES* BESTSELLING AUTHOR

ACCLAIM FOR *A DEADLY BUSINESS*

"The second Mia Quinn mystery is action-packed from the first page. Layers of lies and deception make for a twisting, turning story that will keep mystery lovers entranced. This is a thrill ride until the very end, so hang on tight and enjoy the trip!"

—*PUBLISHERS WEEKLY* REVIEW, 4 STARS

"Wiehl's experience as a former federal prosecutor gives the narrative an authenticity in its depiction of the criminal justice system. Henry's expertise in writing mysteries and thrillers has placed her on the short-list for the Agatha, Anthony, and Oregon Book awards. The coauthors' . . . fast-paced detective series will keep legal thriller readers and John Grisham fans totally engrossed."

—*LIBRARY JOURNAL* REVIEW

"Wiehl has woven a wonderfully multi-layered story that will have readers on the edge of their seats . . . *A Deadly Business* delivers everything we love in a massively good mystery."

—CBA Retailers & Resources Review

ACCLAIM FOR *A MATTER OF TRUST*

"This suspenseful first in a new series from Wiehl and Henry opens with a bang."

—Publishers Weekly

"Wiehl begins an exciting new series with prosecutor Mia at the center. The side storyline about bullying is timely and will hit close to home for many."

—RT Book Reviews, 4 stars

"Dramatic, moving, intense. *A Matter of Trust* gives us an amazing insight into the life of a prosecutor—and mom. Mia Quinn reminds me of Lis."

—Maxine Paetro, *New York Times* bestselling author

"*A Matter of Trust* is a stunning crime series debut from one of my favorite authors, Lis Wiehl. Smart, suspenseful, and full of twists that only an insider like Wiehl could pull off. I want prosecutor Mia Quinn in my corner when murder's on the docket—she's a compelling new character and I look forward to seeing her again soon."

—Linda Fairstein, *New York Times* bestselling author

ACCLAIM FOR THE TRIPLE THREAT SERIES

"Only a brilliant lawyer, prosecutor, and journalist like Lis Wiehl could put together a mystery this thrilling! The incredible characters and nonstop twists will leave you mesmerized. Open [*Face of Betrayal*] and find a comfortable seat because you won't want to put it down!"

—E. D. Hill, FOX News anchor

"Who killed loudmouth radio guy Jim Fate? The game is afoot! *Hand of Fate* is a fun thriller, taking you inside the media world and the justice system—scary places to be!"

—BILL O'REILLY, FOX NEWS AND RADIO ANCHOR

"Beautiful, successful, and charismatic on the outside, but underneath a twisted killer. She's brilliant and crazy and comes racing at the reader with knives and a smile. The most chilling villain you'll meet . . . because she could live next door to you."

—DR. DALE ARCHER, CLINICAL PSYCHIATRIST, REGARDING *HEART OF ICE*

ACCLAIM FOR *SNAPSHOT*

"The writing is strong and the plot is engaging, driven by the desires (both good and evil) of the characters and the reader's desire to know who killed a man decades before, how it was covered up, and whether an innocent man has been charged and imprisoned. The book offers a 'snapshot' of the civil rights movement and turbulent times."

—*PUBLISHERS WEEKLY*

"A pitch-perfect plot that tackles some tough issues with a lot of heart. *Snapshot* brings our world into pristine focus. It's fast paced, edgy, and loaded with plenty of menace. Lis Wiehl knows what readers crave and she delivers it. Make room on your bookshelves for this one—it's a keeper."

—STEVE BERRY, *NEW YORK TIMES* BESTSELLING AUTHOR

"*Snapshot* is fiction. But it takes us along the twisted path of race in America in a way that is closer to the human experience than most history books."

—JUAN WILLIAMS, BESTSELLING AUTHOR OF
EYES ON THE PRIZE: AMERICA'S CIVIL RIGHTS YEARS

"Inspired by actual historical events and informed by Lis Wiehl's formidable personal and professional background, *Snapshot* captivates and enthralls."

—JEANINE PIRRO, BESTSELLING AUTHOR OF *SLY FOX*

"Riveting from the first page . . ."

—PAM VEASEY, SCREENWRITER AND EXECUTIVE PRODUCER

ALSO BY LIS WIEHL

NEWSMAKERS NOVELS (WITH SEBASTIAN STUART)

The Newsmakers

The Candidate

THE TRIPLE THREAT SERIES (WITH APRIL HENRY)

Face of Betrayal

Hand of Fate

Heart of Ice

Eyes of Justice

THE EAST SALEM TRILOGY (WITH PETE NELSON)

Waking Hours

Darkness Rising

Fatal Tide

THE MIA QUINN MYSTERIES (WITH APRIL HENRY)

A Matter of Trust

A Deadly Business

Lethal Beauty

OTHER NOVELS

Snapshot

THE SEPARATISTS

© 2017 by Lis Wiehl and Sebastian Stuart

Published in Nashville, Tennessee, by Thomas Nelson. Thomas Nelson is a registered trademark of HarperCollins Christian Publishing, Inc.

Thomas Nelson titles may be purchased in bulk for educational, business, fund-raising, or sales promotional use. For information, please e-mail SpecialMarkets@ThomasNelson.com.

Publisher's Note: This novel is a work of fiction. Names, characters, places, and incidents are either products of the author's imagination or used fictitiously. All characters are fictional, and any similarity to people living or dead is purely coincidental.

Library of Congress Cataloging-in-Publication Data

Names: Wiehl, Lis W., author. | Stuart, Sebastian, author.
Title: The separatists / Lis Wiehl with Sebastian Stuart.
Description: Nashville : Thomas Nelson, [2017] | Series: Newsmakers ; 3
Identifiers: LCCN 2017004731 | ISBN 9780718037697 (hardback)
Subjects: LCSH: Women journalists--Fiction. | Reporters and
 reporting--Fiction. | GSAFD: Mystery fiction. | Suspense fiction.
Classification: LCC PS3623.I382 S47 2017 | DDC 813/.6--dc23 LC record available at
https://lccn.loc.gov/2017004731

Printed in the United States of America
17 18 19 20 21 22 /LSC/ 6 5 4 3 2 1

THE SEPARATISTS

LIS WIEHL

WITH SEBASTIAN STUART

THOMAS NELSON
Since 1798

For Jacob and Dani, When I look at the two of you, I know there is great hope in the world. While much is left to be accomplished, you two and your generation can do it. I couldn't be a prouder Mom. Now that you're all grown up, I wish for you to always to follow your bliss, be strong, and show compassion for others as you find your way in life. I love you to the moon and back. Mom

PROLOGUE ───────────────────────

STURGES AND MARY BELLAMY ARE sitting in their library, a fire going, enjoying after-dinner coffee—espresso for Mary, who thinks sleep is grossly overrated. They're watching *Antiques Roadshow*. Well, Mary is watching. Sturges is buried in his iPhone, no doubt checking up on stock prices. Or who knows what. He's been so distracted lately. Dinner together is supposed to be inviolate, but the truth is they've both been so consumed with work—of one form or another—that sitting down to eat often seems like an afterthought. On-screen, the appraiser is discussing an Art Deco brooch.

"Isn't that a striking pin?" Mary asks. She wears very little jewelry herself. Just not her style. Too ostentatious. She pats at her hair.

"That primavera was delicious," Sturges says.

"Sarah does such a good job. I think it's time to give her a raise." Mary loves to give their employees raises. The ones who deserve it, of course. One must never reward substandard work. Standards are everything in life. Standards and discipline. And kindness, of course. *Kindness is the language that the deaf can hear and the blind can see.* Mark Twain said that. Such a wise man.

The phone rings. Sturges mutes the TV and answers it. "Oh hi there, Frank." He turns to Mary. "It's Frank Simmons."

Mary looks at him blankly.

"He runs Dakota Salvage for us."

Of course—their vast salvage yard in Fargo. What could he be calling about at this hour?

As Sturges listens, his face grows serious and pained. Then he hangs up.

"What is it, dear?" Mary asks.

"Jerry Swanson, the foreman at the salvage yard, fell into the compactor today."

"Oh dear. The poor man."

". . . his body . . . extracting it . . . ," Sturges says, looking ill.

"We must send flowers."

"He's worked for us for almost a decade."

"Was he a family man?"

"Wife and two daughters."

"We'll do something for them. Maybe a scholarship fund for the girls," Mary says. She puts her coffee down, feeling a little queasy. After all, she considers their employees family. "Did you know him?"

"Met him a couple of times. Last year he gave me a tour of the yard with that banker from Minneapolis. Swanson was a good man." He pauses. "He *was* trying to unionize the place."

Mary *tsks* lightly. She and Sturges look at each other. "It's a terrible tragedy," she says.

On-screen, the appraiser is discussing a Civil War relic, a tattered American flag.

CHAPTER 1 ————————————————

ERICA SPARKS IS STRIDING DOWN the hallway at GNN, heading for the executive conference room. She's got a big ask, and the half dozen men and women she's about to face have the power to grant it. She's keyed tight and her heart is thwacking like a metronome—there's a lot at stake. Yes, her nightly show, *The Erica Sparks Effect*, is still at or near the top of the ratings, but she's getting antsy stuck behind a desk night after night. She's beginning to feel more like a newsreader than a journalist. And that's just not acceptable.

She walks into the conference room, with its walls of windows looking out at midtown Manhattan, the buzzing heart of the American news business.

News *business.*

Remember that word, Erica.

It's a word that Greg, her husband, drilled into her as he helped her with the pitch. They may not be working together at GNN anymore—Greg has started his own consultancy, which has led to some major friction in the marriage—but the man knows how the industry works inside out.

"Good morning, Erica," Mort Silver, the head of GNN, says. He's sitting at the head of the table looking avuncular and self-important. On one side of him are the CFO and her top lieutenants, on the other the COO and his. They're all poker-faced and expectant.

"Good morning, Mort." Erica nods and smiles. It's a tight smile. She's anticipating some resistance to her proposal. She's girded.

Charm, Erica, charm. You attract more flies with honey.

"Good morning, everyone," she says, this time with a warm smile, the smile that has helped her win millions of loyal viewers. Without waiting for an invitation, she sits at the end of the table opposite Mort, whose eyes narrow. She's going to take this meeting by the horns.

"Coffee, water, how about a little nosh?" Mort asks.

Erica hates these silly niceties. She looks at the plate of soggy Danish. Man has evolved. Why do depressing Danish platters persist?

"I'm fine, thanks. First of all, thank you all for coming. I hope everyone knows how committed I am to GNN. This is my home." If there's one thing Erica doesn't romanticize, it's *home*. Home is where the pain was. "This network has given me extraordinary opportunities." She takes a pause and slows her cadence. "And I think the benefits have flowed both ways." She takes another pause to cue up the money shot. "Now I want to take our relationship to the next level."

The suits around the table remain impassive. Considering the millions she pumps into the network's bottom line, Erica was hoping for an encouraging smile or two. But this is a don't-rock-the-boat-or-kill-the-goose crowd, paid to keep the gravy train running on time. What a bore.

Erica stands up. Mort tries to disguise his discomfort.

Sorry, Mort, but go-along-to-get-along isn't my style these days.

"I feel very strongly that fearless, muckraking journalism is a lynchpin of our democracy. It has been for our entire history. The Founding Fathers understood how crucial a free press is, and they wrote its protection into the Constitution. In the search for the truth there can be no sacred cows. And I feel that *all* the news networks have been intimidated and defanged by political pressure, corporate pressure, ratings pressure."

Erica turns and takes a few steps, letting the tension in the room build. Then she wheels around. "Look at the Iraq War. It was based on *lies*. Lies that the press for the most part accepted, cowed by the bullying and belligerence of the White House. And our nation is still paying a price for that acquiescence. This isn't theoretical or hypothetical." Erica can feel her emotions rising, anger and sadness—she is *passionate* about our veterans.

"Tens of thousands of young men are scarred forever, missing their limbs, their eyesight, their sanity. Disfigured, disabled, and traumatized. Their lives have been reduced to endless struggle. I remember one vet I interviewed when I was working at a local station up in New Hampshire. His name was Ryan Taylor. He was nineteen years old. His family had no money, and he'd enlisted so he'd be able to pay for college. He was sent over to Iraq, and one cold morning an IED exploded beside his patrol. He was blinded and lost both arms below the elbow." Erica feels another wave of emotion sweep over her—she will *never* forget the despair on Ryan Taylor's face. She never *wants* to forget it.

Around the table, eyes look down, papers are shuffled, someone coughs. This wasn't what they were expecting first thing on a Thursday morning. Too bad.

"Ryan Taylor's happiness, his future, was snatched away from him. And we in the press bear some responsibility. We didn't do our job. And that's why I asked you here today."

Now the room is pin-drop silent, statue-still. Erica slowly sits down, leans forward on the table, lowers her voice. "I would like GNN to be in the forefront of a new American journalism. One that is truly fearless and follows a story *wherever* it leads—even if it's right to the Oval Office. I propose a monthly, single-issue program dedicated to finding the truth, the whole truth, and nothing but the truth. Each month we'll cover a different subject, and we'll go deep, toppling pedestals and speaking truth to power." Erica slowly scans the faces around the table, looking each one in the eyes, bringing them on board.

"I'd like to call it *Spotlight*—on whichever topic we're covering that month. Corruption. Malfeasance. Greed. Lies. We won't go searching for the controversial and sensational, but if we find it we won't look away."

The room remains quiet. Mort eyeballs Erica, and she sees a mix of skepticism and admiration in his eyes.

Time to hit the bottom line. "I believe we can make great television together. Television that, not incidentally, will have sponsors clamoring for ad time. Television that will also, quite frankly, keep *me* engaged." It doesn't hurt to remind them that she's the network's number one asset. Erica leans back and softens her voice. "You'll all find a mock-up of *Spotlight*'s budget and organization in your mailboxes. As well as a half dozen potential stories." She stands. "I want all of us here to be part of something we can be proud of, something bigger than ourselves. At its best I hope *Spotlight* will not only report news, it will *make* news." Erica pauses. "And maybe even history."

Without loosening the screws, she smiles at the room, a welcoming, even conspiratorial smile. The expressions that meet her are 180 degrees from what they were ten minutes earlier—there are nods, murmurs of approval, smiles of encouragement. "Thank you for your time, and I'm hoping to get a green light within forty-eight hours. Now, I've got a show to prepare."

Erica strides back down the hallway with only one thought: *Onward!*

CHAPTER 2 —————————————————

IT'S LATE THE FOLLOWING AFTERNOON, a little more than two hours before the start of her show, and Erica is in her office at GNN. She's going to lead with a horrific story—the sinking off the coast of Greece of a boat carrying over six hundred Libyan refugees, drowning all onboard. The dead bodies are washing ashore in waves. It's a big story with powerful visuals, one more sad chapter in the largest refugee crisis since World War II. On her computer screen Erica watches footage of the lifeless bodies bobbing in the surf. It's the children that get to her the most; she imagines their last uncomprehending moments as the boat listed, took on water, and then sank in a matter of minutes. And their doomed parents, unable to protect them. Sometimes it feels as if the world is coming apart at the seams.

Erica turns from the screen, picks up her well-worn playing cards, and deals a hand of solitaire—something about the tactile feel of the cards and defined parameters of the game always helps to calm and center her. The world may be a swirl of chaos, but her cards are manageable and familiar. Why hasn't she heard from Mort Silver? Her presentation was flawless. But she knows those people have built their careers on caution. Give them a little more time. Yes, the start-up and production costs of *Spotlight* will run into the millions. So what? The rewards for the network, both monetary and in prestige, are worth it. Still . . . her left leg is bouncing and she feels that familiar restlessness, the one that's tinged with claustrophobia, anxiety, and even panic. It's been her constant companion since her childhood in that leaky double-wide in rural Maine, soggy with booze and pot and pills and mold and rage. Her restlessness drives her, yes—but sometimes it drives her all the way to the edge.

Erica loses the hand of solitaire, stands up and paces, goes to the window. She looks down at the city below—Sixth Avenue is jammed with pedestrians who look like they're moving in three-quarter time, trapped in a blazing hazy, sticky May day when the temperature is approaching ninety-five. Didn't May used to mean flower buds and birdsong? Maybe most disturbing is that temperatures in the low forties are projected for the weekend. When it comes to the climate, all bets are off. And yet still the ostrich chorus denies the science and stymies action. Erica thinks of Jenny, her thirteen-year-old daughter, who lives in Massachusetts with her father. Last summer her favorite swimming hole was closed due to a toxic algae bloom triggered by the brutal heat. This is an issue *Spotlight* won't shy away from. But why hasn't Mort called? What will she do if they nix her proposal? She has no Plan B.

Erica turns away from the window and goes into her small galley kitchen. She turns on the coffeepot and then turns it off again. More coffee is the last thing she needs. She opens a cabinet, and there sits a package of sublime macaroons, those little brightly colored French ones that melt in your mouth. But she needs a sugar rush—and its inevitable headachy crash—even less than she needs coffee. She shuts the cabinet and turns away, then she turns back, opens the cabinet, reaches up and grabs the package, tears it open, and devours one macaroon. Then another. Then a third (they're so small). Feeling triumphantly defiant, she goes back to her desk.

She's been able to book former secretary of state John Kerry and United Nations secretary-general Ban Ki-Moon to discuss the refugee crisis. Now she needs to work on asking them the right questions. Erica prides herself on really delving into an issue, engaging both her viewers and her guests. Just as she's starting to write out questions, Eileen McDermott, her lead producer, appears in her doorway.

Eileen is tall and thin, with enormous darting eyes behind blocky black-framed glasses; her thick auburn hair looks like an afterthought, and her blouses are perpetually half untucked from her pants. But she keeps *The Erica Sparks Effect* running like a well-oiled machine. Right now she looks alarmed. "Supreme Court Justice Mark Rothman was killed in a car accident."

Erica goes still for a moment and then, "When? Where? How?"

"About an hour ago, in Richmond, Virginia, blindsided by a drunk driver making an illegal U-turn."

"Is there footage?"

"Of the aftermath, of course, but none of the actual accident. At least none has turned up yet, and there are no surveillance cameras at the intersection."

"Shoot me every detail we have, including Rothman's bio. I'll start writing a new lead."

"We'll move Kerry and Ban Ki-Moon to the second spot and cut the segments on the Zika virus and that secessionist standoff in Texas. We can run them tomorrow," Eileen says.

"Rothman was the court's one centrist, the fulcrum between the left and right. We can't ignore the politics of this," Erica says. "President Winters has an opportunity to reshape the court for a generation."

"Will she pick a tough conservative to appease the right wing of her party or stay true to her moderate instincts?"

"She's going to be under enormous pressure from the right," Erica says. "Who can we get to comment on Rothman, and on the decision facing the president?"

"I can think of a couple of dozen senators who would jump at the chance," Eileen says.

Moths to a flame, senators to a camera. They bore Erica with their predictability, always toeing the party line. She wants to go deeper and book a guest who could put the challenge facing President Winters in historical context. "How about Leslie Burke Wilson?" Wilson is one of the country's most admired historians and writers, Pulitzer Prize and every-other-prize winner, bestselling author, and one of Erica's idols.

"She'd be perfect, but she's tough to book. She doesn't like to spread herself too thin," Eileen says.

"Can you get me her contact info?"

Eileen is already out the door. Erica takes a moment to gather her thoughts. She remembers Justice Rothman—humble, thoughtful, universally respected, with a fair and brilliant legal mind. The nation has lost one of its preeminent jurists, his family has lost a man they love, and here she is, focusing on the politics of his death and the best way to report it. Erica exhales. The morbid truth is that for journalists, death is one more story that has to be covered. And covered well.

Shirley Stamos, Erica's assistant, appears in her doorway. Shirley has proved herself invaluable—she has an uncanny knack for knowing what Erica needs before Erica does, and she's always happy to work late and take on tasks that border on drudgery. Around forty-five, plump and slightly matronly, with short gray hair and a round face that has never known makeup, she's a very private person. All Erica knows about Shirley's personal life is that she lives alone in Kew Gardens.

"Jenny is on the line," she says. "Are you available?"

This isn't the best time for Erica to take a call from her daughter, but if she doesn't she'll have one of her bad-mother guilt attacks. She nods at Shirley, who leaves. Erica picks up her phone. "Hi, honey. Can't wait to see you this weekend."

"Do you mind if I bring a friend?"

"Of course not. Who is it?"

"Her name is Beth. She's in my class."

"Look forward to meeting her."

"She has a YouTube channel with thirty-five thousand followers."

"That's impressive. What does she focus on?"

"Mom, all YouTubers focus on themselves. That's the deal."

"You mean she just sits there and talks about herself?"

"Yeah, pretty much. I mean, she gives her opinions on music and movies and clothes and boys and stuff. We were thinking it might be fun to do a segment with you."

"Seriously?"

"Yeah. Maybe makeup tips or visit the station or something."

"My GNN contract is an exclusive. And they enforce it." Erica notes that Leslie Burke Wilson's phone number just appeared in her in-box.

"I guess you're super busy."

"A Supreme Court justice was killed today. It's a big story."

"Get to work!" Jenny says with a laugh. A laugh with an edge.

"Greg will pick you up at LaGuardia. Love you." Every time Erica thinks her relationship with Jenny is on an even keel, it gets thrown off-balance, usually by the demands of her job. But Jenny seems fairly happy, and she's doing well in school. They see each other for at least two weekends a month—and with Jenny racing into adolescence, she seems more grown up every visit. It makes Erica both proud and sad. But she has no time to dwell on it right now. She dials Wilson's number.

"Is this Erica Sparks?" Leslie Burke Wilson asks.

"It is. Thanks for taking my call."

"Of course."

"I'll get right to the point. Is there any chance you could come on my show tonight to discuss Rothman's death, President Winters's options, and how former presidents have dealt with similar crises?"

"I have a benefit for the public library tonight. I'm on the committee."

Erica fiddles with a pencil and then says a mild, "I understand . . . It's just that I feel you're uniquely qualified. Your biography on Oliver Wendell Holmes is a classic."

Leslie Wilson laughs, a throaty laugh that sounds sophisticated and ironic. "You know how to reel them in, don't you, Erica? I am intrigued by which direction the president is going to take the court."

"I'd love to hear your thoughts, and so would my viewers."

There's a short pause and then a snippet of that laugh again. "So I'll arrive late at the benefit. No one will notice. And if they do, who cares? What time do you want me at the studio?"

"No later than seven thirty. And I owe you."

There's another pause, and then Wilson says in a lower voice, "That's one chit I'll be sure to call in."

In addition to her intellectual accomplishments, Leslie Burke Wilson is known for being a member of New York's cultural elite. She's pals with the nation's most respected writers, actors, artists, entrepreneurs—the beating heart of the most exciting city in the world. Her husband, Stan Wilson, founded *the* cutting-edge ad agency. Definite power couple.

Erica is fascinated by this rarified tribe, and even admits to herself that she would love to gain admittance. Hasn't she earned it? It would be the ultimate imprimatur of her success, not to mention a source of ideas, inspiration, creative friction, intellectual stimulation, and just plain juice and boogie.

As Erica heads down the hall to hair and makeup, Mort calls.

"Errr-*ica* . . . ," he says playfully. "I'm seeing green. Green gold and . . . green light."

"*Yes!* I'll start putting together a production team. And, Mort— thank you."

"My pleasure. You're the original never-a-dull-moment gal."

Erica hangs up and takes a moment to let it sink in. A new show, new challenges, new stories, a chance to make a difference. It's a delicious feeling, liquid and electric, a shot of adrenaline with a goose bumps chaser. But really, there's no time to savor her triumph. She has a show in a matter of hours and a whole new production team to pull together.

Her immediate instinct is to call Greg and tell him the news, but then she hesitates. He's unfailingly supportive, but . . . but . . . Soon after their wedding eighteen months ago he left GNN and set up his own consulting business, helping local television stations around the country strengthen their news departments. He advises them on organization, hiring, cost cutting, graphics and visuals, logistics, you name it. He works out of an office on Ninth Avenue not far from GNN. While things are going well, and Erica is proud of him for striking out on his own, he's earning less than a tenth of what she is and watching from the sidelines as her star continues to pulse.

When they met, she was the newbie and he was the seasoned and respected news producer. He was an amazing mentor, generous and understanding, and he made her feel safe and valued. And they slowly fell in love, a love based on mutual respect (and some serious physical chemistry). The chemistry has cooled a tad, as chemistry does, and now his male ego is taking a few hits. He's been drinking more. Even bringing alcohol into the house, which he never used to do. Considering Erica's in recovery, it's inconsiderate, even a little hostile and troubling. But at the end of the day it's not a big deal. Right? They're in love. Committed to each other. That's what matters. Isn't it?

She sticks the phone in her pocket and heads down the hall.

Erica greets Rosario, her makeup lady, and Andi, her hairdresser. As she sits in the chair, Greg calls her. He must be psychic. But she can't ignore the call. Rosario and Andi take a discreet step back.

"Any word on *Spotlight*?" he asks.

Erica hesitates a moment before saying, with as little bravado as possible, "It's a go."

There's just half a beat before Greg says, "Erica, that's fantastic news." Do his words sound a little forced?

"I'm excited." Should she ask him about coming onboard as one of the producers of *Spotlight*? But that would make her his boss. And they'd be together virtually 24/7. Better to hold off. Besides, he may not *want* to work for his wife.

"You sound a little subdued, considering . . . ," he says.

"Just a big day, with Rothman's death."

"Are you ready for tonight's show?"

"I think so. I was able to book Leslie Burke Wilson."

"That's a score. Is there anything I can do to help? Do you want me to come over?"

"I think it's all under control."

There's another pause and then he says, "Have a great show." Erica can hear a hint of disappointment in his voice. But if Greg came to the studio it would only complicate things. Eileen might resent his presence. Plus, it would dilute Erica's focus.

"How are *you* in the midst of all this?" Erica asks.

"WPVI in Philadelphia wants me to come down next week to discuss a contract."

"Oh, Greg, that's great news." But helping some local station polish its news department seems like pallid stuff next to Rothman and Wilson and *Spotlight*. Best to change the subject. "Listen, Jenny is bringing a friend down this weekend."

"That's a first. Should be fun. Talk later." He ends the call and Erica sets down her phone.

"Are you okay, Erica?" Rosario asks. The middle-aged, homey makeup woman has become a friend and ally at GNN, always alert for news or gossip that she thinks Erica should know. People's lips tend to loosen when they're in the chair.

"Yeah, I'm okay," Erica says.

Rosario narrows her eyes in skepticism, then picks up her airbrush. As she and Andi work their magic on her face and hair, a phrase coined by Truman Capote comes to Erica: *Beware of answered prayers*. Here she is with two women fussing over her, she's starting a thrilling new project, earning millions of dollars a year doing work she loves and believes in . . . and yet . . .

Has her success put distance between Erica and her daughter? Between Erica and her husband? How ironic it all is. And the job itself can be so draining—reporters aren't paid to report good news, sunshine, and lollipops. No, it's an unrelenting barrage of disasters and bombings and climate crises and human suffering. Death never takes a day off.

Erica looks at herself in the mirror. She's almost camera-ready, except . . . "Rosario, I didn't get a lot of sleep last night. Could you put a little more concealer under my eyes?"

CHAPTER 3

LESLIE BURKE WILSON IS SITTING in the green room going over notes when Erica walks in. Erica stops for a moment—struck by how arresting Wilson is in person. In her midforties, her thick black hair in a layer cut to just below her ears, she's wearing black silk pencil pants, a matching low-cut top that reveals a hint of cleavage, and black sandal-strap heels. Exuding a subtle sensuality, thin and toned and expertly made-up—she's one of those women who trick you into thinking they're beautiful by sheer force of will. And brilliant styling.

"Leslie," Erica says. The two women shake hands.

Leslie's smile is open and warm, in contrast to her look, which seems a bit like armor. She's wearing some amazing perfume—Erica recognizes the top note as citrusy bergamot, but under that is something floral, subtle and seductive, that she can't quite name.

"Thank you so much for coming, and on such short notice," Erica says. "I don't gush, but if I were a gusher, please know I'd be gushing."

"Gush back at ya."

"Are there any questions you'd particularly like me to ask?"

"I think the president is facing one of the most critical decisions of her presidency. She was elected on a promise to bring the country together, but her political future depends on continued support from the right, which held its nose and voted for her. Now they want payback."

"What do you think she's going to do?"

Leslie tilts her head and gives Erica a conspiratorial smile. "Why don't we save that answer for when the cameras are rolling?"

"Bingo."

Leslie takes one of Erica's hands in her own, looks her in the eye, and says, "Listen, I know your story, your history. And then, of course, there are the piddling matters of Nylan Hastings and Lily Lau."

It may be a practiced charm offensive, but it sounds sincere, and Erica feels an immediate emotional connection to this woman—she feels like a friend, or even an older sister. "A gig's a gig."

"No, Erica, for some of us a gig is more than a gig. It's a calling."

"Speaking of which, I see my producer is calling *us*. Ready to rumble?"

The interview goes well, more than well. As with all terrific exchanges, this one takes on a life of its own. Inspired, ignited by Leslie's answers, Erica finds the questions pouring out of her. The two of them touch on the Constitution, the history of the Supreme Court back to its founding, the best and worst justices and their most significant decisions, finally ending up where they started—at today's developments, the president's choices, and their ramifications for the court and the country.

"Well, *that* was fun!" Wilson says as they go to a break.

Erica walks her out of the studio. "You were cooking."

"Listen, if you have nothing better to do Saturday night, Stan and I are trekking down to the Lower East Side to see a chamber opera based on a Toni Morrison short story. It's being done by a new company dedicated to contemporary opera. Fran Lebowitz is on their board, and she's corralling one and all."

Erica feels a frisson of excitement: Leslie Burke Wilson is reaching out to her. Is she going to invite Erica into her heady circle of friends? But then Erica realizes, with a twinge of disappointment, even resentment, that she's not free this weekend. "My daughter will be in town."

"Bring her."

"She's thirteen."

"All the better. Morrison is so remarkable. I just reread *Beloved*. It's staggering."

Erica stops for a second. The Lower East Side? Toni Morrison? A chamber opera? Three undiscovered countries for Jenny (not to mention Erica). "You know what? We'd love to come."

"I'll call Fran and have her put aside tickets for you. Three?"

"Four if possible. My daughter's bringing a friend for the weekend. Now I'd better get back to my desk."

"See you Saturday," Leslie says with that disarming ironic smile.

Erica watches as Leslie strides out of view—and the world seems slightly less alive than it did just a moment before.

CHAPTER 4 ——————————

ERICA, JENNY, AND BETH ARE at the dining room table, Greg is in the kitchen, and they can smell the chicken Provençal he has just taken out of the oven. Erica doesn't cook. Never has. Never will. Her list of man's three greatest inventions goes: the wheel, flight, takeout.

"So, we're heading down to the Lower East Side tonight," Erica says. She feels distracted—and guilty for feeling distracted—but her mind keeps going back to *Spotlight* and the need to hire a production team. They've put out the word that they're hiring an executive producer, and interviews start on Monday. It's a crucial hire, and Erica has been consumed with that and the thousand other details that go into developing a new show.

"An opera, Mom? Seriously?" Jenny says.

"Yes, seriously."

"I guess you're serving broccoli too."

"No way . . . We're having cauliflower."

Jenny smiles and rolls her eyes. She can dish it out, but she can take it. What a great kid. Erica's not so sure about her friend Beth, who's wearing eyeliner and lip gloss and a multicolored, multipatterned jumpsuit that borders on seizure inducing.

"I googled Fran Lebowitz, she's wicked famous," Beth says. "There might be celebrities there. Can I use my cam?"

"I don't think that would be appropriate," Erica says.

Beth shoots a glance at Jenny, who says, "Oh, come on, Mom."

"Absolutely not."

Beth frowns, shrugs, and takes out her phone.

"And no phones at the dinner table."

Beth ignores this admonition, texting and swiping.

"No. Phones."

Beth exhales with a sigh and puts down her phone.

Maybe Erica should do a *Spotlight* on what smartphones are doing to kids' brain synapses. *We're definitely in the nascent stage of some evolutionary leap*, she thinks. *Where is it leading, where will we land?*

"I could use a hand in here," Greg calls. Jenny leaps up and heads into the kitchen. Beth makes no move.

"Just to make it clear, Beth, my contract with GNN forbids me to appear on other networks or channels. Including YouTube."

"But I've seen you on YouTube."

"It's footage of me on GNN that subsequently got posted."

"Can I at least do a Snapchat of this dinner?"

"Beth, I lead a very public life. I treasure my privacy."

Beth clasps her hands on the table and goes silent. She's definitely a bright girl, and ambitious, but there's something calculating about her that Erica finds off-putting. The kid has an agenda. Why has Jenny chosen her to be friends with? Why couldn't she have picked some silly, messy, funny kid, full of questions and spontaneity? Someone who wasn't racing toward adulthood as fast as she can.

Erica feels a pang of guilt and sadness. Her own childhood was such a litany of pain and abuse, she wants Jenny to have some good old-fashioned fun. Adulthood will come soon enough.

"Ta-*da*!" Greg says as he and Jenny appear from the kitchen bearing plates. Erica feels a catch in her throat—Greg looks so adorable in his apron, with his tawny skin and dark tousled hair, smiling broadly, happy to cook and have the family together. Jenny is beaming in adoration. Erica wishes she could file away this moment of happiness, bank it for future withdrawal.

They all dig in. "This is delicious!" Jenny exclaims.

"It's an old family recipe I made up," Greg says. "So, girls, bring us up to date on school."

Jenny engages completely, stories of book reports, science projects, and track meets spilling out. Beth puts in a word now and then, but clearly school is not her chief focus. Her eyes keep darting to her phone. When Greg and Jenny finish clearing the table and bring out the coconut cream pie he made, Beth declines a piece, saying, "Sugar is inflammatory. Miley never touches it."

"Beth is *obsessed* with Miley Cyrus."

"Miley's my big sister, there was a mix-up at the hospital," Beth says with a sly smile.

Well, at least there's a sense of humor under there.

In the cab heading downtown, Erica is keyed tight. She wants to be at her best for Leslie and her friends—will Toni Morrison be there? She's wearing very little makeup and is dressed down in black slacks and a white oxford, her only accessory a pair of sapphire clip-on earrings. (Erica only wears clip-ons—as a teenager there was enough pain at home, she wasn't about to self-inflict more.) She considered wearing a dress, but it's not about how you look, it's about what you do.

She thinks of Archie Hallowell, her brilliant, ancient, chalk-smudged, hairy-eared mentor at Yale. He took her—an insecure kid from an abusive background gasping in the thin Ivy League air—under his wing. He encouraged her to read, to think, to aspire, to fight for what was right, to appreciate art and beauty and literature, to call on her best self and better angels. After one thrilling discussion on democracy, he pressed Leslie Burke Wilson's book on the Founding Fathers—*Self-Evident Truths*—into her hands. And now she's in a taxi on a clear Manhattan night, on her way to meet Wilson at a downtown cultural event.

Oh, Professor Hallowell, dear Archie, if only you could see me now.

Then Jenny asks, "Can we go shopping tomorrow, Mom?"

What Erica really wants to do tomorrow is work on *Spotlight*, but she says, "What about a museum? There's a show on exotic insects at the Museum of Natural History that sounds fascinating. It's filled with live specimens from places like Tasmania and Madagascar. Islands often have their own ecosystems."

Jenny loves science, or used to love science. She's turning into an adolescent so quickly, Erica can't keep track of her changing tastes.

Her daughter's interest seems piqued, but then Beth says, "Why don't we go downtown to the Whitney, then do the High Line and then hit the shops in the Meatpacking District. My parents put three hundred dollars in fun money on my phone."

There's silence. Jenny looks uncomfortable. Beth is wide-eyed and expectant. Well, the girl certainly is fearless. Erica shoots Greg a help-me look.

"The insect show is up for a while, we can go in two weeks," Greg says.

They reach the Lower East Side, a neighborhood of former tenements that has been colonized by cutting-edge boutiques and farm-to-table restaurants, each straining to be more rustic than the next. After all, shouldn't the gritty heart of Manhattan feel like a farmhouse kitchen in Vermont? Squeezed between them are funky bodegas, Jewish delis, and discount catch-all shops that signal the area is still a yeasty mix of classes and cultures. This is a foreign land for Erica, and she marvels yet again at the gorgeous mosaic of her adopted city.

They pull up in front of Dixon Place. There's an expectant crowd out front, the scene is charged with that peculiar New York electricity that never fails to jolt and jazz Erica.

"There's Jesse Eisenberg! And Chloë Sevigny!" Beth coos.

They get out of the cab and Leslie comes over. "Erica!" She has her husband in tow; he's in his early sixties, well-groomed if not handsome, with a slightly distracted air, as if he'd rather be somewhere else.

Erica and Leslie make the introductions. Leslie sticks out her hand

and shakes Jenny's, giving her a big smile, but then turns away quickly. Like many brilliant and successful people Erica has met, she clearly has little interest in kids. She hooks her arm through Erica's as they make their way inside. "I'm so glad you could make it. Apparently the composer is quite a talent."

New York worships talent the way LA worships youth and beauty. Not that those shiny coins don't have currency here, but it does feel more like a meritocracy and Erica loves that, partly because it validates her own success.

The crowd in the lobby has a downtown edge—the clothes are hip and the insouciance is thick. Erica sees writers, artists, and actors she half recognizes. Leslie introduces her to several people, and Erica soaks it all up. Greg and Stan Wilson are deep in conversation. Jenny takes Erica's hand, and she can tell her daughter is a little intimidated by the scene. Erica gives her hand a squeeze.

"Where's Beth?" Erica asks. Jenny shrugs. Erica scans the room, anxiety spiking. Then Beth appears through the crowd, smiling brightly. A little too brightly—Erica's thoughts go to cats and canaries.

"So, Erica, I saw the mention in the *Times* about your new show. Congrats, kiddo," Leslie says.

"We'll see. It's a long way from here to daylight."

"I have no doubt you'll deliver."

Or die trying.

Now a man is approaching them—his face is familiar—he's around fifty, self-consciously rumpled and shaggy, with flashing eyes behind rimless round glasses. "Leslie! You brought one of my favorite journalists," he says.

"Erica Sparks, Eliot Woodson."

Of course—Woodson is a leading essayist and cultural critic, well known for his pieces in *The New Yorker* and elsewhere, which are collected and published in book form every couple of years and regularly win him fancy prizes. Erica has read some of his work—it's penetrating and incisive. He'd probably make a terrific guest on her show.

"What's on your mind these days?" Erica asks.

"I'm fascinated by the secessionist movements we're seeing pop up around the country. I think they speak to a national mood of alienation and dissatisfaction."

Erica leans in toward him. "Say more."

"At their worst, they're about threats of violence and not wanting to pay taxes. At their best, they're a reflection of that yearning for independence, to create something better, that is such a part of our national character."

Erica's wheels start turning.

"What do you think is driving them?" she asks.

"The natives are restless," Woodson says. "They're struggling. Our democracy, as it stands, simply isn't working for them. We really are at the edge of oligarchy. This is only a free country if you can afford it."

"And if you can't afford it, your pain turns to rage," Erica says.

"Exactly. And that rage can lead to violence. Look at the standoff at that ranch in West Texas that's going on right now. That could turn ugly on a dime," Woodson says.

"It all seems very fringy to me," Leslie says.

"All revolutions start at the fringe. Secession was debated and voted on at the last Texas GOP state convention. It lost, but still, that's what you call inching into the mainstream. There's one group in particular that fascinates me. It's in North Dakota. I don't want to use the word *legitimate*, but they seem more serious than some of the crazies, the Cliven Bundys, the white supremacists."

"I've read a little bit about the drive in North Dakota. A couple is spearheading it, I forget their names," Leslie says.

"Sturges and Mary Bellamy," Woodson says. "They're well educated and well heeled, from old ranching families. They're not seizing government buildings and parading around with guns. They've started what they call the Take Back Our Homeland movement and are working through the political process. Which I think makes them far more intriguing. And perhaps dangerous."

Erica knows a little bit about these secessionist and sovereign citizen groups. She ran a piece on the group down in Texas, the Free Texas Rangers, but it was reported by a stringer and didn't go into a lot of depth. In the last few days the standoff has escalated. Maybe she needs to do something more expansive, include secessionist movements nationwide. Interview the Bellamys. Maybe it could work for *Spotlight*.

The lobby lights flicker, and as the audience files into the theater Erica makes a note to do some research on the situation in North Dakota. Greg and Stan Wilson are still in a deep powwow. What are they discussing? Erica sits next to Leslie, with Jenny on her other side and then Beth. As the lights go down, Beth is showing Jenny something on her iPhone. Erica leans over to take a peek, but Beth switches off the phone before Erica can see what's on the screen.

CHAPTER 5 ———————————————

IT'S THE NEXT MORNING, AND Erica is in the kitchen making pancakes. Pancakes she can handle. From a mix. She did throw in a handful of blueberries, so there. Greg is out for a run. The girls are in the dining room, being awfully quiet. No doubt their noses are deep into cyberspace.

Erica is starting to obsess on what Eliot Woodson told her last night about the secessionist movements around the country. The story is multifaceted, has danger, uncertainty, drive—it might be the perfect topic for the first *Spotlight*. She's especially fascinated by the couple out in North Dakota, Sturges and Mary Bellamy, and their Take Back Our Homeland movement. They're the new, rational face of secessionism. And Erica suspects they might be great television.

"Jenny?" Erica calls. No answer. She pushes open the swinging door to the dining room. No sign of them. "Jenny?"

"Coming, Mom," echoes from the bedroom wing.

Erica smells something burning and turns around. The pancakes are smoking. Serves her whole family right for putting her in charge of breakfast. She scrapes the mess into the trash and pours another batch. Then she picks up her phone and dials.

"Erica," comes Leslie Wilson's voice. Suddenly, in the cold kitchen light, Erica feels a little surge of insecurity. She can't keep track of her own daughter or make a batch of pancakes, and she's calling a woman who holds a unique place in the country's cultural firmament on a Sunday morning. Erica plows forward—she didn't get where she is by giving in to her self-doubt.

"I hope I'm not calling at a bad time."

"Not at all."

"Thank you for last night. It was good for all of us."

"You make it sound like cough medicine." The two women laugh.

"The opera was wonderful. Who knew? But listen, can I ask your opinion on something?"

"Always."

"Do you think the country's current wave of secessionist movements would be a strong topic for *Spotlight*?"

"I do. As Eliot was saying last night, it's fascinating and disturbing in and of itself, but equally so because of what it says about our current political and cultural climate. It taps right into a very angry and confused zeitgeist."

"The Trump derangement syndrome?"

"Exactly. There are tens of millions of Americans working their tails off to stay two steps behind. For people who live in rural areas or dying rustbelt cities, well, it can seem like their America is obsolete. That time has passed them by. On television and online they're flooded with images of wealth, technology, and diversity that can seem almost mocking to them."

"In a little more than a decade, we're going to be a majority minority country," Erica says.

"Exactly. And these people don't see a place for themselves in the emerging paradigm. And they deeply resent their tax dollars paying for programs they don't support. Secession seems like a chance to both start anew and regain what they feel has been taken from them— their sense of who they are and what America stands for. But make no mistake—these groups are dead serious about their goals. And will use any means to achieve them. They're *dangerous*."

The danger, of course, is part of what makes them so compelling. Erica inhales and goes for it. "If I do choose it for the first *Spotlight*, would you consider being part of the program?"

"Absolutely. In fact, you can name me as a consultant," Leslie says. "If it would be of any help," she adds in a stab at modesty.

Erica's short hairs tingle. Having Leslie Burke Wilson's blessings and input on the show would be incredibly helpful—in terms of content, of course, but also for publicity and prestige. It's major. "I would deeply appreciate it."

"I hope you know by now, Erica, that I consider you a woman of substance."

"Who saw her first opera at age thirty-five."

They laugh again. "It was a pleasure meeting Greg. What a terrific guy. Stan was quite taken with him."

"What were they discussing?"

"Ad buys on local television stations," Leslie says drily. There's a pause filled with sisterhood.

"Maybe that can be the topic of the second *Spotlight*."

"You do want to throw male viewers a bone."

"Anything to keep them out of our hair," Erica says.

"Naughty-naughty. Fun-fun."

Erica hangs up and flips the pancakes. "Jenny!" Where *is* that girl?

Erica hears the front door open, and moments later Greg breezes into the kitchen, looking pretty darn fetching in his running shorts and T-shirt. She leans in and gives him a quick kiss and gets a whiff of sweat mixed with his pine soap. She'll be glad when the girls are safely on their flight back to Boston—and she and Greg can work off some of her nervous energy.

"Those look good," Greg says.

"I made them not-from-scratch."

"You really are up for anything—skydiving, saving the world, flapjacks."

"Someone's got to do it."

Greg gives her a kiss. "Leslie Wilson is taken with you."

"It's mutual."

There's a pause, and Erica senses Greg wants to say something. She wants to say something too, to talk about where things stand between them, about his feelings on *Spotlight*. But she's afraid if she brings it up, the mood will curdle, and she treasures these Sunday mornings filled with easy affection.

"Where are the little monsters?"

"Up to no good, no doubt."

Just at that moment, Jenny and Beth burst into the kitchen, flushed with excitement.

"First batch!" Jenny cries.

"Don't guests get served first?" Erica asks.

"Excuse me, Saint Mom."

Beth eyes the pancakes and says, "Maple syrup contains trace nutrients."

"Good to know," Erica says. She plates the first batch and hands it to Beth. "The trace nutrients are out on the table."

After the perfectly edible pancakes, Beth announces she wants to "post a quirky little doo-dah from Central Park." Erica begs off chaperone duties—she wants to work on the proposal for *Spotlight: The American Secession Movement*—and Greg offers to take the girls off her hands for a couple of hours.

With the apartment to herself, Erica sits at her desk and gets to work. At one point she looks up and forty minutes have flown by. Then her mind goes to Beth. Something about that girl. An arrogance. Entitlement. She goes to YouTube and watches one of her videos. In it Beth is sitting at a desk in her bedroom, looking (Erica must admit) adorable. She talks fast, lightning fast, the words pouring out, and is indeed quirky and funny as she expounds on some feud between two pop singers Erica has never heard of—both of whom have apparently slept with Justin Bieber, ergo the feud. The whole thing is scarily immature and knowing at the same time.

Erica stands up and heads down to Jenny's bedroom. Beth's bright orange suitcase is open on the floor. Erica hesitates. It would be a violation of the girl's privacy. But Beth is clearly having a big influence on Jenny. Maybe a good one. Maybe not. Maybe a bad one. Erica feels a sudden surge of protective instinct.

Come on, Erica, it's already open.

Erica kneels down, her heart thumping, her ears hyper-alert for the sound of the front door opening. She carefully peeks into the suitcase. Beth brought something like six outfits, and come to think of it, she's worn them all. There is a side pocket. It bulges a little. Erica pulls it open and sees a package of condoms.

CHAPTER 6 ————————————————————

ERICA STANDS UP, RECOILING FROM the evidence. Evidence of *what*? She feels angry and guilty and confused. She walks quickly down the hall, through the living room, and into the kitchen. She pours herself a glass of water and drinks the whole thing.

Now what?

Should she confront Beth? That's not her place, she's not Beth's mother. Does she tell the girl's parents? And what about Jenny? Does she even know about the condoms? She must. Erica walks into the living room, looks around for no reason, and then walks back into the kitchen. She starts to do the breakfast dishes—she could just stick them in the dishwasher, but then what would she do with her hands? She can't go back to work, she's too . . . *freaked out*. Could Jenny possibly be having sex? No. Out of the question. Isn't it? She's never really had The Talk with Jenny. Why not?

Because you're a bad mother. That's why not.

And then comes that echo, that raspy cigarette-scarred echo that can never be silenced, no matter how many years go by, how much success Erica earns: *Just remember, you can change a lot of things in your life, but you can't ever change where you come from. And deep down you'll never be better than any of us.* Erica didn't need to be taught about the birds and the bees—not when there were drug-fueled live demonstrations practiced on the other side of the flimsy plasterboard walls night after night.

The cup she's soaping up slips from her hands and crashes to the floor, shattering into a thousand little pieces. For a moment she's afraid she'll burst into tears. And then she hears the front door open.

Erica goes to the closet and gets the broom and dustpan. She quickly sweeps up the shards and is finishing just as Greg, Jenny, and Beth pile into the kitchen.

"Honey, what happened?" Greg asks.

"Oh, nothing, no big deal. Really. Dropped a mug. Nothing." Erica dumps the pieces into the trash and asks brightly, "How was the park?"

"Awesome," Beth says. "We rented a rowboat and I did a bit with Jenny filming me."

"Why don't you girls go check out the footage," Greg says. As soon as they're alone in the kitchen he asks, "What's going on?" His eyes are so full of concern and Erica feels so at sea. He goes over to her and runs his hand down her hair. "What is it?"

"I found condoms in Beth's suitcase." She breaks away from Greg. "I know, I shouldn't have been snooping. It was wrong."

"Erica, every mother snoops. Jenny is your kid and she brought a friend you don't know into our home." He takes a step toward her. "Anyway, you *did* snoop. The question is, where do we go from here?"

"I have no idea. I just want to get back to work on *Spotlight* and pretend this never happened." Erica collapses into a kitchen chair. "Oh, Greg, what if Jenny *is* sleeping with boys?"

"I think that's highly unlikely. And whatever she is or isn't doing, we don't want to overreact."

"Greg, sex is dangerous at that age, in so many ways."

Greg walks over to Erica, stands behind her and puts his hands on her shoulders, and massages gently. "I love you, Erica. I know this is bringing up a lot for you. Like Susan, for instance."

"I hear her taunting voice. I'm afraid I inherited her mothering gene."

"You are not your mother. You've raised a great kid."

"You mean Dirk and Linda have."

"No, I mean *you* have. You, Erica. You're a wonderful mother and Jenny adores you."

"You've seen how sarcastic she's becoming. And she's angry at me. Again."

"It's called adolescence."

Erica turns and looks up at Greg. With his thumb he gently wipes away some silly wet from her eyes. Erica gulps air, wills herself to grow still, to focus, to replace emotion with reason. She's quiet for a long moment. Then she grasps Greg's hand in her own and holds it to her cheek. It feels warm and soft and rough and safe. She stands up and kisses him lightly on the lips. Whatever professional jealousy he may be feeling seems a million miles away. Their marriage is solid. Isn't it? "Thank you."

Greg follows her out into the living room. They can hear the girls' laughter from down the hall. Erica walks toward the sound, saying, "Jenny! It's my turn for a little walk." She hopes her casual tone masks the apprehension she feels.

CHAPTER 7 ————————————————

NEAL CLARK IS SWIMMING HIS daily laps at the Union Club. How many sixty-four-year-old men swim for an hour a day? He loves the rhythm, the strokes, the breathing; it's a meditation for him, his mind clears and fresh ideas pour in. Neal Clark loves ideas. Ideas are what got him where he is today, which is a long way from where he started. In a dirt-poor nothing of a town in the middle of nowhere. His father worked on the highways—a brutal job in the Manitoba winters, a thankless one in the baking mosquito-ravaged summers. He hated it and took out his bitterness on his only son, while his mother cowered in the corner, afraid of the man she married.

Neal knew from his earliest memory that he was going to get out. School was nothing but a distraction for him, a waste of time. The teachers would chastise him for not doing his homework. Fools in their frayed cardigans and half-glasses. He got his first after-school job when he was nine, shoveling manure on a nearby farm—and he hasn't stopped working since. He dropped out of school at fourteen, the very day after he finally stood up to his father. Knocked him out, he did. Right onto the kitchen floor. That was a lesson learned. He left home a week later and moved to Winnipeg, where he got a room in a musty boardinghouse and found a job unloading freight for the railroad. He kept his mouth shut and his ears open. Saved every nickel he could, and earned more on the side collecting scrap metal. He began studying geology, devouring books and articles by the dozens. Bought his first piece of land when he was twenty, paid cash. Then made his pitch to a local oilman with deep pockets. They put in a well. It gushed. One well led to another, and soon he didn't need a partner.

And today he owns a tasty little chunk of the whole province—logging and gas and oil and mining and pharmaceuticals and a chain of hardware stores and construction and farming. Oh, and politicians. Premiers come and go. Neal Clark endures. Every list names him the richest man in Manitoba. But so what? What's *next* is what he cares about—moving forward, rhythm, stroke, breathe. And that's where his greatest idea—no, *their* greatest idea—comes in. The one that will take his wealth and power to a whole new level. *Power*. He swims harder, faster.

As he climbs out of the pool and grabs his towel, he thinks, *And I've found the perfect mate to make it happen—and to be by my side after it happens.* He smiles as he thinks of her, their hearts and minds in sync. And their bodies, of course. Power is the ultimate aphrodisiac. Mary understands that. That's what makes them such an unstoppable team.

They met ten years ago, at an energy conference here in Winnipeg, and the attraction was immediate. Yes, it was physical—within the hour, they'd retreated to her suite to discuss coal futures. It was a passionate discussion. But they quickly realized they had far more in common than desire. They shared philosophies about personal freedom, government overreach, excessive taxation—intellectual sparks flew and they talked well into the night. Yes, she was married. But Neal and Mary believe in free will. Adults make choices. That's their right. The bond that ignited that night has only grown over the decade, as their grand idea took shape and they began the long process of making it a reality. They are going to do nothing less than redraw the map of the United States. And it's happening. Yes, it is. They've reached critical mass and the snowball is rolling, gathering steam with each revolution. *Revolution!*

At his locker, he wonders if he should call her. Just to hear her voice. He knows how hard she's working on her end. She's such a worker. His Mary. He loves that. He loves her.

But they have to be discreet. For now. Soon enough all the world will know. Neal has learned the virtue of patience. But there is one call he will make.

As he leaves the club, phone in hand, it's just getting dark and the street—a few blocks from downtown Winnipeg—is quiet. The May air holds a promise of warmth. He takes out his phone. Then a man appears out of the shadows. He looks half drunk, his eyes are lidded, his clothes are raggedy, and when he gets close Neal smells him, dank and rancid. He holds out a hand and smiles feebly. "Can you help me out, sir, eh, please?"

Neal looks into the man's hopeful and pathetic eyes—poor old soul, what a wasted life. "Yes, sure I can help you out." He reaches into his pocket and pulls out a ten-dollar bill. He glances up and down the street before holding it out toward the beggar, whose eyes light up. Just as he reaches for the bill, Neal shoves him back, hard, and the man tumbles down onto the sidewalk with an ominous *thud*, crying out in pain.

Neal laughs as he walks away, pockets the bill, and dials the corporal's number.

CHAPTER 8 ———————————————————————————

ERICA AND JENNY ARE HEADING toward Sheep Meadow, Manhattan's backyard. The park is full of New Yorkers enjoying the balmy spring day, playing and biking and picnicking, but none of it registers with Erica; her focus is on Jenny, and her own anxiety. Erica has no makeup on and is wearing sunglasses and a cap, and thankfully no one pays any attention to her.

"So . . . it's been a fun weekend with Beth?"

Jenny nods.

"Do you two hang out together a lot back home?"

"Yes. She's super popular. She's almost famous. Like you."

"Is she popular with boys?"

"Of course."

"Does she date?"

"Why are you asking me all these questions about Beth, Mom? And why are we out on this walk? What's up?"

Erica takes a deep breath and leaps in. "I found a box of condoms in your bedroom."

Jenny stops and makes a face. "What were you doing in my bedroom?"

"You're my daughter. It's my apartment." *Grrrrr*—she knows it's the wrong thing to say as soon as the words are out of her mouth.

"I thought it was *my* apartment too."

"Of course it is, honey."

"Yeah, right. I don't feel at home there anyway."

"You don't?"

"No. It's yours and Greg's house. I live with Dad and Linda."

Erica suddenly feels like she's about half Jenny's age, a confused kid who doesn't understand the big world and just wants to sit on the floor and cry and cry.

"But, honey, you *asked* to live with them, you chose it. It wasn't what I wanted."

"You didn't fight it."

"I didn't fight it because I thought it was what you wanted."

"It *is* what I wanted, but I also wanted you to fight it."

They stand there a foot apart, but Erica feels like a chasm has opened between them.

Reach across it, Erica, reach for your baby.

"I guess I read that whole situation wrong. I'm sorry if I've failed you. I was trying to do what was best for you. You're the most important thing in the world to me. And you know it."

"I know it until a bomb goes off somewhere and you get on a plane."

"It's what I do for a living. It's always been my dream. Can you understand that?"

Jenny is silent.

"If you want me to be a mother, you can't criticize me for acting like one. When I found the condoms I panicked. There are a lot of dangers you can't appreciate yet, and I don't want you to make any mistakes you might regret later."

"It creeps me out that you were snooping in my room. It's pathetic."

Erica takes Jenny's shoulders and lowers her voice. "You listen to me, Jenny, I'm your mother. You show me some respect. I've worked like a dog to get where I am, and to provide *you*, young lady, with a lot of advantages." Jenny rolls her eyes and Erica has an urge to slap her. "What were those condoms doing in Beth's suitcase?"

"Come on, Mom, chillax."

"I don't *want* to chillax. I want to know what's going on here."

Jenny is quiet for a moment and then says, "Mom?"

"Yes?"

"The condoms are not for sex," Jenny says slowly, in the tone a teacher might use to reach a not-wildly-bright student. "They're for the condom challenge."

"The *what?*"

"The condom challenge. It's a big thing with YouTubers right now. You fill a condom with water, then drop it on someone and it wraps around their head and they look like they're in a fishbowl . . . Just google it, Mom."

Erica is gobsmacked, stands there with her mouth open. She feels ancient and ridiculous and left out. Why hasn't Jenny told her about this infantile frat-house prank? Why?

"Did you actually perform this 'challenge'?"

Jenny smiles. "Yeah, we did."

"This weekend? In the apartment?"

"Yeah. I think it's really cool footage."

"And were you the dropper or the dropee?"

"I dropped it on Beth. It worked perfectly."

Erica tries to digest all this information. But does she really believe it? Is there more that Jenny's not telling her? She's about to ask when her phone rings. She decides not to answer it, but then sees who it is. "Jenny, this is Greg."

"Go ahead and take it, Mom."

"How's the talk going?" Greg asks in a charged voice.

"It's going. What's up?"

"The secessionists down in West Texas got into a shoot-out with federal marshals. Two of them were killed, as well as two marshals. It's very ugly."

"Is it over?"

"No. It's all just breaking. Both sides are armed, and the secession-ists won't talk to a mediator."

"This is big." And fits so perfectly with her *Spotlight* plans. "I think I should go down there. We'll head back." Erica hangs up. Suddenly the condoms don't seem so important.

"What's happening, Mom?" Jenny asks, alert and curious. All her snarkiness has evaporated. The two of them turn and start to make time back to the apartment.

"There's a confrontation going on down in southwest Texas between federal marshals and a group of sovereign citizens."

"What's a sovereign citizen?"

"It's someone who doesn't recognize the authority of the federal government. They're secessionists and want their state to leave the union."

"And become like an independent country or something?"

"Exactly. They don't think they should have to pay taxes. They're very militant. Things got violent today."

"Are people dead?"

"Greg said at least four."

"Wow. I agree, you should probably go down there."

Erica takes Jenny's hand and they pick up the pace. Suddenly it feels like they're allies and friends. "Thanks for being so understanding."

"Beth says I can't expect you to be a regular mom."

"Does she?"

"She says that celebrity moms only pretend to be like real moms."

What's a real mom? Maybe someday Erica will find out. But not today.

Erica calls Eileen McDermott. "You've heard?"

"Yes, I've got us booked on a two o'clock flight out of LaGuardia. The car will pick you up in half an hour. We've got a local crew in place."

Erica's apartment building comes into view, and she and Jenny break into a trot. Upstairs, Greg has her suitcase open on their bed. As she starts to pack, Beth appears in the doorway, filming. Erica is about to scream at her—wouldn't that make fun footage on TMZ?—when Greg ushers Beth out, takes her camera, and deletes the footage.

When Erica is finished packing, she, Greg, and Jenny head downstairs to wait for the car. She takes out her phone and starts to read—Eileen has already sent her background material on the Free Texas Rangers. Greg tries to draw Jenny into some small talk, but she stays focused on her mom, her face filled with pride and concern.

The car pulls up. Erica hugs Greg and then Jenny. "Good-bye, Mom. Be careful."

Just as Erica turns toward the car, Greg's phone rings. Erica catches the incoming name: Leslie Burke Wilson.

CHAPTER 9 —————————————————————

AS ERICA JETS ACROSS THE continent, she does her homework on the situation in Texas. The Free Texas Rangers movement is less than five years old and was started by Steve Watson, the charismatic twenty-eight-year-old scion of an oil and ranching fortune. Since his parents' death three years ago, he has racked up a six-million-dollar past-due bill with the IRS. Three months ago a lien was placed on the family's four-thousand-acre ranch, and it's scheduled to be auctioned off by the feds. Since that time Watson has denied law enforcement entry to the compound and has turned the private-plane hangar into an armory. According to federal intelligence, Watson and his supporters have amassed a vast arsenal that includes rocket launchers, armored vehicles, bombs, and other sophisticated weaponry.

Erica watches footage from that morning's shoot-out, which took place just outside the entrance to the ranch. Law enforcement was out in force, basically waiting and watching, hoping the secessionists would run out of food, water, medicine, and, most important, resolve. They know from experience that encampments like this one often run out of steam on their own volition. People have lives they need to get back to, things get cramped and dirty and uncomfortable, tempers flare, passions cool. The feds' goal is to arrest Watson on tax evasion charges, but not by force. Bloodshed is to be avoided at any cost, as it would only turn Watson into a martyr and bolster the sovereign citizen movement nationwide.

Erica watches on-screen as a midsized truck arrives on the scene, carrying supplies. US Marshals in an armored vehicle block its path. Then suddenly the back door of the truck rolls open and some kid with an automatic weapon—he looks like a teenager—starts spraying fire. The feds return the favor, and the shooter and the driver of the truck are dead within seconds, but not before two marshals are taken out and several more injured. The footage is terrifying and ugly. Live reporting shows that in the hours since, an eerie calm has pervaded the scene.

Erica's flight lands in Midland. Eileen has a car waiting, and they set off for the half-hour drive to the Watson ranch outside Odessa. A broadcast van with the crew follows. Erica has never been to this part of the country and it looks . . . flat. And scruffy. And beneath the flat and scruff lies oil, billions of barrels of it. In fact, the entire economy lives and dies by oil; it's the reason the cities of Midland and Odessa came into being in the first place. And it's hot, 107 degrees, sticky and dense, with shade hard to find. They're lucky they have all that oil to pump out of the earth, Erica thinks. She can't imagine voluntarily living here otherwise.

They pass oil wells pecking like hungry science-fiction insects, trailer parks, ranches, mini-malls, billboards featuring hucksters in cowboy hats selling trucks as big as small houses. Erica has never spent more than a day or two in Texas, and it all feels foreign and forbidding with its macho and almost obsessive worship of guns. Erica has a more conflicted relationship with guns. On the one hand, she hates them. On the other, she's been in serious danger more than once and wants to be prepared for it happening again. To that end, she's been taking shooting lessons at the West Side Rifle and Pistol Range on West Twentieth Street. She also got a permit and bought a handgun—she refuses to touch an automatic, she considers them killing machines that should be banned.

Texas suffers from no such ambivalence. Which isn't surprising, considering its violent history. Even the cursory research she was able to do on the flight revealed that Watson is only the latest in a long line of Texans who have no use for a union, any union, and have no hesitation in taking up arms to oppose it.

Texas was a Mexican territory until 1836 when—spurred on by American settlers—it declared its independence from Mexico—*Remember the Alamo!*—and became a sovereign republic. But it wasn't exactly a roaring success—the fledgling nation had no currency, massive debt, and an economy that was just generally in the tank. Despite vehement opposition from many of its citizens, Texas joined the United States in 1845. But its brief period as an independent nation seared itself into the state's identity, and in the 175 years since it has seen many secession movements come and go. Erica is fascinated by how quickly political upheaval can happen—and how slowly the hearts and minds of citizens follow. Look at the Civil War. In many ways it's still being fought today. Still, Free Texas Rangers is the best financed and most violent in the long line of Texas secessionist crusades. According to polls, roughly a quarter of Texans support its goal of reestablishing an independent republic, a figure Erica finds deeply disconcerting.

"Is there any chance we can get an interview with Watson?" she asks Eileen.

"Right now he and his people aren't speaking to anyone but themselves."

"Do we know how much food and water they have?"

"No. And that's a big question."

They arrive at the entrance to the Watson ranch. It's fronted by a stone and metal gate that looks like it could hold off an army, with fencing that seems to stretch forever on either side. Erica and Eileen get out of the car. The hangar is visible about two hundred yards past the gate. There are scores of journalists, broadcast trucks, armored military vehicles, and local, state, and national law enforcement gathered. Erica spots David Muir and Andrea Mitchell. The air is hot and still, people are talking in whispers, leaning into one another, and even in the heat the air is charged with the electricity of anticipation. Erica feels her adrenaline spike.

Eileen points to a middle-aged black man. "That's Jake Gilman, deputy director of the US Marshals Service. He's the guy in charge."

Erica approaches Gilman and introduces herself. He looks serious and shaken, but focused. "Can you tell me where things stand?"

"They haven't gotten any supplies in for six days. We're hoping things are getting dire."

"Do they have a water supply?"

"The hangar is plumbed. However, it is not air-conditioned."

"Can you tell me anything about what happened earlier?"

"The kid who did the shooting was Frank Gordon, seventeen, with two priors for dealing meth. These movements don't always attract the best and brightest. For every sincere member there are two wackos. And the wackos are the ones who drop their everyday lives and show up at standoffs."

"Can I get you on camera?"

Gilman nods.

Erica's crew is busy setting up, she's going to go live in about five minutes. Her phone rings. It's Greg. Erica realizes with a start that she hasn't thought about Jenny or condoms since the moment she stepped into the car for the ride to the airport. What a relief. Her work is not only exciting, important, and fulfilling, it's a potent defense mechanism.

"How is it down there?" Greg asks.

"Intense. Did Beth and Jenny get off safely?"

"With their tails between their legs. Are you okay about everything?"

"Oh, I'm just thrilled that a condom challenge filmed in our apartment is going to be splashed all over the Internet."

"They promised not to identify the location."

"Hooray."

"They're kids, Erica."

"That cuts both ways. I don't want Jenny to be haunted by a video trail. And also, do we know for *sure* that the condoms were only used as glorified water balloons? But I'm about to go live." There's something else that's eating at Erica. "Listen, Greg, I saw you got a call from Leslie Wilson just as I was leaving."

There's a pause and then, "She tried to reach you." Erica doesn't remember missing any calls. "She invited us for dinner on Saturday."

Erica is both flattered and, for reasons she doesn't quite understand, somewhat wary. Can she really hold her own in that world? There's something frightening about its casual, at times caustic, brilliance. Still, it's what she wants. Isn't it? "That would be great."

"She also wants you to call her. She said she'd be willing to do a long-distance interview on the situation down there."

That's a generous offer. "That could be fascinating. Let's see how this plays out."

Erica hangs up just as the soundman hands her a mic and Eileen gives her a go.

"This is Erica Sparks reporting live from the Watson ranch outside Odessa, Texas, which was the scene of a shoot-out this morning between US Marshals and members of the Free Texas Rangers, resulting in the death of two marshals and two movement members. In the distance behind me you can see the airplane hangar where Free Texas leader Steve Watson and his followers have been isolated for almost a week now."

Then suddenly Erica hears shouts of "They're coming out!"

Erica watches as a small group of mostly men, about a dozen in all, walk out of the hangar with their hands up. They look hot and exhausted, scared and defiant. "It appears that members of the movement are surrendering. We can see that more followers are pouring out of the hangar, the total is now about twenty. This story is unfolding in front of our eyes."

Marshal Gilman speaks into a megaphone and his voice booms out, "WALK SLOWLY AND KEEP YOUR HANDS UP!"

And then Steve Watson walks out of the hangar behind his followers. His hands are also in the air, his face looks drawn but determined. "Steve Watson, the head of the Free Texas Rangers, also appears to be surrendering," Erica says.

Just as Watson reaches his followers, Erica notes that he's wearing a heavy jacket—and then there's a *boom* and a flash of light and the ground shakes as Steve Watson blows himself into small gobs of particulate matter, taking his followers with him into the void.

CHAPTER 10 ⸺⸺⸺⸺⸺⸺⸺⸺⸺⸺

IT'S THE NEXT AFTERNOON—THE MONDAY after a very eventful weekend—and Erica is back in her office, in the middle of interviewing potential executive producers for *Spotlight*. After yesterday's suicide bombing, there really wasn't that much to report. The deed was done, the perpetrator known. She flew back to New York, but the horror and pathology continue to fascinate her, especially since her research has uncovered no less than two dozen other secessionist groups in the country. Most are far less radical than Free Texas Rangers, but all share a profound mistrust, even hatred, of government. And the movement is growing in strength.

Erica is feeling a lot of pressure—she wants to get going on the first episode of *Spotlight*. She's already contacted Sturges and Mary Bellamy in North Dakota, and they've agreed to a joint interview about their Take Back Our Homeland movement. Unlike Steve Watson and most of the other secessionist groups, the Bellamys are working through the political process, methodically building public support for their defiance of the federal government. Few in the establishment, from either party, take their quest seriously, but they are well known and admired, even loved, figures in North Dakota, and their message, means, and pedigree make them the most fascinating and potentially dangerous secessionists in the country.

But before Erica can seize the moment and start shooting, she has to hire an executive producer. The half dozen prospects she's met with so far all have strong résumés, but she hasn't felt that spark, that chemistry that's crucial to a successful partnership. There's one more candidate today, and Erica walks into her outer office—presided over by Shirley Stamos—to greet her.

A woman about Erica's age, black, carrying a few extra pounds, wearing a dark suit, stands up and extends her hand. "Gloria Washburn, what a pleasure." Her shake is firm and her clear eyes radiate a focused intelligence.

"Thank you for coming in," Erica says, ushering Washburn into her office. They sit across from each other at Erica's desk. "So you've been working at WJLA down in Washington for the last six years?"

"Yes, I started as an intern. One thing led to another. For the past three years I've been executive producer of *Washington Undercover*, our investigative series. We've exposed corruption by local and national politicians, in multinational corporations, and in metro DC agencies. Our work has led to over a dozen arrests and convictions, and institutional reforms." She recites these facts simply, without an ounce of boasting. She doesn't even mention the Peabody Award her show has won; after all, it's right there on her résumé.

"Impressive. Can you tell me what drives you, what makes you jump out of bed in the morning?"

Washburn leans forward. "Erica, I believe journalism is *vital* to our democracy."

Erica feels a surge of excitement. Washburn's passion and sense of mission are just what were missing from the other applicants.

"What do you think is the most important quality in a producer?" Erica asks.

"Results. If you don't deliver, you're not doing your job. I'm not interested in reinventing the wheel, in trendy new theories of leadership or management. I'm interested in what *works*. A producer has to be obsessed with detail, has to respect her staff, delegate authority, encourage initiative, and stay one step ahead. And of course, remain flexible. In our business you never know what's going to hit you next. And the blows can come swiftly and from out of left field."

Erica is drawn to Gloria's combination of quiet confidence, energy, and openness. She's not sucking up to Erica, yet she's created an immediate rapport, a relationship of peers. The two talk for another ten minutes, but Erica has seen enough. She doesn't want to play her hand until Washburn's background check has been completed, but she's confident she's found her woman.

Erica escorts Washburn out of her office. "Thank you so much for coming in. We'll let you know as soon as the decision is made."

Washburn leaves, and Erica turns to Shirley. "What do you think?"

"I think very highly."

Erica walks back into her office just as Greg calls. She winces. The subtle, unspoken strain that *Spotlight* has put on their marriage is only increasing. She's embarking on this great adventure without him. He's certainly qualified to produce the show himself, but Erica feels strongly it would be a bad idea. Home and work boundaries would blur. Erica loves Greg, he's brought her happiness, but there's some part of her that she has to hold back. No doubt it dates back to her traumatic childhood, when she had no one to turn to, no one she could depend on but herself. Little by little, as she grew up, she developed an identity—part armor, part motivator—as an independent girl and then woman. She wasn't going to wholly rely on anyone, ever. Some part of her strength and drive comes from that sense of self. If she was working with Greg, together virtually 24/7, she's afraid she would lose it, get claustrophobic, feel suffocated.

Greg senses her reticence, but Erica isn't sure he understands the reasons for it. Sometimes when they're discussing *Spotlight*, a look of confusion tinged with hurt will come over his face. Does she owe him an explanation? She's afraid that if she opens that can of worms, a lethal snake—green and angry—might slither out. The fact is, her career continues to soar while his plods along, successful at a much lower level and not fully engaging for him. She knows he misses the hurly-burly of being in the trenches. He's not really cut out to be a consultant, and Erica wonders if his male pride is keeping him from admitting it. Managing that pride requires a delicate balance of support and discretion. Oh, what a roiling mass (mess?) of subtle adjustments and seesawing emotions marriage is.

Erica sits at her desk. "Hi there."

"How's the search going?" he asks.

Erica pauses. "It's progressing. There's a lot of talent out there."

Greg pauses. "No one leapt out at you?"

Erica closes her eyes and exhales. "A couple of candidates seem promising."

"You seem preoccupied. Are you sure you're not taking on too much?"

"You know I thrive under pressure," Erica says.

"It can be a thin line between thriving and cracking."

Well, *that* was unnecessary. "I'll try my best not to cross it."

"You know I'm always available to troubleshoot. Even if it's only short-term. It might take some of the pressure off."

The truth is Erica's North Star—but sometimes you have to head south. "That might be very helpful. Let me look at the budget and timetable. If one of today's candidates gets hired, of course, everything changes."

"Of course."

Erica hangs up and walks over to the window—down on Sixth Avenue, the city is its pulsing, indifferent self. There was definitely an edge in Greg's voice. Jealousy. Erica's first marriage failed because of her drinking, her ambition, her final terrible fall. But she's older now, and wiser. Not as impulsive. She understands where her self-destructive instincts come from—the toxic quicksand of her past. She's better now, isn't she? She's made some peace, her sobriety is solid, she's built a strong foundation to replace the house of cards. Right?

She looks down at the streetscape, and a wave of vertigo sweeps over her. She moves away, goes into the kitchen, and puts her hand on the refrigerator door. As she opens it, she imagines—for one delicious effervescent second—being greeted by a shiny bottle of champagne.

CHAPTER 11 ————————————

GLORIA WASHBURN WALKS OUT OF the GNN building and quickly merges with the swarming lunchtime crowds. She takes out her prepaid phone and calls.

"How did it go?" the male voice asks. Hearing it, Gloria feels that familiar wave of desire ripple over her body—and her soul.

"I think it went well. We don't want to count any chickens, but our preparation paid off."

"When will you know?"

"In a couple of days."

"What did you think of her?"

"She's very pretty."

"That's it?"

They laugh. Their shorthand laugh. The one they've developed during the two years of their beautiful relationship. No, partnership. Their beautiful partnership.

"She's sincere, hardworking, and . . . troubled."

"We do love them troubled, don't we?" he says, lowering his voice into that seductive whisper.

Gloria has pleased him, which is what matters most. More than anything. She lowers her own voice. "Yes, darling, we do love them troubled," she says with a satisfied smile as she reaches the curb and prepares to step out into traffic.

CHAPTER 12 ————————————————

LESLIE AND STAN WILSON LIVE in one of those Richard Meier glass buildings facing the Hudson in the far West Village. The apartment is enormous and open, with a large Mondrian competing with the view of the glittering river and the towers of Newport City on the far shore. The space is impossibly chic, streamlined, midcentury, and Erica feels a stab of insecurity—her own apartment seems so old-fashioned, even dowdy, in comparison.

There's another couple there—Frazier Stone, the painter, and Veda Alexander, the designer—as well as Elle Walker, a youngish screen-writer known for her wit and for the string of men in her life. All three of them are dressed in striking outfits that look to Erica as if they should be hanging on gallery walls, not human bodies. She defiantly (defensively?) fingers one of her clip-on earrings.

They're sitting around on vast low sofas, Leslie is in the kitchen.

"To an artist, truth is subjective," Frazier says, Scotch-and-water in hand. He's burly and virile, with a booming voice, larger than life. "My work is my truth, it makes its own rules—and then breaks them. I don't concern myself with absolutes."

"I *so* agree," Elle Walker says. "You can't let the truth stand in the way of a good story."

"Of course, in advertising, truth is a tool, to be used selectively. 'The whole truth and nothing but' may be fine for the courtroom, but it could put me out of business," Stan says.

Everyone laughs. Except Erica. She finds the discussion disheartening but stays on the sidelines, intimidated by the casual assurance, clubby and cool.

"Well, in the news business we play by different rules," Greg says. "The truth isn't the means to an end, it *is* the end. And it is absolute."

Erica is proud of him for speaking up and feels a wave of affection and respect.

"You've just proved my point. The truth means different things to different people," Frazier says.

"Every woman who has ever faked an orgasm knows *that*," Elle says, to great laughter all around.

Leslie walks in, looking both chic and homey in a short pearl dress—what amazing legs—and a blue chef's apron, her trademark bergamot perfume kissing the air. "I could use a little help in the kitchen."

Erica practically leaps out of her seat—not easy from the low-slung sofa—and follows Leslie into the sleek, if diminutive, kitchen. These condos are clearly not designed for the Julia Child crowd.

"So, how is *Spotlight* coming?" Leslie asks as she takes down plates and picks up a serving spoon. There's a pot of paella on the stove.

"Well. I hired an executive producer, and I'm flying out to North Dakota next week to meet with the Bellamys."

"Terrific. Whom did you hire?"

"Her name is Gloria Washburn, she's been the executive producer of *Washington Undercover* for the past three years."

"I've heard terrific things about that show. Weren't you tempted to hire your husband?"

Erica wasn't expecting that question. She ignores it, gesturing around the kitchen and asking, "What can I do?"

"How about tossing the salad? Back to Greg. Who isn't resting on those divine looks—he's bright and has something to say. Terrific guy."

"He is. He's wonderful."

"If he were mine, I don't think I'd let him out of my sight."

"You know he's got his own business. I'm not sure he'd want to be around me 24/7."

"From what he told Stan, the consultancy is fine, but he feels a little bit . . . irrelevant. He said he misses the excitement, the high stakes of being at the center of things."

Odd that Greg would tell that to Stan—whom he's known for all of two weeks—when he's never brought it up directly with Erica. But it does confirm her suspicions. She pours on the dressing, picks up the salad servers, and starts to toss.

"Erica," Leslie says with a laugh, "they're greens, not enemies of the state."

Erica stops cold. "I'm sorry. Was I tossing too vigorously?"

"Lettuce does bruise," Leslie says drily.

People bruise too.

"How's your new book coming?" Erica asks to change the subject. Leslie is working on a biography of Michelle Obama.

"It's always a slog at this point. My research is done; now I have to organize it, pull it together, and force it into a coherent narrative."

"Somehow you turn history and politics into page-turners."

Leslie smiles, stops plating the paella, and takes Erica's hand. She leads her into the back of the apartment and opens the door to her office. The room is book-lined, every available surface is strewn with articles and papers and jotting-covered legal pads. The shelves are dotted with miniature giraffes of various sizes and styles, and in the middle of the room there's an enormous table entirely taken up by a wooden box filled with research, with markers dividing it by category and subject. The contrast of this clutter with the rest of the apartment is striking.

"Welcome to my id," Leslie announces.

"Mine's a lot messier."

"We'll have to discuss that at some point."

"So this is where the it's-not-magic-it's-hard-work happens."

"Thank you."

"And your dreams are populated by galloping giraffes."

"My parents took me on safari when I was seven."

Erica knows that Leslie comes from privilege; both her parents were academics, but there was old money in the family.

"I just fell in love with the giraffes. Here is this creature with the most awkward anatomy, and yet . . . they are the soul of grace." Leslie fusses with her hair and then looks down. "I was never the prettiest girl. So I've had to . . ."

Erica is touched by Leslie's admission. Underneath her sometimes brittle brilliance is a kid who's had to work hard to accept herself. She reaches out and gently touches her arm. Leslie gives her a disarming smile.

"Oh, rats, the food!" Leslie exclaims.

Leslie has placed Erica between Frazier and Elle at the table. Frazier thinks that Erica "*must* do a *Spotlight* on the art market, it's as corrupt as the Kremlin." Greg is on Leslie's left, and she spends most of the meal leaning into him, chatting in a low exclusionary tone, laughing and making him laugh.

Leslie and Stan clear the plates. Erica looks over at Greg and he gives her a big smile. Someone's having a very good time.

Leslie comes back to the table and stands behind Greg. "Now who's up for some dessert?" she asks, casually putting a hand on his shoulder.

CHAPTER 13 —————————————————————

IT'S A LITTLE PAST ELEVEN, and Erica and Greg are in their bedroom, getting ready for bed. Greg has had too much to drink—his movements are emphatic and jerky. On the ride uptown he was silent, even a little sulky. He wanted to stay longer but Erica insisted they head home—she's exhausted and wants to get right to work on *Spotlight* in the morning.

Greg takes off his jacket and shirt and tosses them on a chair. It's annoying—he knows Erica likes a neat room. And that she dislikes what happens to him when he's tight. His charm dissipates and then rematerializes as a chip on his shoulder. And she hates the smell of alcohol on him. Hates it because it's so seductive and unfair.

Erica takes off—and hangs up—her blouse and skirt and heads into the bathroom. She looks at herself in the mirror and sees insecurity in the corners of her eyes. The evening has left her feeling a little confused, even conflicted. Leslie and Stan were so welcoming, Erica feels like a door to a whole new world is opening for her. It's both flattering and intimidating. Leslie is just so polished and sharp and knowing, but there always seems to be something unspoken going on below the surface. And her financial and academic pedigrees trigger memories of Erica's days at Yale, the casual confidence of her class-mates, their not-so-subtle digs at her background. *"You're from rural Maine? How picturesque."*

Erica, stop it! You're more famous than all of them put together. And your work may not hang in museums or get nominated for Academy Awards, but it makes a difference in the real world.

Erica washes her face and brushes her teeth. In the bedroom, Greg has gotten into bed and turned out the bedside lights. Erica climbs in beside him. She lies on her back, staring up at the ceiling. The room feels dark and lonely.

And then Greg reaches out and pulls her to him, roughly, and his hot whiskey mouth is on hers, his tongue insistent. Erica pulls away.

"What's wrong, not in the mood?" he asks sarcastically.

"No, *you're* not in the mood. Make that state of mind."

"Oh, so now I'm not allowed to have a couple of drinks?"

"And I'm not allowed to say I don't want to have sex?"

There's a pause and then Greg says, "You know, sometimes it's not a lot of fun being Mr. Erica Sparks."

"I'd say you more than held your own. And you certainly looked like you were having fun."

"I'm a nobody with that crowd. I run a two-bit consultancy. That Frazier guy never said a word to me."

"Leslie certainly made up for that."

"Jealous?"

"No," Erica says too quickly.

She can't believe they're arguing like this. They almost never argue. She *hates* fighting, she saw enough fighting as a kid to last her three lifetimes. It's ugly and sad and a big fat waste of energy.

There's a pause and Greg props himself up on an elbow, and when he speaks his tone is soft, if slightly slurred. "I'm sorry I'm being such a jerk."

"It takes two."

"Nah, I started it. It's just that, well, you're putting *Spotlight* together and I'm trying to win a contract with a station in Akron to run team-building exercises."

Erica feels a wave of guilt. She could hire Greg for *Spotlight*. But her gut tells her it would be a bad idea. Yes, they were an amazing team *before* they got married. But a ring changes everything. As empathetic as Greg is, he also has an ego. While they were equals at the start of her career at GNN, today she's top dog. And she *wants* to be top dog, without apology. And he *is* angling for a team-building gig in Akron.

They look at each other in the dim diffuse light coming in through the room's windows. "I'm proud of your success, and who knows where it will lead," Erica says. "I'm also exhausted."

"We're doing okay, aren't we?"

Erica feels her throat tighten and tears well up behind her eyes. She reaches up and touches Greg's cheek. "Yeah, we are."

He smiles, lopsided, and turns away from her, curling up. Within a minute he's fast asleep. Erica lies there, trying to control her anxiety.

CHAPTER 14 —————————————————————

GENERAL FLOYD MORROW STRIDES DOWN the Pentagon hallway, enraged. *How dare they?!* It's despicable, a disgrace! He reaches his office, storms in, and slams the door behind him. Then he kicks the wastepaper basket across the room. His temples are pounding and he feels a massive headache forming behind his eyeballs. There are no standards anymore. The country is going to ruin. No soap in the men's room dispenser! How is a man supposed to wash his hands after doing his business? Germs are spreading. Antibiotics are becoming useless. It could lead to an epidemic. Some idiot might say it's a small thing. There are no small things! *Only small people!* It's emblematic of everything's that's wrong with this country!

The whole USA is sick, sick in the head. It disgusts him.

Well, he's not going to take it! He's going to fight back and fight hard and fight dirty if he has to. And he's got the means to do it. Oh yes, he does. And nobody knows. Well, James knows, of course. He's the one who brought Morrow into the movement. Fine young man. And Neal knows. Another upright fellow. A strong man. A self-made man. Knows what he wants and how to get it. And, of course, the Bellamys know. Mary is a good woman. Great woman. Classy lady. Old school. And

Sturges. A real gentleman. Yup. He, James, Neal, and the Bellamys are quite the team—the dream team that's going to be this crummy country's worst nightmare.

Just thinking about James and Neal and Mary and Sturges brings down his blood pressure. He goes to the window and looks out at the vast parking lot. Useless fools, every one of them. Rats on a sinking ship. Well, they can have this country 'tis of thee. He doesn't want it. Not anymore.

General Morrow looks over at the map on his wall. It's a map of a quadrant of North Dakota. It shows Devil's Lake. And the peninsula that sticks into the lake and is home to Camp Grafton, the army reserve base and training center. Great place. His fiefdom, his baby, his bailiwick. Under his command. He wishes he could be out there full-time, but the stupid army wants him here, stuck behind a desk, running things from afar. They say it's a low-priority facility, that his one week a month out there is enough since the base is quiet in between periods of reserve training.

That's going to change soon. (Ha! Is it ever!) He's put in his third request to be stationed at Grafton full-time, permanently. Ironically—cleverly!—he used the Take Back Our Homeland movement as his reason. Look at what happened in Texas, and with some of these other wacko militia movements, he told his (inferior) superiors. It could happen in North Dakota. (Ha-ha, could it ever.) He's expecting an answer any day, but he was forceful and convincing, he knows that. He's been getting encouraging signals.

Floyd is starting to feel much better. He takes out a stick of Juicy Fruit, unwraps it, bends it in two, and puts it into his mouth. Yeah. He's got a good feeling about this transfer.

And his other duty? Helping to keep track of a certain reporter who doesn't understand that when you play with fire, you get scalded. Also going well. James, who happens to be his colleague here in the Pentagon, has got a source practically embedded in Erica Sparks's head. Embedded where her head is. Floyd laughs.

His office phone rings. He stands up straight.

"General Floyd Morrow here."

"This is General Smithers." Three-star general Gwen Smithers is his commanding officer.

Yes, she's a woman. And, yes, that rankles. Patton must be turning over in his grave.

"Yes, General."

"Your application to be stationed at Camp Grafton has been approved."

Floyd feels adrenaline surge through his veins with the velocity of a fighter jet. Yeah, baby, yeah! "Happy to hear it, General. You won't regret it."

"Your points about the . . . *unpredictability* of the Homeland movement were persuasive. We need to keep a close eye on things out there. You'll send me a written report every Friday, and as needed."

"Yes, General."

"Your file has been sent to Relocation. Expect to be out there within two weeks. Don't let your country down, General."

Floyd hangs up. *His* country. This steaming pile of political correctness and mediocrity isn't *his* country anymore. He wants *out*. And that's exactly where he's going.

He takes out his special phone and calls Mary Bellamy. He keeps his voice calm, businesslike, the way Mary likes it.

"General Morrow."

"I've received orders to relocate to Camp Grafton."

Floyd is sure he can actually hear Mary smile. "This is good news, isn't it?"

"Very good news."

"You've been doing such a good job with preparations. This will take things to a whole new level."

"I hope so, ma'am."

"I'll call Neal. He'll be delighted. Will you call James and tell him?"

"Of course. Things are taking shape, aren't they, ma'am?"

"They are, General, they certainly are."

Floyd hangs up. Then he looks around at his office, his confining, constricting office, and he imagines all the other cookie-cutter offices in this mausoleum to America's lost greatness. Bunch of third-rate paper pushers, the whole lousy sissified American military. You can all kiss my butt!

Then he gets to work writing a memo on the fact—*the outrage!*—that the soap dispenser in the men's room has run out twice in the last month.

CHAPTER 15 ───────────────────

ERICA'S FLIGHT APPROACHES BISMARCK, NORTH Dakota. Gloria Washburn sits next to her, absorbed in her work. They've only been colleagues for a week, but Erica already has a comfort level with her. The woman works hard, seems tempered with a sly sense of humor that she lets pop out now and then, and knows the news business inside out. *Spotlight* is on its way, and Erica is jazzed by a sense of momentum and challenge.

She's also glad to be out of New York. She and Greg have been tip-toeing around each other all week. She can feel his festering resentment. And she's starting to resent it. They're civil enough, but every discussion is a minefield. Which means she hasn't been able to talk about *Spotlight*, which is what's happening in her life right now, and where he could be genuinely helpful. The search for safe topics leads to tense, desultory dinners filled with pauses and way too much pride, on both sides.

Out the window Erica sees the North Dakota capitol, a grace-ful Art Deco skyscraper that's got to be one of the few state capitols without a dome, columns, and other clichéd classical flourishes. It's refreshing. Bismarck sits in the south-central part of the state on the banks of the Missouri River, and the landscape around the small city is low, grassy, and hilly. And these days the town is jumping, thanks to a booming economy driven by the state's vast gas and oil deposits, much of it being sucked up out of the earth by fracking. Whatever the means, the oil—and the gold it brings—are flowing. North Dakota has the nation's lowest unemployment rate and among the highest wages.

"Odd that a state that's doing this well should be fertile ground for sovereign citizens and secessionists," Erica says to Gloria.

"Sometimes when you're prosperous, you have time to nurture your grievances. I think there's some collective greed here too. This is an independent-minded state that doesn't feel it should have to pay for other states' sins. It gets fewer dollars back from the feds per dollar paid in taxes than any other state. And the Bellamys aren't preaching the same level of raw anger and grievance that Trump and Sanders tapped into in 2016. They're talking more about self-reliance and local control of local resources. These are bedrock Western values."

"And do the Bellamys really want North Dakota to secede?"

"They're being very careful with their language. The closest they've come to secession is talking about the state being granted more autonomy from the federal government."

"How can they possibly hope to accomplish that?" Erica asks.

"Our job is to answer that question. We're meeting them at their office at one."

"Have they made any demands on us?"

"I have to say they've been very cooperative."

The plane touches down. Outside, the air carries a hint of the tawny grassland and cattle farms that cover much of the state—but then, under that, there's another smell, faint but unmistakable, something darker, burnt and acrid and oily. As the car drives from the airport to the Bellamys' downtown office, Erica is struck by how small and white the city is—it feels so homogenous and bland, with none of the diversity that enlivens the East and West Coasts and the large cities in between. Yet an important story is building in this nondescript setting. You just never know. Which makes journalism such a thrilling profession. You're not only an eyewitness to history, you're often a part of it, influencing and even driving events.

They arrive at the midrise office building that houses the Bellamy Foundation and ride up to the sixth floor.

The receptionist announces their arrival, and within moments a robust, ruddy man in his late fifties appears, a welcoming smile on his face.

"Erica Sparks, what a pleasure. Sturges Bellamy." They shake hands. "Thank you for trekking out to the Great Plains to see us."

Introductions are made, and then Erica and Gloria follow Sturges down the hall and into a large, orderly office that has two desks and a seating area. One wall is lined with bookshelves filled with awards, citations, commemorative belt buckles, and other mementos of the Bellamys' long careers as businesspeople and philanthropists. The other walls feature oil paintings of the harsh and beautiful North Dakota landscape. Bottles of water, a pot of coffee, and a platter of cookies sit on the table.

Then Mary Bellamy appears, a welcoming smile on her face. Like her husband, she looks like she spends time outdoors—her handsome, freckle-splashed face is framed by an incongruous mane of well-coiffed auburn hair, and striking red lipstick is her only makeup. She's wearing jeans and a Western shirt with pearly snap buttons. Together, the couple radiate wealth, warmth, the West, and an eagerness to engage.

"*What* a pleasure," she says in a voice that holds hints of fancy schools and country clubs. "Let's all sit down and get to know each other a bit, shall we? Coffee? Water?"

Erica takes a cup of coffee, Gloria helps herself to a cookie. Erica loves that Gloria owns her weight—she's not one of those larger women who pick at their lunch salads and then go home and devour an entire key lime pie in one sitting.

"These are from my grandmother's recipe," Mary says.

Half out of politeness and half craving some sugary carbs, Erica bites into a cookie.

"Grammy would be so happy to see this." Mary's movements are deliberate, and she has a charming habit of tilting her head for emphasis. The total package is persuasive, although Erica can sense the artifice behind the art.

"Oh heck, I feel left out," Sturges says, reaching for a cookie. Mary laughs indulgently as he devours it—the Bellamys are brilliant at creating a convivial mood.

But enough about cookies. "I'd love to hear about your motives and plans," Erica says.

"First of all, that terrible business down in Texas bears absolutely no resemblance to our mission or means. We're nonviolent and turn away anyone who isn't," Sturges says.

"Martin Luther King is one of our great inspirations," Mary says, treating Gloria to a small empathetic smile.

"We also have a dream. And we're rolling up our sleeves to make it a reality," Sturges says.

"Both my husband and I are descended from North Dakota's original settlers. We *love* this land and the people who live on it." Mary moves forward in her chair, clasps her hands in her lap, and grows serious. "And we have watched with alarm as the federal government has usurped more and more of our autonomy, freedom, and self-reliance. What works in New York or California may be all wrong for North Dakota. And Governor Snyder is complicit in all of it. He's a tool of the Washington establishment."

Sturges says, "The sad truth is we have one federal agency after another coming in here and telling us what we can and can't do. Where we can graze our livestock, what land we can build on. They tell us how to run our schools and businesses and treat our sick neighbors. And they tax us from here to the North Pole and back. They're using our success to pay for a lot of programs we don't want or need."

Their demeanors belie their strong words. They're both so down-to-earth, sincere, and engaging—it's like they stepped out of one of those baked beans commercials filmed around a campfire, filled with warmth and camaraderie and simple wisdom. While they may be home-spun, Erica also senses they're spoiling for a fight.

"As you know, we're experiencing an historic energy boom," Mary says. "We feel that we should be able to use the proceeds to help our own citizens. We have Native American tribes with horrific poverty and alcoholism rates. The health care they're receiving is substandard. The federal government bears a lot of responsibility. We're going to take care of our own."

"I understand all this. But can you tell me what your *goals* are? Do you want North Dakota to become an independent nation?" Erica asks.

There is a pause, and the Bellamys exchange a glance, as if gauging how much they should reveal. "We want some form of autonomy, for which there is precedent in numerous other countries. Regions that have their own identity and history and goals, and are permitted to run their own shops, so to speak," Mary says. "The Alto Adige region of northern Italy, for example, was part of Austria before the First World War, and today many of the schools are still run in German and the local government makes almost all decisions pertaining to the region, with no interference from Rome." She sounds like the soul of reason, her green eyes alive and fervent and lovely, all topped off by that disarming charm.

"And how do you propose to do that?"

Mary Bellamy leans back in her chair, an expectant smile on her face. "Well, here's where you and I have to start negotiating, Erica."

Erica feels her own excitement rising—clearly this woman has some news she wants to break, and she wants to control its rollout. "I'm listening."

"This is all *strictly* off the record," Mary says, looking at Gloria.

"Of course," Gloria says.

Mary turns to her husband and gives a small nod. "Come with us," she says, standing.

Mary leads them not to the elevators but to a stairwell. They go down a flight of steps and come to a door with a punch-code lock on it. Mary hits the keys and then opens the door.

They're standing in a full-floor open space. There are about twenty rows of tables and chairs, with a phone and laptop at every place. Additional tables are also set around the perimeter; a large coffee urn sits on each one. There is an enormous banner along one wall that has a map of North Dakota with the word *Homeland* superimposed on the image. The room is filled with a sense of expectancy, as if behind the entry door hundreds of people are waiting to pour in and get this party started.

Then Erica notices a young man sitting at the far end of the room. Tacked on the wall behind him is a large county-coded map of North Dakota. He's so engrossed in his laptop that he doesn't notice their presence.

"That's what concentration looks like," Mary says approvingly. "Wendell," she calls.

The man looks up. Then he waves distractedly and goes right back to his work.

Erica and Gloria exchange an excited glance: this could be big. "What is all this?" Erica asks.

"We have a marvelous tool here in North Dakota. It's called a gubernatorial recall election," Mary begins.

Sturges takes over. "You write up a recall petition. Then you gather signatures that total 25 percent of the turnout in the last gubernatorial election—in our case that's about seventy-five thousand signatures. We've made that threshold as well as added a cushion of approximately five thousand more. We're going to present our petitions to the North Dakota secretary of state tomorrow. He will then certify the signatures. That should take about a week. Once the signatures are validated, the secretary of state is obligated under our constitution to schedule a recall election."

"And is it a straight up-or-down vote?" Erica asks.

"No, this is what makes it interesting—and exciting," Mary says. "The sitting governor runs against any other candidates who file."

"So it's basically a whole new election in one fell swoop?" Gloria asks.

"Exactly."

Sturges puts an arm around his wife. "And Mary Bellamy will be on that ballot."

"As soon as our signatures are certified, we're going to roll out the Take Back Our Homeland campaign. Our message is simple: Governor Snyder is little more than a puppet of Washington DC. He was in Congress for eight years and sold his soul—and his state," Mary says.

"But he's not going to roll over for this," Sturges says. "And neither will the powers that be, mostly multinational energy companies, who own the legislature and run this state like it was their personal fiefdom. They're going to spend some serious money to try and stop us. It's going to be a fierce, hard-fought campaign."

"And what happens if you win?" Erica asks.

"We're going to reclaim our homeland," Mary says in her softest voice, making it sound like she's going to tickle a wind chime. Then she smiles modestly.

"After all, a woman's place is in the statehouse," Sturges says. "Which brings us to *us*. We'd like to give you the story to break. *If* you make it the centerpiece of the inaugural *Spotlight*."

"I can't make that promise," Erica says.

"Now, Erica," Mary says, giving Erica's hand a squeeze. "I'm sure every other network would love to have this story. But we want to give it to *you*."

"The day after the election is scheduled this room is going to be wall-to-wall with volunteers. We've got them fired up and ready to roll. It's the only political story in the country right now. MSNBC, FOX, CNN are going to be all over it," Sturges points out.

Erica and Gloria exchange a look—these Bellamys are a savvy duo. "Like I said, I can't make any promises about placement or emphasis. But we would like the exclusive. It will certainly be part of the first episode."

"I want the lead," Mary says with a smile.

"May Erica and I talk privately for a moment?" Gloria asks.

"Of course," Mary says, gesturing to a far corner.

Erica and Gloria walk out of earshot, and Gloria says, "I think we can give them the lead. We're not making any commitments on tone or how much total air time we give them."

"I'm not prepared to guarantee them the lead."

"I can't think of a stronger angle to start with," Gloria says with a fervor that surprises Erica. "We could begin with a flyover shot of the state, talk about a Great Plains rebellion. It's a strong way to frame the show. And they'd make compelling television."

Erica considers. Leading with the Bellamys makes perfect sense, and they're not compromising the actual reporting. Erica would *hate* to see another network get this. She nods at Gloria and they walk back to Mary and Sturges.

"We'll give you the lead," Erica says.

A great flush of excitement sweeps over Mary, and she seems to grow taller by three inches. "You won't regret it. We're going to reclaim the homeland and remake the map." She looks around the room in triumph. "Now come and meet Wendell."

As they cross the room, Erica thinks, *It's all so well planned, impressive, confident, calculating, cold.* She wonders what happens to people who cross the Bellamys. The thought makes her uneasy.

Reclaim the homeland and remake the map.

CHAPTER 16

WENDELL BRODSKY LOOKS ABOUT SEVENTEEN but is probably in his early twenties. He has that semi-distracted manner Erica notices in a lot of people his age—they never fully engage because they never fully *dis*engage from their phones, pads, apps, and laptops. They may be talking to you, but you sense you're just an interruption from their real lives, which are lived online. Even their experiences—climbing mountains, eating at quirky restaurants, chasing tornados, lolling at exotic beaches—become secondary to the documenting and instantly sharing of the experience. Life isn't meant to be lived, it's meant to be recorded. Where will it all end?

Wendell stands there, awkward, not making eye contact, shuffling a little.

"This young man is a genius," Sturges says, patting him on the back. "He's tracking every voter in the state."

"We're putting together the most comprehensive database ever constructed. By the use of extensive online and phone polling, and Internet data-sweeping that mines their interests and previous votes, we are able to determine who will . . ." Wendell looks at Mary Bellamy. "Am I allowed?"

"Erica and Gloria know about the recall. *Off* the record."

"Do you think it will pass?" Erica asks.

"Gubernatorial recalls are notoriously difficult. There have only been two successful ones in American history. Oddly, the first one was right here in North Dakota in 1921; the second was in 2003 when California voters recalled Gray Davis," Wendell says. "It's going to be tough. The numbers are against us at the moment. This is a traditional state. Convincing its citizens to embrace radical change is going to take some doing."

"So, will you be able to pull it off?" Gloria asks.

There's a pause. Both Sturges and Wendell look to Mary Bellamy. She smiles coyly. "We have a secret weapon."

"Which is?" Erica asks.

"Now, if I told you it wouldn't be secret, would it?" Mary says. "However, I will reveal it during our interview on *Spotlight*."

CHAPTER 17 ———————————

IT'S FRIDAY, AND ERICA IS at her desk at GNN, prepping for tonight's *The Erica Sparks Effect*. Her trip to Bismarck was last Thursday. The secretary of state certified the recall petitions yesterday and scheduled the recall election for August 1, just under eight weeks away. Erica will be flying out over the weekend to film her interview with the Bellamys. She's burning with curiosity about what they plan to reveal. She and Gloria have brainstormed and suspect it may be an endorsement from a prominent politician, maybe even a former president. That would give the movement a new level of legitimacy.

The rest of the first *Spotlight* is coming together nicely, thanks to Gloria's talents. Her research has uncovered a Pandora's box of fringe groups: a militant organization in northern New Hampshire that advocates for an armed insurrection against the federal government; one in Alabama that wants to divide the state in two, turning half of it into an all-white nation. And working with the Southern Poverty Law Center, she has uncovered literally scores of sovereign citizens groups, many of which operate underground and engage in military training. At the less extreme end of the spectrum, Erica is going to interview the Texas Republicans who introduced the secession platform at their last state convention and explore nascent but growing mainstream movements that—guided by the Bellamys' example—have sprung up in Montana, Idaho, Wyoming, and South Dakota. The episode will be strong and disturbing, and it will be framed and capped by the Bellamys—the rational, methodical, telegenic Bellamys—and by Erica's interview with Leslie Wilson, who will put the movement in context and perspective. GNN has been heavily promoting the series debut, and Erica is hoping to establish a show with real legs—*60 Minutes* is her model.

Her phone rings. It's Leslie. "I had a couple of thoughts on *Spotlight,*" she says.

"Shoot."

"I think our interview should be the last thing you shoot. That way you can get my reactions to all the other footage and personalities."

"Makes sense. I think you'll be fascinated by the Bellamys. They're somewhat inscrutable. They present as reasonable and rational, but I sense something darker going on behind the camera-ready façade."

"One wonders what their ultimate game plan is if she's elected governor. Do you think she'll win?" Leslie asks.

"I don't know. They're well known and liked in the state, but the establishment, both out there and in Washington, is aligned against them. That said, they're very well organized and funded. It's going to be a tough battle."

"With enemies like that, they're playing with fire," Leslie says. "And there are the national implications, of course. The federal government isn't going to sit idly if Bellamy wins and tries to secede or even demands some new level of state autonomy. It could trigger a domino effect, with other states making similar demands."

"It could get ugly."

"Which makes terrific television. On another matter, is there any chance you and Greg can come for brunch on Sunday? David Remnick, Frank Rich, and Lena Dunham are coming."

Erica practically swoons at the name David Remnick, the brilliant editor of the *New Yorker*. And Rich and Dunham are hardly slouches. "I wish we could, but I'll be out in Bismarck."

"Our loss." There's a pause, and then Leslie says casually, "Oh, you're such a great sport, Erica."

Where did that come from? "I try."

"The video is very amusing. Your daughter's little friend is quite the talent."

"What video?"

"Oh, you haven't seen it? It's on YouTube." Leslie laughs. "I mean— Garnier Fructis?! Really, Erica. Please tell me this Beth child planted it."

Erica feels like she's on a small boat that just got hit by a big wave. Garnier Fructis? Planted? What on earth is Leslie talking about? But she's too confused and embarrassed to ask.

"Anyway, I wouldn't worry about it. It will all be a blip in the end," Leslie says.

"Yes," Erica manages.

"I'm so happy to be part of *Spotlight*. Talk soon."

Erica sits frozen for a moment with her mouth open. Then she goes to Beth's YouTube channel. There's a video, posted yesterday, called "Sparks Will Fly." With a sense of dread, Erica clicks it. There's Beth in Erica's bedroom, talking so fast that she verges on unintelligible, moving around the room with the camera following. Which means Jenny was doing the filming.

"Hi, everyone, I'm in Erica Sparks's *bedroom*. Yes, *the* Erica Sparks, the one who only saved the world, like, *twice* and by the way she's super pretty in person but she should maybe cool it on the mascara—did I see a little clumping?—and anyway she's very down-to-earth and cool and nice and she makes *horrible* pancakes and won't let you text at the table, that is so, like, *retro*, get over it, it happens, anyway, check out this bedroom, it's like bigger than a tennis court or whatever, *sickening*, freaky, like, does she think she's Miley or something—Happy Hippie shout-out—so here's her closet, it's not a walk-in, it's a sleep-in, or a slumber party in, or have a rave in or *whatever* and check out this dress, what is happening with these sleeves, I think you could frost a cake with them, not that I *ever* eat cake, unless it's a day that ends in Y, and I think I know what's in this drawer—*ooooooohhhhhh*, no I won't open it all the way, that would be *too* twisted sister, and check out these sweaters and blouses and shoes, should I 'borrow' a pair and wear them to school, and how sick would *that* be because Mrs. McGough, that's my homeroom alleged teacher, would never know, I think old McG is on the spectrum anyway, stay tuned for that one, and now let's go into her *bathroom* and here's her shower, marble, here's her body wash and shampoo—wait, I just died, she uses *Garnier Fructis*, that is *tragic*, if I find Cover Girl I am *so* going to drown myself in this bathtub . . ."

Erica clicks it off, she's seen more than enough. Her stomach hollows out and all the blood drains from her head to her feet and she thinks she's about to faint. Or throw up. Jenny betrayed her, completely betrayed her. And now her bedroom and closet and bathroom have had, oh dear, the video's had forty-seven thousand hits already . . .

Erica leaps up from her chair and starts to pace. She wants that video taken down! Now! She calls Beth's parents at their home number. They both work, and she doesn't have their cells. But even if it is taken down, it's out there, in cyberspace, downloaded and shared, it can never, ever be killed. Erica feels her anger overtaken by another emotion, and she sits down in a chair in the corner of the office, one she's never sat in before.

Jenny . . . why, baby girl . . . why?

And then the tears start to slip down Erica's cheeks . . .

Jenny hates me, she wants to hurt me . . .

And that voice again. *Just remember, you can change a lot of things in your life, but you can't ever change where you come from. And deep down you'll never be better than any of us.*

And then, slowly, the tears stop, but Erica remains in the chair, the chair she has never sat in before . . .

CHAPTER 18

FIVE MINUTES LATER ERICA IS on the phone with her lawyer, Gary Halpert. "I want YouTube and Beth London to pull that video *immediately*. Or I'll sue."

"That shouldn't be a problem, Erica. The video is an invasion of your privacy, and it's causing you emotional pain and distress. YouTube doesn't want legal trouble, and I doubt that this Beth London—or her parents—want to get hit with major lawyer bills. I'll have the cease and desist letter to them within the hour."

"Thanks, Gary. Let me know ASAP."

Erica hangs up and dials her old friend and IT whiz Mark Benton out in Portland, Oregon, where he works for Nike. She quickly explains the situation. Mark knows Jenny, and Erica can sense his shock at what she's done, but he's too kind and discreet to say anything.

"I can scrub the video off the Internet. It's been out there for almost a day, so we can't get rid of it entirely—no doubt it's been downloaded to some personal computers—but I can make it very difficult to find."

"I can't tell you how much I appreciate this, Mark." She and Mark have been through a lot together—he was almost beaten to death helping her unmask Nylan Hastings as a dangerous megalomaniac.

"Are you okay there, Erica?"

"Yeah, I'm okay."

"I'm sorry this happened."

"I was blindsided."

"I'll get right on it."

Erica hangs up. Her instinct is to get on the next plane up to Boston and have it out with Jenny. But that would only give the video—and Jenny's acting out—more power than it already has. Jenny wants to get her goat. Well, Erica's not going to give her the satisfaction. In fact, she's not even going to mention the video. Jenny will learn soon enough that it's been pulled and that Erica has threatened a lawsuit. Let Jenny bring it up. And apologize. Erica has worked and struggled and sweated for everything she has, she's *earned* it all. Jenny is basically a rich kid at this point, with a mother who makes millions of dollars a year and gives her everything she wants. She's spoiled, and Erica doesn't like it one bit. And it's going to stop.

Good moms don't raise spoiled brats. Who put their mothers through emotional wringers for sport. Good moms practice tough love. Because it's a tough world out there. And the sooner Jenny finds that out, the better off she'll be. Enough second-guessing and guilt and tears and trauma.

That's right. Enough! You try your best, and if that's not good enough, Jenny can just stuff it. You're a good mother. A kind, caring, generous mother.

As Erica bolts up her from desk and strides down to the studio, she can almost convince herself that she believes those words.

CHAPTER 19 —————————————————————

MARY AND STURGES ARE IN their office at Bellamy Foundation headquarters. It's evening and the employees have all gone home. A roll-down map of the United States is on one wall. The contiguous states of North Dakota, South Dakota, Idaho, Wyoming, and Montana are outlined in red so as to form one giant land mass, one nation really, one glorious stretch of tomorrow, the ultimate Homeland. Did anybody really think the Bellamys would stop with North Dakota? How small-minded that would be.

The speakerphone is on and Mary is talking. Her voice is a mix of honey and steel. "This has been a very productive chat, as they all are. To review, Wendell Brodsky will be sending you his voter-mining software and protocol. It will allow you to profile and classify every voter from 'never' to 'definite.' Thus you'll be able to concentrate on the groups in between, the persuadable. What we're doing here is just the beginning. We are building what will be the eighth largest nation on the planet. I'm so proud of all of you."

They all chime in their thanks and their expressions of support and pride. Some of them Mary actually likes. Jason Erickson, the head of the Montana Homelanders, is a particular favorite—he *gets* it. A couple of the others will have to be . . . Well, let's just say politics is a blood sport. They're useful now, but the day will come . . .

"You may have seen some polls that show me behind in the recall. Ignore them. We have a couple of secret weapons." Oh, indeed they do. *Top secret.* Mary smiles to herself. "We can deploy them if needed. We're going to win this. You can count on it. Until next week's call, stay strong."

"You were brilliant. As always," Sturges says. Mary looks at him with that peculiar expression—affection sprinkled with contempt—that has come to define her marriage. He's her lapdog. Neal, on the other hand, is her wolf.

And Mary hears the call of the wild.

CHAPTER 20

ERICA AND GLORIA ARE IN the lobby of the Staybridge Hotel, Bismarck's finest—think a Holiday Inn with delusions of grandeur—waiting for the broadcast van to arrive and take them to their interview with the Bellamys. There's something about the quiet and vastness of the state that unnerves her. She thinks of *In Cold Blood*, Truman Capote's true crime masterpiece about the Cutter family, prosperous farmers who were brutally murdered at their isolated farmhouse in western Kansas. The wife and two teenagers were shot through the head and the father's throat was cut. Later one of the killers said, "I thought he was a nice man. I thought so right up until the time I slit his throat." It's a story of pure evil in a lonely landscape. A landscape like North Dakota. Erica shudders. She's become obsessed with what the Bellamys are going to reveal in the interview. It has to be something big. But what? Where is that van?

There's a vibrating noise from inside Gloria's bag. But she has her phone in her hand. Odd. She makes no move to answer it, although Erica senses she wants to.

"Feel free to take that call."

Gloria waves it away. "I'm sure it's my niece; she's pretty much the only one who uses that number. I'm putting her through college. She also thinks I'm her therapist."

"That's very generous of you."

"It's the least I can do. My sister was caught in a shoot-out between two gangs. Wrong place, wrong time. Shonda was six at the time. Her dad has tried his best, but his best isn't very good."

"So you stepped in?"

Gloria nods. "She's turned out to be worth the investment. She's finishing her first year at Penn. It's been a . . . tough adjustment. To go from the projects to the Ivy League is a real culture shock."

Boy, can Erica relate to that. She feels a wave of emotion toward Gloria and her niece.

The phone is still vibrating. A look of yearning flashes across Gloria's face.

"Are you sure you don't want to take it?"

"Like I said, she thinks I'm her on-call shrink. If I answer this I'll be sucked into her latest drama. Sometimes it's best to let kids stand on their own two feet and figure things out for themselves."

Those words are just what Erica needs to hear. No more mollycoddling. She wonders if she should open up about Jenny, but decides to hold her tongue.

The phone finally stops, and Erica sees rueful regret flash across Gloria's face. "Speaking of adjusting, how are you finding life in New York City?"

"I'm loving it. I do miss my . . . *fiancé*." Gloria says the word somewhat tentatively, as if it were a beautiful piece of clothing she was trying on but wasn't sure she could afford.

"Oh, I didn't realize you were engaged."

"Um . . . yes, yes, I am," she says, almost as if she's trying to convince herself.

"What does he do?"

"He's a corporal in the army. He works at the Pentagon."

"Oh, what does he do there?"

Gloria looks down and bites her lower lip before answering. "Oh, something dull and rote. He's not planning on staying there forever." Gloria is trying to sound casual, but there's nothing casual about the way her eyes are darting around.

"Have you set a date?"

Gloria frowns. "Not yet . . . Oh, Erica, he's *so* wonderful. But I worry about him. He's driven and wound pretty tight. I work so hard myself that when I'm off I want to relax, really relax. Which isn't easy for him."

Erica is starting to realize that Gloria is wound pretty tight herself. Some of her reactions seem off, even inappropriate. She's emotional but tries to disguise it, and at times she seems oddly insecure and awkward. Erica senses that she wants to talk about her fiancé but is afraid. What could that be about? Well, she doesn't want to pry. And a little instability is worth it—Gloria has been working brutal hours getting *Spotlight* on its feet. Erica feels prepared for today's interview thanks to the background research and suggested questions Gloria sent her.

The van arrives with the crew and takes them to the Bellamys' large, old brick Edwardian that sits atop a hill in Bismarck's wealthy River Road neighborhood. It's a stately house that harkens back to North Dakota's early days, when hardy pioneers made farming and mining and mercantile fortunes and wanted to show them off. As they pull up in front, both Sturges and Mary Bellamy come out to greet them. Mary's hair is expertly done and she has on some understated makeup.

"Welcome back to the Homeland," Mary says—her welcoming smile and soft voice can't quite disguise the cold cunning that flashes in her eyes. She's definitely keyed tight, a woman with a secret she's about to reveal.

The Bellamys show Erica, Gloria, and the crew into the house. It looks like a museum of North Dakota history, with oil paintings, sculptures, photographs, and glass-fronted cabinets filled with artifacts, all bearing testimony to the stark beauty of the Plains, and to the courage and culture of both the Native Americans and the settlers who displaced them. They move into a sunroom, and the crew begins setting up for the shoot.

"I'll sit in this chair. Sturges, you sit next to me; Erica, you're across from us, of course. Can we get someone to stand in for me so I can check the lighting?" Mary says.

The woman has no problem taking charge, and Erica shoots a look at Gloria—without speaking, they agree to let Mary do her thing. The more comfortable she feels, the better the interview will be.

When everyone is ready, they start.

"I'm here in Bismarck, North Dakota, with Mary and Sturges Bellamy, leaders of the state's Take Back Our Homeland movement, which has initiated a recall election against sitting governor Bert Synder," Erica says to the camera before turning to the Bellamys. "What do you say to critics who feel that sovereign citizen movements such as yours use the threat of violence to achieve their ends?"

"I say come to the Homeland and meet us and our followers," Mary says. "We renounce any sort of violence. We are working through the political process. As you said, we have initiated a recall effort against Governor Snyder, who is little more than a puppet for big-money interests and the federal government in Washington. It's time to take back what is rightfully ours."

"And you're running to replace him?"

"I am, yes," Mary says simply with a head tilt and a smile.

"I understand your opponents are about to go up with ads that call you irresponsible, even radical."

"Do I look radical to you? Honestly, I wish they would stick to the core issue here, which is *freedom*. But if they want to play hardball, well, I'm not going to let them besmirch my good name without fighting back."

"My wife is a formidable woman, Erica. When she sets her mind to something, it gets done."

"There are enormous risks inherent in what you are attempting to do. Do you really believe there are enough North Dakotans willing to take those risks for you to win the election?"

"I certainly hope so. But we aren't doing it alone. We have supporters all across the nation."

"I suppose they can send contributions, but your campaign is well financed already."

"Oh, they can do a lot more than make a contribution. And this is more than a campaign, Erica. It's a *movement*." Mary takes a pause and leans forward in her chair; her voice stays soft but grows fervent.

Here comes the money shot, Erica thinks.

"And we are inviting our supporters to come and settle here. And vote. We have jobs that go begging. We have open spaces, inexpensive housing, great natural beauty." Mary looks directly into the camera. "So I put out a call to all Americans who support our goals: Be a twenty-first-century pioneer. Come to the Homeland, make it your own, and join us as we make history."

Erica is stunned. Standing to the side of the cameraman, Gloria nods and pumps a fist—this is great, news-making television. Erica feels a surge of adrenaline.

"Let me make sure I heard you correctly: You're asking people to move to North Dakota for the express purpose of bolstering your recall drive?"

"We're inviting them to come for the express purpose of strengthening the Homeland movement and setting an example for the rest of the country."

"And you'll help them settle?"

"Yes. We've hired a staff of social workers, employment specialists, and relocation experts. We're setting up hundreds of temporary trailer homes. We're opening a processing center in a warehouse here in Bismarck. We take care of our own."

"This sounds like a very expensive endeavor. Where is the funding coming from?"

"From my husband and me. Nobody owns us. Not Washington,

and not the special interests." She turns to the camera again. "We need you, we want you, we love you. Please . . . pack up your family and come to the Homeland. Come *home*."

They finish up the interview—it's all an anticlimax after Mary's stunning invitation—and the Bellamys walk them out to the van and wave as they drive away. Their camera-savvy charisma and bold call to arms have blown Erica away. She has landed a big fat scoop. But she senses there is more here than meets the eye—there's something eerie about the Bellamys; they seem like wax figures come to life. In spite of their repeated embrace of nonviolence, they seem unyielding, and under all the soft smiles is ruthless resolve. Watching this election play out is going to be riveting. And make fantastic television. But there's a catch.

"There's no way we can contain this story," she says to Gloria. "Now that the recall election has been scheduled, Bismarck will be crawling with reporters."

"Mary has promised us she won't reveal the invitation to move here until *Spotlight* airs. It's in their interest to build anticipation."

"True, but with reporters nosing around we could easily get scooped."

Gloria is silent for a moment and then says, "Why don't we throw together a promo clip for *Spotlight*, a teaser that promises a bombshell. We can get it up on the network today. That'll keep us in control of the story."

"Good! Send the footage to our editor in New York as soon as you get it from the cameraman. Ask him to tighten it and get it back to us within an hour."

"We're cooking," Gloria says.

"This should really drive the ratings for the premiere. Listen, do you get the sense that the Bellamys are holding something back?"

Gloria looks down and then out the window before saying, "My research hasn't turned up anything."

"It's nothing I can put my finger on, but I've seen overweening ambition before. It's there. In Mary Bellamy's eyes." Erica's phone rings. "My husband . . . Hi there."

"How's it going out there?" Greg asks.

"Really well. How are things there?"

"Good. Leslie Wilson called. Stan is down with the flu, she wants me to escort her to some party."

"Some party?"

"It's a publication party for a biography of Mike Nichols."

"Where is it?"

"At Peggy Noonan's. She's an old pal of Diane Sawyer, Nichols's widow."

Erica feels a stab of jealousy, both toward Leslie and about missing a party that will be filled with fascinating people. She exhales. "Well, have a good time."

"I'll miss you."

"Leslie is pretty good company."

"She is, isn't she?" Greg says, and then he laughs.

Erica doesn't get the joke.

CHAPTER 21 ————————————————————

IT'S NINE THAT NIGHT AND Erica is in her soulless hotel room at the
Staybridge, feeling lonely. She just did a half hour of vigorous Tae Kwon
Do and it didn't help. She started the practice while at Yale, almost
on a whim, and it has turned out to be a lifesaver. The concentration,
discipline, and physical prowess she gained make her feel powerful—
both physically and emotionally better able to defend herself. She moves
to the window and looks out at the scenic parking lot, a distant mall,
and a black horizon. Greg is at that party right now, no doubt charming
some . . . other woman. Leslie Burke Wilson maybe. Erica remembers
the way Leslie laid her hand on his shoulder at their dinner; yes, it was
casual on the surface, but there was something proprietary, even challenging, about it.

Oh, Erica, cool it. That *part of your marriage is solid. Grown-ups flirt.
It's all in fun. Don't be a square.*

Erica turns from the window, sits at the desk, and opens her laptop.
The day was productive, but she has an itch about the Bellamys, a sense
that there's another secret, one they're holding close to the vest. She
searches Mary Bellamy. Scores of articles come up, but most of what she
gleans she already knows, thanks to Gloria. But Erica keeps reading,

even the articles in obscure North Dakota newspapers and websites. Her eyes are starting to ache, she's exhausted, but she keeps pushing on. Then exhaustion overtakes her and she walks over to the bed and flops down. Just as she's escaping into the arms of Morpheus, the hotel phone rings.

"Is this Erica Sparks?" a woman's voice asks in an urgent whisper.

"Who's this?" Erica asks, sitting up, instantly alert.

"My name is Joan Marcus. I have to talk to you." She sounds on the verge of tears. "I'm down in the lobby. Can I come up? I'm scared."

Erica feels a wave of foreboding. The woman sounds unhinged. "I'll come down."

"Hurry."

Erica exits the elevator into the lobby and scans the space. It's generic, depressing, and almost empty, an expanse of garish carpeting and wood-veneer trim; an instrumental cover of "Yesterday" oozes from ceiling speakers. No wonder America's suicide rates are soaring. There's a smattering of people in the bar/restaurant, mostly exhausted-looking businessmen in ill-fitting suits. But no sign of this Joan Marcus. The woman sounded desperate, and Erica's anxiety is spiking, she can feel her heart thumping in her chest. She rushes outside. No one. Just that endless parking lot dotted by lonely streetlights—one of them is flickering and making a low hissing sound that seems to be mocking Erica's rising sense of dread.

And then, from the far end of the parking lot, a car, a dark sedan, speeds away, gunning its motor. It's too far away for Erica to make out the model.

She races back into the lobby and up to the front desk. A blond clerk wearing too much makeup looks up from Overstock.com and smiles.

"Have you seen a woman?"

"Gosh, Miss Sparks, I'd need a little more detail than that."

"Her name is Joan Marcus. I was supposed to meet her here."

"What does she look like?"

"I don't know."

"I haven't seen anyone. Did you check the restaurant and lounge?"

Erica nods.

"What about the ladies' room?"

Erica heads across the lobby, down a short hallway, and into the ladies' room.

There's a middle-aged woman on the floor, slumped against the wall, her legs splayed out in front of her. Her throat is slit and she's sitting in a thick pool of blood, her head back, her tongue hanging out, her eyes rolled up so only the whites are showing. The tiles around her are streaked with blood, as if she made a final desperate attempt to stand up.

Erica feels bitter bile at the back of her throat and fights the urge to heave. She kneels down and checks the woman's pulse. Flatline. She looks at the woman's face—it's bloated and blotchy—a drinker. Erica stands and gulps air. That's when she notices an 8 x 10 manila envelope on the floor near the body. She wants to pick it up, look inside, but that would be tampering with a crime scene, it could compromise evidence. She scans the bright sterile room and sees a small triangular piece of paper on the floor, no bigger than a Post-it, really. That couldn't possibly be relevant, could it? Is it a gum wrapper? She picks it up—it's a fragment of a photograph. She replaces it on the floor; it too could be evidence. She takes out her phone and takes a picture of the scrap of paper. Then she takes several of the corpse.

CHAPTER 22 ———————————————————

ERICA AND GLORIA ARE SITTING in a corner of the lobby, across a low table from Bismarck detective Peter Hoaglund. He's in his thirties, tall and balding and earnest. In contrast to the big-city detectives Erica is used to dealing with, he looks as wholesome as Andy of Mayberry. But there's something knowing in his eyes that makes Erica think he's at least peeked into the heart of darkness.

"Is there anything else you can tell us?" Hoaglund asks.

"Not that I can think of," Erica says. "What can you tell me about Joan Marcus?"

"She's from Jamestown, about a hundred miles east of here. Fifty-six years old. Divorced and currently unemployed. Two emergency room admissions for acute alcohol poisoning in the last six months. Which coincide with her leaving her job at Oil Field Solutions."

Something in Erica's earlier research comes back to her. "Isn't Oil Field Solutions owned by the Bellamys?"

Hoaglund hesitates before answering. "They own it with a Canadian businessman named Neal Clark. He has several joint ventures with the Bellamys."

"Did she leave Oil Field Solutions or was she fired?"

"She quit."

Erica and Gloria exchange a glance but keep their mouths shut. A gurney carrying Joan Marcus's body is wheeled across the lobby. Several local television crews are reporting live from the scene.

"Erica, we've got to file a report," Gloria says. "The crew is waiting."

Erica nods. All three of them stand. Hoaglund hands Erica his card.

"What do you make of the manila envelope and the scrap of a photograph?" Erica asks.

"The manila envelope was empty. Of course we'll check it for fin-gerprints. I'm not sure what scrap of a photograph you're referring to?"

"It was on the floor, about two feet to the left of her body. A small triangular piece of a photograph, on glossy paper?"

Hoaglund looks blank. Erica feels her anxiety spike. "Come on," she says, heading toward the ladies' room. The door is open, blocked by police tape. Erica points to a spot on the floor. "Right there, it was on the floor right there."

Hoaglund shakes his head. "I was the first one to arrive on the scene, and I didn't see it. I'll check the police photographs."

For a moment Erica thinks she should take out her phone and show him the pictures she took. Then she thinks again.

CHAPTER 23

"ERICA, ARE YOU ALL RIGHT?" Gloria asks as the cameraman runs a light check.

Erica is shook up. Bad. Walking into that bathroom and seeing the corpse. She's been up close and personal in other horrific situations—the Staten Island Ferry crash, Kay Barrish's death, the bombing at Case Western University—but no matter how many times it happens, it throws her into an existential free fall, a sense that she's hurtling away from the here and now into some other, darker place, falling, falling, into a void that knows no boundaries, no limits.

"I'll be okay," she manages.

"To be honest, Erica, you look a little spooked," Gloria says. "Listen, the report can wait fifteen minutes, a half hour, whatever. As of now, this is a local murder—gruesome, yes, but hardly a national story. Why don't you go up to your room, take a few minutes, maybe take a hot shower, run a brush through your hair? We'll be here."

Erica feels a wave of gratitude toward Gloria, and she is pulled back into the moment, grounded a little bit. And Gloria is right. Joan Marcus's grisly death wouldn't even make the national news if Erica wasn't part of the story. But she is part of it. She feels a terrible wave of foreboding.

"Maybe I will take ten. I'll be back ASAP."

Up in her room, Erica sits on the edge of her bed, closes her eyes, and takes deep breaths. As it sinks in.

You're part of this story, Erica. Joan Marcus came to see you, to tell you something. You own it now. For better or worse. Better or worse . . .

Erica exhales with a sigh. She wants to talk to Greg, tell him what happened, hear his reassuring voice. She calls his cell. It rings and rings and rings, a lonely echoing sound. Of course, there's no answer—he's at that party, the party with Leslie Burke Wilson and all the fascinating people, the lucky people who live their lives and do their work and enjoy their success and don't discover women with their throats slit sprawled on bathroom floors.

And then: "Hey there, Erica." Greg sounds so up, and in the background she can hear laughter and clinking ice and voices, excited, speedy, intriguing New York voices. And she's in the middle of nowhere in the middle of a story that just became ugly and personal.

"Greg . . . I thought you weren't going to answer . . ."

"I'm always here for you. I'm talking to Charlie Rose. Want to say hello?"

"Not right now please."

"Listen, Leslie just appeared and she's giving me the hairy eyeball . . ."

"You're committing a social *sin*," Leslie states in a voice that sounds loose and liquid. "Who *is* that?"

"It's Erica."

"Er-i-*ca*," Leslie says into the phone. "Where *are* you?"

Erica feels like she's talking to people on another planet, in a parallel universe. "Bismarck, North Dakota."

"Oh, of course. I want a full report," Leslie says in a suddenly sober voice. "Thank you for loaning me your husband."

"Just make sure you return him."

"Bergdorf's allows you to wear a dress once and still return it."

"Then think of me as Macy's. They have a much stricter policy."

Leslie laughs and then Greg takes back the phone and asks with concern, "Is everything all right out there?" Erica is about to answer when he says, "Listen, they're shushing the room. Peggy Noonan is about to say a few words. I'll call you back a little later. Okay?"

". . . Yes. Sure. It's fine."

The call leaves Erica feeling even more lonely. She looks out at the parking lot and remembers the car that sped out of it. It was a sedan, dark, but that's all she can bring up. She only saw the sides, not the front or rear, which would have given her a glimpse of its license plate or medallion. She picks up her phone and checks the picture she took of the little scrap of photograph. It's a black-and-white picture that looks, from the thickness of the white border, like it was torn from the corner of an 8 x 10. The top of the scrap is dark and then below it, at the corner, there's a diffuse gray light and what looks like the edge of . . . something. An object? A building? A vehicle? It's so small, so indistinct, that it's impossible to make any sort of supposition or even guess about what it depicts.

Now that she's turned her mind to concrete details, to questions that need to be answered, Erica feels on a somewhat more even keel. She takes a quick shower, slaps on a little makeup, and heads down to the lobby to get to work.

When she steps off the elevator, she sees a woman across the lobby, hysterical, shaking, weeping, contorted with grief. A female police officer is holding her up, talking to her, trying to console the inconsolable.

Erica turns to Gloria. "Is that . . . ?"

"Yes, it's the victim's daughter."

Her mother is dead. Killed in a brutal murder. Some lives end in the blink of an eye. Others are just irrevocably altered, into a *before* and an *after*. This woman has just entered *after*. Erica has an urge to go to her, offer condolences. But it would only make matters worse.

"Erica?" Gloria says.

Erica is pulled out of her reverie. "Yes, Gloria, I'm sorry, let's go."

She picks up her mic and begins, "This is Erica Sparks reporting live from Bismarck, North Dakota, where a little over an hour ago I received a frantic call . . ."

Erica continues her report, shocked that she manages to get the words out, words that don't seem real—because all she can hear is the sobbing behind her.

CHAPTER 24 ————————————————

ERICA ARRIVES BACK AT LAGUARDIA on Sunday evening, and she and Gloria get into a waiting car. She's still feeling shaky, she can't get the image of Joan Marcus on the ladies' room floor out of her mind—the tongue hanging out, the rolled-up eyes, the livid throat wound, the smeared blood on the wall, the blood, the blood.

After dropping Gloria at her rental on Eighth Avenue and Fifty-Fourth Street, the driver takes Erica up to Central Park West. As they approach her graceful prewar building, lights glowing in the windows, she allows herself a moment of sentiment: *There's no place like home.*

And then she hears Susan's bitter mocking laugh: *Home? Ha! Home is where the crap is.* Will it haunt her forever? Shouldn't it stop, finally? After all, she bought her mother a townhouse outside Bangor in a spiffy new development, she pays the monthly fees, and her accountant sends Susan $2,500 a month. Yes, it's all done out of guilt and shame and, yes, Erica resents the money. Why should she take care of a woman who never took care of her? Who left her to fend for herself all during her childhood, to scrounge meals, often subsisting on blocks of government cheese and food pantry peanut butter and Hamburger Helper without the hamburger? Who took her clothes shopping—to the Goodwill—once every two or three years? Who thought slapping your kid across the face—sometimes, most times, not for misbehavior, but because Susan was in a hungover raw-nerve state—was acceptable parenting?

Still, Erica (through her lawyer) dutifully sends the checks—her only stipulation being that Susan go to NA meetings. On some level she enjoys the monthly reminder to Susan that her daughter got out, she made something of her life, she's not a pathetic loser. But still the sad, sick bond remains, like invisible shackles around her heart and soul, the bond forged in a thousand nights in that cramped, filthy, moldy, drafty double-wide. And with it comes the tiny, faint flickering hope that somehow things could get better, that the sliver of affection—love even, maybe—that Erica felt from and toward her mother a couple of times during her childhood could be rekindled, that redemption is possible. Because when you're a mother and daughter, there is no escape.

Home, bitter home.

Erica walks into the apartment. The front hall is dark and the place is eerily silent. "Greg?"

There's no answer. Erica tenses. She switches on the hall light and walks down into the living room, which is also dark. "Greg?"

Still things are silent—and then, "I'm in here, honey."

Why didn't he answer her first call? And take so long on her second? Erica walks down to the guest room, one corner of which Greg has turned into his home office. He's sitting at his computer in the dark, his face looks ghostly bathed in the gray light from the screen. He makes no move to stand up and greet her.

Erica stands behind him, rubs his shoulders, leans down, and kisses him.

"I'm just finishing up this proposal," he says, not turning to her kiss.

Erica takes a step back. "Sorry to interrupt."

"I just want to get this nailed. We're having horseradish-encrusted salmon for dinner."

He cooked! "Yummy."

"With asparagus and baby potatoes."

"I'm starving." They'll sit down to a nice dinner and catch up, she wants to hear all about last night's party and to fill him in on the Bellamys and on the murder. She wants to feel supported and engaged and . . . loved. She *needs* it right now.

He finally turns to her and takes her hand. "Are you okay? You had a pretty eventful little trip." Before waiting for an answer, he turns back to his computer, saying, "Just give me ten minutes."

"I'll go unpack. Meet you in the kitchen."

"If I'm not there, just take the containers out of the fridge and nuke 'em for a minute. Everything is from Whole Foods."

Down in their bedroom, Erica fights to control her disappointment and hurt. She gathers her dirty clothes and then heads down to the washer/dryer closet. As she's about to put her stuff in the washer, she notices a shirt in there. One of Greg's. A cool black-and-white striped one, Marc Jacobs. He must have worn it to the party last night. Maybe it got a little stain on it and he zapped it with Shout and then stuck it in the machine. Erica lifts it out and holds it to her nose. The smell of bergamot is unmistakable.

CHAPTER 25 ———————————————————

IT'S MONDAY, AND ERICA IS back in her office. She hasn't heard a peep from Jenny. So be it. Is she being a little stubborn? Maybe. But tenacity has been a big part of her career, and it might be time to apply it to her parenting. As for the Doubt Demon that likes to perch on her shoulder and whisper nasty nothings in her ear about what a crummy mom she is—*Get lost, you slimy little creep!*

Gary Halpert was able to get both YouTube and Beth London to pull the video, and Mark Benton has pretty much scrubbed it off the Internet.

But of course, Erica thinks ruefully, the video is only a symptom of a relationship that's at a low point. Hardly its first dip, but Erica is afraid puberty and adolescence—all that intensity and hormones and sarcasm and anger and rush toward independence—will only further rend their bond. She folds her arms on her desk and rests her head for a moment, closing her eyes as sadness washes over her.

Oh, Jenny, my baby girl, I love you so much, just know that, please. And I feel as lost as you do.

There's a gentle knock on her open door.

"Is this a bad time?" Gloria asks softly.

Erica sits up, shakes her head. "No, no, of course not."

Gloria walks over to Erica's desk. "You've been working like a dog on a triple-espresso IV. Are you sure you don't need a little break?"

"You've been working just as hard as I have."

"Yeah, but I'm not the majordomo, public face, anchorwoman, et cetera."

"We don't have time to take a break." GNN agreed to push the first episode of *Spotlight* up two weeks. Their hand was forced by Take Back Our Homeland's still-undisclosed invitation for "twenty-first-century pioneers" to move to North Dakota and join them. It's a hot story and they want to break it. But it does mean twenty-hour days for everyone connected with the show.

"The promo is up," Gloria says.

"Let's take a look."

Gloria clicks on Erica's office television and then sends the video from her phone to the set. It opens with a quick shot of Steve Watson blowing up his supporters and himself, cuts to Mary Bellamy talking about the Homeland, and ends with a crowd of Alabama white-supremacist secessionists holding a protest outside the statehouse.

"It's scary. And the Bellamys aren't going to like it. It makes secessionist movements seem militant and dangerous," Erica says.

"Actually I think they come across as the soul of reason in a sea of hate."

"Yes, but it does lump them all together. There's definitely some guilt by association."

"Well, that will draw people to watch her interview, which gives her a huge platform to demonstrate how different Take Back Our Homeland is from these fringe groups."

"Good point. And good job."

"We're running this on GNN and eight other cable channels. A week from Thursday is our big night. We want to come out of the gate with a bang."

"Exciting. Listen, I'm going to head out to North Dakota again on Saturday."

Gloria looks momentarily taken aback. Then quizzical.

"I want to do a little digging on Joan Marcus."

She takes this in and then nods. "Okay. Would you, um, like me to come?"

"I want to keep a low profile."

"Okay. Okay." Gloria steps closer to the desk and her face fills with concern. "I want you to be careful out there. Stay in close radio contact."

"I will. And thank you."

Gloria leaves and Erica feels a wave of affection. Gloria has her back.

CHAPTER 26 ———————————

GLORIA HEADS OUT OF THE GNN building and merges with the sea of pedestrians heading south. She walks down two blocks and turns west on Fiftieth Street before taking out her prepaid and dialing.

"Yes," comes the taut baritone. And with it, that jolt of desire and longing.

"She's going out to North Dakota this weekend."

"I thought the filming was done."

"It is. She's going alone. To look into the Marcus murder."

He curses in Russian—he loves to show off his fluency. "That was grossly mishandled. Marcus was supposed to be dealt with *before* she reached the hotel. The deliveryman was incompetent. Well, he won't be incompetent for long."

"I offered to accompany her, but she wants to go alone."

"Don't worry, we'll keep a close eye."

Gloria comes to a pocket park and walks in. She goes to a wall and huddles facing it, lowering her voice. "I miss you. When will I see you?"

"You know I never mix business with pleasure."

"I thought I was both."

His voice softens. "Of course you are. Good work. Keep it up."

And then he hangs up and he's gone and Gloria is overcome by a wave of loneliness. Well, it will all be over in due time and then . . . then she will be rewarded with James's love—*oh, James, my James*—and all those years of being the Good Little Girl, the best in class, hand up at every question, polite and discreet and dull . . . those days will be over and she will verily play in the fields of plenty with the man she lives for.

Gloria smiles to herself and then heads over to the food kiosk, where she orders a double bacon cheeseburger and onion rings. She's always had a fierce appetite.

CHAPTER 27 ———————————————————

ERICA SPENDS THE NEXT SEVERAL hours working on tonight's show, but she's haunted by the murder of Joan Marcus and the disappearance of that torn corner of a photograph. She supposes it could have simply been overlooked in the initial response to the crime, maybe stepped on and kicked aside—it was so small—but if that's the case, it's sloppy police work. If that's not the case, what happened to it? And the police have made no progress with identifying the car Erica saw speeding out of the parking lot. And who *was* Joan Marcus? What did she so desperately want to tell Erica? And, of course, who slit her throat?

Erica calls Detective Hoaglund. "Any progress?"

"Not much. The parking lot surveillance camera was shot out. Her car was in the lot, so she drove herself to the hotel. Her killer or killers were following her. They waited outside in the shadows while she called you on the house phone, then they walked into the hotel and either forced or lured her into the bathroom and killed her."

"And nobody in the lobby saw anyone?"

"No. As you know, it was pretty deserted at the time."

"No fingerprints?"

"None."

"No one saw Marcus earlier in the day?"

"We're still looking. There's a lot of country out here, and Marcus lived in an isolated house. You can go weeks without seeing another person."

"And the search of her house?"

"A lot of vodka bottles, a lot of pills. No evidence."

"Listen, I'd like to fly out there this weekend and poke around."

There's a pause and then, "We're in the middle of a police investigation here. Your presence might be disruptive."

"No cameras. Nothing. Just me." There's another pause. "Listen, Detective, Joan Marcus wanted to see *me*, to talk to *me*, she had something to tell me. I was the last person to speak with her. I'm coming out there."

"I can't spare anyone to escort you around. We're dealing with a murder here. And I certainly can't guarantee your safety."

CHAPTER 28 —————————————————————

NEAL CLARK IS ON HIS Harley 750 speeding along Route 7, heading north, past the Winnipeg suburbs. Is there anything more exhilarating than being on a bike, going eighty miles an hour, whipped by the wind, feeling the power of the machine between your legs merging with your own power, your own strength? It's pure freedom.

He's on his way to visit Prairie Health, his vitamin and supplement operation (not to mention the unmentionable). It's a surprise visit. The best kind. Catch everyone unaware. See what's really going on. Of course, production has been running smoothly, the numbers are great, he has built Prairie Health into the largest vitamin and supplement manufacturer in Canada. Neal believes that the body is a temple and that supplements are an offering. They keep us rockin' and rollin'—young and vital and virile. He's a running, swimming, motorcycle-riding, love-making testament to his ethos.

The only thing missing is the woman he loves. If only Mary were on the back of the bike, her hands around his torso, moving with him like his shadow.

Patience, Neal, patience.

He exits the highway and heads east for eight miles on Route 17 before reaching the vast Prairie Health complex, which is set back from

17 and reached by an access road. He pulls into the parking lot, dismounts, takes off his helmet, and surveys the property. *His* property. With graceful landscaping, immaculate buildings, lots of glass and steel, it projects health and serenity and strength. And it's safe—there are a half dozen Province Security cars parked strategically around the campus. His own private police force. All of them trained, armed, and ready. Nobody messes with Neal Clark.

Set about a quarter of a mile past the main building is the laboratory, a sprawling low-slung, single-story building. The lab is top secret—the supplement industry is famously cutthroat and competitive—and set behind a high fence, reached through a manned gatehouse. It's where his scientists are inventing new tools for better, healthier, longer living.

Neal laughs out loud at the beauty of it all.

Tools for better, healthier, longer living.

Well, I suppose you could say that. Depends whose living you're talking about. He keeps laughing. It's so funny. And so beautiful. And so *powerful*. And so close. So tantalizingly close.

He'll visit the lab second—save the best for last. As he walks toward the main building he feels like the Master of the Universe. And why shouldn't he? Wherever he goes in the province he sees land, businesses, and buildings that he owns. And he built the empire himself; he's not one of those coddled types (like Sturges) who was born on third base and thinks he hit a triple. And after Mary wins the election, his empire is going to have a new crown jewel—he's going to tap into the mother lode. Let it flow, let it flow, let it flow—he's going to ride that inky tide right into the Buffett/Gates/Koch league.

Once inside headquarters, Neal is greeted by the usual obsequious array of middle managers. Such a sad lot, like little lapdogs, so eager to please, so transparent, so easy to manipulate that there's no challenge really. They bore him. But he feigns interest—because it's in his own interest. He visits various departments—operations, quality control, IT, public relations, the assembly line—nodding his head, asking the occasional question and offering praise when earned. Praise is a wonderful tool of manipulation. If he's the Master of the Universe—and he is—they're his slaves. Working their tragic little butts off to pay the mortgage, get the kids through school, take a little vacay in August. It's poignant really. Almost touching. But ultimately pathetic.

When he's done talking about calcium and melatonin and some new study on the benefits of milk thistle and whether the Newfoundland market is big enough to warrant investment, he takes his leave.

That chore out of the way, he walks back toward the laboratory building, his excitement growing with every step. He passes through the gatehouse, where another slave waves him through. Inside the building, Anton Vershinin is waiting to greet him. Anton isn't a slave, he's an equal, a better even, one of the most brilliant scientists on the planet. And he works for Neal. And for the Homeland, of course. Luring him over from Russia took some doing, but James—amazing James—handled it so beautifully, doing his research on Anton, finding out he felt unappreciated and unpaid by the Kremlin. Then making the connection, the clandestine meetings, slowly seducing Anton with visions of glory and freedom. And, of course, it's amazing what a suitcase filled with five million dollars in cash can accomplish.

The building is an engineering marvel. It's one story above ground and four stories below. Anton, as always, insists that Neal don a hazmat suit. He's so meticulous. As they ride down in the elevator, Anton is keyed up, his gray eyes alight with scientific fervor.

The main lab, four stories down, never fails to awe Neal. It's a mass of pipes and tanks and vats and compressors and refrigeration rooms, with a low, soothing hum that belies the power of what is being created. Anton excitedly details their progress. Neal listens and nods and pretends to understand. The science is gibberish to him, but he knows enough to stroke his resident genius.

After the tour they go into Anton's office and take off their hazmat suits.

"I know what you are going to ask me, Neal: When will we be ready?"

"We're under the gun here."

"I understand this fact."

"And?"

"Soon."

"Soon is too indefinite," Neal presses.

Anton looks down at his hands. He's a lean, almost gaunt, man, in his forties with close-cropped gray hair, and—as his psychological profile detailed—he's an obsessive compulsive with no hobbies or interests outside his work. Anorexic, asexual, and amoral. Perfect for the job. When he looks up, his eyes are electric with excitement. "Very soon." He smiles, a dry smile of imminent accomplishment. "Unfortunately I cannot give you a minute or an hour, but I will give you a day: July 15th."

That's two weeks before the recall election. *Perfect* timing.

The men shake hands. "You're a genius, Anton."

Anton looks down in a failed attempt at modesty.

On the ride back to Winnipeg, Neal feels like he could raise the handlebars of the Harley and lift off into the ether, ecstatic.

CHAPTER 29 —————————————————

IT'S FRIDAY NIGHT, AFTER HER last show of the week, and Erica is walking home, heading uptown on Sixth Avenue. She's wearing khaki slacks, a blue oxford, and a straw hat pulled low. She gets some looks, but no one stops her or rushes up for an autograph. She loves how blasé New York is to celebrity. When she's out in the hinterlands she sometimes feels like a freak, or a specimen—*Celebritorus americana*—or even public property, available to any crazed fan who wants to shove his face in hers, gushing like a goose on meth. No, she'll take Manhattan, the Bronx, and (one-of-these-days-she'll-get-to) Staten Island too. It's a warm night, close and humid, almost oppressive; there's an air-quality warning, the new normal, but still Erica treasures the sense of freedom, the chance to people-watch. And what a cool melting pot this town is! No wonder New York is the center of the known universe—it embraces *all* God's children. And diversity equals strength.

Erica is hoping the walk will calm her restless mind and taut nerves. Her plate is full, but she'll deal with things as best she can with—she hopes—smarts and grace and hard work. All well and good, but not quite enough to tame her disquiet, her fears—for her marriage, her relationship with Jenny, and her own life. Joan Marcus's throat was slit from ear to ear like a pig at slaughter. Someone *really* didn't want her talking to Erica. But who? Why?

"We think you're wonderful," come the words, delivered with a lovely Indian lilt.

Erica looks over and sees a family—mother and father and three teenage children. They're all smiling, beaming goodwill at her.

"I know we're being tragic tourists, but we watch you every night back home in Sacramento," the mother says. "Thank you for fighting for the truth."

"You inspire me," the daughter says.

The air between Erica and the family is filled with simple kindness and humanity—and she feels her eyes welling, her throat tighten.

"*You* inspire me," Erica says.

The family moves on, and Erica tries to hold on to the gift they've given her. She takes out her phone and calls Jenny.

"Mom," is the first surly word.

"How are you, baby?"

"I have asked you *not* to call me baby."

"How are you, Jenny?"

"Oh, I'm just great, Mom, just great. You cost me my best friend, who dropped me like I had Zika, and now she's leading a cyber campaign to make me the most unpopular girl in the school. Yeah, I'm just great."

"That snake, that creepy little snake. What is she doing?"

"What *isn't* she doing? Facebook, Snapchat, Twitter, Instagram. I'm the spoiled little wannabe who relies on her famous mother to have friends. I'm ugly and stupid and have crummy hair and *thanks, Mom, thanks a lot*!"

"Now you listen to me, Jenny, that Beth London is a nasty kid. I'm going to contact the school and her parents and put a quick end to this."

"Dad already did."

"Has it stopped?"

"Too soon to tell."

"Why didn't you call me?"

"Because you were out in I-don't-know-where being famous and rich and saving the world. I knew you wouldn't have time for me."

Erica feels her stomach hollow out, and now the city that moments ago brought her a measure of solace seems to be mocking her. In that familiar voice she recognizes, a voice that makes her nauseous with dread and sadness. She hears:

Ha-ha, got too big for your britches, didn't ya, Little Miss Perfect. Well, you got all that fame and money and fancy clothes and blah-blah-blah, but your own daughter hates ya, ha-ha-ha.

Erica picks up her pace, she needs to get away, away from the voice . . .

"Oh, Jenny, please don't hate me, please . . ."

"I have to go. *Game of Thrones* is on. Good-bye."

And now Erica breaks into a run, running past startled pedestrians, not caring about their stares, running away from her pain, running away from her past, knowing even as she does how futile it is, but still she runs, sucking air, fast faster, away away from it all . . .

But, Erica . . . where are you running to?

CHAPTER 30

IT'S MIDDAY ON SATURDAY. ERICA surveys her room at the enchanting Bismarck Holiday Inn—the decorator must be color-blind, how else to explain the pairing of mauve and chartreuse. But the thought of spending the night at the Staybridge made her shudder. And hideous room or not, the truth is she's glad to be out of New York, away from Greg, even if it's only for one night. Their home life has been reduced to desultory dinners filled with polite chitchat. She has so much she wants to talk about, but any mention of *Spotlight* triggers a chilly response. And when it comes to Jenny's behavior, he shrugs everything off with the all-purpose "it's adolescent acting out." For her part, she resents his flirtation—or whatever it is—with Leslie. It seems like midlife male acting out. And if he's so eager to get back into the producing end of the news business, well, GNN isn't the only network out there.

Speaking of Leslie, that's a call Erica's been putting off, but time is getting tight. She sits on the edge of the bed and dials.

"Erica, how are you? We missed you terribly at Peggy Noonan's."

"I'm back out in North Dakota."

"Yes," Leslie says in a way that lets Erica know she already knew that. "Productive?"

"We got terrific footage of the Bellamys. Gloria sent you a rough cut of the whole show. There should be enough fodder there for you to formulate your thoughts and opinions."

"I'll look at it post haste."

It's been in her mailbox for almost twenty-four hours, and now she'll look at it post haste? Two weeks ago, Leslie was an eager little camper, offering Erica and *Spotlight* all sorts of help. Now she's turned into a cool customer.

"Can we film you on Tuesday?"

"Yes. Can you come down here?"

"I was thinking the studio might work better. Your apartment is so spectacular it may distract from your words."

There's a pause and then, "I actually think it gives me more authority. You know I hate the stereotype of the fusty academic. Probably because underneath these absurdly expensive clothes and my weekly massage, I *am* dull and fusty."

Erica knows when she's been disarmed. "Your apartment will be fine."

"Greg was an absolute gentleman at the party. He charmed one and all."

"Thank you for getting him out of the house."

There's a laden pause and then Leslie says drily, "It *is* fascinating. This whole *secession* business. The wanting to break away, to start anew, to declare independence."

"Sometimes people don't realize how good they have it."

"Yes, and sometimes they do. But they're *bored* with the status quo."

"There are risks involved in reckless action."

"This nation was built by risk-takers," Leslie says with the authority of a Pulitzer-winning historian.

"I think we've survived because the Founding Fathers *minimized* the risk that we'd split apart."

Leslie makes a funny little sound of surprise at being challenged before saying, with finality, "And then the Civil War happened." There's a tense pause before she adds, "So, I'll dive into the rough cut and send you some suggested questions."

"I'll be happy to take a look at them. But when I do an interview, the questions are always mine," Erica says in a tone that lets Leslie know it's the final word.

There's a reproachful pause and then Leslie says, "You're a curious creature, Erica Sparks."

And then she laughs—that knowing, ironic, and entirely mirthless laugh.

Erica hangs up feeling naïve, confused, and bested. Is her marriage really shaky? And so soon? She knows one thing: if Greg does stray, she's not going to be one of those look-the-other-way wives. No way no how. She's going to change the locks.

Erica feels resolve flowing through her veins like an elixir. And it works. For a moment or two.

Because somewhere, deep under her denial, Erica knows that Greg cheating on her would shatter her world.

CHAPTER 31 ————————————

ERICA STANDS UP, PUSHING LESLIE and Greg out of her mind. She has work to do. She turns on the local news as she changes out of her travel clothes, getting ready for her meeting this afternoon with Joan Marcus's daughter, the woman she saw sobbing in the lobby of the Staybridge. A somber male newscaster is on:

"In our top story, there have been no leads in Thursday's gangland-style execution of drifter George Lundy. Lundy was shot in the back of the head as he slept in his room at the Expressway Motel in east Bismarck. Police have no explanation as for why Lundy, whose last known address was a boardinghouse in Winnipeg, Manitoba, was in Bismarck. They are looking for any possible link between his murder and last Saturday's brutal murder of Jamestown resident Joan Marcus in the ladies' room at the Staybridge Hotel. The two crimes have turned Bismarck into a town on edge."

An old mug shot of Lundy appears on-screen—he looks skinny and angry and scared. "Local resident Janice Marks, who lives across the street from the Expressway Motel, spoke with WKRX earlier today."

An obese young woman in a housedress appears on-screen. "We're all just terrified. This is *Bismarck*, for heaven's sakes. We don't even lock our doors. Well, we do *now*. What's going on around here? That poor woman with her throat cut open? I don't let my kids leave the block when they're out playing."

Erica mutes the set and calls Detective Peter Hoaglund.

"Hello, Ms. Sparks," he answers in his laid-back way, which is starting to get on Erica's nerves. In her experience it takes energy and engagement to solve a murder.

"Please, call me Erica. Why didn't you tell me about George Lundy's murder?"

"I've been busy."

"A phone call takes thirty seconds. Have you found any new evidence?"

"Not a thing." Peter Hoaglund is not a man with much imagination or curiosity. Or if he is, he's willfully not exercising them. Which is a troubling thought. "And no one has claimed Lundy's body."

"That's kind of sad," Erica says.

"I'm not shedding any tears. George Lundy has a rap sheet a mile long, including aggravated assault and attempted murder."

"What kind of car was he driving?"

"A black 1998 Honda Civic."

"Four door?"

"Yep."

"That could definitely have been the car I saw racing out of the Staybridge parking lot. Keep me posted."

Erica hangs up, puts on her jacket, and unmutes the TV in time to hear another Bismarck resident say, "I think there's a psychopath on the loose. *Anyone* could be his next victim. My little girl woke up screaming last night."

Erica clicks off the set and heads out the door, thinking, *There may be a lot more screaming before this story is over.*

CHAPTER 32

ERICA DRIVES NORTH OUT OF Bismarck on Route 32 for six miles before turning into a small subdivision of prefab homes. She's expecting neglect spiced with squalor but instead finds a tidy little neighborhood with flower boxes, garden gnomes, and ornate mailboxes. Apparently when your economy is as hot as North Dakota's, some of it trickles all the way down to the prefab crowd. That sure didn't happen in Maine.

Erica parks in front of #45, gets out, and knocks on the door. A young woman she recognizes as Marcus's daughter opens it. She's wearing a loose dress that looks like it just came out of the wash. She doesn't seem particularly comfortable in it. She doesn't seem comfortable, period. She seems dazed and scared.

"Cathy Allen?"

"That's me. And you're Erica Sparks. In my doorway." She laughs nervously. Erica hates it when she intimidates people; it can throw up roadblocks to the truth.

"Thank you for seeing me."

Cathy sticks her head out the door and scans the street. "Come in, sit down."

The house is neatly furnished, heavy on the plaid furniture, with bookshelves filled with science fiction and fantasy, a lava lamp, magazines and catalogues in perfect symmetry on the coffee table. There's also a loaf of sweet bread and a pot of coffee on a trivet.

Erica sits in a plaid recliner, Cathy on the sofa. She looks at Erica and smiles wanly.

"How about a cup of coffee? I made a banana bread."

"Coffee sounds great. And so does a slice of the banana bread." Erica hates banana bread.

Cathy's hand shakes slightly as she pours the coffee and cuts the loaf, and she laughs to cover the shaking. "I'm sorry, I don't like being here alone. My husband's at the hospital, he's a nurse. I'm a para, a teacher's assistant at Guthrie Elementary. You know, it's funny, you wanting to talk to me. My mom watched your show every night. She said you kicked butt. Do you think they'll find her killer?"

She hands Erica the coffee and cake. Erica takes a bite. "This is delicious." It isn't.

"I add a little cinnamon and yogurt. My mom taught me to jazz up recipes."

"Is there anything else you want to tell me about your mom?"

"You may have heard that she had a drinking problem. Well, I mean, she did, but she didn't always. She was a wonderful mother when I was little, when I was big too, it's only been the last year or so that she started drinking like that. I didn't know what to do, she'd promise to stop but something was wrong in her life and she drank . . ." Cathy's eyes well with tears and she looks like she's an inch away from hysteria. She gulps air and says, "I'm sorry, pay me no mind."

"Cathy, you just lost your mother." This interview feels so intrusive, Erica has half a mind to cut it short—make that a quarter of a mind. She's a journalist with a job to do. She can't solve this murder if she walks away now. "Do you mind if I ask you a couple more questions?"

Cathy shakes her head.

"Was there some incident in her life that coincided with the start of the heavy drinking?"

Cathy blows her nose. "It was her work. Her job. Oh, she was making some serious money. But she paid a price for those dollars."

"You mean with Oil Field Solutions?"

Cathy nods. "She wanted to cash in on the boom, like everyone else. They were paying her forty-five dollars an hour. Before that she was working in an insurance agency in Jamestown for fifteen."

"What exactly was she doing for Oil Field Solutions?"

"She did bookkeeping and operations. She kept track of expenditures, expenses. Capital spending. And shipments. She tracked shipments. Mom was smart and organized. She knew how to put two and two together."

"What do you think it was about the job that made her drink?"

Cathy stands up and goes to a window and looks out. Then she sits back down. "At first she liked it, although she told me she was seeing some ugly things. And the hours were brutal, they worked her like a mule, twenty hours straight sometimes. They were on three shifts a day, place never stopped. So she was exhausted. Then there was the mess."

"The mess?"

"Oh yeah. The wastewater was being drained into streams, all these fracking chemicals treated haphazardly, spilling all the time, people were coming down sick, it was nasty."

"Why didn't she leave?"

"She earned six figures."

"Was your mother going to expose the pollution?"

"She talked about it. But decided not to."

"Then why do you think someone would want to kill her?"

"It wasn't only the chemicals and stuff. They had her doing bookkeeping and shipment tracking for other companies they owned, and some they didn't even own. Canadian companies. The Bellamys are tight with some billionaire up there. It's shady. She saw something she shouldn't have. It scared her."

"Do you have any idea what it was?"

Cathy stands up and goes to the window again, scanning the street. "We're moving to Florida. We're putting this place on the market this week. It's gotten all weird up here. There's too much money coming in too fast. Money makes people do crazy things. We're getting out."

"Cathy?"

She turns from the window, but she can't look Erica in the eye. She starts to walk around the room straightening things that are already straight. "That's why it's so neat in here. I'm trying to sort of *stage* the place. There's going to be an open house. Frank has a job lined up down in Jacksonville. You can buy a pretty decent house down there for 150,000. And no snow. Imagine that?"

When she finally turns to Erica, her eyes are full of fear and her words come in a rush. "Why did they have to slit her throat like that? I had to go down and identify her body. They tried to cover up her neck, but I could see it. She looked like a carved-up animal. She was a good mom. She always told me I was smart and pretty and could do anything and now . . ." She takes a throw off the back of the sofa and wraps it around herself. Then she walks back to the window.

"Cathy, what did your mother find out that made them kill her?"

Cathy whirls around. "*I don't know! I swear I don't know! She didn't tell me!*" Cathy looks shocked by her own outburst. Her shoulders slump and she sits on the sofa, legs curled under her, and pulls the throw tight around her. When she speaks her voice is soft and flat. "All she told me was that it was big. Real big."

CHAPTER 33

STURGES AND MARY BELLAMY ARE at their ranch, riding horses against the backdrop of low hills, grazing cattle, and an endless blue sky.

"You know, Mary, this land is in our blood," Sturges says. He looks so handsome, burnished, the afternoon sun striking the planes and angles of his weathered face, his thick gray hair picking up glints of light.

"It certainly is, Sturges. My great-grandfather settled here in 1894. Built a farmhouse. Bred cattle. Raised a family."

"CUT!" the director—Corey James, long-haired, lanky, flew in from LA, only the best—calls from the open truck that is about twenty feet in front of the Bellamys, filming them as they ride. "Interference." He points up to the sky, where a low-flying prop plane can be seen and heard. Everyone freezes until the plane passes. "All right, from the top." The horses resume their saunter.

"You know, Mary, this land is in our blood."

"It certainly is, Sturges. My great-grandfather settled here in 1894. Built a farmhouse. Bred cattle. Raised a family. He was all about hard work and integrity and your word being your bond. Those same values are what guide me today. But they're under attack from outsiders. From Washington politicians who want to control our lives and our pocketbooks." Mary—a potent mix of soft, sincere, and passionate—looks right into the camera. "If you elect me governor on August 1st, I promise you we will take back our homeland. Once and for all."

"CUT! Terrific! It's a wrap."

A sound tech takes off Sturges's and Mary's microphones. Instead of dismounting, they turn their horses toward the horizon and nudge them into a trot, leaving the film crew behind.

"This is what it's all about, Sturges—a horse, the land, you and me," Mary says in what she thinks of as her "Sturges voice"—loving, nurturing, *convincing*. She could have been an actress. Of course, it only works because Sturges plays *his* role so well.

"There is nothing more perfect than freedom. I'm so proud of you, darling."

"I would be nothing without you," Mary says.

———

Actually, it's her dad, the one and only Morris Adamsson, who gets that credit. He was the strongest person Mary has ever known, a pillar of rectitude, one of the most respected and wealthiest men in the state. Mary's mom, Ingrid, died when she was three, plunging her father into an abyss of grief. But he never gave in to his sorrow, he bore it with such grace. He got up every morning and did what he had to do. He poured all of his love into his only child. But it wasn't a soft, spoiling love, it was a toughening-up love. Because life is unpredictable and harsh and heartbreaking. He knew that. And he wanted Mary to be prepared.

Once every month or so—starting when she was just a little girl—he'd take her to the slaughterhouse on their ranch. They'd stand on a small platform, and he'd pick her up and they would watch as the cattle, the terrified cattle, were herded through a shoot. Mary can still hear the cries and moans and braying of the doomed beasts as they were prodded along—they knew what was coming. Then they were jolted in the head with a stun gun, a jolt that rendered them insensate. Theoretically. It worked some of the time. Other times it didn't.

Next they were strung up, their feet were cut off, and their throats slit. They bled out. Except the ones who weren't stunned were still alive when their feet were cut off and their throats slit. And they cried and screamed until they bled out. Her dad was animated by it all; he would breathe heavily and get red in the face, excited by the deaths and the suffering and the cries. Maybe it was his rage toward a world that took away the woman he loved.

At first Mary hated to watch; she cried the first few times and turned her head away—but Daddy didn't like that. Not one bit. He took her chin in his big hand and turned her face toward the dying animals. He told her to be strong, now and forever. That she was his daughter and that meant something. He told her that the cattle made lots of money for him, and for her. And that money was power. He told her if she watched the cattle die, she would be ready for life, ready to do big, important things.

And so Mary trained herself to look, to watch as the animals' throats were slit. To hear their cries and moans not as agonized last throes but as the sound of money being made, power being acquired. Before too long Mary loved their ritual visits to the slaughterhouse.

Afterward they'd go into town for ice cream sundaes.

———

"We're quite a team, aren't we?" Sturges says.

"We are indeed," Mary says, smiling to herself. She slows her horse to a walk and Sturges follows suit. The tone in her voice changes subtly as she says, "Isn't that Erica Sparks a lovely young woman?"

"Isn't she?"

"So bright. I admire her. Coming from that terrible background. She's completely self-made." Mary never takes her privilege for granted. Work is the great leveler. And Erica, like Mary, is a workhorse. "You know, she's one of those people I just instinctively want to help. And she's already proven very valuable to our cause. When *Spotlight* airs, we're going to be the talk of the nation."

They walk in silence for a minute before Sturges says, "She's very curious, isn't she? Like a bloodhound."

"Yes. How else do you explain her flying out here last weekend? Meeting with that Marcus woman's daughter. She'll probably want to look into that drifter who was murdered, what was his name again?"

"George Lundy."

"Yes. It's an open-and-shut case. You heard Detective Hoaglund's statement. Lundy and Marcus were involved in some sort of shady deal that went bad. I honestly don't know why Erica would waste her time." Mary frowns. "Although I suppose it's that kind of doggedness that got her where she is today. But still . . ."

"She might have called us. Just to say hello," Sturges says.

"One would hope." Mary stops her horse and looks over at her husband. "We have to keep a close eye on her, don't we, darling?"

CHAPTER 34 —————————————————

IT'S EIGHT THIRTY THURSDAY NIGHT and the premiere of *Spotlight* starts in a half hour. GNN is hosting a viewing party at the Paris movie theater on West Fifty-Eighth Street just off Fifth Avenue. The lobby is jammed with the city's media elite, half of them wishing Erica every success, the other half wishing her every failure. Erica is making her way through the throng, smiling and greeting people, trying to project confidence and warmth—in fact, she's paddling like mad below the surface, tense, uneasy with all the attention, knowing how much is at stake, and repeatedly tugged back to events in North Dakota. What could Joan Marcus have seen when she was working at Oil Field Solutions, a company co-owned by the Bellamys and a Canadian billionaire? Whatever it was, it cost her her life.

She wishes Greg were by her side, but he's across the lobby, networking with a vengeance. He's made a tentative decision to look for producing work, and she knows how important contacts are . . . but still, tonight of all nights, couldn't he keep the focus on her?

And then Leslie Wilson sidles up to her, snaking her arm under Erica's in a besties gesture that's clearly meant for public consumption. "Isn't this exciting?"

"It is." Erica is grateful to Leslie. The shoot at her house went so well; she was articulate and penetrating in her thoughts about the secession movements, and her footage elevates *Spotlight* in a way few other contributors could. In fact, a fair amount of the buzz around the show—online, in print, and on TV—has been generated by Leslie's participation. Still, it's Erica's show, her baby. If it flops, she'll be tainted and will probably never be given another chance at an in-depth investigative program. Leslie, on the other hand, will simply get back to her work and move on with her life.

Erica spots Gloria and waves her over. "Big night," Gloria says.

"It wouldn't have happened without you."

"I'm hardly the irreplaceable one, Erica."

"I was hoping your beau would make it."

"That makes three of us. But the Pentagon never sleeps," Gloria says, momentarily looking a little bit lost and forlorn. You don't need to be a couples counselor to figure out that it's a fraught relationship. And that her mysterious fiancé holds most (all?) of the cards.

The lights flash, and the audience makes its way into the theater. Erica is going to watch the screening from the back of the room— fewer people will see her wincing at tiny details that could have maybe been improved. As she watches the audience file in, she gets a text from Jenny.

Good luck tonight, Mom. I'm watching and wicked proud

Thank you, dear heart

I don't want to secede from you;)

A thousand xxxoo's

Erica's throat tightens, her eyes well. It's the most pleasant exchange she's had with Jenny since that awful weekend. *Maybe we should only text*, she thinks with a rueful smile.

Greg finally appears and puts an arm around Erica. It sits there self-consciously. Erica takes a half step away and Greg retracts his arm.

"Peggy Malkin, CNN's head of production, wants me to come in for a meeting next week," Greg says.

"That's wonderful, honey," Erica says.

On her way into the theater, Leslie dashes over and gives Erica's hand a quick squeeze. "Bon courage." Then she looks at Greg, smiles, and purrs, "And you." Then she's gone, leaving a whiff of bergamot behind.

Just as Erica is about to say something about Leslie, the lights dim in the theater and her cell vibrates. It's a North Dakota number. Erica moves to a corner of the lobby and answers.

"Erica, it's Peter Hoaglund in Bismarck."

"Not the best time. What's up?"

"You said you wanted to be kept in the loop, so I thought you'd want to know that Cathy and Dennis Allen were killed today when their propane tank exploded."

Erica feels the blood drain from her head and an icy shiver races down her spine.

"Are you there? Erica? Ms. Sparks?"

"Yes. Does it seem suspicious in any way?"

"Well, um, considering . . . You know, propane tanks don't just spontaneously combust."

"Thanks for letting me know." Erica hangs up and stands there, stock-still.

Greg waves to her from across the lobby as ushers close the doors to the auditorium. "Erica, come on, it's starting."

But his voice seems to come from far away and Erica doesn't move.

CHAPTER 35

ERICA STANDS IN THE AISLE at the back of the theater as the first episode of *Spotlight* plays on-screen, trying to contain her restless anxiety. Not about the show, which is playing well, but about the deaths of Cathy and Dennis Allen. She quickly checked out the Bismarck *Tribune*'s site on her iPhone and saw pictures of the propane explosion—their house was leveled, nothing was left but a slab piled with detritus. Somewhere under it lie their mangled, lifeless bodies. She was with Cathy less than a week ago, sitting in her living room. And now she's dead. Cathy was giving Erica important information about her mother's murder. Someone didn't like that. Erica feels a bead of sweat roll down from her left armpit. She shivers and ducks out into the lobby, gulping air. She takes out her phone and calls Mark Benton out in Portland.

"Hey, Erica, your show starts in two hours out here. I'm recording it. Congrats."

"Thanks, Mark. Listen, if I sent you a picture I took with my iPhone of a photograph, or part of a photograph, could you enlarge it?"

"Sure. I can't make any promises on clarity and definition, but I'll do my best."

Something about talking to Mark always grounds Erica. He's been such a stalwart friend. And the fact that he's out in crunchy, laid-back

Portland, working and windsurfing, and not here in New York desperately trying to reach the top of the greasy pole, is comforting, a reminder that there is more to life than a career.

Yes, Erica, like a child and a husband.

Erica feels a wave of guilt and knows that she could never be happy in Portland, winsome and windsurfing, she *needs* the adrenaline rush of the news business, the sense that her work matters.

"Can I send it along now?"

"No time like the present."

"Hold on." Erica messages the picture to Mark.

"It's dark, Erica."

"I know."

"I'll try and lighten it up. Still . . ."

"It could be important, just do your best." Erica realizes she's once again pulling Mark into a case in which she is directly involved and that has already produced four corpses. "And please don't let anyone see it or know what you're doing. Okay?"

"Gotcha."

Erica slips back into the theater. It's near the end of the show and on-screen she's interviewing the Bellamys. The audience is pin-drop silent, with many people leaning forward in their seats.

Mary Bellamy is speaking: "People are just plain fed up. And not just in North Dakota. We have supporters all across the nation." She leans forward and her voice grows fervent. "And we are inviting them to move here to help us. We have jobs that go begging, we have open spaces, inexpensive housing, great natural beauty. So I put out a call to all Americans who support our goals: Be a twenty-first-century pioneer. Come to North Dakota, make it *your* homeland, and join us as we make history."

The audience gasps as one. Then people turn and start whispering to each other, a great surge of energy ripples through the theater, phones come out.

On-screen Erica is closing out the episode, saying, "Although it's only one of many, the North Dakota secession movement is certainly the most serious and advanced in the nation. Where will it lead? At this point, that question is impossible to answer. Polls have consistently shown Mary Bellamy trailing Governor Snyder. Will Bellamy's call for 'twenty-first-century pioneers' to move to North Dakota affect the outcome? The White House has refused to comment on the situation, but sources inside the administration say they are watching developments closely. Behind the scenes, both parties are working to defeat Bellamy, whom they view as a threat to national unity. We will, of course, be following the story closely and will bring you any updates as soon as we have them. Thank you for watching *Spotlight*. We'll see you next month."

As the lights go up, the audience seems to rise as one and pour up the aisle: the cat is out of the bag and everyone has joined the chase. Erica is quickly surrounded by colleagues and admirers. Mort Silver muscles his way close and says, "Brilliant, Sparks, brilliant. You *created* news here. And I just got a text: ratings are high, very high."

Erica finds the crush oppressive and feels a surge of claustrophobia; she looks around for Greg. There he is, walking up the aisle with Leslie Wilson, who has a hand on his arm as she leans in to tell him something.

Erica breaks through the throng and intercepts them.

"Masterful," Leslie says simply.

"A lot of credit goes to you," Erica says.

"We're a team. Listen, why don't we all go out for a late supper?"

"I've got to get home. I've got my show tomorrow and I'm flying out to Bismarck on Saturday."

"You didn't tell me that," Greg says.

"I just decided." Erica's instincts tell her to play it close to the vest, even with Greg. "Every network is going to have people out there, some are probably on their way to the airport as we speak. We broke this story, and I want to own it." She also wants to investigate the string of murders, albeit it far more quietly.

"Isn't Jenny coming down this weekend?" Greg asks.

Erica clenches her teeth in chagrin—she had completely forgotten.

CHAPTER 36

IT'S SATURDAY MORNING AND ERICA looks out the airplane window at the endless plains below. It's as if someone took the crumpled eastern landscape and stretched it tight across the globe, expanding it seemingly forever. It all looks so lonely to Erica, all that empty space, desolate and frightening, and she turns away from the window to her computer, where she is reading anything she can find on the murder of George Lundy, the drifter who may have killed Joan Marcus.

When she next looks back out the window she sees the suburbs and then the skyscrapers of Winnipeg, rising from the plains like a vertical mirage. She's meeting Gloria and her crew in Bismarck this afternoon. While she's not completely sure she wants the second *Spotlight* to be devoted to the Homeland movement, she wants to shoot footage just in case. And she's also going to be filing live reports. Eileen is down with a killer flu, and Gloria generously offered to oversee the live feeds too. Her work ethic is earning her a lot of chits very quickly.

Erica begged off flying out with Gloria, saying she wanted to spend a few more hours with Jenny, and then booked this flight without telling anyone.

She made good use of those hours with Jenny; they paid a quick visit to the exotic insect exhibit at the Museum of Natural History, just the two of them, and it went well. Didn't it? Jenny was full of questions about secessionists and the Bellamys and North Dakota, proud of the success of *Spotlight*, but still . . . somehow it felt to Erica as if they were playing a game of mother/daughter, each sticking to her role for fear that if they broke character the whole show would fall apart, degenerate into sarcasm, passive aggression, and mutual resentment—the truth is the Beth video still rankles. But they made it through the museum and then Erica delivered Jenny back to the apartment—where Greg is going to entertain her for the rest of the weekend—and took off for the airport, hoping her relief wasn't too obvious.

The plane lands at Winnipeg airport, and Erica—passport (and celebrity) in hand—quickly goes through customs. She steps outside and gets a cab to the Edgecomb Hotel. As they drive through the city toward downtown, Erica is impressed by how clean and orderly it is; even the pedestrians seem well behaved, with little of the nudging and rushing and weaving so common on the sidewalks of New York. They reach downtown and then move into a run-down old neighborhood in its shadows. So many cities seem to have these Skid Rows next to their downtowns, once-thriving neighborhoods left to fester as the cities expanded outward. They pass bars, check-cashing convenience stores, drunks, druggies, derelicts, the down-and-out. The driver stops in front of a circa-1920s hotel that has clearly seen better days.

"Can you wait for me here? It shouldn't be long. Then I'm heading right back to the airport." The driver nods and Erica gets out.

The lobby of the Edgecomb Hotel is high-ceilinged and expansive, with rococo detailing and cool architectural details, all of it covered in a thick layer of dust, dirt, and defeat. A sputtering television hangs on the wall, and the sagging chairs and sofas are home to about a half dozen empty-eyed men and women who look like extras in some low-budget zombie movie. Were these sad souls really once innocent children?

Erica approaches the front desk, which is manned by a thin, sallow, middle-aged man who is methodically clipping his fingernails. He glances at her with feral eyes and then goes back to his chore.

"Hi," Erica says.

He purses his lips expectantly.

"I'm looking for information about George Lundy."

"George Lundy is dead."

"I know. Can you tell me anything about him?"

The man focuses on Erica for the first time. There's no sign of recognition. ". . . I *might* be able to tell you a thing or two." His lips purse again.

In her travels Erica has learned to come prepared. She takes out her wallet, removes a fifty-dollar bill, and slides it across the counter. The man puts the flat of his hand on the bill and slides it over to his side, and then, in a strangely agile move, right into his pants pocket.

"Lundy lived here for about six months. Kept to himself. Most do." He nods toward the dazed denizens.

"Did he ever have any company? Did you ever see him with anyone?"

"Can't say as I did. I will say he got agitated his last week here, before he was . . . shot in the back of the head, wasn't it?"

Erica nods.

"Way down in Bismarck. That's kinda weird, isn't it? I mean, we're not exactly sister cities."

"How was he agitated?"

"Just kinda jumpy and nervous, going in and out a lot."

"Can I see his room?"

"That's strictly against hotel policy."

Erica slides another fifty across the counter. The man scratches behind his ear, looks around the lobby, then turns and takes down a key. "Room 411. Don't dawdle."

As the elevator—with its tarnished gold filigree—rumbles upward, Erica thinks of her mother, ensconced in the cookie-cutter townhouse development with its community center and immaculate landscaping.

If Erica hadn't been a success, would Susan have ended up in a dead-end hotel like this one? And what about Erica herself? Where would she be if she hadn't gotten sober and pulled her life together? The world is full of Edgecomb Hotels, the last stop on the loser train.

The fourth-floor hallway is the color of tobacco spit, dimly lit, and smells like some mix of cigarettes and urine and canned spaghetti. Erica passes an open doorway and looks in—an ancient man in his underwear is sitting on the edge of his bed. He leers at Erica and then cackles toothlessly.

There's a strip of police tape over the doorway to room 411. Erica unlocks the door, ducks under the tape, and shuts the door behind her. The room is surprisingly clean, and the only personal touch is a Star Wars poster taped to the wall, which Erica finds poignant somehow. The place has obviously been searched by the police—the dresser drawers are open, their contents jumbled, the bedsheets are a tangle on the floor. Erica makes her way through the room and small bath, examining every nook and cranny, looking under the sink, in the toilet tank, behind the radiator, removing the dresser drawers, going through the pockets of the three sad jackets that hang in the wardrobe. Nothing. Anywhere.

Frustrated, she heads back down the hallway. As she hastens past the open door, the ancient man barks, "I seen 'em." Something in his tone, the certainty, makes Erica stop. She turns, walks back, and looks into the room. The man smiles with lascivious satisfaction.

"Who did you see?"

"Come in, honey, I don't bite."

Erica takes a half step into the room; it smells like baby powder and Vaseline.

"Yeah, I seen 'em."

"Who?"

"Lundy and Freddy."

"Who's Freddy?"

"I warned him to stay away from that Freddy McDougal. But nobody listens to Elmer anymore."

"Who's Freddy McDougal?"

"He waves a couple of Gs in some sad sack's face and the guy does some dumb crap and winds up with a hole in the back of his head."

"Where can I find this Freddy?"

"Eager, eh? Like a filly at the gate. A real pretty filly."

"Listen, I don't have much time. I need to find Freddy."

There's a buzz, and Elmer picks up his cell phone and reads the text message. He smiles to himself, then turns his attention back to Erica. "Freddy's got a luncheonette on the next block. Not that he cares if he ever sells another BLT. Don't tell him I sent ya." He looks at his phone again. "Listen, I got a hooker coming up in twenty minutes. Unless *you* want to make a few extra bucks." Then he cackles.

As Erica heads down the hall, Elmer shouts after her, "Watch your step, sweetie."

CHAPTER 37

FARLEY'S LUNCHEONETTE IS A THROWBACK, with a U-shaped Formica counter, leatherette stools, and a row of booths along one wall. There's also a large framed photograph of the premier of Manitoba, Pearce Johnson. The place is pretty crowded, and the clientele looks a step or two up from the Edgecomb. Erica sits at the counter. She asked the cab driver to wait a little longer, but she has to make her flight and time is tight.

A waitress who looks alarmingly like Elmer's twin sister comes over.

"What can I get ya, eh?"

"Just a cup of coffee. I'm looking for Freddy McDougal."

The waitress cocks her head toward a booth in the back. Freddy is middle-aged, looks like he's in good shape, wearing a sports coat, respectable. He's leaning across the table, deep in conversation with a man in a nice suit.

Erica walks over. "Hi, Freddy."

"Didn't your mother ever tell you it's not polite to interrupt?"

"She didn't, actually. But I'm pressed for time. Could I possibly have a couple of minutes of yours?"

"I know you."

"I guess I know you too."

Freddy shoots his boothmate a glance and the man gets up, saying, "We can finish this later." He casts an appraising glance at Erica, as if he's imprinting her on his mind, and walks away.

"Have a seat, Erica Sparks. What's on your mind?"

Erica scoots into the booth. "George Lundy's murder."

"I heard about that."

"You knew him, didn't you?"

"Never met the guy."

"You were seen with him in the Edgecomb Hotel."

"I *own* the Edgecomb Hotel. I'm in and out all the time. I also own this place and a decent chunk of this whole neighborhood." He smiles. "There's a lot of money in poverty."

"So you never had any dealings with George Lundy?"

"I collect rent from people like Lundy, I don't socialize with them."

"And you have no idea who sent him down to Bismarck to murder Joan Marcus?"

"I can see how you got where you are, Erica, but no, I have no idea." His eyes are clear and his matter-of-fact manner doesn't suggest guilt. Still, there's something about him . . . He's too relaxed by half. "Listen, you're not the only one who's busy. I'm meeting with a prospective retail tenant. This area is coming up, and I'm going to ride it all the way home." He stands and buttons his sports coat. "It was a pleasure meeting you, my wife is going to be thrilled." Then he walks out of Farley's.

The waitress comes over and puts a cup of coffee in front of Erica. Then she puts a menu and pen on the table. "Could we get your autograph?"

Erica looks around and sees that pretty much everyone in the place is staring at her. She throws a five on the table and splits.

CHAPTER 38 ———————————————————

THE CAR TAKES ERICA FROM the Bismarck airport to an industrial park north of town. It's late afternoon and the place is jumping. There are hundreds of cars parked in the lot, more are driving in, and there are at least a half dozen broadcast trucks. The car pulls up to a vast hangar-like building and Erica gets out.

She heads inside—the cavernous space is filled with hundreds of people, upbeat music is blaring, there are banners and balloons and signs, a festive fervent mood that borders on zealous, that carries a tinge of the cultish, the mob, as if this energy could go either way, tinder waiting for the match. Erica scans the space for Gloria and her crew. She spots them and races over. Gloria has a look of concern on her face, which turns to relief when she sees Erica.

"Thank goodness you're here. I was worried. Didn't you get my messages and texts?"

"I was busy, I ignored everything. But I'm here on time."

Gloria looks at her watch. "Barely. I was so worried I called the airlines. You weren't on any of the flights to Bismarck. Texting me back would have taken two minutes. There is such a thing as professional courtesy."

Gloria isn't afraid to stand up to Erica, and she loves that. It makes her trust and respect the woman even more. Still, she ignores her questions and grabs her mic. "Let's go . . . This is Erica Sparks reporting live from an industrial park on the outskirts of Bismarck, North Dakota, where Mary Bellamy has established headquarters for her Homeland Pioneers campaign. As you can see around me, this vast space is serving as a welcoming, processing voter registration and housing and job center for 'pioneers' from across the country who have responded to Bellamy's call to move to North Dakota to strengthen her chances of winning the governorship in the recall election on August 1st. The mood is festive, even raucous, and very determined. Let's meet some of the newcomers."

Erica moves to one of the dozens of stations lining the perimeter of the facility; each is identified by a large sign—*Housing, Voter Registration, Jobs, Medical, Gun Registry*—and each has a line snaking in front of it. Volunteers are moving up and down the lines, handing out water and soda, coffee and doughnuts. There's an enormous banner hanging down from the rafters that reads *Welcome to the Homeland*. Erica approaches the end of the line waiting in front of a housing station. A young couple, the mom carrying a baby, is patiently waiting to register. They're clean-cut and nicely dressed, poster people for Bellamy's movement.

"Hi, what are your names and where are you from?"

"I'm Phil Davis."

"I'm Lonnie Davis, and we're from Seattle."

"And what brought you here to North Dakota?" Erica asks.

"We think the federal government is too big and intrusive. We believe states should run themselves," Phil Davis says.

"The Bellamy campaign is asking every pioneer to register to vote and to pledge to support her in the upcoming election. Are you willing to do that?"

"Absolutely. We love her," Lonnie Davis says.

"And you're hoping that you can get help finding a place to live?"

"The campaign has promised us housing, even if it's temporary. I hear they've brought in trailers like FEMA did after Katrina. We're fine in a trailer, we just want to be part of this."

"Thank you," Erica says, moving away from the Davises and over to a voter registration station, where Wendell Brodsky is keeping a watchful eye on things. "Now, let me see if I can grab a few words with Wendell Brodsky, who is the strategic and statistical brain behind this campaign . . . Do you have a minute, Wendell?"

"Of course, Erica."

"Can you break this all down by the numbers for our viewers?"

"Well, in the last North Dakota gubernatorial election, voter turn-out was just over 300,000. Right now Mary trails Governor Snyder by approximately four points in the polls. We're hoping to welcome and register between twenty-five and thirty thousand pioneers, whom we believe will provide us with a comfortable margin of victory."

"But you have no guarantee they'll vote for your candidate. The voting booth is private."

"I don't think these people would pick up their lives and move here unless they were passionate about our cause."

"Can you tell me how many people in total you've processed?"

"As of fifteen minutes ago, 6,820. That's in three days, so we're on track to meet our goals."

"Those are very impressive numbers. But in order to vote, someone has to have lived in North Dakota for thirty days. Which means you only have another eight days to register people."

"We're confident we're going to reach our goal. Pioneers are pour-ing into the state," Wendell says.

Erica spots Mary Bellamy holding a tray of coffee and doughnuts, cheerfully—with just a trace of noblesse oblige—offering them to those waiting in line. Her modest endeavor is undercut by the adoring throng who hover around her. "Thank you, Wendell Brodsky. Now let me see if I can get a few words with Mary Bellamy herself, the leader of the Take Back Our Homeland movement."

"Erica," Mary says in her understated way, "how about a cup of coffee and a doughnut? I've got plain, frosted, and chocolate."

"Maybe later. What do you make of all this?"

"Well, I think it's the most wonderful thing I've ever seen. *This* is democracy in action. Just look at all these lovely families who want to be a part of it. They're the *new pioneers*. Together we are making history."

"Isn't there a danger that you're weakening our nation by dividing people, creating an us-versus-them mentality?"

"We're *strengthening* the Homeland," Mary says deftly. "This movement is about freedom. The federal government wants to control our lives. We believe North Dakotans know what's best for North Dakota. Now, if you'll excuse me, Erica, I've got doughnuts to give out."

The woman is measured, homespun, self-effacing, but under it all Erica senses that steel, that ruthlessness. It's the tightness at the corners of her mouth, the eyes that tend to dart, the imperious tilt of the chin. Erica has seen the lust, the thirst, the *need* for power before. And it never fails to terrify her.

In the van carrying them back to the Holiday Inn, Gloria asks, "Now are you going to tell me where you were this morning?"

Erica hesitates for a moment, some instinct telling her to hold back. But this is Gloria, for goodness' sake. "I made a little detour to Winnipeg."

"For?"

"That was the last known location of George Lundy."

"I thought we were here covering the Bellamys and their movement. Not the murders of Marcus and Lundy."

"And don't forget Joan Marcus's daughter and son-in-law."

"That's classified as an accident, as of now."

"Exactly: *as of now.* The point is I'm not sure that the Bellamy story and the four deaths aren't related."

Gloria leans back in the seat and her eyes get very wide for a moment. But she recovers quickly. "I wish you'd let me know, I would have offered to help."

"I appreciate that, but this is all at the embryonic stage. Sometimes stealth is the best choice."

"Do you have any evidence that might link the Bellamys or the Homeland movement to the murders?"

Erica hesitates again. This time she trusts her instincts. "One step at a time, Gloria, one step at a time."

CHAPTER 39 ———————————————

ERICA IS IN HER ROOM at the Holiday Inn, playing solitaire and going over what she learned today. Freddy McDougal seems to be an important piece of the story. But what story, exactly? Is Joan Marcus's murder really somehow connected to the Bellamys? Was she about to expose environmental crimes committed at Bellamy-owned companies? If so, it surely would have torpedoed Mary Bellamy's campaign for governor—it's tough to sell your state as capable of self-regulating and then flood it with cancer-causing chemicals. Or did Marcus uncover something when she was tracking shipments in and out? Is it possible drugs were laundered through the company? That could happen without the Bellamys even knowing.

But no matter what the malfeasance, are the Bellamys capable of murder? You're taking a big risk when you kill. They're working through the system. Would they really put it all in jeopardy to off a bookkeeper? But *someone* ordered the murder of Marcus, and then Lundy. Which leads her back to McDougal.

Erica loses the game and tosses the cards aside. She goes over to the dresser and picks up the barely edible turkey sandwich she picked up at the small shop in the lobby. She and Gloria had agreed to go out for a nice dinner, but then Gloria begged off, saying she had a lot of paperwork to do. She seemed oddly distracted after Erica told her about her detour to Winnipeg. Maybe she was trying to figure out how newsworthy, nationally, the Marcus/Lundy story is. Gloria likes to stay one step ahead of the game, which is a valuable quality in their business. Still, Erica is seeing another side of her producer: moodiness, flashes of suppressed anger, impatience. She's probably just lonely; she's been working so hard, and she misses her man.

Erica sits down at the desk and googles *Fred McDougal Winnipeg*. There are stories about his development plans for downtown, but then, on the Winnipeg *Free Press* site, she reads:

BREAKING NEWS:
Winnipeg businessman Frederick McDougal, 52, was killed this evening in a hit-and-run accident downtown. McDougal, who owns numerous properties and businesses in and around downtown Winnipeg, was struck by a black pickup truck as he crossed the intersection of South and Lovell Streets. His body was thrown over 30 feet. The pickup then sped away. Witnesses say the truck was traveling at high speed when the accident occurred. The Winnipeg police have no further details at this time. McDougal leaves a wife, Janine.

Erica's breathing goes shallow and she closes her eyes as she absorbs this news. A hit-and-run? Yeah, right. Freddy McDougal was murdered because he spoke to Erica.

And then there were five.

CHAPTER 40

ERICA IS BONE-TIRED WHEN SHE gets back to New York on Sunday evening. As the car approaches her building all she wants is a hot bath, a chunk of dark chocolate, and some affection from her husband.

She's been following the McDougal hit-and-run "accident" all day and there have been no new developments, except that his funeral is scheduled for early Monday. In the morning Erica appeared via feed on *Face to Face*, GNN's Sunday morning interview show, to discuss the Take Back Our Homeland movement. And all day she was haunted by her own role in these unfolding events. Now she just wants to forget all of it and relax.

Good luck on that one, Erica.

She walks into her apartment. All the lights are on and Bing Crosby is softly crooning "Night and Day" through the speakers. "Hi, honey!" Erica calls.

No response. Erica strides into the living room, filled with expectation.

Sitting on a couch, glass of wine in hand, looking very much at home, is Leslie Burke Wilson.

CHAPTER 41 ———————————————

"ERICA," LESLIE SAYS, GETTING UP, putting her hands on Erica's shoulders, and giving her an air kiss. Erica tenses.

"Where's Greg?"

"He should be home any minute. He drove Jenny out to LaGuardia." Erica looks at her blankly. "Oh, didn't they tell you? I thought they would surely have told you. Maybe they didn't want to make you jealous. I was able, through some miracle of fate, to score three tickets for today's *Hamilton* matinee. One was for you, of course, but you were out in the hinterlands. By the way, I thought your reporting was terrific, and you were marvelous on *Face to Face*. *Spotlight*'s been fantastic for me too—my publisher wants me to write a book on American secessionist movements. They're waving fistfuls of money in front of my face. So *thank you*!" Then she plops back down on the sofa.

Erica feels like an interloper in her own home. Okay, so they went to *Hamilton*. Did that mean Leslie had to come back to the apartment with Greg and Jenny?

"Erica, what is it? You look pale."

"I'm just a little tired. Been a long weekend."

"Oh, I wanted to talk to you, but we can do it another time."

"Give me five," Erica says, heading back to her bedroom without waiting for an answer. She drops her bag on the bed and goes into the bathroom, splashing cold water on her face again and again. She looks at herself in the mirror and sees an overwhelmed, confused, hurting woman staring back at her. *Hamilton* with Jenny? And Greg. And here *alone*, in Erica's apartment, the one she paid for with her salary, the salary she *earns* by regularly putting in seventy-hour weeks. How could Greg let this happen? What kind of game is he playing? Yes, Leslie was important to the success of *Spotlight* and, yes, Erica covets entrée into her world. But at what price?

Erica changes into a pair of loose shorts and a T-shirt and walks back out into the living room. Leslie is still sitting there, still looking very much at home. "I won't stay a minute, Erica, but . . ."

"I'm going to make myself a cup of tea," Erica says, heading into the kitchen to turn on the kettle. Leslie follows. Erica actually wants something a lot stronger than tea, like a tall glass of vodka with a splash of tonic—on second thought, hold the splash. But green tea will have to do.

"I'm tremendously grateful to you, Erica."

For loaning you my husband?

"I feel the same about you," Erica says.

"I've done my share of television, but *Spotlight* gave me a whole new platform. We're a strong team. I would love to come on board as a permanent consultant."

Erica pours the boiling water in her mug a little too vigorously and some splashes out, scalding her fingers. She bites down to avoid yelping—she doesn't want to yelp in front of Leslie. She turns on the cold water and holds her hand under it.

"Are you all right?"

"I'm fine." *I want this woman out of my apartment.* "I think it's too soon to make any decisions on *Spotlight*. Yes, the ratings were good, but they could drop off if we don't sustain what we've started."

"That's where I think I could be helpful. I've drawn up a list of six possible topics for future episodes. I can draw on a deep well of contacts to help you book the most prominent and insightful thinkers on each one. Want to hear my ideas?"

No!

Thankfully the front door opens. "We're in the kitchen, honey," Erica calls.

Greg walks in, looking casually handsome in cords and a well-worn denim shirt. "Did I interrupt something?" he asks.

"We were just brainstorming ideas for future *Spotlights*," Leslie says.

(A) That's not true, and (b) Leslie is trying to co-opt Erica's show. It's the last straw. "Listen, I had an exhausting weekend. I'm running on fumes, not really thinking straight. Let's pick this up another time."

Leslie is suddenly all empathy—funny how that happened as soon as Greg walked in the door—and she says, "I'm sorry. I was just so revved up I forgot my manners." She crosses to Erica and gives her a little kiss, then lowers her voice. "Jenny is so bright and curious and funny and, best of all, *interesting*. You've done a *wonderful* job. And she *adores* you. Now get some rest. Talk soon."

And then she's gone. As soon as Erica hears the front door close, she wheels on Greg. "Are you sleeping with her?"

Greg takes a step backward and then says, "No."

Erica just stands there looking at him. Is this the same man she fell in love with? Or have the stresses of their marriage twisted him into someone else? "I'm not sure I believe you."

He steps a step toward her. "Honey, please—"

"Don't touch me!"

"Erica, I have *not* slept with Leslie Wilson. Do you really think I would jeopardize our marriage that way?"

"Well, it's a pretty serious flirtation then. How do you think it felt to come home from a tough weekend to find her alone in the apartment?"

"I hinted that she should leave, but she really wanted to talk to you. She's on a big high because of *Spotlight*. She has some ideas, I thought it might be fun for you to hear them."

"I don't think we should see any more of Leslie and Stan for a while."

Greg looks away and rubs his chin. "I'm not sure that's a good idea."

"Why is that?"

"Because I need them, *we* need them. They're very . . . *helpful*."

Greg's point is well taken, even if she doesn't tell him so.

"Erica, you know this consultancy business isn't making me happy, that I want to get back into the action. Stan Wilson can be very useful. Just being in their circle is useful. It's certainly helped *you*."

"Greg, I do not need Stan and Leslie Wilson. I have the highest-ranking news show in the country."

"Leslie's participation gave *Spotlight* a real jolt of prestige, even cache, and you know it. Look at the reviews, they all mentioned her."

"So you're basically saying we should *use* them?"

"I wouldn't put it that bluntly. It's a quid pro quo."

"I'm not sure I belong in their world. I'm not sure I *like* their world."

"Well, I do!"

"That's pretty obvious!"

Suddenly, as if from out of nowhere, Erica is hit with a wave of exhaustion so strong she puts a hand on the counter to steady herself. *Spotlight*, Winnipeg, Bismarck, the murders, *Face to Face*, Leslie sipping wine, it's all just too much for her.

"Erica . . . ?"

When she speaks it's in a deliberate monotone. "Listen, Greg, I'm going to go pass out. Would you like to sleep in the guest bedroom or should I?"

CHAPTER 42

IT'S THE NEXT AFTERNOON AND Erica is in her office. Greg slept in the guest bedroom and she slept like the dead—and woke up feeling half alive. Still, she's happy to be at her desk, at work—her refuge, her salvation. Leslie Wilson aside, she does have to pick a subject for the next *Spotlight*. Mort Silver sent her a memo saying the network is thrilled by the response to the first and wants to know the topic of the second show, which needs to go into production immediately. Erica is inclined to devote the second show to what's unfolding in North Dakota—the whole nation is now following the story and Erica is their go-to source for the latest developments. The election is still almost two months away, but interest in the story is only increasing, and the secession movements in neighboring states are gathering steam. On the other hand, the polls remain iffy, with Mary trailing by the mid-single digits. If it looks like she's going to lose, the nation will turn its fickle attention elsewhere. A new batch of polls is due out midweek. She'll meet with Gloria then, and they'll make a decision.

It's a busy week. She's going up to the Kennedy School of Government in Boston on Wednesday to be part of a symposium on the current state of journalism. It's a prestigious gathering, and she's going to be on a panel entitled "The Whole Truth and Anything But"—Tom Brokaw is moderating. She wishes she hadn't accepted, but pulling out at this late date is out of the question.

She told Jenny about it and invited her. Will she show up? Erica hopes so, even though they're still estranged. Jenny's sweet texts the night of the *Spotlight* premiere helped, but Jenny and Beth's video stunt ripped the lid off Erica's denial: Jenny wants to hurt her, resents her work, is jealous of her. Erica is still waiting for an apology. Although a part of her wants to call Jenny and tell her she loves her and spoil her rotten, Erica is holding her ground. She wants Jenny to understand that actions have consequences. That privilege isn't a license to behave badly. And that her mother deserves respect and consideration. Which is why she hopes Jenny makes it to the symposium—she wants her daughter to see her at her best.

Erica's phone rings: it's Mark Benton out in Portland.

"Mark."

"I just sent you the image blown up thirty times. Take a look."

Erica clicks on the attachment and it fills her screen. On first glance, it looks the same as it did as a small scrap—black at the top, bleeding into a muddy gray section at the bottom. But is that something, barely discernible, in the black field?

"Is that some kind of delineation or margin in the black there?" she asks.

"I saw that too, but it's so indistinct."

"Does it look a little circular to you?"

"It does."

"This is tough."

"I think what we need, Erica, is to take this to the next level. There are experts in the field of reading photographs who use sophisticated technology that can heighten contrast. Law enforcement uses them all the time. I'll see if I can track one down." There's a pause, and Mark lowers his voice. "Listen, Erica, I've been reading up on Joan Marcus's murder, and George Lundy's, and the 'accidental' deaths of Marcus's daughter and son-in-law and Freddy McDougal. Are you putting yourself in danger again?"

"I'm more concerned that I may be putting *you* in danger."

"I don't think anyone is going to be gunning for me because I blew up a photograph. You, on the other hand . . ."

"I appreciate the thought. I'm being careful." *Are you really, Erica?* "And I appreciate *you*, Mark." Erica feels a sudden and unexpected wave of emotion, affection, for Mark. He's been there for her again and again, a steadying force, an ally, and she's feeling so lonely right now.

"Will you promise me you'll stay in close touch?"

"Yes, sir!" Erica says with good-natured bravado that feels completely false.

Erica hangs up, goes into the kitchen, and makes herself a cup of tea. Then she returns to her desk and calls Moira Connelly, her best friend from her first days in the business. They worked together at a local Boston station; Moy had been there for a few years and she mentored Erica generously, kindly. And when Erica fell, and she fell so far, Moy was right there to pick her up, almost literally—she got her into that respected rehab, drove her out to it, kept tabs on her, and picked her up after twenty-eight days. Moy is the sister she never had. These days Moy is anchoring the local news out in Los Angeles, so the two don't see each other all that often, but when they connect they effortlessly pick up right where they left off.

"Hey, doll," Moy says.

"Rag doll at this point."

"You've got yourself back into it, haven't you? With the Marcus murder."

"Tell me about it. Listen, you have good contacts with law enforcement, don't you?"

"Yeah, they're pretty good."

Erica brings Moy up to date on the scrap of photograph, Lundy's murder, and the rest of her nascent investigation. Then she sends Moy her images of both the original scrap of paper and the blowup.

"This all looks so hazy," Moy says. "There is a guy in forensics down at police headquarters, Detective Chester Yuan, he has an amazing eye. I've covered a couple of trials where he's been called as an expert witness. I've seen him show the jury a blowup that looks like the inside of an impenetrable fog bank. Then he'll pick up a pointer and five minutes later the jury is slack-jawed in amazement at what they're seeing. I could ask him to take a look."

"That would be fantastic."

"So listen, are you sure you're okay?"

Erica gets up and goes to the window and looks down at the city, the city that never stops *demanding* your best. The city that inspires and energizes, that drains and depletes.

"My marriage is in the tank." Just opening up, saying the words to Moy, makes her feel a little less alone.

"Those are strong words. Things may not be going well, but *in the tank*?"

"He's been spending a lot of time with Leslie Burke Wilson."

Moy sucks in air. "Okay. Yes, she was brilliant on *Spotlight*, she's brilliant in general, but something about that woman scares me."

"She's reached out to us socially, and it's flattering, but . . ."

"Are they . . . ?"

"He denies it, but I'm not sure I believe him."

"Erica, don't get ahead of yourself. People flirt. Greg is a pretty great guy, and he adores you. I just don't see it."

Erica wants to believe Moy, she wants it so badly. She turns away from the window. "Enough about my traumas and dramas. How's *your* love life?"

"Actually kind of amazing at the moment." Moy has been dating Jordan Monk, a television writer, for about a year. "We're *thinking* about getting married."

"Oh, Moy, that's wonderful," Erica says, and then she has a moment of jealousy. Moy seems to glide through life, whereas for Erica it's always a push. Moy grew up in a stable household in south Boston with a black mom and an Irish dad, both cops. She's always known she was loved. Maybe that's why it's so easy for her *to* love, and Erica has been a beneficiary of that love. Her jealousy evaporates as quickly as it struck, and she feels a surge of happiness for her dear pal.

"Listen, I'm going to call Chester Yuan right now. Talk soon," Moy says.

There's a knock on Erica's open door, and she looks up to see Gloria standing there. In contrast to her usual professional manner, she seems keyed up. And she's wearing a flattering dress and her hair looks just-done.

"Bad time?" she asks.

"Not at all."

Gloria comes in and sits opposite Erica. "I'm just looking ahead. We don't have a lot of time to pick the next *Spotlight*. We want to make sure our researchers and associate producers have time to prepare."

"Let's wait for the midweek polls out of North Dakota. If Mary Bellamy's numbers are up, I think we should do a second show on the situation out there."

"I agree. If it looks like Bellamy is going to win, things are going to get *very* interesting. By bringing in all these so-called pioneers, she's basically building herself a rock-solid political base. It will overwhelm any opposition to her agenda in the state legislature. But . . ."

"Yes?"

"I think we need a backup topic. If polls show Governor Snyder with a growing lead, we'll have to pivot quickly. I think we should be moving forward on parallel tracks, then we're ready no matter what happens."

"What would I do without you?"

Gloria smiles and smooths out her dress. Then she says, "There are the literally thousands of earthquakes in Oklahoma that are being caused by fracking. That story has a lot of compelling elements—climate change, science denial, human interest, political drama."

"Yes, it's strong. I also like the idea of 'Infrastructure in Crisis.' It's compelling—and a needed call to arms. But it does lack some of the human interest. Then there's Zika. Which is almost too full of human interest."

"It's heartbreaking, isn't it? And terrifying."

"I'm thinking Zika is our strongest choice. It's a horrific threat to hundreds of millions of people, and is also related to climate change. Yes, let's go with Zika."

"I like the way your mind works," Gloria says. Then she lowers her voice. "Listen, I have a doctor's appointment and was going to take the afternoon off. I'll put some Zika research in motion before I leave."

Oh, so she dressed up for her doctor. "Sounds good."

Gloria stands up and is heading out the door when she turns and asks, "Oh, any follow-up on your trip to Winnipeg?"

Erica hesitates before saying, "No, not really. George Lundy was definitely a marginal and shady character, but how and why he ended up in Bismarck is still a mystery."

Gloria nods and leaves.

Erica stands up and paces; she suddenly feels uneasy. She was evasive with Gloria, probably because she's learned about loose lips the hard way. And the trip to Winnipeg unnerved her. Her instincts tell her she's dealing with the tip of the iceberg here, and what's submerged is deadly indeed.

She picks up her phone and calls Eileen McDermott. "Listen, I think I should head out to Bismarck again on Thursday or Friday for an update on the recall. It's the number one story in the nation."

"You mean hosting *The Erica Sparks Effect* from Bismarck?"

"Yes."

There's a pause and then Eileen says, "That's a big undertaking, and you want to do it in a couple of days. We have to find the right studio, hire local techs, book long-distance guests, bring out at least a dozen staffers. The expense will be through the roof. If you want updates, well, we've got field reporters for that."

As executive producer of Erica's show, Eileen has the right, the responsibility even, to raise these issues. Still, Erica doesn't like hearing them. Her mind races as she tries to make a decision. She can hardly admit her ulterior motive: to continue investigating the murders. If need be, she supposes she can fly out on the weekend and file reports on the weekend shows. Which will also leave her time to poke around.

"Your points are well taken, Eileen. If I feel absolutely compelled to go out there, I'll go on the weekend."

"I really appreciate this, Erica. I hope you don't think I'm being hard-nosed."

"Sometimes hard-nosed is needed."

Erica hangs up and starts to focus on her notes for tonight's show. After all, North Dakota isn't the only story on the nation's radar. There's the unprecedented flooding in Miami Beach, with talk of a partial evacuation. There's the moralistic senator just arrested for lewd conduct in a men's room. There's the profile on London's popular Muslim mayor and how his success is impacting global Islamophobia.

Shirley Stamos appears in her doorway.

"What is it, Shirley?"

"You just got a call from a woman who says it's crucial that she talk to you. She sounds a little unhinged. Or maybe *distraught* is a better word. I have her on hold."

"She didn't give you any other information? Her name?"

"Her name is Janine McDougal. She says you knew her husband."

"Put her through." Shirley leaves and Erica picks up her phone.

"Is this Erica Sparks?" The voice is quavering, as if her whole body is shaking.

"It is. And this is Janine McDougal?"

"You met my husband on Saturday morning. The same day he—" And she starts to weep, heaving bitter sobs.

"I'm so sorry about his death. He was a charming, dynamic man."

"Oh, he was one heck of a man, let me tell you. Came from nothing. Earned every penny through hard work." There's a pause and the sobs subside. "Well, most every penny," Janine says in a tone inflected with insinuation and bitterness.

These are the pennies Erica wants to hear about, so she says nothing, knowing that silence can trigger an unburdening.

"I warned him a thousand times."

"Warned him about what?"

"About some of those . . . *scumbags* he was associating with. Oh, they cleaned up pretty as a picture in their fancy suits and cars. But they were bad men. Bad men. They did this to my Freddy."

"Who? Who are they?"

"He never told me their names, but they'd pick him up, take him off to meetings late at night. Then a month or so later he'd have some construction permit he needed, or some alcohol permit, or some such."

"So you think your husband was doing favors for the men he was meeting with?"

"What do *you* think? Stupid fool he was! I told him a hundred times to keep his hands clean. What goes around comes around. In the form of a black pickup truck. He looked like a broken doll lying there on the sidewalk. I'll never get the picture out of my mind. His head split open, the blood coming out of his ears. Oh, my Freddy, my poor Freddy." And then she starts to sob again.

"Listen, Janine, please calm down and listen to me a minute." The sobbing continues. *"Calm down and listen!"*

Janine McDougal goes silent. There's a long pause and then she asks, in a tiny terrified voice, "What?"

"I want you to get out of Winnipeg. *Today.* Pack some things, go to the airport, and get on a flight."

"But where would I go?"

"Not to a relative's. If you can, fly to Europe, or at least to the US. Get out of Canada. Register at a nice hotel and just lie low for a couple of weeks. Will you promise me you'll do that?"

"I . . . I . . ." Erica can hear her sucking air.

"I'm serious, Janine. Your life is in danger. You *must* get out of Winnipeg."

"Okay . . . okay."

"Is there *anything* else you can tell me about these men your husband met with? Anything at all?"

"He . . . he said they were fancy men. Big shots. One time we were watching TV and the premier of Manitoba came on, Pearce Johnson, and Freddy said, 'There's my buddy.' I thought he was joking, didn't give it a second thought. But a lot of those permits and such came from the province, eh."

"So you think your husband was doing favors for the premier?"

"Freddy came up through the streets. He knew some dicey characters. If you needed dirty work done, well . . . you know what I'm saying."

"I do know what you're saying," Erica says. She hangs up, stands, and walks over to the window, then suddenly imagines what it would be like to fall out and tumble through the sky to the sidewalk below.

CHAPTER 43 —————————————————————

CARRIED ON THE WAVE OF her desire—cut with fear, fear that only heightens her senses—Gloria rushes across town.

She feels guilty—kinda, sorta—about Erica. She's so nice and supportive, really an upstanding person. But she's strangely naïve, too, believing in goodness and the power of journalism to make the world a better place and all that blah-blah-blah. Give me a break. Gloria saw it a thousand times in DC. Fighting greed, corruption, subterfuge, even evil, was a waste of time, an exercise in futility, the ultimate game of whack-a-mole. You knock it out somewhere and it pops up somewhere else. The world is a cesspool, and once you understand that, well, they say that the truth sets you free.

Gloria reaches Second Avenue and turns north for several blocks before reaching the undistinguished white brick postwar apartment building. She scans the street before ducking inside. The doorman nods discreetly, of course he's been informed that she's coming. To this strange, anonymous apartment that belongs to . . . who? Who cares?

In the elevator heading up, she pulls out her compact, checks her lipstick and hair, her whole body almost vibrating with expectation. It's been six weeks since she's seen him, six endless, agonizing weeks.

The elevator doors open and Gloria steps off, throws back her shoulders, takes a deep breath, and wills herself to *cool it*. She doesn't want to come off like some goo-goo-eyed teenager. She's a career woman, a woman of accomplishment, for goodness' sake. This delusion lasts as long as it takes her to think it. Then the truth comes pouring out: she is insanely in love with this man, this man who took her—an uptight, goody two-shoes bundle of repression—and led her into womanhood, one ecstatic evening after another.

They met at that bar on Dupont Circle where she sometimes went after work, alone—she's always been a loner, too busy working to nurture friendships—and nursed her Chablis at the far end of the bar. She saw him first, who could miss him—he looks like a movie star, a young Harry Belafonte, with that proud Pentagon posture—he just took her breath away. And he saw her watching him and he smiled at her. No man had ever smiled at her like that before, and she was gone, just gone, gone baby gone.

And now here she is, doing such important work for him, she's more valuable than she's ever been. He needs her now too. The balance has shifted, hasn't it? No, not really. Because in the end all that matters is being in his arms.

She rings the buzzer and waits. He always keeps her waiting. She rings again. Still no answer. She feels sweat break out on her brow. Does she have time to get a tissue from her bag? What if he answers the door to find her wiping sweat from her forehead? Then another door opens at the far end of the hall, and she feels panic rising inside her; they can never be seen here together, that's the rule.

And then he opens the door and ushers her in and he's standing there in his expensive slacks, shirtless, and his sculpted chest and abs and his arms and his smile and his bracing citrus smell and . . . and . . . and Gloria feels herself flooded with want, a want that overpowers reason, and she goes to him and he takes a step back and smiles.

"Now, now, there's no hurry."

She makes a hasty attempt to pull herself together, tries a casual laugh, brushes her dress. "No, no, of course not. We have all afternoon."

She follows him into the generic living room that looks like a model room at some second-rate suburban furniture store. All the shades are down; they're linen shades and they cast the room with a sultry rosy glow and all Gloria wants to do is kiss him and touch his skin and . . .

"How about a glass of wine?" he asks.

"Yes, um, sure." It's early in the day, too early to drink, but he always likes her to have a drink or three. He never has one himself. He never loses control. She does. She can't help it.

She sits on the hard sofa and he brings her the glass of wine and looks down at her. She smiles up at him—is her mouth quavering?—and takes a sip. And then another and another.

He walks across the room and sits in a straight-back chair. It was so cruel of him to take his shirt off, how can she concentrate on what she knows he's going to ask?

"What do you have for me?" he says in that voice that is both matter-of-fact and steely, that military voice.

"I'm sorry, I don't have that much."

He frowns.

"You said I did a good job, getting the Winnipeg information, George Lundy and everything."

"That turned out to be actionable, yes. The old freak in Lundy's hotel, Elmer, had an encounter with Ms. Sparks, he led her to McDougal. But is she still prying?"

"I think so. She wants to go out to Bismarck this weekend. She says it's for her show, but I think she wants to snoop around."

"But she hasn't *found* anything new, has she?"

"Not that I know of."

"You're going to have to do better than that."

Gloria feels like she might burst into tears—*he's so demanding*—and at the same time she can feel the wine loosening her up, its warmth flowing through her veins and muscles, all up and down her body. "I will, I promise I'll do better. I'll find out everything there is to know."

He stands up and crosses to her, refills her wine glass, looks down at her. "I'm counting on you, Gloria. We're *all* counting on you."

She looks up at him and he smiles, that tight smile of his, and there is his body, glowing in the diffuse light, a beacon, calling her, she needs him, she needs him more than she's ever needed anything in her life and longing surges through her and she wraps her arms around his torso and pulls him close and buries her face in his abdomen. "Please make love to me, *please* . . ."

And he gently tilts her head back and smiles down at her and this time his smile is different. Why is it different, it is a smile, isn't it? And he cups her face in his hands and then runs them down her shoulders to her breasts and her breath stops.

But why, as he leads her into the bedroom, does he laugh?

CHAPTER 44

AS ERICA GETS OFF HER flight from New York to Boston and walks into the terminal, she gets the text from the limousine company:

Your driver is waiting outside in Car 17

She goes out to the curb and there's the car. The driver, a middle-aged white man wearing a chauffeur's cap and dark glasses, opens the door for her with a smile.

It's a lovely summer day in New England, and as they drive from Logan toward Cambridge, she looks out the window at the graceful Boston skyline and the Charles River with its scullers and bankside amblers. It's such a pleasant place. But appearances can be deceiving. Boston has a dark, even nasty and brutish side—the Irish Mafia is no myth and its tactics are no fun. Plus, the town is staid and judgmental and classist and insular.

Erica has such mixed feelings about the place. It's where she had her first big success. She was hired by WBZ as a writer pretty much straight out of Yale. Soon thereafter her boss asked her if she'd ever considered going on camera. Of course she had. She started as a substitute for sick or vacationing anchors and she just leapt off the screen, the station was flooded with e-mails from fans. Four months later she was named anchor of the 6:00 p.m. and 11:00 p.m. news, and quickly became the most popular newscaster in New England.

Moira Connelly was an amazing mentor and hand-holder during Erica's first year, but it was still too much too soon for a kid who'd left a big chunk of her psyche back in that moldy, rage-filled trailer up in Maine. She was wracked by self-doubt and felt as if she were carrying a sick secret. To the world she was one person, to herself another. At first the drinking was fun, a lark, she was the new kid in town, invited to all the best parties and benefits—the wine and then champagne and then vodka helped ease her nerves and ignite her wit.

Then one Saturday when she and Moira were on a guided tour of a Cezanne show at the MFA, she met Dirk Loudon. He was so attractive, funny, smart, and idealistic, a high school history teacher who didn't care about her fame and success, someone with whom she felt she could let her hair down. Marriage ensued and Jenny came along a year later. And then . . . and then the stresses of balancing work, baby, husband, all started to get to her and her drinking escalated. Slowly but steadily.

Finally, she and Dirk separated, she was fired for on-air intoxication, and then it all went south in a big snowball, culminating in that awful night when—after downing six of those darling little nips of vodka—she spirited Jenny out of Dirk's house under a babysitter's nose and drove her to some anonymous motel in Framingham, where she left Jenny alone in the room while she went out to pick up some "ice cream." Ha-ha. She was headed to the nearest liquor store when she rear-ended the pickup in front of her, sending herself first to the hospital, then to the courtroom, and finally to rehab.

Now they're on Storrow Drive right along the river and Erica feels a moment of trepidation, a sense of inadequacy. A symposium at the Kennedy School is something Leslie Burke Wilson should be doing. Yeah, Erica's a good journalist, she cares about the truth, but she's not an intellectual, not particularly articulate; she's going to be out of her league, make a fool of herself. And it all might happen in front of Jenny.

The driver approaches the JFK Street exit, which will take them right across the bridge to the Kennedy School. But he keeps going, he doesn't turn off; in fact, he speeds up.

"Excuse me, that was our exit."

The driver says nothing, is completely impassive as he speeds down Storrow. Erica gets a text from Shirley:

Are you at the airport? The driver can't find you.

Panic sweeps over her.

"Turn around now, that was our exit!!" No response. She reaches for the door handle. There is none. "Let me out, let me out of this car!"

A tiny smile plays at the corners of the driver's mouth. Erica makes a move to climb into the front seat and at just that second the other half of the backseat flies down and a man in a ski mask slithers out from the trunk. Erica cries out in shock. He has something in his hand, fabric, black fabric, and his arms come up and then everything goes black. Erica grabs at the blindfold but then her arms are twisted behind her and her wrists are bound together. She screams and the man slaps her hard across the face. "Shut up!"

"No marks!" the driver says.

Erica swings her body sideways and starts to kick wildly, blindly. Both men laugh as she kicks at air and then one foot connects and the man yelps in pain and grabs both her legs and he's strong, very strong, and he twists her body around and shoves her headfirst through the hole and into the trunk.

Now she's in the trunk and she hears the seat click back into place and she's alone in the hollow blackness. The car takes a sharp turn and she's tossed around and she struggles to break her wrists free but the binds are so tight, so tight and strong, and she gulps air and fights her growing claustrophobia. She'd scream but what's the use? Is she going to die? Are these men going to take her somewhere and kill her? Slit her throat the way Joan Marcus was murdered? Put a bullet through the back of her head the way George Lundy died? Run her over? Strangle her?

Oh, Jenny, your mother loves you, I love you so much.

Stop! Think! Erica wills herself to breathe, in and out, in and out. *Try and make sense of what's happening. You're in the trunk of a car. Two men are taking you somewhere. They're going to open the trunk and pull you out. That's your chance.* Erica wriggles her body into position and pulls her legs up to her chest, ready to kick. She holds the position as the minutes tick by and then suddenly the car is bouncing, it's on a rutted road, and she tenses, coils her whole body, waiting.

And then the car stops. Two doors slam. The trunk pops open and Erica senses where the man is and then she lets loose a hard, fast kick and connects with his torso. "*AHHH!*" followed by a thudding fall and spitting curses. And Erica steels herself and clenches her teeth and knows this might be her last breath and . . . *Jenny, my Jenny . . .*

"Haven't you ever heard of standing back?" one of the men says.

"I want to rough her up," the other man says, wincing in pain.

"No, no damage." Then the voice is closer, he's leaning into the trunk. "Listen, Erica, we're nice guys. Just playin' with you a little."

"Who do you work for?"

"We may not be Harvard professors, but we're not that dumb. I can tell you this—you're just one more gig for us. Come on now, take it easy." The man reaches into the trunk and lifts Erica up. She doesn't struggle. He stands her up on her feet and leans into her, so close that she can feel his hot breath, and runs his hand down her cheek. "I'm putting your purse down next to you. See, perfect gentleman."

"We do have a message for you—consider it friendly advice," the other one says. "You can't bring the dead back to life. So why die trying?"

And then there are footfalls and the car doors slam and the car drives away. Silence. Then a slight breeze and leaves rustle. And Erica realizes she's alive and in one piece and then she starts to shake, to shake all over, uncontrollably, almost violently, and then she heaves and bends over and a thin stream of bile pours out of her mouth. She struggles with her wrists but they're bound with plastic cuffs. Then she walks slowly, slowly, sliding one foot and then the other out in front of her. Her left foot bumps into a tree and she slowly, slowly lowers her head and leans into the tree with her scalp until it bumps gently against the trunk and she moves it around slowly until she feels a knot on the trunk. Then she so slowly, so carefully brings her head up until . . . until . . . the bottom of her blindfold catches on the knot. Then she moves her head down and the blindfold slowly peels back—and she can see!

Erica looks around. She's in the woods. She listens. It's so quiet. Then traffic, faint but steady. There's her purse. She stands with her back to it, squats down, grabs the handle with her right hand, and picks it up. Then she begins to walk down the dirt track toward the sounds of civilization.

CHAPTER 45

IN ABOUT FIVE MINUTES ERICA comes to a quiet suburban road. Asphalt never looked so good. The kidnapping car turned right onto the dirt road, so Erica turns left, heading back. As she walks she pulls her thoughts together. Someone just sent her a message—it came through loud and clear. But who? She's obviously getting too close for their comfort, but she still feels a thousand miles from any answers.

She comes to an enormous old colonial with an expansive front yard dotted with specimen trees and bordered by an old stone wall. All those empty rooms. Empty rooms scare her. A little farther on, a stately brick Edwardian sits on a rise. *This is a tony suburb*, she thinks, Concord maybe, Belmont or Lincoln, judging by how long she was in the car. She's about to approach one of the houses when, behind her, she hears an oncoming car. *Fear fear.* She ducks into the woods. The car passes, it's an SUV, going about thirty miles an hour; the driver is a woman about Erica's age, alone in the car, well dressed.

Erica rushes back onto the road and yells, "STOP! PLEASE STOP!"

The car does stop, and the woman twists around and looks at Erica. Then she backs up and Erica runs over to her window. The woman zips it down. "Are you all right?"

172

Erica takes a deep breath and says, "Yes."

"You look a little . . . Wait, aren't you Erica Sparks?"

"I am."

"What happened to you? Oh my goodness, you're handcuffed. Hang on." The woman pops open the rear door, gets out of the car, and retrieves garden clippers from the back. It takes a few tries, but she cuts off the cuffs.

Erica rubs her sore wrists. "*Thank* you."

"What happened to you?" Erica hesitates, and the woman adds, with New England discretion, "If I may ask."

"I had a little run-in with . . . It's a long story."

"Would you like me to take you to the police station here in Belmont?"

"What I'd really like is a lift to the Kennedy School. I'm on a panel that starts in twenty minutes."

CHAPTER 46

THE WOMAN, WHOSE NAME IS Adrienne, pulls up in front of the Kennedy School.

"I can't thank you enough for this," Erica says.

"I'm guessing you don't want me to tell anyone," Adrienne says with a knowing smile.

"Good guess."

On the drive over Erica reapplied her lipstick, ran a brush through her hair, and put on a favorite pair of clip-on earrings. Her dress is a little worse for wear, but who cares? She also called Shirley to tell her she was in one piece, and to please not tell anyone about the car mix-up.

The panel is being held in the school's main hall, and Erica is directed to the green room, where she finds Tom Brokaw, Katie Couric, Joy Reid, and Brit Hume. Brokaw quickly runs down his plans as moderator. He's deeply concerned that lying has become commonplace among politicians and that journalists have become complicit, rarely challenging the lies and thereby devaluing the truth. It's a vicious cycle. He'll get things started with a couple of examples and then let the panelists run with it "in any direction you want." He'll only jump in with a new topic, angle, or question when the previous one has been exhausted.

Erica is at the craft services table, fidgeting with fruit and trying to focus on what Brokaw is saying. She's still fighting to compose herself after her little joyride, and equally anxious to find out if Jenny is in the audience.

A stage manager ducks his head in the room. "You're on."

They all file into the lecture hall and take their seats at a long table. Erica scans the capacity audience. And there she is! There's Jenny near the back of the hall! Erica waves and Jenny waves back. She's sitting with a thin, older woman who is wearing a red mohair sweater, a little too much makeup, and whose hair is salon colored and coiffed.

Who is that woman? Now she waves at Erica and smiles.

Erica knows that smile. And that's when it hits her.

It's her mother.

CHAPTER 47 ───────────────────────

ERICA SITS BACK IN HER chair, reeling. Brokaw is talking, but his voice sounds a million miles away. Susan waves again, beaming. Now Joy Reid is saying something, something about the truth.

The truth is, Erica, your mother brought your daughter to see you.

Jenny has only met Susan once, when she crashed Erica's wedding. Erica hired a car to take Susan back to Maine that same day and she hasn't seen her since. Until now. How did this happen? What is going on? Did the two of them conspire to do this? No, no, this can't be happening.

"Erica, do you have anything to add?" Tom Brokaw asks.

Erica looks over toward Brokaw—he, Couric, Reid, and Hume are all looking at her with concern. She picks up the glass of water at her place and takes a long drink.

Pull it together, you have to get through this.

"Well, um, Tom, with so many different so-called news outlets, including all forms of social media, there's no central arbiter of what is true and what isn't. And so lies go unchallenged. And they get repeated. Each faction of our Balkanized society has its own cultural landscape and echo chamber. They're able to create, in effect, their own 'truth.'"

Erica can hardly believe she's capable of speech, let alone thought. She drinks some more water, wills herself not to look at Jenny and Susan, and forces herself to listen to the other panelists, even though her heart is pounding in her chest and her left eyelid is twitching and all she can think is: *What now?*

Somehow she makes it through the hour without making a total fool of herself. The panel ends and she steps down off the stage as people are filing out. As she walks toward Jenny and Susan she feels like she's having an out-of-body experience. She was able to stay coherent for Tom Brokaw; will she for her own mother and daughter?

And now they're all together, three generations, standing awkwardly in the aisle. Jenny seems tentative, maybe abashed. Susan looks like a different woman—she's shed thirty pounds, has found a terrific colorist, a better dentist, and looks like she gets regular massages and facials. But a little bit of the sow's ear is still showing—under her too-assertive perfume, she smells like an ashtray.

"So . . . ," Erica says, "how did this happen?"

"Aren't you going to give us a hug, honey?" Susan says.

Erica gives her mother a perfunctory hug, mostly because they're in public and she sees cameras out. Then she hugs Jenny.

"Hi, Mom."

"How did I do?"

"Joy Reid was better." *Thanks, I needed that.* Jenny sees Erica's stricken look and adds, "But you were okay too. You were good."

"So, again, how did this happen?"

"Gosh, Erica, I follow you on Facebook and Twitter and everything, and when I saw you would be in Boston, I thought, well, why not just get in my new Intrepid, I lease it, honey, only $259 a month, and by the way I got this sweater at Nordstrom Rack, you see, honey, I've changed. Thanks to *you*, of course." She leans in close and whispers, "I go to my meetings. I have eight months clean and dry. I don't want to be a pathetic loser anymore." She leans back and raises her voice. "After all, I'm Erica Sparks's mother. That means something in this world. Oh, you should see my townhouse, how I have it fixed up with a sectional and my art glass collection. Maybe someday you and Jenny will come visit."

Erica keeps looking at Jenny, who is looking at her grandmother with a puzzled and fascinated expression on her face, like you might look at some exotic animal at the zoo. By now the lecture hall is mostly empty. Not as empty as Erica, though. She feels like she's in some realm beyond shock and surprise and fear and anxiety, she's just flatlining emotionally.

"So you called Jenny and then picked her up in Dedham, and the two of you drove here together?"

Jenny nods.

"That's just exactly what happened," Susan says.

"And your father was all right with it?"

"I told him I wanted to see my grandmother, and he said that was understandable."

Erica doesn't have much time, she has to catch her flight back to LaGuardia and do her show. She wanted to go out with Jenny, for ice cream or a sandwich or something, but she's not sure she can handle the thought of Susan being there. She was thinking about Henrietta's Table, the nice restaurant in the Charles Hotel, just a block away. But it's always filled with well-known Bostonians, and no doubt a lot of people who were at the panel discussion will be there. Erica will be fussed over and have to make small talk. And worst of all, she'll have to introduce this peculiar woman as her mother.

"This is such fun, us all being together," Susan says with forced brightness. "Oh, Erica, look at my new front teeth." She smiles too widely and then she tugs at her skirt and frowns and looks around as if she's lost, and Erica sees how deeply insecure the woman is, how fish-out-of-water she is, sober, in a place like Harvard. This is a distant planet for her. The poor, sad creature never had a chance, really—her childhood with a boozy, illiterate mother and boozy, crude father who was overly affectionate and not in a good way. Erica is glad she takes care of Susan, buys her things, sends her money. The woman *is* her mother. The only one she'll ever have.

Erica flashes back on a spring Saturday when she was about six. Her father had been AWOL for a couple of weeks, and with him away Susan had cleaned the place up a little, was a little less manic, took fewer pills, smoked less pot, and it was raining that day, it was a warm spring rain, and Susan took Erica's hand and led her outside and they played a crazy game of tag in the rain, which turned into a downpour, and they kept chasing each other and laughing until they were sopping wet and then they went inside and stripped their clothes off and Susan dried Erica with a big towel and then made them hot chocolate from little packets she had stolen from the coffee bar at the 7–Eleven.

Erica had loved her mother that day, and on other days too. When she walked her to school or picked her up. She even tried to help with her homework a few times. She was just unequipped to be a mom. She had no example to follow except abuse, poor thing.

"Listen, I don't have a lot of time, but there's an IHOP across the street," Erica says.

"I'm going to get chocolate chip pancakes," Susan says, taking Jenny's hand and heading up the aisle.

"Not me, I want peanut butter!"

Susan turns and looks back at Erica, an indulgent smile on her face, and in that moment she almost seems like a real grandma, bemused and loving and . . . happy. Could they all be happy together? Susan does look so much better, maybe she's aged out of her wild impulsiveness, maybe her anger has dissipated with the years, maybe having a successful daughter has been good for her sense of self and inspired her to clean up her act, to rise to the bar Erica has set.

Standing there in the now empty auditorium, Erica's heartbeat seems to be echoing back to her and she feels hope for the three of them, the three generations, hope that out of all the chaos and pain and hard work and bitterness and disappointment, they can forge something . . . meaningful, even beautiful.

"Come on, Mom!" Jenny calls from the doorway.

"Coming!" Erica says. Then her phone rings.

"Hello, Erica, it's Detective Chester Yuan of the LAPD. I've been analyzing that photograph you sent me and I've come to a disturbing conclusion."

CHAPTER 48 ───────────────────────

"ONE SECOND, DETECTIVE." ERICA CUPS the phone and calls to Jenny and Susan, "You go ahead, I'll be right over." They turn and look at Erica and then smile at each other conspiratorially as Jenny says, "Take your time, Mom."

How sweet. But Erica has bigger fish to fry than her three-headed maternal monster.

It is bigger, isn't it? Well, it's safer anyway. At least emotionally.

"I'm eager to hear your thoughts, Detective."

"I'm going to send you a copy of the photograph that I enhanced. Will you be able to look at it?"

"On my phone."

"That's better than nothing . . . Did you get it?"

". . . Okay, I've got it." On first glance, it looks exactly the same to Erica, but then she begins to see what looks like an outline of some object, a tiny portion of some large object; is it tube-shaped?

"Can you see the delineation about a third of the way up in the black part of the picture?"

"Yes, I do, I do see it. It looks round to me."

"Yes, it is. It's the base of an object. Now you probably can't make it out on your iPhone, but there are some barely discernible numbers and letters on the side of the object."

Erica can feel her adrenaline kick into overdrive. She loves *nothing* more than taking a step toward the truth.

No, that's wrong, of course. She loves Jenny more. Doesn't she?

"I can't see any letters or numbers."

"They're very faint. I can't read them right now, but I'm going to try and enhance them further. I'm pretty sure they're identifying numbers. And that the object is a ballistic missile."

Erica grabs the top of the nearest seat and then sits down in it, absorbing the words. She was expecting evidence that Oil Field Solutions, the Bellamys' company, was violating environmental laws. But this? A ballistic missile?

"Detective, can we talk confidentially?"

"Of course. And call me Chester."

"Do you know how I came into this scrap of a photograph?"

"Yes, Moira Connelly told me. Ugly murder. Of course, it's hard to find a pretty one."

"Joan Marcus was trying to tell me something. Something about a . . . *missile.*"

"I think the next step, Erica, is to try and track down this missile. If we can discern the identifying marks, we'll be well on our way."

"It must be in North Dakota, don't you think?"

"Probable, but by no means definite."

Chester Yuan is both matter-of-fact and dynamic, and talking to him is just what Erica needs. "Do you have any thoughts on how I could trace the missile?"

"I have a couple of contacts in the Pentagon. Let me see what I can do."

"I can't tell you how much I appreciate this."

"This is a big story, Erica, and a dangerous one. If this missile has fallen into the wrong hands . . ."

Something occurs to Erica, and it sends a fear rat scurrying up her spine. "Do you think this missile is capable of delivering a nuclear warhead?"

There's a pause before Chester Yuan says, "Yes, I do."

CHAPTER 49 ———————————————————

ERICA SITS IN THE BOOTH at the IHOP (what is an IHOP doing in the middle of Harvard Square?) watching Jenny and Susan devour their stacks of pancakes, chattering away, trading bites. Erica feels a little like a third wheel. But this wheel is turning a million miles an hour trying to make sense of what she learned from Chester Yuan. *A missile capable of carrying a nuclear warhead.* This story is darker—far darker—than she imagined, and sitting in a restaurant that seems to be constructed entirely of plastic that serves food guaranteed to send you into sugar shock, she feels herself falling into the grip of paranoia. There have already been five murders. She is obviously in their sights, whoever *they* are.

She looks around the place; it's filled with families pretending to be happy, just like hers is. People are looking at her and whispering. Right now she hates being famous, she wishes she were a print reporter who could go anywhere unnoticed. She needs to get back out to North Dakota pronto. But the thought of that vast bleak state, ravaged by oil wells and fracking and instant trailer towns, fills her with dread. Sitting with her mother and daughter, not sure what to say to either one of them, she feels trapped between a rock and a hard heart. Erica takes a deep breath and rubs her temples. The only way out is to keep searching for the truth.

What was that Shakespeare quote Archie Hallowell used to admonish her with: *Screw your courage to the sticking place and you'll not fail.*

"You seem really distracted, Mom," Jenny says.

"The secessionist story is turning out to be much bigger than I expected."

"The se-what-onist story?" Susan asks. "I'm sorry, I don't follow politics and all that."

Jenny shoots Erica an incredulous look.

"I'm sorry, I'm just trying to keep the focus on my recovery, you know."

There's something touching about her honesty and her terrible insecurity. "There's a political movement in North Dakota that wants the state to break away from the union," Erica explains.

"Oh, of course, I heard about your new show—*Spotlight*, right? I wanted to see it, but I had a meeting that night. First things first. Do you mean break away like in the Civil War?"

"On a smaller scale, but yes."

"Well, what do you know."

Looking across at her mother and daughter, Erica feels at a loss. They should bring her solace, but they only bring confusion. Now that Susan is making a sincere effort to get clean, to pull her life together, shouldn't she be supportive?

As if reading her mind, Susan reaches across the table and takes Erica's hand. "I owe your mother some serious amends, Jenny. I was not a good mother to her." Susan's eyes well. Her hand is shaking. "In fact, I was a dirty, lousy, rotten mother and I know it."

Erica feels her throat tighten. She wasn't expecting this. And she can't cry, not here, not in public, not with Jenny watching.

"You did your best," she manages.

"Well, my best was downright crummy. All I can do, sweetheart, is say I'm sorry. And try and be some kind of . . . well, I guess *friend* is the best word, to you from here on out."

Could it be possible? Could the three of them form some kind of chain, a chain of . . . love? Erica knows she's the middle link—between her uneducated, addict mother and her privileged, well-spoken daughter. It's up to her to hold them all together. And that will take an emotional fortitude and flexibility she's not sure she possesses. It will also take a lot of forgiveness. And that will be the hardest thing of all.

Erica's phone rings. It's Shirley. "Erica, your driver's been waiting outside for half an hour. Your flight leaves in forty minutes. You've got to get out to the airport."

Erica hangs up, feeling a surge of relief. "I've got to run or I'll miss my flight."

"You better hurry, Mom."

Erica stands and grabs her bag.

"I'll make sure this precious little girl gets home safely," Susan says.

Erica stops and looks down at her mother and her daughter, sitting side by side in the booth. She feels a welling of emotion that threatens to overwhelm her. "I'm happy we all got to be together."

And even happier that I'm leaving.

CHAPTER 50 ————————————

IN THE CAR ON THE way to Logan, Erica calls Boston Police Detective Pat Halley, an old contact from her days as a Boston anchor.

"Sparks, as I live and breathe, to what do I owe?"

"A kidnapping."

"Who was 'napped?"

"Me."

"O-*kay* . . . ?"

"This morning at Logan, at approximately ten thirty, on the arrival sidewalk outside of Jet Blue."

"But you're in one piece?"

"I am. Would it be possible to get the surveillance video of the area? There was a man posing as my driver. There was a second guy in the trunk of the car, but he obviously won't be on the video."

"So two thugs picked you up and then what?"

"We went for a little drive out to some woods in Belmont. They were delivering a message. I'd like to find out who it was from."

"Erica, we may need to file a report on this."

"Pat, I would *really* appreciate it if that didn't happen."

There's a pause and then, "This call never happened. Although I just gotta say, I've been following your career and I'm proud of you. You were a good reporter and you made it, you made it to the top."

As her car pulls up in front of Jet Blue, Erica thinks, *Making it to the top was the easy part. It's staying there that's the killer.*

CHAPTER 51 ———————————————

MARY BELLAMY IS ALONE IN her library, watching *The Erica Sparks Effect*. Erica is speaking to the camera: "The Take Back Our Homeland movement, and its offshoots and copycats, continue to gather steam, not just in North Dakota, but nationwide. In what political operatives are calling 'brilliant political theater,' the leader of the movement, Mary Bellamy, has organized what she is calling 'twenty-first century wagon trains filled with new American pioneers.' Here we can see one of these wagon trains in Oregon and another in Arkansas."

The screen fills with footage of a stream of cars, campers, SUVs, and RVs moving in a line down an Oregon thruway. Banners hang from the sides of many of the vehicles proclaiming *We're Heading Home* and *New American Pioneers*. Then Arkansas pioneers are shown.

Cut back to Erica at her desk: "Bellamy claims that caravans are arriving from all fifty states and that the movement is three-quarters of the way toward meeting its goal of thirty thousand new North Dakota residents and voters. With the election just weeks away, the fervor is only growing, though the latest polls show Governor Snyder holding on to his narrow lead. The Bellamy camp blames the numbers on the millions of dollars in television and online attack ads with which her opponents are blanketing the state. The White House continues to refuse to comment on the developments. Administration insiders say that President Winters is convinced that even in the unlikely event that the movement does prevail in the election, Mary Bellamy is a reasonable woman who will moderate her positions and goals. These sources point out that the Bellamys are among the state's wealthiest residents and that any radical action could jeopardize their extensive holdings. However, those who know Mary Bellamy best and have dealt with her over the years are cautioning that she is a woman of her word and that her commitment to her cause is unshakeable. Off the record, the White House is convinced Bellamy is going to lose. The answers to these provocative questions will become apparent in the coming weeks and months. But first she has to win the recall election. When we come back, the latest developments in the historic drought gripping the Northwest."

Mary Bellamy clicks off the television. That was a troubling update, and slanted. How many times did she have to mention the polls? Mary's speeches have been drawing large crowds. The pioneers are getting registered. That Erica Sparks is starting to annoy her. Sturges is down at headquarters. They missed their nightly dinner-and-TV ritual. It's one of the things that holds their marriage together. It's certainly not passion. Never has been, really, has it?

Mary has a sudden itch on her left leg, and why wasn't the fireplace cleaned of its ashes? She goes to the bar and pours herself two fingers of Scotch. She takes a sip, well, a swallow, well, a gulp. Its burning warmth floods her chest. This is all unacceptable, these poll numbers, the mere thought that she might lose. She won't lose, she can't lose. Out. Of. The. Question.

Mary pulls the library's pocket doors closed. Sarah, their cook, and Julie, the second maid, are still in the house. She sits down, takes out her special phone, and dials.

"My darling, I was just about to call you," he says in that virile voice of his. The one that's thrilled her since they met at that energy conference in Winnipeg almost a decade ago. Their rapport was instant.

Two kindred spirits who share ambition and smarts and courage. And disdain for big government.

"Neal."

He can hear her anxiety. "Your wagon train idea is creating so much momentum and excitement, and it's dominating coverage. It's pure genius."

It's a kind thing to say, but she hates sugarcoating. "You've seen the polls."

There's a pause, filled with gravity. "I have."

"They're troubling."

There's another pause and the mood changes between them. When they speak their voices are low and charged. "But we planned for this contingency, didn't we?"

"We did," Mary says.

"I think now is the time to put the plan into action."

"Yes, yes . . . ," she says, almost vaguely, as if they were discussing what to have for dinner tomorrow night. Their minds think alike. She finds that so reassuring. They really don't need to delve or elaborate, enough has been said, wheels will start turning. "I adore you, Neal."

"You do know we're going to win, don't you?"

"Yes, yes, I do. Of course."

"We always win, darling. That's the kind of people we are."

"Well, I'd better get to work."

He lowers his voice to a purring growl. "I can't wait to hold you."

Mary switches phones and calls Sturges at headquarters. "How are things going down there?"

"Everyone is very pumped up!" he says in a pumped-up voice. His plastic enthusiasm is annoying. "We're going to win this thing!"

"Yes, we are," Mary says in a soft voice. "Listen, darling, Julie Hassan, who's running the phone banks in Fargo, thinks it would be terrific for morale if you could show up tomorrow and spend some time making calls. Nothing inspires the troops like seeing the generals in the fray."

There's a pause, and she can hear his wheels turning, making his own plans, the plans he so often makes when he's on an out-of-town trip. "Well then, I suppose I should drive out tomorrow. I can stop in at Dakota Salvage and see how the new foreman is working out."

"Excellent idea. Of course, evening is the best time to make calls."

"Yes, yes, it is. So I may as well stay overnight."

"You may as well."

They hang up. What a silly man he is, really. Not that she's bitter. Well, maybe she is bitter. Yes, she is. He married her under false pretenses. And she was madly in love with him, thought he would be her one and only. One and only. How ironic that is. Oh, it was more than once, of course, but not that much more, and for the last decade or so it's been her none and only. *Never mind, silly girl.* Neal has made all that so insignificant.

Still and all, they have been married for thirty years. Mary goes back to the bar and pours herself another two fingers of Scotch. Poor dear Sturges. But he really does have it coming.

CHAPTER 52 —————————————————

IN NEW YORK, ERICA HAS just finished her show and is walking home up Sixth Avenue. The July night is dense and sticky, but after the over-air-conditioned studio she welcomes the heat. It doesn't relax her—it's humidity, not a miracle worker—but it does feel good against her skin. Her skin. It's nice to feel *something* sensual. After all, she and Greg haven't . . . well, it's been a while.

The two of them have been ships in the night. Friendly enough, no overt hostility, just a distance that seems to grow larger with each passing day. It confuses Erica on good days, and fills her with a terrible sadness on bad ones. The lack of resolution, the sense of her marriage being suspended between its early happiness and . . . and *what?* As she moves through the crowds of tourists, Erica thinks ruefully, *Motherhood isn't the only thing I'm lousy at.* Why isn't there a manual that explains it all: *Being a Grown-up for Dummies.*

But it's not time management that she's bad at it, it's heart management. When it comes to Jenny and Greg and even her mother, her emotions cloud her judgment and she says and does the wrong thing, making matters worse. It's ironic that to the world she seems the very picture of a winner, one of those celebrities who grace the cover of

People—she's been on it three times—and are featured on gossip web-sites and badgered for beauty and workout tips. Erica feels a wave of loneliness sweep over her. If only her fans could see who she really is: a woman who often feels at sea, like an imposter, a failure at what matters most.

But what does matter most?

She passes a large rowdy tavern. The television set over the bar shows a map of North Dakota and then footage of one of the instant trailer towns that the Bellamys have financed to house their pioneers. And suddenly—yes, it happens that quickly—she feels the loneliness evaporate, her concerns about being a good wife and mother fade. She has a mission in life: *to find the truth.* Right now that means uncov-ering the labyrinthine machinations that led to Joan Marcus's savage murder in a hotel ladies' room. *What* was that poor woman trying to tell her? And was it somehow connected to the Homeland movement? Something big and nasty is going down in North Dakota. Erica is fly-ing out there on Wednesday to cover the campaign. Her instincts tell her it's going to get ugly. Make that *uglier.*

Her phone rings.

"This is Erica."

"Pat Halley up in Boston. Listen, we got the surveillance video from Logan. It shows you walking right into the lion's den."

"And do you know the lion is?"

"Name is Desmond Riley. He's a flunky, works for a guy further up the sleaze chain, name of Pete Nichols. Nichols is a tough one, and wily as hell. His fingers are in a hundred mud pies and he always comes out with his hands clean."

"Do you know where Riley is?"

"We know where he isn't. At home. Or at any of his regular water-ing holes."

"He may have been offed."

"Definite possibility. Although Nichols is known for his blood loy-alty. He knew there'd be surveillance video of Riley. My guess is Riley is holed up in some isolated cabin in the Maine woods. Or he could be hiding in plain sight, wearing a disguise and walking the streets. Nichols loves to play games, tease us. He's got that leprechaun gene."

"I need to talk to him."

"Erica, this isn't a game."

"I was the one who was stuffed into a trunk. Where do I find Nichols?"

"He works out of Charlestown."

"Text me his phone and address."

There's a pause and then a sigh and then, "Will do."

Erica quickens her pace, striding uptown, toward the truth.

CHAPTER 53 ————————————————

STURGES CHECKS INTO THE HILTON Garden Inn in Fargo at just after eleven. The staff is so cheerful and welcoming. He often feels like Mr. Mary Bellamy, so it's good for him to get out alone now and then and see that he's loved too.

"Well, well, look who's here, honey." A tall young man in a cowboy hat crosses the lobby to Sturges, hand out. "I just want to shake your hand, sir. We're pioneers, arrived in Fargo two weeks ago from Missouri."

Darn, Sturges thinks. The only thing he wants is to get upstairs and . . . he stops his thoughts there, before they cloud his judgment.

"Well, welcome to the Homeland," Sturges says, clasping the man's hand.

"I'm Travis Cotton and this is my wife, Carrie."

"Could we get a selfie?" Carrie asks.

"Of course," Sturges says, gritting his teeth into a big smile.

Then he heads upstairs to his fourth-floor room. He told the "event planner" to get a room on the same floor. They're planning an event all right. As he walks down the hallway he looks at each door he passes and wonders if it's the one. If *he's* in there.

Sturges reaches his room and swipes his card. Is his hand shaking a little?

In the room the first thing he does is pull the curtains closed tight. Then he calls Mary, their nightly ritual when they're apart. "I made it, honey. I'm in my room about to hit the sack."

"I just spent two hours working the phones. Boy, the Homeland is full of the nicest people. Now you get a good night's rest, dear boy."

"I love you, dear girl."

They hang up. She knows. Of course she knows. She's known for years.

Sturges takes out his prepaid and texts:

I'm here. Room 412

And then he waits, trying to control his nerves, why does he always get so nervous? He's not committing a crime, for goodness' sake. He goes to the minibar and pulls out a nip of whiskey and downs it in one swallow. Then another. He feels the warmth and relaxation spreading through his chest. Everything is going to be fine.

There's a knock on his door. He goes and opens it. He's standing there, Derek Strong (that can't be his real name). He's even more handsome and muscular than he looks in his online videos, wearing a suit and tie, just as Sturges stipulated. Good quality too. Well, at 3K plus airfare from LA, he can afford a good suit. And it just looks more professional, in case . . . well, you can't be too careful.

"Derek?"

"Mr. Bellamy."

"Come in."

Derek steps in, and Sturges sticks his head out into the hallway. No one. He closes the door behind him.

"So, thank you for coming. Would you like a drink?"

"I'm good."

"I asked you here to discuss your proposal for the victory celebration on election night. We want the best."

"Of course you do. And I am the best."

"You look it."

"Everything will be *top* of the line." Derek smiles.

Sturges can't believe how handsome this young man is. "Listen, would you like to take off your jacket?"

"It is a little warm in here."

"It is, isn't it?" Sturges sits on the edge of the bed. "Are you sure you don't want a drink? Or a snack?"

"No thanks, I'm not hungry." Derek steps closer to Sturges. "Are you hungry?"

"Um, yes, yes . . . I, I . . . ah, I am hungry."

Two minutes later he hears a muffled click and looks up to see that Derek is filming him.

CHAPTER 54 ————————————

IT'S SATURDAY AROUND NOON. ERICA grabbed an early flight to Boston, then she cabbed over to Charlestown. At first glance the Gem Spa looks interchangeable with a thousand other small convenience stores in Boston—surviving on sugary sodas and lottery tickets and cigarettes. But then you notice that the shelves are barely stocked and that the refrigerator case is home to some sad-looking potato salad and coleslaw and a couple of blocks of meat and cheese—they'll make you a sandwich if you ask nicely. The place smells like stale coffee, fresh cigarettes, and timeless venality. They're clearly selling a lot more than sugar, smoke, and scratch-off dreams.

A young kid is behind the counter, he's wicked skinny and jumpy, with greasy hair and eyes that are permanently averted.

"I'm looking for Pete Nichols."

The kid narrows his eyes in semirecognition. He doesn't look like a *news* junkie. "I don't know no Pete Nichols."

"Yes, you do."

"You telling me what I do and don't know, lady?"

"Yes."

The kid sort of leaps back, like a jittery cricket. He looks down and grimaces. "You on TV?"

"Erica Sparks."

"Oh yeah, I heard of you."

From the back of the store Erica hears whistling and then a good-looking guy in his thirties, muscular but going to seed, with a gut and dark circles under his eyes, appears. "Erica!" He comes over, and before she can step back he enfolds her in a hug. He smells like sweat with a metallic, chemical afternote. "I thought we might see ya."

Erica breaks away. "Have you seen Desmond Riley?"

"Whoa. Where you rushing to, the grave? Relax a minute, enjoy some hospitality. How about a nice piece of jerky and a slushie? Sean, get the lady a snack."

Sean grabs a couple of candy bars, a can of Mountain Dew, and a vacuum-packed rope of mozzarella. He presents them to Erica. She puts the candy and cheese down on the counter, cracks the soda, and takes a sip. Pete whistles during this dance.

"I'm looking for Desmond Riley."

"Oh, Desmond's in the back. He's looking forward to seeing you again . . . *Kidding!*" Then he laughs and then Sean laughs in support, like one of those sidekicks on the late-night talk shows.

Erica is losing her patience with this jokester. "Where is he?"

Nichols makes a great show of taking out a vape pipe and taking a long pull. He exhales the "smoke," and Erica realizes where his metallic smell comes from—those vape fumes smell like an aluminum factory on the outskirts of Bogota. Then he takes out his phone and scrolls through with exaggerated nonchalance, whistling away. He finds what he's looking for and turns the phone to Erica. "Recognize your pal?"

And there's Desmond Riley sitting on a beach, sipping a bright blue cocktail and grinning at the camera.

"I hope he's not overdoing it. You Irish burn so easily," Erica says.

"Do we?"

"You push your luck and then it runs out."

"I think you might have us confused with nosy reporters."

"Where is he?"

"Puerto Vallarta. Cheap hotels, cheap drinks, cheap women. It's like Vegas—what happens there, stays there. Unless it's the clap." He laughs, and Sean does his sidekick bit.

"Was he working for you?"

"I'm not going to answer that question."

"You just did. And who were *you* working for? Who paid to have me kidnapped?"

"I have no idea what you're talking about." He takes another vape and smiles. "I just run my little store here, mind my own business."

"Someone is minding mine, and I don't like it."

"Nowadays we're all being watched."

"Just know this—I'm watching you."

As Erica turns and walks out of the Gem Spa, Nichols gives her a sly, almost conspiratorial look and whistles her on her way.

CHAPTER 55

IT'S PAST TEN AT NIGHT, Saturday night, the staff is gone, the house is quiet, and Mary is waiting in the library for Sturges to get back from his trip to Fargo. He called and said he was running a little late and she should go to bed, but she wants to stay up and see him. She filled a glass with whiskey so he could have a drink after his long drive—she wiped it down so there'd be a clean palette for his fingerprints. She's gotten some troubling news—the latest round of internal polling isn't looking good. Voters have mixed feelings about Mary. They see her as a strong leader but also as somewhat outside the mainstream. Her opponents have succeeded in painting her as a risky choice, someone who could lead the state off a cliff. The race is still winnable, the earlier influx of pioneers is keeping it close, but . . . well, she'll explain it all to Sturges. He'll understand.

And now she hears the front door open, quietly, as if someone is trying to sneak into the house. Then she sees Sturges crossing the entrance hall, again quietly, with measured steps.

"Darling," she calls.

He whirls in shock, then walks slowly into library. "I thought you would be in bed."

"No. I decided to stay up. You look pale, darling. Is everything all right?"

". . . Oh yes, fine. Just a little tired, it's a lot of driving."

"It is a lot of driving. And we're not kids anymore. Remember when we *were* kids? Our honeymoon in Bermuda?"

"We must get back there," Sturges says sadly. He's sweating now, on his brow, and the house isn't warm. And his whole body looks so tense. And the house is so quiet.

"How did the phone banking go?"

"Well, it went well. The volunteers are terrific. Just super." His enthusiasm seems so forced and desultory, and he looks so distracted, so worried, spooked.

Mary says nothing, but pats at her hair. "Have a seat, darling. There's something we need to discuss."

Sturges's eyes open wide and he inhales sharply. To cover his anxiety he looks down and rubs his hands together. Then he sits down, unable to look her in the eye. "What's that, dear?"

"I poured you a drink."

He reaches for it and takes a sip.

"It's the latest polling," Mary says, and Sturges sighs and his body relaxes.

"It could be better," he says.

"It *will* be better. I believe we have momentum."

"Oh, so do I. We have momentum." He keeps looking down at his hands.

Outside, the prairie wind gusts and the house creaks in response. Through the doorway, the darkened entrance hall is visible, full of shadows and the kind of heavy wood furniture no one wants anymore, and heavy maroon velvet drapes and matching upholstery. It's like a mortuary from the 1940s. And then the wind stops, and quiet settles back over the house like a shroud.

"The thing is, there's something that *could* stop our momentum. In fact, it would basically ensure that we would lose."

"What's that?" Sturges asks, finally looking at her. But he can't hold her gaze.

"It's this." Mary picks up her phone and taps it. Then she turns the screen to Sturges. There he is. In his motel room in Fargo. With Derek. He looks for a second and then turns away. Mary keeps playing it. She keeps playing it.

White-hot shame pours over him like molten lava and now he's suffocating in his shame, his whole body covered with prickly heat and panic and dread and . . . sadness. A terrible sadness.

Mary finally puts down the phone. She sits there looking at him. The man who married her under false pretenses. Well, it's time to pay the piper. Just like Mary paid Wendell to hack into Sturges's computer and learn of his liaison with Derek. Who was only too willing—for 5K in cash—to do her bidding.

There's a long pause filled with quiet and the final acknowledgement of what they've both known for many years. And then, when they speak, it's in low, intimate tones.

"Our opponents have gotten hold of this. They're threatening to release it," Mary lies. Sturges winces. She loves the power of her lie.

"I'm sorry," Sturges says finally, simple and heartfelt. He struggles to keep from crying. That's pretty pathetic.

"If this comes out, my chances of winning the election will be zero."

"I'm sorry," he repeats. Like a broken record.

"There's only one way to salvage this situation," Mary says. "To salvage our dream."

"I'll hold a press conference and come clean and ask for forgiveness," he says, his voice high as he fights to control his desperation and fear.

"Do you really think that would help? Do you really think the voters of this state want to have a First Man who's . . . *homosexual*?" She watches as he struggles to retain his composure. Her voice remains calm, composed. "Well, do you? *Answer me!*"

Sturges shakes his head as tears start to stream down his face. Then his body starts to quiver, almost to convulse.

Mary reaches for a small vial and opens it. She shakes out a pill and places it on the side table between them. "It will all be over in less than sixty seconds. It will look like a heart attack. I'll come down in the morning and discover your body. You were down here having a nightcap, weren't you? Carney Mortuary will come and, as per your wishes, you'll be cremated. I'll be a brave widow, stalwart in my grief, never forgetting my responsibility to the people of this state. Who will then elect me as governor."

The pill sits there between them as Mary waits serenely and Sturges cries and shakes.

CHAPTER 56 ⸺

STURGES LOOKS OVER AT THE pill, through a scrim of tears, and knows that Mary is right. He deserves to die—for the sin of his cowardice.

Sitting there, with minutes to live, what comes washing into his mind is that afternoon, his senior year at Groton back East, when he and Bruce Clark, they were such close friends, everyone remarked on it, inseparable since freshman year, Bruce was a lovely boy—smart and funny and kind, who grew up to be a lovely man—he lives in Ojai now, a retired lawyer, with his partner of thirty years, and that afternoon, that fall afternoon after soccer practice when they raced not to the locker room but into the woods behind the playing fields, driven by . . . love. Yes, love. And they fell to the leafy ground and kissed and the world opened up for Sturges and he knew he was where he belonged, on the dappled earth kissing the boy he loved.

But then they separated for the summer, and in the fall Sturges went to Cornell and Bruce to UCLA, they were so far away, and the pressure from his family, he was the scion, the heir, he carried the Bellamy name. And he carried his shame. And he retreated, buried his nature and his dream, and became someone he wasn't. That's what cowards do.

Oh, Bruce, I will always love you.

Sturges reaches for the pill and puts it in his mouth as Mary says, in her sweetest voice, "Bite down, darling, bite down." And he does bite down and then his body goes rigid and he can't breathe and everything goes black and he falls to the floor and his last thought is of Bruce and he smiles . . .

CHAPTER 57 ———————————

MARY SITS CALMLY WATCHING, IT'S quite riveting actually, to watch someone die just a few feet away from you. It's brief, just as James assured her it would be. A little too brief, really. She would have enjoyed savoring the moment, the strange gurgling noises he's making, watching him clutch his throat as his skin turns the color of a high gray sky. She's a good person, a decent person, a kind person. He deserved it. Besides, in the end it's not really about Mary or Sturges. It's about the history they're writing. They're creating a more perfect union. Mary smiles—a perfect union. That's what the world thought she and Sturges had. What delicious irony.

Now he's slumped down on the floor, askew, his head and shoulders against the chair, his tongue hanging out, his eyes rolled up. Dead. He's dead. Bye-bye. Not a pretty picture. But an affecting one.

Mary picks up her phone, her special phone, and texts Neal their code phrase: Sweet dreams, darling.

Never sweeter, he texts back.

Mary smiles again and pats at her hair. Then she gets up and walks out of the library—and into her future.

CHAPTER 58

IT'S SUNDAY AFTERNOON, AND ERICA is at home. Greg is out running. She just finished an hour of rigorous Tae Kwon Do and is now at work at her desk, feeling swamped. Gloria and her team were working on Zika for the second *Spotlight*, but Sturges's death triggered an outpouring of sympathy for Mary, and the most recent polls show a wave of momentum in her direction. The altered mood has forced her opponents to pull their negative ads for fear of generating a backlash. Erica and Gloria decided—in a series of morning phone calls—to switch back to a follow-up report on the election and its aftermath. Should she win, Mary Bellamy has been promising to take some bold steps during her first days in office, and the whole country is burning to see what they will be. Will she declare some form of autonomy for her state? If so, the ramifications would be historic. With the election just a month away, the suspense and interest are only growing, and Erica is flying out to Bismarck on Wednesday to file an update from on the ground.

But Erica is still obsessed with the murders, the missile, her kidnapping, and of course any possible links of all these to the Bellamys. She feels a little like she's wrestling with an octopus, but it's called investigative journalism. Her trip to Boston was frustrating. She didn't learn what she most needed to know, hitting a dead end in the form of an overgrown Charlestown punk with a penchant for whistling.

Right now she has to prepare for the week ahead. She has her show tomorrow night and she's running behind on prep. She's booking a roundtable to discuss the election, including Leslie Burke Wilson, Bob Woodward, and Karl Rove. She's also going to do an in-depth piece on the Zika virus. As she starts to read material put together by her researchers, Pete Nichols's mocking whistle keeps intruding. There's something familiar about the melody. She brushes off the thought— what does it matter what song it was?—and gets back to work. Twenty minutes later the blasted melody comes back. It's living rent-free in her head, and the only way to evict it is to figure out why it's so persistent. She whistles it herself a few times.

Then it hits her! She remembers it from her childhood. The song used to play in that soggy, drafty double-wide—not play, blare, with her mother wailing along. She tried to muffle it, putting a blanket along the bottom of her bedroom door, but the beat, if not the lyrics, pounded through. She hates that song. Now it's come back to haunt her. The only way to exorcise it is to know what it is. And there's only one person who could answer that question.

Erica, after hesitating a moment, picks up the phone and calls her mother.

"Erica, honey, is that really you? Calling your old mom?"

"Hi, Susan."

"Wasn't that fun at the Harvard University? I was so proud of my baby girl."

"Thanks."

"I'm still clean and dry, honey, ninety-eight days."

"*I'm* proud of *you* too. Listen, I have a question for you."

"You do? Really? I'm tickled. What is it?"

"There was a song you used to sing when I was little, I'm trying to remember what it is. It went like this—" and Erica whistles it as best she can. When she's about halfway through, Susan starts to belt out:

"Glor-ia
Glor-ia
I think I got your number
I think I know the alias you've been living under . . ."

Erica sits there, motionless except for the twitching of her left eyelid.

CHAPTER 59 ———————————————————

ERICA SPENDS THE NEXT TEN minutes pacing around the apartment. Was Pete Nichols whistling "Gloria" as some kind of sick head game? It's hard, no impossible, to imagine that Gloria could have hired him to arrange her kidnapping. Isn't it? Isn't it impossible? Then Erica remembers that day a phone rang in Gloria's purse while she was holding another phone in her hand, and she looked anxious and refused to answer the ringing one. And her almost obsessive curiosity about Erica's movements, pressing her with questions about her trip to Winnipeg. And was it more than consideration that drove Gloria to cover for a sick Eileen and come to Bismarck? And she was so distracted and keyed-up that day she got dressed up for her doctor's appointment. Is it possible that Gloria is spying on her? *Why?* What could her motive possibly be? Erica tries to push these doubts out of her mind. *I mean, "Gloria" was a popular song, it's just one of those crazy coincidences.* But then she sees that sly look Pete Nichols gave her as she was leaving his store and he was whistling away.

Restless, confused, moving from her office to her bedroom to the living room, Erica doesn't know whom she can trust anymore. Moy, of course, Mark Benton, and Gr—? *Can* she trust Greg? She's been so busy, out of town so often . . . She and Greg are sharing a bed again, if not much affection. She hates dwelling on it, using denial to protect herself from what's happening between them. It starts so small, doesn't it, the deterioration of a marriage? A few harsh words exchanged and suddenly you realize all the unspoken hurts and wants and disappointments that have been smoldering, festering below. Like her lingering resentment over the fact that he cheated on her when they were engaged, slept with that Laurel Masson down in Sydney.

Erica goes into the kitchen, pours herself a cup of coffee, and breaks off a big piece of some organic-chic chocolate bar she was gifted. Just what the world needs, another stupid artisanal chocolate bar.

The front door opens and Greg appears in the kitchen. He heads right past her to the fridge and pours himself a glass of filtered water.

"How was your run?"

"It was good. I did the reservoir twice."

"I've just been working. We switched the next *Spotlight* to the Bellamys."

"Probably smart. It's a hot subject."

They're both being polite, tiptoeing through the minefield, there in the gleaming kitchen that cost Erica north of 150K, a picture-perfect front for a messy life. The tension is thick and Erica just wishes he would go away. She wants to be alone.

"How about some pasta for dinner? There's that new Italian place on Amsterdam," she says halfheartedly.

"I've got to go down to the office later, get some work done, pick up some papers. I'll grab a sandwich there."

So he's going to disappear. Fine. His office is the perfect place for an assignation.

"I'm heading out to Cincinnati in the morning," he says.

"Oh, I forgot." *That was a stupid thing to say.*

Greg shoots her a glaring look. "Hardly surprising."

"How long will you be out there?"

"Two nights."

"Interesting gig?"

"The station wants to rebrand."

"How's the job hunt going?"

"Really, Erica, don't you think I would tell you if anything was happening there?"

"When I don't ask you accuse me of not being interested, when I do you bite my head off."

"Because I feel like you're just asking out of a sense of duty. You don't really care. Your success is turning you into a narcissist. You live your life in color, the rest of us are in black and white."

"You want me to apologize for my success?"

His brow furrows as he tries to find an answer. "Whatever. At this point *I* don't really care!" He storms out of the kitchen and Erica hears the door to the guest room slam shut. He'll take his shower in there. Good! He's living in the lap of luxury thanks to her. He should remember that when he's complaining about her success. Erica breaks off a third piece of chocolate—she's way over her limit—and sits down at the kitchen table.

Beware of answered prayers.

Sitting there, gulping coffee and chomping chocolate, she realizes she doesn't really feel at home in her own home. She shares it with a man she may be falling out of love with. Who may be having an affair with Leslie Burke Wilson. But she just can't face sorting out her marriage right now. Her relationship with Jenny is shaky, she's working harder than she ever has, *Spotlight* is still finding its sea legs, she's concerned, even frightened, for her own safety, she's investigating a string of murders and her own kidnapping. Now is not the time to take on what could be either a salvage or dismantling job. It would be the straw that broke the camel's heart. Sometimes you have to take the path of least resistance. Erica stands up and throws the rest of the ridiculous chocolate bar down the disposal, making a decision: she doesn't want to know if Greg is having an affair. She feels an immediate wave of relief.

There's another elephant in the room, of course, but it's one that Erica has a lot of practice managing, and that's loneliness. That aching sense of solitude and longing. No matter how busy she is, there are moments in every day when she feels it, that yearning for companionship, for a mate, for Greg, for their relationship to be what it once was. Will it ever be again?

The *Sunday Times* is sitting on the table, and she sits down and idly opens the Style section. Just her luck: the Day in the Life feature is about Leslie Burke Wilson. She's everywhere, isn't she? Erica reads about Leslie's Sunday-morning ritual of going out to a "divine bagel place" in the morning, her afternoon swim, her obsessive/compulsive work habits, her new book on Michelle Obama, which she has just finished, and her next one, on American secession movements. In the last paragraph she reveals that she and her husband, ad man nonpareil Stan Wilson, are separating. It's amicable and they've both starting "seeing other people."

Erica feels dizzy for a moment, almost as if she might faint. But her decision serves her well: she doesn't want to know what is or isn't happening between Greg and Leslie. A wall goes up, and the slings and arrows bounce right off it. She stands up and heads back to her desk to get to work. As she strides down the hallway, she hears echoes of her mother's singing:

Glor-ia
I think I got your number . . .

CHAPTER 60 ———————————————

GENERAL FLOYD MORROW KNOWS CAMP Grafton well, he's visited scores of times, but his new second-in-command, Corporal James Jarrett, doesn't, so he's giving him the complete tour. It's not an enormous army base, and because it's home to the North Dakota National Reserve there are long stretches when it's quiet. But it's strategic. *Oh, is it strategic.*

It's Monday morning, just two weeks before the recall election. The camp is pretty empty—there are no active training sessions in progress. It's a hot day on the North Dakota plains, but the base sits on a peninsula that dips into Devil's Lake, and the water has a cooling effect. Not that Floyd is fond of cool. He prefers heat, passion, drive, action.

"Those are the barracks. Empty today. But they'll be filling up soon, won't they?" He smiles at James, that angry smile that looks more like a grimace.

"Yes, sir, they will."

The two men drive in an open cart past a shooting range, an obstacle course, a lagoon, mock-ups of houses and small factories, classroom buildings, bunkers, tunnels. Everything that's needed to train men and

216

woman in how to kill their fellow human beings. The general loves war. It excites him. And soon he'll be, well, if not at war exactly, then on high alert. Training recruits, young men and women who will be willing to lay down their lives for the Homeland.

"It's magnificent, isn't it?" he says.

"Yes, sir, it is."

"And it's *ours*," Floyd says with another one of his feral smiles.

James smiles back, but his is a movie-star smile. The smile of a man who is going places. Floyd likes Corporal Jarrett. He's a good man. A good African-American man. A credit to his race. A credit to his country. They've been working together closely for the past year. When Floyd was finally transferred out here, he made sure Jarrett got assigned his second-in-command. The two men first met on a shooting range outside DC. They were both in uniform and Jarrett was so polite, coming up and introducing himself to his superior. Turned out they both worked at the Pentagon and were both students of war. They went out for drinks. They clicked. They both hinted around their political persuasions that night, showing soldierly discretion. But they exchanged e-mails and agreed to meet out at the range again. This time it was drinks and dinner afterward.

Over the coming weeks and months they opened up. Shared their concerns about how the autocratic federal government was usurping states' rights, attacking Americans' basic freedoms, taxing them into penury. About how wrong it was, and how angry it made them. And how they wanted to change it. And how Sturges and Mary Bellamy were the country's best hope for igniting that change.

Floyd drives the cart over to a gate with a soldier standing sentry in front of it. The soldier salutes, and Floyd and James return it. The gate is sided by fencing topped with barbed wire. Beyond the gate, standing in a row, are four vast hangar-like structures.

"That's where the munitions are kept. Tanks, machine guns, armored vehicles, rocket launchers, ammo. That's it, baby, enough gunpowder to blow half this state to smithereens." Floyd's eyes are giving off some firepower themselves, and his voice is charged with an excitement that sounds a lot like lust. "And see those?" he says, pointing past the hangars to a series of large concrete pads. "Those are our aces in the hole. Properly outfitted, those babies can take out Manhattan." He stares at the pad as if mesmerized, reverent, then lets out a strange moaning yelp of a "Yeaaah," guns the cart, and speeds them back to their residences.

CHAPTER 61

WHILE FLOYD, WHO IS DIVORCED with three grown children, has a substantial house to himself, James has a far more modest but still perfectly comfortable ranch house. He heads inside and finishes unpacking. Then he goes into the kitchen and pours himself a glass of a Zinfandel that he read about in *Wine Spectator*. He takes a nice sip and lets it sit in his mouth a moment before swallowing. It's quite interesting, he thinks, even evocative, the balance of oaky and floral, the lingering afternote. Superior, no doubt. Not cheap at forty dollars a bottle, but not exorbitant. And worth it. The better things in life are always worth it. Mary Bellamy taught him that.

James has known the Bellamys for almost twenty years, since he was at West Point and won a grant from their foundation to fund his post-grad studies in Foreign Affairs at Penn. They liked to meet the recipients of their largess, and of course James practiced his practiced charm on them. The charm that had taken him from the dead-end streets of Gary, Indiana, to West Point . . . and beyond. Mary Bellamy was quite taken, of course, with his race and his manners—oh, he knows just how to punch that ticket. And Sturges Bellamy, recently deceased, was, well, the vibe from him was slightly unsavory, but again, it wasn't the first time James had worked that angle. It's all about leverage, isn't it? When the Bellamys were in the East, they would take him out for dinner. A bond developed, based on mutual respect and a shared worldview that they discussed in oblique terms, using dog whistle phrases, being oh-so-discreet.

Mary really mentored him—on wine and food and cheese and clothes and manners, yes, but it went far beyond that. She's a woman with real standards. She believes in hard work and ethics and the transcendent power of simple human kindness. *Not* to be confused with weakness. And she believes in a better tomorrow. And power. She believes in power. Mary taught him that in the end, *everything*—from a simple transaction between two people to a great leader igniting a movement that changes history—comes down to power.

And James is a man who knows *his* power and isn't afraid to own it. A master of seduction. Look at Gloria. Look at General Floyd Morrow, who really is a dangerous man to the movement, a loose cannon who fires before he aims. Mary and Neal Clark don't play that way. They're aiming for respect on the world stage. Floyd is a foaming-at-the-mouth type. Floyd's a disposable commodity. But not yet. Right now they need him. And so James has been cultivating him, flattering him, charming him. The seduction started on that day they "accidently" met at the shooting range.

The wine warms James and he feels a rush of euphoria.

Tomorrow belongs to us. All hail the Homeland.

Sitting on the counter is the welcome basket that Mary sent. She's so thoughtful. He opens the wedge of Beaufort d'Ete and the box of English water biscuits—Mary taught him that you don't want fine cheese competing with an assertive cracker—and puts them on a small cutting board. There are also chocolates from Belgium and cornichons from Germany and a small bag of Doritos. That's been a running joke since they first met—she's a Doritos gal, he's a potato chips guy. That Mary.

James savors the cheese and wine—and the sense of expectation that is surging through his veins. The election is only the first step, of course, but it's a big one. And it's happening. He takes his wine and the cutting board, walks into the living room, and sits on the couch. It faces an enormous picture window framing a view of the base, the lake, and the endless plains beyond. The perfect canvas on which to write the future.

His safe phone rings. The incoming number is blocked.

"Yes?" he says.

There's a snippet of whistling, which is annoying, and then, "I have some information you might be interested in."

"Who is this?"

"Oh, come on, you're too smart to play dumb. I'm trying to do you a favor here."

It's true, James does know who it is. He came highly recommended. But *he* wasn't supposed to know who James was. That's what middlemen are for.

"How did you get my number?"

"That's part of the information."

"I'm listening."

"I'm not in the business of giving away the goods."

James feels his mood curdle. How dare this jerk ruin his Zin and cheese? "How much do you want?"

"10K."

"That's ridiculous."

"You people have deep pockets."

Whatever this two-bit creep knows could be very valuable. James exhales. "Okay."

"Smart man. I just texted you a PayPal account. As soon as the money is in there, my lips will start flapping."

James is boxed in. He clicks on the link in the text to the PayPal account and transfers ten grand from an untraceable bank account in the Cayman Islands.

"Bingo! Got it. Thank you, amigo."

"I'm listening."

"Your emissary got a little sloppy. She called me on her regular cell phone. Oops! Her bad. My tech guy hacked into her phone records. Presto, you appeared. So it wasn't the first time she got her phones mixed up. Tsk-tsk. Anywho, the Boston cops IDed one of my subcontractors, told Sparks, and *bang!* she shows up at my little gourmet shop. You do the math." Then he whistles again.

James hangs up in disgust. He's lost all interest in the wine and cheese. He's not going to waste them in this mood. Things suddenly got a little more complicated. He's traceable. But he's also level-headed and smart and methodical. He'll work it all out. He's done it before. One step at a time.

Step one: call Gloria.

CHAPTER 62 ———————————————

IN NEW YORK, ERICA IS at her desk at GNN, preparing for tonight's show. Of course, the recall election will be the lead, but she can't ignore the heat wave in India. Temperatures have hit 130 degrees, the highest in the nation's history—people are dying by the thousands, in the streets, in their homes, in hospitals, the old, the young, dehydrating, shriveling up, their bodies going into shock, their hearts giving out. Erica looks out the window. It's a sunny day—remember *fun in the sun?* How quaint those days seem. It's terrifying and ominous. What kind of planet is she leaving Jenny? And all the world's children?

"Knock-knock." Gloria is in her doorway. She smiles brightly. Too brightly.

Erica feels a stab of nausea. Can she trust this woman? Should she ever have trusted her? "Come in," Erica says.

"How was your weekend?" Gloria asks.

Erica pauses. Gloria has this look of innocent curiosity on her face. Yeah right.

"It was okay."

"Did you do anything special?" Gloria asks, trying to sound casual.

"Not really, no. Did you?"

"I'm still exploring New York. I visited the Neue Gallerie. There was a show of Weimar paintings."

"I've seen some of those. They're very dark. Depraved."

"It was disturbing. I had nightmares. I wish I hadn't gone."

"It's hard to un-see something, isn't it?"

"It is."

"But there's an honesty to it. Nobody is pretending to be someone they aren't."

Gloria

I think I know the alias you've been living under.

"I know what you mean," Gloria says, looking uncomfortable.

"It's unrepentant decadence, evil even. It can be very seductive."

Gloria clears her throat, shifts from one foot to the other. "I wanted to go over the checklist for our trip to Bismarck. We'll be shooting footage for *Spotlight*, of course, and want to make sure we don't interfere with *The Erica Sparks Effect*."

"You really should be having this conversation with Eileen."

A look of hurt flashes across Gloria's face. She suddenly seems much less mature to Erica. "I have spoken to her, of course, but I wanted to see if you had any thoughts or requests. Am I right in assuming we're going to be focusing solely on the election? You're not going to be covering Joan Marcus's murder, are you?"

Erica leans forward on her desk. She hasn't invited Gloria to sit. Let her stand. "I'm not sure, to tell you the truth."

"But the Bismarck police haven't made any progress. There's nothing there to report or to investigate, is there?"

"It wouldn't be the first time the police had missed a clue or gone down a dead end."

"So you *will* be spending time on that case?" Erica doesn't answer, and Gloria looks down and frowns. Sweat appears on her brow. "I'm only asking because I'm trying to shape *Spotlight* and want to get a sense of time management, et cetera."

"I really don't want to be tied down to a rigid agenda, Gloria. That would rule out any unexpected developments, wouldn't it? I like to stay flexible. You know, sometimes evil proudly shows its face, like in the Weimar paintings. Sometimes it hides. And in the unlikeliest places."

Gloria is rocking back and forth slightly, a repetitive, unconscious movement that almost makes her look like an autistic child.

"Are you all right, Gloria? You seem . . . concerned."

Gloria snaps to, is suddenly 100 percent present. "I'm sorry, I'm just . . . ah, a little tired."

"Are you sure everything is all right?"

"Well, ah, yes and no. I actually got some bad news."

"What's that?"

"My fiancé has been transferred out to Camp Grafton, the army reserve base that, coincidentally, is in North Dakota."

Erica leans back in her chair, her mouth open in surprise. There's a pause as she gathers her thoughts—and her suspicions. "Well, what are the odds of that happening?"

"I know, right? He's second-in-command at the base."

"What's his rank?"

"Corporal."

"And I'm not sure you've ever told me his name?"

Gloria hesitates for a moment before saying, "It's James. James Jarrett. Corporal James Jarrett. I'm very proud of him."

"No doubt. Maybe you'll get to see him this week."

"I hope so," Gloria says, looking a bit lost.

The kid has it bad for this Corporal Jarrett. Whoever he is. The room grows quiet. Gloria touches her brow, where the sweat is glistening.

"So, ah, about *Spotlight* . . . I've been in touch with Leslie Burke Wilson. She had an idea that I think is promising."

"She's a font of ideas, isn't she?" Erica says.

"She thought we could put together a panel of experts who would comment on the election and its aftermath in live segments."

"So we'd cut from the film to a live panel?"

"Exactly."

"I think that's confusing and will dilute the narrative thrust of the story. Nix it."

"Are you sure? She threw out some intriguing names."

"I've got a lot to do here," Erica says, picking up and reading a page she's already read. Gloria leaves.

Erica googles *Corporal James Jarrett* and finds an article from *West Point*, the military academy's magazine, that details his rapid rise in the military and describes him as Mary and Sturges Bellamy's protégé. It seems awfully coincidental that he's been transferred out to Camp Grafton. And the posting—at a training base in the middle of nowhere—seems like something of a comedown for his rising star. Unless . . . unless . . .

. . . Erica stands up and paces, goes to the window and looks down at the blistering city, sits back down at her desk, takes out her deck of cards, and deals a hand of solitaire . . .

Unless . . .

She was hoping the cards would calm her racing imagination. No such luck.

Unless . . . unless Camp Grafton will no longer be training *American* soldiers . . .

CHAPTER 63

ERICA, EILEEN, AND GLORIA ARE in their car, being driven from the Bismarck airport to the Holiday Inn. Every room within fifty miles of the capital is booked, with media from all over the country and a decent chunk of the world descending on North Dakota. The latest polls have shown Mary Bellamy a point or two ahead of Governor Snyder. While Synder could still pull it out, people are starting to focus on what Bellamy's first moves as governor will be. She has already created the most successful secession movement in American history. Soon she may have real power. What will she do with it?

Erica looks out the car window. The excitement is palpable, people holding Homeland and Bellamy signs line the sides of the roads, shouting and high-fiving passing motorists. Everywhere Erica looks she sees Bellamy bumper stickers, lawn signs, vehicles festooned with bunting, speakers on their roofs encouraging voters to support Bellamy. Clearly Mary Bellamy's campaign has incredible momentum; she doesn't want to just win, she wants a landslide, a mandate. And she wants to send a message to the rest of the country. There are secession movements in every state, but they're strongest and most vocal in those contiguous to North Dakota, where the leaders are following Mary's example, eschewing violent and extreme rhetoric for victory at the ballot box. Could she be advising, even coordinating, them?

Looking out the window at the raucous scene, Erica sees the darkness under the signs and screams, the hoopla, the near hysteria. Her adrenaline starts pumping, and part of what it's pumping is fear. This state is not a safe place for her. She's in their sights. Whoever *they* are.

"I've never seen anything like this," Eileen says. "It's going to be intense."

Gloria says nothing. She sits there looking troubled and frightened and trying to disguise it. That's been her default expression all week. When Gloria was pressing Erica on her investigation of the murders, she probably didn't realize she was the current focus of it. Erica suspects that somehow Gloria has found out that her liaison with Pete Nichols has been uncovered. But Erica has no proof, no evidence other than the whistling of a two-bit hood with a sadistic streak. It's time to turn the screws, but she has to do it artfully, gently. She's starting to question Gloria's emotional stability, and things could turn ugly. When people are cornered they become desperate and take irrational, even violent, action.

The women stop at their motel just long enough to drop off their bags, then they head downtown. Without a studio of its own or a local GNN affiliate, Eileen has rented a downtown storefront and set up temporary shop. It's a great visual, with Erica sitting at a desk in front of two huge corner plate-glass windows that have a view of the downtown's busiest intersection.

"This looks great, Eileen, good work," Erica says. "I think we should get out on the street to try and capture the energy and excitement, do a few on-the-spot interviews. We can shoot that segment ASAP and run it tonight."

"Gotcha," Eileen says. Gloria is standing there, looking like a third wheel; it gets a little awkward. "*Spotlight's* offices are up on the third floor," Eileen reminds her.

"All right. I guess I'll head up there. I want to get organized and then take a crew out and get some establishing shots of the Bellamy house and the capitol."

"I'll head up with you, I have a few thoughts," Erica says.

"Are you sure you don't want to stay down here and prepare for tonight's show? We have a lot more time to pull *Spotlight* together."

"No. I want to talk to you," Erica says firmly.

They step into the elevator and the doors close behind them. Erica stands with her back to the controls, blocking them. Gloria has almost wedged herself into the far corner of the car. She can't look Erica in the eye, and Erica sees her brow start to glisten.

"Gloria, is there anything you want to tell me?"

"Tell you?"

"Yes, tell me."

Gloria starts speaking very fast: "Nothing pressing. I'm sure a lot of questions will come up but right at this moment I can't think of any, I want the second *Spotlight* to be as strong as the first, no slump for us, ha-ha, so I really want to get some expert analysis on what the long-term ramifications of Bellamy's win will be, that's why I thought Leslie Burke Wilson's idea might work and . . . *Erica, why are you looking at me like that?*"

Erica lets her twist in the wind for a few endless moments. She looks afraid. Well, Erica was afraid in the trunk of that car. Erica is afraid now. For herself. For her daughter. So, Gloria, what goes around comes around.

"When I went up to Boston for the symposium at the Kennedy School I was kidnapped, stuffed in the trunk of a car, and taken on a terrifying ride."

Gloria's mouth drops open in a semblance of surprise. Then her eyes well with tears. And is she shaking? "Erica, I'm sorry. I'm not in the best shape these days. The pressures of the show are getting to me. This is the big leagues—in DC I was swimming in a much smaller pond. I just feel overwhelmed. And personally, I'm feeling, well, I *love* James Jarrett. Oh, Erica, I'm so in love with him, and, well, I'm not sure how he feels about me."

"I thought you were engaged."

"That's what I told people, but . . ."

Now *that's* weird. Erica feels slightly queasy. And then there's a momentary surge of pity for poor Gloria, who clearly isn't the woman Erica once thought she was.

"I'm sorry," Gloria says. "I let you down."

Erica has no *proof* that Gloria had a role in her kidnapping. Looking at her now, cowering in the corner of the elevator, she hardly seems capable of such twisted machinations. Pete Nichols could have been playing a double head game, a feint, with his whistling. Sending Erica down a rabbit hole in search of a wild goose. And Gloria's recent erratic behavior *could* be attributed to work pressure and lovesickness.

"So you didn't know anything about my kidnapping?"

"*Me?* Your kidnapping? No, of course not, how could I?"

Gloria sounds so sincere, looks so stunned. What if this is all Erica's paranoia running away with her? In any case, she has a show to prepare. It suddenly feels as if the elevator walls are closing in on her, she feels dizzy with confusion. And under it all, the telltale beating of her frightened heart. She turns away from Gloria and presses the Open button. The doors open, but the two women don't move.

Gloria takes out a tissue and dabs at her eyes, wipes her brow, stands up straight. She gives Erica a forlorn smile. "If you'd like me to resign, just say so."

Keep your friends close and your enemies closer.

"We're heading up to Grand Forks tomorrow to cover Mary Bellamy's final rally. We need that footage for *Spotlight*."

"You want me to stay?"

"We'll revisit this when we're back in New York."

Erica steps out of the elevator with long strides, her shoulders back, hoping that her posture will project confidence—and keep her from drowning in a sea of doubt.

CHAPTER 64 ———————————————————

MAKING HER WAY THROUGH THE claustrophobic backstage labyrinth of the Alerus Center in Grand Forks, Erica can hear the crowd in the arena yelling and stomping—it's so loud and intense that the building vibrates. An old man racing down the corridor yells at her, "Go back to New York, we don't want your kind here!" Other people she passes give her either dirty or dismissive looks, creepy and threatening, or smiles that are too bright and eager, as if they were blissed-out cult members. She makes it to an elevator that takes her up to the broadcast booths. As she steps into the GNN booth, she stops cold. The sight of the packed arena—with a capacity of twenty-one thousand, it's the largest in the state—is electrifying. And there are thousands more Bellamy partisans filling the streets outside and watching on jumbo screens. Looking down on the pulsing, roiling sea of humanity, Erica is awed and disquieted. People's faces are twisted and grimacing with anger, there is screaming and fist pumping, signs and T-shirts with slogans like *F' the Feds*, *Power to the Homeland*, *Nuke the IRS*, and *Free North Dakota*. There are far more men than women, and macho bravado fills the air like toxic gas—there's nothing celebratory here; this crowd wants revenge, it wants blood. In fact, it looks more like a mob than a crowd.

As an American Erica is disturbed. As a journalist she can't help being riveted, a witness to history. And as secession movements in other states grow larger and more mainstream, this story is still in its infancy. Erica sits at her desk and checks her notes.

Eileen McDermott comes over. "You ready for this?"

"I've never seen anything like it."

"We're a go in two minutes."

"I'm just going to do a brief intro and then I think we stay live on Bellamy's speech."

"That's the money shot."

"Blood money," Erica says, looking down at the crowd. She watches the GNN feed from New York and then it's thrown to her.

"This is Erica Sparks reporting live from the Alerus Center in Grand Forks, North Dakota, where the tumultuous recall election of Governor Bert Snyder is entering its last day. We're here at the final rally of insurgent Mary Bellamy, the leader of the controversial Homeland movement, and as you can see and hear, the capacity crowd is pumped up to a fever pitch. Let's listen as State Senator Michael Haydn, who bolted the Republican party and endorsed Bellamy, finishes his intro-duction of the candidate."

Senator Haydn, white-haired and folksy in a bolero tie, leans for-ward on the podium and intones, "I have known this woman for three decades, and I truly believe she is the last best hope we have to escape the tyranny of the federal government. She is a force to be reckoned with, and believe me, after tomorrow night our enemies in Washington *will* be brought to heel. It's an honor to present the next leader of the North Dakota Homeland, Mary Bellamy!"

As Mary walks onstage the place goes berserk. It truly feels like the crowd might blow the roof right off the vast arena. Then they begin chanting—a war chant—"MA-RY! MA-RY! MA-RY!"

Mary Bellamy, looking subdued and humble in a simple blue dress, stands there letting it all wash over her. She waves a couple of times, and each wave triggers a new round of screams and cries. Finally, she starts to hush the crowd. And hush it does, until all that is heard is a low hum of excitement, as much vibration as sound.

"Hello, fellow pioneers," Mary says with a smile. And the place erupts again. Again she hushes it. This time she grows serious. "Last month I lost my husband, my dear Sturges, who so many of you knew and loved. He was my best friend and my partner, and this movement belongs to him as much as it does to me. In the first days after his death I wondered if I could carry on without him. I prayed for guidance. And the answer came to me. I will fight on in his name *until my last breath*."

The arena erupts again, cheers and chants and signs and screaming. And again Mary is able to hush it, as if with a magic wand.

"My friends, we are in the middle of an epic battle. It is nothing less than a battle between freedom and bondage, between yesterday and tomorrow, between good and evil. And the righteous shall prevail. And *we* are the righteous!"

"MA-RY! MA-RY! MA-RY!"

"The federal government has conspired with special interests to strip away our ability to control our own destinies. They have turned us into a nation of the few, by the few, for the few. And *we have had enough!*"

"MA-RY! MA-RY! MA-RY!"

"Tomorrow, everything changes. When you go into that voting booth you will be altering the course of history. You are nothing less than the Founding Fathers of the new Homeland!"

"MA-RY! MA-RY! MA-RY!"

"They will stop at nothing to prevent us. But they will fail. Because we are prepared. And *we* will stop at nothing *to free ourselves from their tyranny!*"

"MA-RY! MA-RY! MA-RY!"

With each new explosion, the crowd grows more hyped up, hopped up, unruly, on the edge of . . . *what?* Violence? Mob rule? The speech goes on for another ten minutes, building to a crescendo—"Go forth tomorrow and vote, for we are an army of believers and, my friends, we are going to take back what is rightfully ours! *The future belongs to us!"*—until the crowd is on its feet, standing on chairs, screaming, stomping, in a fever, a frenzy, a fit of what feels very close to collective madness.

Erica is spellbound and filled with dread. She hears Joan Marcus's voice, imploring, tearful, and terrified: *I need* to talk to you. *I'm down in the lobby. Can I come up? I'm scared.*

. . . the scrap of photograph, the missile, and the murders and the kidnapping, and Joan Marcus's throat slit open, the gaping wound, the blood smeared on the tiles as she fought to stand . . .

Music blares and balloons pour from the rafters as the crowd streams toward the exits, driven by righteous rage. GNN cuts to the crowd outside the arena. Many of them hold burning torches that light the night and speak of a terrible darkness to come.

CHAPTER 65

IT'S MIDAFTERNOON ON ELECTION DAY, and Erica is at her desk on GNN's temporary set back in Bismarck. All day she's been reporting on the massive voter turnout across North Dakota; officials are saying it is sure to set a state, if not a national, record, with over 90 percent of eligible voters going to the polls. The nation has never seen anything like this. Mort Silver called to crow about how high the ratings are, and Erica is the country's go-to reporter on the story.

She has a half hour before her next update, and she's familiarizing herself with some of the day's other big stories. India is still in the grip of the worst heat wave in human history, and the death toll has reached the many tens of thousands. In addition to the dead and dying, doctors, hospitals, and public health officials are grappling with hundreds of thousands of cases of heat delirium, a syndrome characterized by hallucinations, seizures, and suicidal and homicidal impulses. The footage from the subcontinent is horrifying and profoundly disturbing to Erica. She decides then and there that the next *Spotlight* will focus on climate change. She owes it to Jenny.

Jenny. There are so many dangers out there—she needs to speak to her, to warn her to be careful, to not speak to strangers. She calls her.

"Hi, honey, how are things going?" Erica says, trying not to let her anxiety color her voice.

Jenny giggles. That's odd. She's not a giggler. "Going great. Everything's cool." Hip-hop music is playing in the background.

"What have you been up to?"

"Oh, just hanging out." More giggles.

"Where are you?"

"Just at my friend Julie's house now. She has a pool."

"I haven't heard you mention her before. What do her parents do?"

Jenny starts to laugh. "What do her parents *do*? What is this, an investigative report? . . . Julie, *my* parent wants to know what *your* parents *do*." Now both girls are laughing.

Erica has a jolting realization: *they're on pot*. She stands up and starts to pace. She can't get into a confrontation or make an accusation without proof.

"Jenny, listen to me for a minute," she says in her most serious voice.

Jenny goes quiet for a moment and then asks, "What's up, Mom?"

"I want you to be very careful. About where you go. Who you talk to. Never ever talk to a stranger. Be on the alert. Will you promise me you'll do that?"

"Yes, sure."

"And the bullying has stopped?"

"I don't need Beth and her stupid friends anymore," Jenny says. Then she giggles again. Then the music is turned up.

"I gotta go, Mom."

"Be careful. I love you."

After hanging up, Erica goes to Jenny's Instagram feed. The most recent pictures show her by a pool with a group of friends, boys and girls, laughing, looking goofy and bleary-eyed. *Stoned.*

She dials Dirk's number and then hangs up before it rings. She doesn't want to overreact. Every kid smokes a little pot these days, right? Still, it freaks her out. There's so much addiction in the family. It can start with pot, it does start with pot. It can end with pot too. Look at

Susan and the morning joint she sucked down almost every day of Erica's childhood. Jenny may well be drinking, too, for all Erica knows. And pills. Now her imagination is running away with her. She feels at a loss, at sea, a mother without a clue. She'll call Dirk later and discuss it, when she's calmed down.

She sits back down at her desk just in time to see Leslie Burke Wilson stride into the studio.

"Erica!"

Trying to disguise her shock, Erica stands up and accepts Leslie's air kiss. What is she doing here?

"I couldn't stay away, I'm *obsessed* with this story. I think it's *the* current American narrative. The natives are way beyond restless, they're in the midst of a full-blown mutiny. If Bellamy does win this, and it looks like she will, what does the president do in response? How far is Bellamy going to go? Is this a bluff, designed to position herself for a run for the White House? Could she actually set a precedent for some sort of semiautonomous state? One that other states could follow? There are models of that elsewhere in the world. The questions just keep coming, each more intriguing than the last."

Erica feels like a tornado just blew in. It's highly unusual, even unprofessional, for Wilson to show up like this, out of the blue, without being invited. Even though Erica resents this little power play—and the woman who may be trying to seduce her husband—she'd be a fool not to exploit Leslie's star power and intellectual heft.

"Would you join my panel tonight? We're going to be reporting the returns live from outside the statehouse, where Bellamy is going to be addressing her supporters."

"I'd be honored," Leslie says. Mission accomplished. Book contract in hand, she clearly wants to establish herself as *the* authority on secession.

There's an awkward pause. Then Leslie sits opposite Erica, reaches across the desk, and takes her hand. "It's *so* good to see you. How are you?" She looks at Erica with some mix of interest and pity and condescension.

"I'm mostly very busy," Erica says, shuffling some papers.

"And what would we do if we weren't?"

"I've got a live update in a couple of minutes."

"Of course. I'm going to go out and explore, I want to *inhale* this zeitgeist. Something momentous is happening." But she doesn't get up, she grows pensive. Then she leans in to Erica and lowers her voice. "Did you by any chance see the piece on me in the *Sunday Times* Styles section?"

"I did."

"So you know that Stan and I have separated."

"I'm sorry."

"It's difficult. And complicated. And sad. But in the final analysis, I view the end of our marriage as an opportunity."

An opportunity to sleep with my husband?

"I really have to get my game face on for this update," Erica says.

"Would you like to do a quick interview with me as part of it? Sort of a teaser for tonight's show?"

That's a good idea, actually. "No, I think we should save you for the main event," Erica says, turning toward the camera.

CHAPTER 66

IT'S THAT NIGHT, ABOUT AN hour after the polls have closed, and Gloria is in *Spotlight*'s makeshift office on the third floor of the downtown Bismarck office building. Outside, the whole city, the whole state, seems to be celebrating Mary Bellamy's historic landslide win in the gubernatorial recall—her vote total is over 75 percent, soon she'll speak to the huge crowd that has gathered at the statehouse. Cars are honking, boisterous bands of partisans are roaming the streets, the booms and dazzle of exploding fireworks fill the air and light the sky.

Yet it's strangely quiet in the office. Gloria is alone, having sent her crew and two producers out to cover the scene at the statehouse. There are three televisions, all showing GNN, and Gloria watches Erica in triplicate, reporting from a rudimentary set on the statehouse grounds, with Leslie Burke Wilson and Bob Woodward beside her. Gloria has the sound turned off. She needs the quiet. She needs to think. No, she needs to *feel*. She's been doing too much thinking, overthinking. What she really needs is to be in James Jarrett's arms, the only place where she feels safe.

Erica has found out somehow. She's sure of it. Why else would she have cornered Gloria in the elevator like that? Did Gloria mess up on one of the protocols? She tries to follow James's directives to the letter. How much does Erica know? Lovely Erica, who gave Gloria the biggest break of her career, who has been nothing but supportive and generous and considerate. And now Gloria has betrayed her. But that's all right. Because James told her to. He guided her every step of the way. And he'll make everything better. He'll make it right again. Like it was before. He's only 175 miles away, at Camp Grafton. She could get in her rental car and be there in three hours. She could be in his arms in three hours. *In his arms.*

She takes out her only-James phone and dials.

"Yes," he answers in that rich baritone, and her whole body quivers with desire.

"Hello, darling."

"Who is this?" he demands.

Gloria tries for a casual laugh but it comes out as a strangled cry. "Don't be silly, James, it's *me*."

"I have no idea who this is."

"James, it's *me*, Gloria."

"Oh. You."

He's acting so odd, so distant, so cold. Well, he has to be discreet. Being in the army and all. There could be someone in the room with him. That's it. Someone is in the room with him. He has to be discreet.

"You're not alone, are you, darling?"

"As a matter of fact, I am alone."

"Oh. I just thought . . ."

"You just thought what?"

"Never mind. I'm only 175 miles away, James. I could be there in three hours."

"Why would you come here?"

"So that we could be together, you and me, just the two of us, together, the way it's always been . . . Please, my darling."

"Stop calling me your darling."

Gloria lets out another anguished cry and she feels a terrible weight on her chest—is she having a heart attack?—and she can't breathe, she feels lightheaded, is she going to faint?

"But, James, you *are* my darling . . ."

"You mean nothing to me. Less than nothing."

And Gloria starts sobbing. This can't be real, this can't be happening, the world is collapsing. "What happened, what did I do, what happened, I don't understand, I love you, I love you so much—"

"Pull yourself together. This is embarrassing. You're pathetic."

Tears are pouring down Gloria's face, which is all contorted, spittle bubbles at the corners of her mouth. *"What did I do? Please tell me what I did."*

"You messed up. You used the wrong phone. I got traced."

"OH NO! I'm so sorry, my sweetheart, I'm so sorry . . ."

"You're dead to me."

And then he hangs up.

Gloria sits there going into shock, she can't move, and then suddenly she's freezing and she starts to shake, her whole body starts to shake, like a tender leaf in a hurricane, and the world stops and she sits there both still and shaking . . .

And then—is it a minute later or an hour?—she stands up, walks over to the back staircase, down three flights and out through a fire door, out into the night. And all around her, people are screaming and honking and waving flags, and fireworks fill the night sky and she walks past the plate-glass windows and there's that woman, what's her name?—*Erica*—on a bank of television sets, in another world, a parallel universe, and she keeps walking, through the screaming and honking and flags and fireworks, and she's dead to James, she's dead, and up ahead there's a bridge over that big river, the Missouri River—see, she remembered, she's a good girl, a straight-A girl—a steel truss bridge, a workhorse bridge. She's a workhorse, isn't she? She's worked so hard, since kindergarten, hand up, straight As, homework done, good girl, Best Little Girl. But she messed up. Too bad. So sad.

But she can make it right, can't she, by being a good girl, she's still a good girl, even if she's dead to James she can be a good girl and she takes out her phone and calls Erica and her voicemail picks up and Gloria says, "I'm sorry, Erica, for being a bad girl. I did hire that man in Boston to kidnap you. I have to tell you something else though, they're bad people, worse than me even, and they're"—and a car peels by and the driver is leaning on the horn and Gloria can't hear herself speak and then she drops the phone because it doesn't matter anyway, nothing matters anyway . . .

And now she's on the bridge and cars are streaming by, people leaning out windows, screaming and waving flags and honking and the whole night is alive, it's so alive, and she's dead to James, she's dead to James . . . And she stops and leans over the railing and looks down at the river below and it's swirly, such pretty swirls, and suddenly a burst of fireworks lights the sky and makes the pretty swirls glow, the pretty glowing swirls, they're welcoming her, inviting her, and she climbs over the railing and stands there for a beautiful suspended moment and then she lets go and leaps, down, down . . . down into the bright pretty swirls . . .

CHAPTER 67 ———————————————

"I'M HERE ON THE STATEHOUSE grounds, and as you can see and hear, tens of thousands of North Dakotans are packed into the plaza, celebrating Mary Bellamy's landslide recall of Governor Bert Snyder and awaiting her victory speech. Bellamy aides have told us she has received a concession call from Snyder and will be appearing shortly. I'm joined by Leslie Burke Wilson and Bob Woodward. What do the two of you make of all this?"

"I believe we may be witnessing a transformative moment in American history," Leslie says. "The populist fervor that has been growing for the past two decades seems to be coming to a head here tonight. It may be, in fact, that our union is no longer viable in its present form."

"I agree. The peasants have not only stormed the castle, they've anointed their queen. Our nation is so polarized that it may be close to ungovernable. Could we split not into North/South but Blue/Red? Would that be such a terrible thing? The questions raised are almost existential for our nation. Of course, much will depend on Mary Bellamy's actions as governor," Woodward says.

"This puts the president in a very difficult situation, doesn't it? What are her options?" Erica asks.

"I think she'll take a wait-and-see attitude at first. Her number one goal has to be national unity. However, North Dakota's Homeland movement and other secession movements across the country want no part of that. In fact, breaking up the union is their guiding mission," Woodward says.

Erica notices Eileen—who is standing beside the cameraman—looking distressed.

"We'll be right back after this short break," she says.

As GNN goes to a commercial, Erica gets up from the desk and hurries over to Eileen, who tells her, "Eyewitnesses saw a woman matching Gloria Washburn's description jump off the Liberty Memorial Bridge about a half hour ago."

"*No!*" Erica stands there, numb. "Has a body been found? Is there any confirmation?"

"Not yet. There's no answer on her phone. An intern went and checked our offices downtown. She's not there. There's a police boat out on the river, and divers are searching for a body."

"Keep me posted." Erica checks her phone and there's a message from Gloria: "I'm sorry, Erica, for being a bad girl." She starts to sob. "I did hire that man in Boston to kidnap you. I have to tell you something else though, they're bad people, worse than me even, and they're"—and then a blaring car horn drowns out Gloria's voice. And then the phone goes *thunk!* And then Erica can hear honking and screaming and fireworks and then the line goes blank. Erica returns to her desk and Eileen gives her the one-minute sign.

Poor Gloria, poor sad Gloria . . .

"Erica, are you all right?" Leslie Wilson asks.

Erica's first impulse is to tell Leslie the news, but she checks herself. "I'll be okay."

Pandemonium erupts around them as Mary Bellamy ascends the platform in front of the statehouse. Eileen signals Erica as GNN cuts from a commercial to live. "Mary Bellamy is taking the stage to make her victory speech," Erica says, giving wordless thanks for Bellamy's timing, which gives her a chance to gather herself.

Erica looks out over the sea of screaming, chanting humanity and thinks of Gloria's last moments, her despair, the fragility of life, the sadness, the loss of innocence. And then the evil, the threats, the danger. *Jenny. Me.*

Someone drove Gloria to suicide, probably whoever put her up to the kidnapping. And what was she about to tell Erica when the horn drowned her out?

Mary Bellamy silences the vast crowd, their faces filled with hope and reverence and resolve and revenge. She smiles softly and then says, "When we woke up this morning, North Dakota was one of fifty. When we wake up tomorrow morning, we will be the one and only Homeland!" The response is deafening, and Mary lets it play out before raising her arms and hushing her followers. "It's been a long, hard-fought campaign, and I want to thank each and every one of you for your support. We have a lot of work ahead of us. We are going to set a new standard for freedom, self-reliance, and strength. Tomorrow we hit the ground running. Thank you all, good night and God bless you—and God bless the Homeland."

Erica throws leading questions to Leslie and Woodward and lets them pontificate with their trademark erudition. Her own mind is elsewhere—obsessing on Gloria Washburn's final words.

CHAPTER 68

IT'S THE NEXT MORNING AND Erica—after having done a half hour of Tae Kwon Do—is having coffee in her room, pacing and trying to figure out what her next steps are. Gloria's body was recovered from the Missouri River, not far downstream from where she jumped in. Her family is making arrangements to have the body shipped back East after the coroner performs an autopsy.

Her phone rings, it's Mort Silver.

"Great job out there, Erica. I'm sorry about Gloria Washburn."

"Yeah, me too."

"We have to start looking for her replacement."

"Mort, her body is still warm."

"We're trying to establish the best investigative show on television. The first *Spotlight* drew tremendous ratings. We need the second to do even better. The show needs an executive producer."

On some level Erica knows he's right. But it's ghoulish. The world is ghoulish. "I'll start interviewing candidates on Monday."

"You don't sound like yourself, Erica."

"It's been a grueling couple of days."

"This is a grueling business. If it stopped being brutal, we'd be bored."

Erica hangs up. Mort's right. Erica thrives in the pressure cooker. It obliterates—well, assuages anyway—self-doubt, memories, pain, sadness. Even her fear gives her juice. She makes a decision: she was scheduled to fly back to New York today, but she'll stay out in North Dakota—correction, *the Homeland*—over the weekend. Her instincts tell her there's a link between Joan Marcus's murder, the subsequent murders, and Gloria's suicide, and somehow . . . *somehow* . . . the trail may lead to Mary Bellamy. The newly elected governor—or premier, as she has christened herself—has scheduled a news conference for 1:00 p.m. Hopefully it will be revealing.

A call comes in from Boston police detective Pat Halley.

"Erica, I wanted to let you know that Pete Nichols was murdered last night. He was shot by a drive-by killer as he walked home from his weekly poker game."

Erica can't shed any tears for the likes of Pete Nichols. "There goes that source and possible witness."

"Listen, Erica, you've got to be very careful. You're dealing with people who consider murder just another day on the job."

She hangs up and calls Sentinel Security in Boston, a company she's used before. She reaches its president, Dave Garrison.

"What can we do for you, Erica?" Dave asks.

"The same thing you did last time—watch my daughter."

"You want 24/7?"

"I do. Be as unobtrusive as possible, but if comes down to it, let your presence be known."

"Gotcha. She's in good hands."

"I'm counting on it."

Next Erica calls Dirk.

"What's up, Erica?"

"Has Jenny seemed . . . *herself* to you lately?"

"What's that supposed to mean?"

"We spoke yesterday and she seemed . . . a little *too* happy."

"What are you implying?"

Erica doesn't want to go down this road, not right now. She has bigger fears to fry. "Listen, I'm in the middle of something ugly. I'm dealing with people who are ruthless. There's danger. So I've hired that same security firm to keep an eye on Jenny."

Dirk exhales with a sigh. "So you've put our daughter in danger again."

"I have absolutely no indication that she's targeted, I'm doing this as a precaution." Erica hopes she sounds more convincing than she feels.

Dirk is a basically decent guy, but there are residual resentments on both sides. He exhales with a sigh. "Okay."

Erica hangs up, sits down at her computer, and googles directions from Bismarck to Camp Grafton.

CHAPTER 69 ———————————

PREMIER MARY BELLAMY WALKS INTO the state capitol's pressroom, followed by a half dozen aides who line up against the wall as she walks to the podium; one is in a military uniform. The room is thick with journalists, charged with anticipation. Erica sits in the third row, her legs crossed, her upper leg bouncing.

"I'm going to make a short statement and then I'll take questions," Mary says. She looks smart and pulled together in an expensive wool suit, her hair done, her lips red. "First, I have written a declaration of independence to President Winters, informing her that the Homeland of North Dakota is now a self-governing entity." There is a collective gasp from the room. "We are no longer under obligation to obey federal laws or edicts or to pay federal taxes. We are ready and willing to work with the president and the federal authorities to make this transition as seamless and painless as possible. But our status is nonnegotiable.

"This morning I signed an agreement with Neal Clark, president of Trans-Canada Energy, to jointly build a pipeline that will carry the Homeland's oil and natural gas to Winnipeg, where it will be processed, stored, and sold to the world."

Mary points to a handsome older man standing along the wall.

Neal Clark raises his hand in a modest wave and beams at Mary, who beams back. Is Erica the only one who senses that their relationship transcends natural gas?

"All revenues generated by this enterprise will be used for the benefit of the citizens of the Homeland. We expect the number to be in the trillions over the next decade.

"I would also like to speak to all Americans. Over thirty-five thousand pioneers have been welcomed to the Homeland. Please know we have room for many more. I have signed an executive order turning Camp Grafton on Devil's Lake into a processing and temporary housing facility. Camp Grafton will remain under the authority of its current commanding officer, General Floyd Morrow."

There's another gasp from the room. Bellamy points to General Morrow, standing along the wall. He looks too intense, his eyes are darting, his jaw clenching, a light film of sweat glistens on his brow.

"General Morrow has renounced his allegiance to the United States of America and taken an oath of allegiance to the Homeland of North Dakota. He will make sure that all our new pioneers are well taken care of. We think of Camp Grafton as the Ellis Island of the Great Plains. Every American who believes in our cause is invited to make the Homeland your home. I will now take questions."

Erica's hand shoots up. Mary points at her, a slight, almost imperceptible smile playing at the corners of her mouth. "Erica?"

"Have you spoken to President Winters?"

"I have not. But I welcome her call. The people of the Homeland have made their decision. I hope she will respect it. Gregory?"

"Yes, do you really think the Pentagon will allow you to commandeer one of its bases?"

"We have already taken control of Camp Grafton. Including its weaponry. In addition, the Homeland is going to establish a self-defense force—the Great Army of the Homeland. General Morrow has formulated a training protocol that will be initiated within a week at Camp Grafton. It is capable of training a thousand citizens at a time in all aspects of combat. The first thousand recruits have already signed up."

"What about the North Dakotans who didn't support you and want to remain part of the United States?"

"They are welcome to leave. If they stay, we expect them to show allegiance to the Homeland and to obey all of our laws."

As more hands go up, and more details of Mary Bellamy's mind-blowing power grab emerge, Erica's mind races over the murders of Joan Marcus, George Lundy, Freddy McDougal, Cathy and Dennis Allen, and Pete Nichols, and Gloria's suicide. The scrap of photograph showing a missile. A missile capable of carrying a nuclear warhead. Erica realizes that Joan Marcus's desperate attempt to contact her had nothing to do with toxic chemicals and environmental crimes. No, she was on to something much, much darker.

When the press conference ends and Mary Bellamy leaves, the journalists sit there in collective shock, trying to grasp the ramifications of what they've just heard. Erica has to get downtown to the temporary studio and deliver an update. It's 2:00 p.m. now. If she can get it written and on the air by three she'll still have plenty of time to get to Camp Grafton before dark.

CHAPTER 70

PRESIDENT LUCY WINTERS IS IN the Oval Office with a half dozen of her top aides and advisors. She's leaning against the side of her desk, dumbfounded by Mary Bellamy's press conference. Winters picks up the remote and mutes the bank of televisions.

"You know, when I ran for president I imagined all sorts of difficult decisions, crises, emergencies. ISIS, climate change, the economy, gun control, the list goes on and on," Winters says. "I never in my wildest imagination thought I'd be dealing with a state that wants to secede from the union. And a neighboring state to my own, no less."

Winters is a fifty-six-year-old farmer's daughter from Minnesota who worked her way up the political pole the old-fashioned way. Volunteering for her local GOP, getting elected to the state legislature, then Congress, then the Senate, and finally the White House, which she won in a landslide after her Democratic opponent, Senator Mike Ortiz of California, was revealed to have been brainwashed while a POW in Iraq. She prides herself on her strength, integrity, fairness, moderation, and commitment to unifying the country. And now this.

"What are my options?" she asks her aides, who are all people she trusts explicitly.

"We could reach out to Bellamy and start negotiations," Dave Burrows, her chief of staff, says.

"A military response should definitely be on the table," says General Maria Sanchez, her top military aide.

"I *hate* the idea of negotiating with a woman who has just thrown down the gauntlet and expressed her disdain for the United States of America," Winters says. "As for a military response—contrary to what Bellamy may believe, the citizens of North Dakota are still Americans. I can't imagine going in militarily."

"Madame President, Bellamy has fired the first shot," Paul Adams, her chief national security advisor, offers. "She is establishing her own military force. If you let her get away with this, even in the short term, it will embolden copycat movements across the nation. We know they are burgeoning already in South Dakota, Idaho, Montana, and Wyoming. I can envision a regional confederation of former states. This must be nipped in the bud. And nipped forcefully."

"We could do a strategic strike—moving in with a small stealth team—and take Bellamy and her closest aides into custody," General Sanchez says.

"That would trigger such outrage from her supporters, not only in North Dakota, but across the nation. It would be instant martyrdom. She was elected fair and square," Winters says.

"She was elected governor of North Dakota, not premier of some quasi-nation. And she may have won fair and square, but her actions today violate federal law," Elise Manning, the president's chief counsel, says. "And announcing that pipeline deal with Neal Clark was a piece of work. She's got *cojones*, I'll give her that. The pipeline will certainly provide her vast financial resources with which to fulfill her agenda."

"General Morrow, of course, should be court-martialed. And will be as soon as this is over. The man has well-documented temperament issues," Sanchez says.

"Then why did the army put him in charge of Camp Grafton?" the president demands.

"Because it is—or was—a low-risk, low-priority appointment. He's made some influential friends over the years and this was his reward," Sanchez explains.

"I need a little time to think about all this," Winters says. The president prides herself on making considered decisions, and those take time and thought.

"We have to make some sort of statement. The press is clamoring and the nation is waiting," White House press secretary Josh Holden points out.

Winters stands up and begins to pace. She walks over to a bowl of apples on a sideboard, takes one, polishes it on her sleeve, and puts it back in the bowl.

Then she turns and looks into the expectant faces of her staff. That's the thing about being president—the buck really does stop with her. She welcomes advice, even—especially—contradictory advice, but in the end it's her call. And this is the biggest crisis of her presidency. She sits back down at her desk and starts to write on a legal pad. Within five minutes she looks up and says, "How about something like this: 'Today the newly elected governor of North Dakota, Mary Bellamy, took illegal and provocative actions that threaten the unity, integrity, and future of our nation. We are the *United* States of America. And we shall remain united. My administration will deal with her actions in a timely and appropriate manner. In the meantime, residents of North Dakota—and indeed the whole country—should be aware that any actions taken in support of Governor Bellamy are also illegal. I urge all Americans to stay calm during this difficult period. We will prevail.'"

"I think it's strong, and it buys us a little time," Josh Holden says.

"I think you need a little more big stick. Remember, she has asserted control of Camp Grafton. Her so-called pioneers are going to receive combat training," General Sanchez says.

"I think there's a degree of bluster. She has to show her supporters she means business. Bellamy may be soft-spoken, but many of her supporters are loud and angry. They're going to demand that she make good on her campaign promises," Chief of Staff Burrows says.

"I don't think she would actually engage militarily. It would be suicide," Paul Adams says. "I think we need to concentrate on infiltrating her inner circle. We want to know what their plans are in real time."

"Good point, Paul. I authorize the immediate use of covert action to gain information on Mary Bellamy's administration," Winters says, standing up.

"Okay, people, let's get this statement out in the next ten minutes," Holden says. "I'll take a few questions from the press. I don't think the president should have a news conference, it will only give Bellamy more oxygen."

The president's staff make for the door—then General Sanchez's military phone rings. She answers, listens, and then hangs up. "Bellamy has just deputized the first thousand soldiers of the Great Army of the Homeland and issued them weapons."

The room falls silent. Finally, the president says, "She's escalating."

She turns to the window and looks out at the Rose Garden—the roses are blooming, but all she sees are the thorns.

CHAPTER 71

ERICA LISTENS TO THE PRESIDENT'S statement as she races across the state on I-94. She thinks it strikes the perfect balance of tough and measured. She's glad that someone of Winters's caliber is in the Oval Office. Still, she feels her anxiety skyrocketing. Things are intensifying quickly. A standoff seems to be inevitable, especially considering Bellamy's defiant arming of the first thousand recruits for the Homeland army. How far could it go? Does Bellamy really think she could take on the American military?

Then she replays Gloria's final message on her cell phone, spoken in the last minutes of her life: *I have to tell you something else though, they're bad people, worse than me even, and they're . . .* and then that deafening honk, completely obscuring her final words.

Erica says, "Call Moy," into her phone. The number rings.

"Erica, wow, what is happening out there?"

"A lot."

"Are you safe?"

"No, but I wouldn't be safe anywhere. Listen, I got a last-minute phone call from my producer, Gloria Washburn, before she jumped off the bridge. But her final words are unintelligible because a car was honking right next to her. Do you know a forensic audiologist?"

"LAPD has one, Momar Neezan. I've interviewed him. Smart guy, they say he's the best. I'll call him right now."

"Thanks, Moy."

"Stay scared, old friend."

Erica hangs up and puts a little more pressure on the accelerator. The landscape around her is so flat and featureless, endless grassland and tiny towns visible from the highway, just small, random collections of buildings. Who lives in them? Why would anyone? There's something unsettling and frightening about the vastness of it all. It's so lonely. No one would hear you scream. No wonder people huff meth or eat ten thousand calories a day or get hooked on Oxy. There's more than one way to die.

Erica is troubled by the fact that Canadian billionaire Neal Clark was at Bellamy's press conference. He's from Winnipeg, which raises her suspicions. That pipeline alliance has clearly been in the works for some time. Announcing it on her first day was a stroke of brilliance on Bellamy's part, serving notice that she can handle the former state's economy, that she can bypass adjoining states and go directly to Canada, and that she has a ready market for the Homeland's oil and gas that will only increase its prosperity and stability.

At Jamestown she heads north on 281, past Pingree and Edmunds and Carrington, all of it spooky, flat, and deadening. She feels as if she's driving into uncharted territory, another world. She read somewhere that North Dakota is the least visited state in the nation. She understands why.

It's staggering to think that the Bellamys actually pulled it off. Secret planning had to have been going on for years. It's all blatantly illegal. Was that why there were so many murders, to keep things under wraps? Well, the wrapping has been torn off and the prize revealed. It's power. And lucre. North Dakota is sitting on gas and oil worth the ransom of a thousand kings. It doesn't need federal largess. As for the murders, clearly they're all links leading up the food chain, just as they were with Nylan Hastings and Lily Lau. Right now, she's at Gloria

Washburn and Freddy McDougal—and she has to peel the next layer of the onion.

Erica drives into the enormous Spirit Lake Native American Reservation, which stretches right up to the southern boundary of Devil's Lake, the largest lake in the state. She turns right on Route 57 and speeds past small clusters of mobile homes, blank and desolate, with dead cars and plastic toys strewn around—you can almost smell the despair. She passes Spirit Lake Casino, a depressing dollop of gaudy awful in the midst of the monotony. She crosses the lake and there, to the west, is Camp Grafton. The traffic starts to pick up, and many of the cars have bumper stickers reading *Bellamy 4ME* or *Heading Homeland*.

Erica gets off the road and joins the traffic heading to the base entrance. There's a gate and a guardhouse. A soldier is checking identification. Erica waits in line, noticing how young many of the pioneer families are. *I guess it's easier to pack up your life and move when you're young.* She reaches the front of the line. The soldier is also young and sturdy, wearing a dark blue uniform with *Homeland of North Dakota* embroidered on the chest. *They even had the uniforms ready.* The soldier narrows his eyes in recognition.

"I'm here to see Corporal James Jarrett."

"Is he expecting you?"

"Yes," Erica lies.

"I'll need to see some identification." Erica hands him her driver's license. "Okay. I know you. Don't like you, but I know you."

Erica holds her tongue as he goes into the guardhouse and picks up the phone, returning a few moments later. "Go down and take your first left, the corporal's house is the third one on the right. Don't go wandering around."

"Can I ask you a question?"

"Guess so."

"Are you a native or a pioneer?"

"I'm a pioneer. Been here two months. From Iowa."

"What drew you?"

"Hatred of the federal government."

"And you believe in the Homeland?"

His face sets and darkens. "I would *die* for the Homeland."

The base is a beehive—killer bees—of activity as it welcomes the first pioneers who are making it their temporary home and recruits who are going to undergo combat training. Supply trucks are making deliveries, cleaning crews are power-washing barracks, volunteers are carrying tall piles of sheets and blankets, grounds crews are trimming shrubs and repairing walkways.

Erica doesn't see a soul taking a break, having a smoke, chatting with a coworker—the focus and energy are palpable. When people's eyes do meet, they exchange big bright-eyed smiles that speak of unquestioning, cult-like devotion. This place is a lynchpin of the nascent Homeland, and it feels ominous and eerie, like an episode of *The Twilight Zone*. Soon thousands of young men and women will be subjected to rigorous training, to marches and gunfire and barked orders and lessons in the art of killing.

Erica feels her blood pressure spike, a fear rat scurries across her shoulders and she has an urge to turn around, to drive out of here, back to Bismarck, to get on a plane home, to let someone else cover this story. *Save yourself.* Instead, she takes a deep breath and pulls to a stop in front of James Jarrett's ranch house.

He comes out of the house, and Erica is struck by how handsome he is, how lithe, what incredible presence. No wonder Gloria fell so hard. He walks down to her car as she gets out and extends his hand. "James Jarrett, what a pleasure."

His smile is heartbreaking, knee-weakening, and too practiced by half. Erica doesn't trust him. He's a movie star, no doubt, but it's a creepy movie. She's never liked creepy movies. Life at home was chilling enough.

"A lot going on around here," she says.

James looks out at the base and all the worker bees doing their jobs.

"We're getting ready for big things. I thought Mary did an amazing job today."

"She was certainly forthright and forceful." Erica looks him in the eye and sees dry ice.

Jarrett grows grave, and again it feels too polished. "I've been expecting you. I'm sorry it's under such sad circumstances," he says.

"It's a loss. For both of us."

"Please, come in," he says, leading her into the house. "Can I get you a cup of coffee, water, a glass of wine?"

"I'm fine, thanks," Erica says, looking around. The house is immaculate and ordered. Sunlight is blaring through the picture window, and the living room feels close, even claustrophobic. They stand there silently for a moment. There's an enormous fly buzzing against the window, trying to escape.

"Please, have a seat. I don't have a great deal of time, for obvious reasons." He waits for Erica to sit on the living room couch and then he sits in a chair. There's another pause, the only sound is the buzzing fly, the desperate flapping of its wings.

"You must be devastated by Gloria's death," Erica says. She wants to tread softly, ease her way in.

"Gloria was a wonderful woman. And she worked so hard to get where she was."

"She was responsible for the success of *Spotlight*."

"Terrific show. It was very helpful to Mary and Sturges."

"Was it?"

"They came across as the reasonable people they are. Were, in his case."

Clearly this "reasonable people" label is strategic. Breaking away from the republic and forming your own army hardly seems reasonable.

Erica crosses her legs and brushes at her skirt. The air is so heavy in the house. The fly is still buzzing frantically. "Do you have any idea why she would kill herself?"

Jarrett looks down, rubs the back of his neck. "Gloria put a lot of pressure on herself. All her life. I found that touching—her determination, her discipline, her sincerity. But she didn't have an outlet, even a hobby, really, to help her relax. I encouraged her to take up the piano or yoga or photography, but all she cared about was work. The anxiety just built and built. I think this time she just snapped."

Sounds plausible. And Erica doesn't believe a word of it. "I got the impression she thrived on the work. I think it was something else that drove her to jump off that bridge." They lock eyes for a moment. "You know she was in love with you. And claimed you were engaged. She called you her fiancé."

Jarrett can't contain a small narcissistic smirk. "I'm afraid that was a fabrication of her imagination. But we did have fun together."

"So she did have an outlet?" Erica sees that icy look again.

"Well, after she moved to New York, we obviously saw much less of each other."

"But you did get together at times?"

"Now and then."

"In New York?"

A look of annoyance flashes across his face. "Is the *where* really important? The woman is dead."

Now the fly is knocking itself against the window, buzzing and knocking. Erica wants to press her advantage. "Can you tell me about your role in the Homeland movement?"

"I thought you were here to express your condolences."

"Let's just say I'm multitasking."

"As I said, I don't have a lot of time."

"Neither do I." Erica pauses before saying drily, "I have to get back to Bismarck and file a report." The room seems to be getting warmer and the trapped fly more desperate, buzzing and knocking, buzzing and knocking.

Jarrett smiles at her, that tight, chilling smile, and stands up. He casually picks up a magazine off an end table, takes two steps—then suddenly *smacks* it against the window. Silence. All that's left of the fly is a mushy blotch about the size of a thumbnail.

"I'm second-in-command of Homeland's self-defense."

"Did Gloria know that? All she ever told me is that you worked at the Pentagon in military intelligence."

"I'd rather talk about the future."

"Do you know someone named Pete Nichols?"

Erica's curveball has the desired effect—Jarrett blinks but instantly recovers. "No. Should I?"

"We have evidence that Gloria used him to arrange a kidnapping."

"Whose kidnapping?"

"Mine."

"I'm sorry about that. But you look like you're in one piece."

"I'm pretty resilient. But it was no fun."

"Arranging a kidnapping doesn't sound like Gloria."

"No, it doesn't, does it?"

"What are you getting at?"

"Hopefully, the truth."

"Then we're both on the same page."

"Are we? I think someone put Gloria up to it."

Jarrett sits back down, leans back in his chair, and says, "And you think that someone is . . . ?"

"Someone close to her."

"Look, Erica, Gloria is gone. What's happening here is greater than any one person."

"You've moved on very quickly."

"I have a lot of responsibility."

"How did you get involved with Homeland?"

"Through the Bellamys. Their foundation financed my graduate work at Penn. I've known them for twenty years. So I've had two losses in the last few weeks."

"What will you do if President Winters orders military action against the Homeland?"

"I don't think it's going to come to that. We're reasonable people. So is the president."

"You call withdrawing from the union a reasonable action?"

"Why are you here?"

"Because six people connected to the Bellamys have been murdered. No one has been arrested for the crimes."

"I'm sorry to hear that. But it has nothing to do with me."

This guy is hard to rattle. Erica notices a book in Cyrillic on the coffee table. "You speak Russian?"

"I'm trying to keep it up. I learned it at West Point. Then I was a military attaché at the American embassy in Moscow for two years."

This is new information to Erica. "What was that like?"

"You can read all about it in my memoir."

"So you don't use the Russian much these days?"

"Now and then."

"Oh. When?"

Jarrett stands up. "Listen, I've really got to get back to work."

"Would you consent to an interview for *Spotlight*?"

"Yes, of course. We have nothing to hide."

"Everyone has *something* to hide."

CHAPTER 72

IT'S ABOUT TEN MINUTES LATER and Erica has just crossed Devil's Lake and driven past the Spirit Lake Casino. She's piecing together what she just learned. The whole place is so disturbing—it's really happening, this insurrection. And James Jarrett is a merciless man. But she still has no *proof* that he's connected to the murders, or that he put Gloria up to the kidnapping.

What Erica is struck by again and again is the calm confidence of Mary and her inner circle. They're basically giving the middle finger to the greatest power the world has ever known. If she wanted to, President Winters could annihilate them the way Jarrett did that fly on the window. Of course, it's far more complicated than that, both politically and logistically, but still it's David versus a thousand Goliaths. Do they have a magic slingshot? Or some kind of secret weapon?

It's a missile. A missile capable of carrying a nuclear warhead.

Her phone rings. It's an LA number she doesn't recognize.

"This is Erica."

"Hello, Erica, this is Momar Neezan from the LAPD. I got a call from Moira Connelly."

"Of course, thanks for getting back to me so quickly. Did Moy explain what I need?"

"She did. And I would be delighted to try and help. Can you send me the message?"

"Of course. I'll do it as soon as we hang up."

"I'll get back to you ASAP."

Erica is about to forward the message to Neezan when she hears a funny sound, a rustling, rattling sound. It's not loud but it's unmistakable. Is it coming from the engine? The dashboard? No, it sounds like it's coming from under the passenger seat. She looks over and sees a large snake slither out from beneath the seat, with a rattle at its tail.

Erica screams but there's no one to hear her. Then another snake slithers out, then a third, then a fourth, and now they're a slithering rattling mass and one hisses at her and raises its body, poised to strike. Erica jerks the car off to the side of the road and leaps out, racing away from the car, hyperventilating, her heart thwacking in her chest, her body trembling, sweat breaking out all over her. She doubles over and retches but nothing comes out. She wants to cry, but what good would that do? She stands there sucking air as her blood pressure slowly returns to some semblance of normal. But why are her hands still shaking and why is sweat still pouring down her back?

She slowly walks around the driver's side of the car, keeping a safe distance. The door is open and now she can see at least a dozen snakes, slithering and rattling over the seats, the console, the dashboard, her bag. Her phone is in the bag. Her phone with Gloria's last message on it. The car is still running, but she's afraid to reach in and turn it off or grab her bag.

Then a pickup truck pulls off the road behind her. Her fear ratchets up. She remembers the man in the pickup truck in Marin County, he picked her up as she was fleeing Lily Lau's compound, she was running for her life and he pulled over, pretended to be her friend, told her he would take her to safety and she got in his truck, but then he turned it around, he was a minion of evil and he was going to take her back to Lau's lair. But he had a gun and Erica grabbed it and blew his brains out. But she doesn't have a gun now. She doesn't even have the mace she keeps in her bag.

A lean, almost gaunt Native American man of about sixty gets out of the pickup and approaches her. "You all right here?"

Erica doesn't trust him. What if he's one of them. *Them?* She doesn't even know who *they* are. She won't get into his truck, that's for sure. She looks at him. His face is deeply lined, his deep-set eyes look weary but concerned.

"You look pretty shook up," he says.

Erica points to her open driver's door. The man walks over and looks in. "Oh wow, you got something there. They look angry. Those are prairie rattlers, they're not from around here. They only live in the western side of the state. Are you coming from there?"

"No, I was just up at Camp Grafton."

"Oh man, lot going on up there. But no rattlers, that's for sure. How in hell did those things get in your car?"

How did they? Jarrett said he was expecting her. Erica feels dizzy and the sun is so bright and she can't really handle it all anymore, it's too much, it's just too much. She wants out. O-U-T *out*. But there's something she wants more than out—and that's the truth.

"Somebody must have put them there while I was up at Camp Grafton."

"I wouldn't be surprised. I don't trust those people for a minute. Didn't vote for them either. But listen, I can get rid of them for you."

"Please."

He goes back to his pickup and puts on a leather barn jacket, which he buttons to the neck, then turns up the collar. He walks back, pulling on cowhide work gloves.

"Okay now, stand back." He kicks the driver's door shut and comes around the other side of the car. He quickly opens the passenger door, reaches in, grabs a snake, and flings it backward. The snake flies through the air about thirty feet and lands in scruffy prairie grass and slithers away. He repeats this lightning move again and again and again. Then he squats down and peers under the seats. "I think we got 'em all." Then he stands up. "Well, that was intense."

"Can you check the trunk?"

The man reaches in and pops the trunk, then goes and takes a look. "Empty," he says.

Erica walks close to the car and looks inside. No sign of any snakes, but somehow the car, with its motor running, her bag knocked over, looks dangerous to her, like a crime scene just before the crime is committed. Can she really get back in there and drive all the way to Bismarck? Does she have a choice?

"I can't thank you enough."

"Hey, we're all in this together."

As Erica drives away, she laughs bitterly at his sentiment. Then she feels a stab of panicked nostalgia for the young woman who once believed it.

CHAPTER 73

IT'S SUNDAY NIGHT, AND MARY, Neal, General Morrow, and James Jarrett are sitting in the library at the Bellamy house enjoying a bottle of Veuve Cliquot, oysters from Prince Edward Island, paté from Perigord, and caviar from the Caspian Sea. Just a little celebratory snack. They've certainly earned it. There's a roaring fire in the fireplace and the air-conditioning is on.

"We also have Triscuits and peanut butter if anyone would prefer that," Mary says, and they all laugh, although Morrow looks a little wistful. He's such a rube, really. He wouldn't know paté from lard.

Mary is savoring this moment, both for what has been accomplished and for what is to come, soon, tonight. Something terribly exciting. Something that will advance the Homeland. She raises her glass. "To the three of you, the best team that anyone could have. Thank you from the bottom of my heart."

What heart? Mary thinks, smiling to herself. They all toast and sip.

"Now is when we redouble our efforts, parley and leverage this success to bring more states into the Homeland. I spoke to our state directors today in Montana, South Dakota, Idaho, and Wyoming, and they're all deluged with pioneers. We are their example and inspiration. And we are just beginning."

"You better believe we're just beginning!" the general exclaims. He's so florid and emotional.

Mary thinks of the scene in *Hamlet* where the Danish prince instructs the actors: *In the very torrent, tempest, and, as I may say, the whirlwind of passion, you must acquire and beget a temperance that may give it smoothness.* Morrow has too much unbridled id. It's unbecoming. And dangerous. He's a loose cannon, really. Oh well, he won't be for much longer. He was so instrumental in securing Camp Grafton. But sadly, he's outlived his usefulness.

The general takes a bite of caviar and squelches up his face. The poor man looks like he might gag. Shouldn't his last meal be a little more to his liking? Mary reaches out her foot and presses a buzzer on the floor. Within a heartbeat Claire, a day maid doing night duty (at time and a half, you *must* pay help fair wages) appears.

"Claire, could you bring in the Triscuits and peanut butter? And see if there's any luncheon meat to be found, and some sort of cheese, in a hunk, and rolls."

"Of course, Mrs. Bellamy."

"Oh, do you like mustard and mayo, General?"

The general nods eagerly.

"So we'll add those to the order, Claire."

The general smiles in relief as Claire disappears. Mary really is so terribly kind and thoughtful. And a marvelous host, so attuned to her guests' wishes.

"I might have a little sandwich myself," Neal says, smiling at the general. What a thoughtful gesture! Now the general won't be self-conscious eating his bologna and Swiss.

Mary reaches over and squeezes Neal's hand. They're being discreet because the general doesn't know the full . . . *extent* of their relationship. James does. James knows everything. James is brilliant and beautiful, and Mary's been half in love with him since the day they met at West Point twenty years ago. And how richly he's rewarded her faith in him.

The mood in the library is effervescent, laced with heady triumph, a cocoon of charged anticipation. Claire returns with the sandwich fixings on a tray and places it on a table next to the general, who digs right in. Watching him eat sets Mary's teeth on edge. He's crass. She's so glad that she's arranged his murder. The way she did. Talk about two birds. It's genius, plain and simple. She is a genius, isn't she? Really, one of the most extraordinary women in history. A beacon to feminists all over the world. See, ladies, men aren't the only ones who can kill.

Mary is so much more formidable than that lightweight Lucy Winters, that phony, folksy farmer's daughter who's playing way above her pay grade. Mary really can't stand the sight of her; with her earnest voice and that helmet haircut, she looks like an assistant principal at an elementary school. Well, she better not mess with Mary if she knows what's good for her.

"James, I think we should call Anton," Mary says. "To firm up plans. Just in case."

James is so good with Anton. He found him. In Moscow. He charmed him. He reeled him in—of course, five of Mary's many millions sealed the deal. And now he's doing such extraordinary work for the Homeland.

"Will do." James takes out a phone and dials. He immediately starts speaking in Russian. Such an odd language. It sounds like gibberish. Mary expects Putin to recognize the Homeland, and sooner rather than later, if only to embarrass the United States. The quaint, outdated, obsolete United States. It was a silly concept to begin with. To think that such a vast land with such disparate populations could possibly function as a unified whole. The Civil War proved that it couldn't, of course. Although it did buy it another one hundred and fifty years. Then the Homeland was born. And nothing will ever be the same again.

Sitting in the library in front of the roaring fire, Mary isn't sure if she's ever known a moment of such complete contentment. It's the trifecta—celebrating a victory, planning her next move, and having an imminent murder to look forward to. She feels a little shiver of bliss race up her spine. She watches as the general stuffs—*literally*—the sandwich into his mouth. His cheeks bulge like a chipmunk's. A soon-to-be-dead chipmunk. Perhaps she should send Claire out for some Little Debbie cakes for a grand finale to his last meal. She can't suppress a little titter at the thought.

"Anton says he just needs two to three more days," James says. "He and his people have been working twenty hours straight to get it done."

"Tell him how *deeply* grateful we are," Mary says, beaming at Neal and the general.

James hangs up. "So, we should be ready for launch by Thursday. If need be."

"It's so important not to be making claims one can't back up. And we won't be," Mary says, shooting James and Neal a conspiratorial glance. "All systems are go across the board."

"Across the board," James says.

Now the three of them are quiet as the general chomps away. *He's making mouth noises.* He deserves to die for that alone. Neal gets up and tosses another log on the fire. Mary loves how quickly he's becoming the man of the house. Of course, they can't go public with their relationship just yet. Why, Sturges's ashes are probably still warm. But they can certainly go private with it. Later tonight. Oh, she'll be in a wild mood.

Mary steps on the foot buzzer and Claire reappears.

"Do we have any cookies or candy in the kitchen?"

"There are those marzipan elves."

"I don't expect the general is a big *marzipan* fan. Are you, General?" He shakes his stuffed face.

"There's a box of Oreos," Claire says.

"Can you put a dozen in a bag, nicely folded, for the general to enjoy on his drive back to his motel?"

Claire nods and leaves. What a thoughtful gesture. The general will be sent packing filled with cookie-fueled anticipation.

Oh, Mary, you think of everything.

"I'm afraid I'm fading," Mary says.

"I'm amazed you've held up this long," Neal says.

"Well, I did want to have this small gathering, just the four of us, the *first* four. The Founding Fathers, if you will. It's so important to celebrate achievement."

Claire comes in with the cookies in an adorable little bag from Fortnum & Mason. Neal knows how much she loves the bags, and he has them sent to her by the dozen.

The general has mercifully finished his sandwich. He's staying at the Staybridge. Where that Marcus woman was murdered. James is staying at the house. There are house dogs and there are motel dogs. That's simply the way things are.

"Here you go, good sir, for your midnight snack," Mary says, pressing the little bag on the general.

"I appreciate that."

"We appreciate *you*."

"Guess we all better get our sleep," the general says. "Like you said, we're just beginning."

Actually, some of us are just ending.

The men shake hands. Then the three of them stand there looking at the general. It grows a tad awkward. Then Mary lightly touches his arm and leads him through the entry hall to the front door. His car is parked down on the curb across the street. He walks down the brick path, then turns and waves at Mary one last time. She waves back, calling, "Drive safely."

Then she turns around, goes back inside, and closes the door behind her. The three of them walk into the dining room, which is farther from the street. They're only there a moment before there's a flash of light and a deafening boom. Windows shatter in the library and parlor opposite.

"What was that?!" Mary cries, rushing to the front door. James and Neal follow, Mary opens the door, and they see the tangled remains of the general's car, engulfed in flames. Mary can just make out his body, or what's left of it. It's sort of writhing and twisting. Is he still alive, or are those movements involuntary? Whichever, they're thrilling to watch.

CHAPTER 74 ───────────────

JAMES HAS HIS PHONE OUT and calls 911. "Yes, there's been a car explosion in front of Mary Bellamy's residence. One fatality."

Mary leaves the front door open, and the three of them head into the library. The floor is littered with shattered glass.

"This is outrageous. The Winters administration will stop at nothing to undermine us. Assassinating the head of our military. I have no doubt this is the work of the CIA. James, call Steve Wright, our head of communications. I want a statement ready within a half hour. Ask him to bring it over personally. Also, call Judy Born, my legal counsel. I want her here too. And Terri Bertolo, our social media director. Get her on the phone immediately. And Detective Peter Hoaglund. Neal, can you go into the kitchen and ask Claire to put out sandwiches and an urn of coffee in the dining room? Press will be here within minutes. And have her call Morgan, my handyman. I want these rooms cleaned up and the windows boarded. No wait, scratch that. Leave everything as it is. It's a strong visual. Tell Steve and Judy I'll read the statement from the front steps as soon as the press is here in force. *This will not stand.*"

Neal and James watch Mary with raw admiration. They've both seen her go into overdrive before and it never fails to awe them. Mary catches their looks and thinks, *No wonder they're both in love with me.*

James gets Terri Bertolo on the phone and hands it to Mary, who moves into an alcove and lowers her voice.

"Terri, General Floyd Morrow has just been assassinated by federal agents. I want to blanket social media. Ask our supporters to join a vigil outside my house *now*. Tell them to bring candles, that we want to mourn the general. Use this wording: *Illuminate his commitment to our cause and light the way to a better tomorrow.* After everything is posted, get over here and join the crowd out front. When I'm done with my statement—your cue is 'sing thee to thy rest'—start to sing 'Amazing Grace.'"

The next half hour is a whirlwind of emergency vehicles, phone calls, preparations, quick rewrites, press, camera crews. Mary is finally happy with the statement. There's a thicket of press outside and a growing crowd of Homelanders, swelling by the second, filling the street, and still they're arriving, pouring in. Mary peeks out the window: it's so moving and thrilling, the somber faces, many tear-streaked, lit by candlelight. The television crews are filming it all, it's being broadcast live all over the nation, the world. Mary is swept by a wave of exhilaration—*Kristallnacht has nothing on me.*

She takes a minute to pop into the powder room. She looks in the mirror and smiles at herself—with all these people here, the general's Oreos would have come in handy. *Oh, Mary, you are naughty.* Her hair was done yesterday, so she musses it a little, going for the distraught-but-coping look, sort of Maggie Thatcher after that hotel bombing. Then she pinches the web between her right thumb and first finger, digging in her nails so hard that her eyes water. All set.

Statement in hand, she steps out onto the house's front porch as cries of "We love you, Mary! We love you!" come from the crowd.

CHAPTER 75

ERICA IS AT HOME IN her living room, watching it all unfold. She's on the sofa, Greg is in an armchair across the room. It's so shocking and disturbing. It's only five days after the election, and already violence has reared its twisted head. Erica wishes Greg were sitting beside her. But she's not about to invite him.

Erica watches as Mary Bellamy waits until an expectant hush falls over the crowd and then she begins, "Tonight I lost a dear and trusted friend, General Floyd Morrow. But we all lost something greater: a man of extraordinary gifts who was committed to building a strong Homeland and a better world. Floyd was murdered in a savage and unprovoked attack. An attack that was intended to frighten and intimidate us. An act of terrorism. Whoever is responsible will be brought to justice. I have instructed Detective Peter Hoaglund, whom I have appointed director of the Homeland Bureau of Investigation, to stop at nothing to uncover the perpetrators. For, make no mistake, this *was* an attack on the Homeland. And on our supporters in other states. We are a nonviolent movement, but never doubt our resolve: we will not sit back and allow ourselves to be attacked without retribution."

Mary pauses, looks down, fights to control her emotions. Then she looks out over the crowd. "But tonight is a night to remember a great man, a friend to all of us, a visionary, a leader, a man I loved for his passion, his friendship, and his idealism, a man who never failed to inspire all who knew him. *A Homelander*. Good-bye, Floyd, may flights of angels sing thee to thy rest."

And then, from somewhere in the crowd, it starts softly, the singing of "Amazing Grace." At first it's just one voice, and then a dozen and then a hundred and then thousands, thousands of mournful voices singing in the candlelight, a beacon in the darkness of the endless Plains night:

Amazing grace!
How sweet the sound
That saved a wretch like me!
I once was lost,
But now am found;
Was blind, but now I see.

"She's very compelling," Greg says. "She understands the visceral power of an emotional moment. She's bonding with her followers on a profound level. The woman is a brilliant performer, a brilliant politician."

"She is, isn't she? She frightens me. I don't believe it, I don't buy it. There are too many unanswered questions. Too many dead bodies. How do we know that car bomb wasn't planted by Mary's allies? That James Jarrett is her lead fixer. And putting Peter Hoaglund in charge of the investigation, when he's pledged his fealty to the Homeland? If that's not a fox and a chicken coop, what is?"

"What exactly do you think her goal is?"

"Power. It's always power. Or money. Or sex. She's got money. She's got Neal Clark. This is a woman who wants to play on the world stage. I will say I think she actually believes in what she's fighting for, this idea of splitting up the country into groupings of like-minded states. So in that sense she's at least sincere. But I've seen it in her eyes, the same thing I saw in Nylan Hastings and Lily Lau. The heart of darkness. If she goes through with establishing a viable Homeland, she'll force President Winters to step in militarily, and the death toll could number in the tens of thousands. And it would wrench the country apart politically, culturally, morally."

"But if she forms a viable country and we invade it, that will make us occupiers. Guerilla groups, clandestine militias will spring up. And they'll be able to cast themselves as freedom fighters," Greg says.

"There are so many layers to this story, and so many possible outcomes."

Erica realizes, with a small start, how much she values Greg's thoughts, his insights. Discussions like this one used to be the norm for their marriage. She misses them, a casualty of their recent distance. This is a man she loves and treasures on so many levels. Still . . . she can't ignore the riffs, the envy, the flirtations with other women.

And now Detective Peter Hoaglund is on-screen, being interviewed by GNN stringer Alicia Walden. Erica curses herself for flying back to New York this morning. She should be on the ground out there.

"I'm here with Detective Peter Hoaglund of the Bismarck Police Department. Can you tell us your thoughts on this bombing?"

"Actually, Alicia, I'm director of the Homeland Bureau of Investigation."

"Of course."

"This crime was a heinous act of cowardice and terrorism. The Homeland has been attacked. We will use all of our resources to track down the person or persons responsible," Hoaglund says.

"Do you have *any* leads, clues, or suspicions at this point?"

"We know that the general arrived at the Bellamy house at approximately seven thirty this evening. He left shortly after nine. Someone planted this car bomb during that interval. We have already begun canvassing the neighborhood to see if anyone observed suspicious activity. Now I have to get back to work."

Erica mutes the television. "I need to get back out there."

"Erica, you can't solve every crime. And—PS—the home fires need a little stoking."

She doesn't like the tone of his voice. And how many glasses of wine has he had? Greg gets up, crosses to the wet bar, and refills his glass. "And there's something I need to talk to you about."

"Is it Leslie Wilson's recent separation?"

"What? No."

"I know that she and Stan have both starting seeing other people."

"Of course you know it, she stated it in the *Sunday Times*. There are no secrets here."

"There aren't? I don't know what you do when I'm out of town."

"That covers a lot of territory. You're gone more than you're here."

"You're beginning to sound like Jenny."

"Well, I can certainly see her point."

"Well, I'm not sure *I* can see the point of this anymore," Erica says, standing up and gesturing around the room, the apartment, encompassing their marriage.

Then her phone rings. It's a Los Angeles number, and she recognizes it as being Momar Neezan, the forensic audiologist out in Los Angeles. Erica forwarded him Gloria's last message yesterday.

"Momar, have you had any luck?"

"This tape is very difficult to decipher. The background noises are almost impossible to segregate out because they come from multiple sources. Deafening fireworks exploded at the exact moment that the car horn, which was only feet from Washburn, sounded. Then there is the rumbling of the traffic on the bridge and the screams and shouts of the celebrants leaning out of car windows."

"Is it hopeless?"

"No. Not at all. I've made some progress. And I'm going to keep working. But let me play you what we have so far." He turns on the recording. Gloria's voice has been slowed down, and it sounds elongated, as if she was on a drug of some kind:

"I'm sorry, Erica, for being a bad girl. I did hire that man in Boston to kidnap you. I have to tell you something else though, they're bad people, worse than me even, and they're working with a Russian scientist up in Canada and"—then the fireworks explode and Gloria's last words are inaudible and then the phone hits the ground and goes blank.

Erica tries to digest what she's just heard. *A Russian scientist? In Canada?* But what were Gloria's final words? She clenches her jaw in frustration. "We need the end, Momar."

"Yes, I know. I'll keep working. I thought this much might be helpful."

"It is, and I'm very grateful. But something big is going down, and I think it's on that tape. We *need* that information."

Erica hangs up, and Greg crosses to her. "Erica, what is it? You suddenly turned as white as a sheet."

She moves away from him and collapses on the couch.

"Erica, please, tell me." His face is full of concern. And she needs him right now. Leslie Wilson or no Leslie Wilson.

"Gloria said that Mary Bellamy is working with a Russian scientist up in Canada."

"What does that mean?"

"I don't know. I would guess they're probably working with the scientist to develop a weapon of war. It could be chemical weapons. Poisoning agents to use on a civilian population, maybe in the water supply. A nuclear warhead. Take your pick."

"No . . . ," Greg says.

Greg goes and sits next to her, takes a hand in his. Erica says, "Don't tell Leslie, don't tell *anyone*. First of all, we need corroboration, we need Gloria's last words. Second, if it is true, the more people who know, the more likely it is that Bellamy will find out. And the more danger I'll be in."

"Of course. But what's our next step?"

Our next step, Greg, really? His support feels a day late and a dollar short.

Erica is at a loss. She needs to think, to calm down and think. She gets up and strides into the kitchen and pours herself a glass of water and downs it in one gulp. Greg follows her. "If it's in Canada, Neal Clark is the key here, I'm sure of it."

"Shouldn't you call the police, the FBI, the Canadian authorities?" Greg says.

"I'll call the FBI tonight. Canada doesn't have a federal police force, things are left to the provinces. And I think Neal Clark pretty much owns Manitoba. Plus, all we have are Gloria's words. Not a shred of evidence. I *have* to get back out there. I have to find the truth."

Greg looks glum and left out.

"What did you want to talk about?" Erica asks.

Greg hesitates, as if he's about to jump into the deep end. Then he says, "I've been offered a job running the news department at KHOU in Houston."

Erica is surprised, shocked even. He never told her he'd applied. "Okay. And . . . um, are you inclined to take it?"

"It's the country's fifth biggest market. The station has a healthy news budget. I'd be running the whole show."

"In Houston."

"True, but it would be a springboard to get me back to New York."

"I'm sure they want you to sign a contract."

"Two years."

"That seems like a long time right now. And why did you have to hit me with this tonight, after what just happened in Bismarck, what I just learned about Gloria? You know how invested I am in this story. A woman's throat was slit because she was going to tell me something."

"Oh sorry, I'm not allowed to have a life because there's breaking news?" He paces before saying, "Listen, Erica, we both know this isn't working. I feel like I'm coming home to a meat locker. A little separation might do us good."

Erica feels a splitting headache coming on. She closes her eyes and breathes. And then a terrible sadness washes over. She loved Greg, she loves him, he was her everything just two years ago. And now this. It's hurt. Pure hurt. Tears well behind her eyes. But tears aren't fair. To Greg or to herself.

"Oh, sweetheart, I'm sorry it's come to this," Greg says. He crosses the kitchen and cups her head in his hands. They look at each other. Is it still there? The love? Part of her yearns to fall into his arms, to let go . . . Can she let go? Can she ever let go? She's wound up so tight, bound by the pain of her past, her childhood, her mistakes, her fall, her mothering. In the end, she has only herself. That's all she's ever had. Loneliness opens up in front of her like an abyss. She breaks away from Greg, goes to the sink, and washes a mug and two small plates. She can't turn and look at him, she's afraid if she does she'll dissolve into a puddle of tears.

"I . . . ah, I think I'll take a little walk," he says.

"Okay," Erica manages, drying the plates and mug even though they're already dry.

"I'll sleep in the guest room tonight. And I'm inclined to take the job in Houston."

Greg walks out of the kitchen, and Erica waits to hear the front door close. Then she looks longingly at the wine rack. She'd like to open a nice red and drink it straight from the bottle, just guzzle down the whole thing. For starters.

CHAPTER 76

IT'S 3:12 A.M. AND PRESIDENT Winters is lying in bed wide-awake, staring at the ceiling. Sleep is out of the question. Beside her, First Man Ed Winters is sleeping like a baby, and she envies him. Nights like this she envies just about everyone. But she fought to win the job, and no matter how awesome the responsibility, she is going to serve the citizens of this country. She throws back the covers, puts on a robe, and walks into her adjoining office.

After watching coverage of General Morrow's murder earlier in the night, she called Paul Adams, her national security advisor, and pressed him on whether it was the work of the FBI or CIA. If it was, she would be *profoundly* disturbed. Actions of that gravity must be cleared with the president, and assassination is never an acceptable means. Adams made some calls and then assured her that no one in the government had anything to do with the bombing.

That begs the question, who *was* behind the murder? Well, who gained the most? Mary Bellamy, of course. Her so-called Homeland— just saying the word to herself raises Winters's blood pressure—suddenly has a martyr. How convenient. From the dossier on Bellamy that the FBI prepared for her, the president knows she is a ruthless businesswoman who has had over a dozen complaints filed against her with the National Labor Relations Board. They came from employees at her various companies who alleged discrimination, underpayment of wages, sexual harassment, and dangerous working conditions.

Winters hates that kind of corporate behavior. You can make billions in profit and have plenty of money left over to treat your employees fairly. It's a moral issue, and it goes right to the heart of the president's philosophy. She also knows that Bellamy's late husband, Sturges, was a closeted homosexual who, despite having passed his last physical with flying colors, died of a sudden heart attack and was cremated before an autopsy could be performed. And that Bellamy is currently romantically involved with Neal Clark, the Canadian billionaire who just signed an agreement with the Homeland to build a pipeline that will guarantee the breakaway state billions of dollars in revenue. Oh, she's smart, Bellamy is. But Lucy Winters is not going to let her play this president for a fool.

She goes to the window and looks out at the White House South Lawn, the Ellipse, and the Washington Monument beyond. It's a stunning view, a reminder of our nation's greatness. Democracy is messy and hard, just look around the world, but somehow we've made it work. Because men and women of goodwill, no matter what their differences, came together, compromised, and took actions that kept us united and moved us forward, kept the arc of history bending toward justice.

But there are times when compromise is weakness. And this may be one of those times. If the president's suspicions are correct, she's dealing with a psychopath. Which means all bets are off.

Lucy Winters hugs her robe around her, closes her eyes, and looks deep into her soul. She loves her husband and her children more than life itself, but she loves her country just as much. And she's not going to let it be torn asunder by a madwoman.

She picks up her phone, calls Paul Adams and General Maria Sanchez, and orders them both to report to the White House immediately.

CHAPTER 77

ERICA ARRIVES AT GNN ON Monday morning. She called the FBI last night and was assigned a contact, but they also informed her that they have no jurisdiction in Canada and can't pursue a case there. It would violate a treaty between the two nations. As she walks into her office, Erica calls Mort Silver even before she sits down.

"Mort, I want to move *The Erica Sparks Effect* out to North Dakota for the week."

"Erica, it's Monday morning. There just isn't enough time. The logistics."

"This story is about to get bigger. Much bigger. We want to be out there. Trust me."

"We've got our stringers. Alicia Walden is doing a terrific job. And just what do you mean by *much bigger*?"

"Confrontational."

"You privy to some classified information?"

"You might say that."

"What is it?"

"You're going to have to trust me." Time to put the screws on. "Mort, either we move the show out there or we find a substitute host for me for the week. Because I'm going to Bismarck. Your call."

"You're threatening me."

"I'm being the best journalist I know how to be."

Mort exhales with a sigh of surrender. "Do you know how much this is going to cost?"

"A lot less than it would cost if we got scooped."

"Good point."

Erica hangs up and calls Eileen McDermott. "You're going to hate me, but we're heading back to Bismarck for the week."

There's a pause. "I can tell from your tone of voice that resistance is futile. I'll pull it together. We'll just use the same set we used last week. Let me get to work."

Erica's next call is to Neal Clark.

"Erica! Terrific job last week. And on *Spotlight*. You're our favorite journalist."

Hooray. "Listen, I want to do a little piece on you and your relationship to the Homeland."

"All I've done is be a smart businessman."

"By providing the Homeland with a ready outlet for their oil, you're helping to bankroll them." Erica pauses before getting a little closer to the bone. "And I want to examine your relationship to Mary Bellamy."

Clark coughs uncomfortably. He's not naïve enough to deny what's an open secret. "Can I be honest with you, Erica?"

"That's all I ever want."

"Off the record?"

"Off the record."

"We have to be discreet. At least for now. You may not know this, but Mary's marriage was more of a partnership than a love affair. Sturges Bellamy was gay. Once a little more time has passed since his death, we'll go public with our relationship."

He's a clever fellow. His admission is disarming. But Erica's got more than one arrow in her quiver. "When we discuss your relationship with Bellamy, we'll stick to the business side."

"I really prefer to stay out of the limelight as much as possible."

"I'm going to do my piece, with or without your cooperation. If I do it without, it will change the angle I approach it from. I will, of course, have to inform viewers of your refusal to appear on camera."

The vibe between them grows tense. "Hardball, eh?"

"Call it what you will."

"I call it a threat, and I don't like being threatened. What do you want?"

"I want a filmed interview."

"You're *not* our favored journalist anymore."

"My loss."

"Call my secretary, she'll tell you my availability."

"You're a privately held company. I'd like to see as much information as possible on your holdings."

"I'm under no obligation to provide that."

"Either you provide it or I go out and find it. And if it's the latter, well, once again, viewers will be informed of your resistance. When you and Mary do go public, that could cause you both some serious problems."

"You're a bulldog."

"I'm a journalist."

Erica hangs up and gets ready for her trip. She has a clothes closet at work, kept filled and up-to-date by her great pal Nancy Huffman, GNN's former wardrobe supervisor, who struck out on her own as a designer thanks to exposure Erica gave her. She now works for Erica on a freelance basis, and it's some of the best money Erica spends. She grabs a few outfits and tosses them into her carry-on.

She and her team are going to have to throw together tonight's broadcast on the fly. She'll lead, of course, with General Morrow's assassination and its aftermath. There's also a major drought in Argentina and Chile, flooding in London, and an unrelenting heat wave in Chicago that has already killed dozens of seniors. The planet is coming apart at the seams, and it fills Erica with a pervasive anxiety that flares and wanes and flares and wanes in a never-ending cycle.

She heads down to hair and makeup. Eileen will arrange for local freelancers in Bismarck, but might as well get today's over with now. A good application and comb-out will last all day, and Rosario and Andi are the best.

As she's striding down the hall her phone rings. It's Dirk. Erica feels her anxiety spike. She stops in her tracks.

"Hi, Dirk."

"I have some upsetting news, Erica."

"What?"

"Jenny's been caught with pot."

"Caught? By whom?"

"By the police. At the mall."

"Was she arrested?"

"Yes. As a juvenile, of course."

"They're not holding her, are they?"

"I posted bail."

"I'll hire her the best lawyer in the state. I suspected she was smoking. I didn't want to blow it out of proportion, though. Every kid today tries pot."

Yeah, Erica, but every kid doesn't have both a mother and a grandmother who are addicts.

"It's not that simple, unfortunately."

"What do you mean?"

"Jenny wasn't just smoking pot. She was selling it."

Erica closes her eyes and leans against the wall.

Someone, please tell me this is a nightmare and I'm going to wake up.

"Where is she now?" Erica asks, heading back to her office.

"She's at home. I've grounded her for the rest of the summer."

"Isn't that a little harsh?"

"In the last couple of months she's pulled that stunt with the YouTube video, she's been involved in a major bullying battle, and now she's dealing pot. I'm worried about her."

"Listen, the Homeland story is about to blow up big-time, and I have to head out to Bismarck today."

There's a long pause. "Figures. Why don't I call your assistant and see when we can schedule a call?"

"That's not fair."

"Yes, it is. You've abrogated your duties as a mother."

Erica is hit by a tsunami of guilt. Then comes anger. And sadness. And hopelessness. Then she hangs up with Dirk and calls Sentient Jet and books a private plane to Boston, leaving as soon as she can get out to the airport.

CHAPTER 78 ————————————————————

IT'S MONDAY MIDMORNING AND MARY Bellamy is in her office at the state capitol, surrounded by a half dozen of her closest aides. There's an enormous amount to be done, tasks both large and small, including issuing decrees and orders, hiring staff, getting the Homeland website up, changing signage, meeting with legislators—some of whom are recalcitrant about switching their loyalty to the Homeland—and dealing with scores of media requests from the United States and the world. There have been reports of North Dakotans unhappy with her ascension moving away. Good riddance. Having them gone will only solidify her power. The people around her are all veterans of her recall campaign. Dan Lundgren is her chief of staff—he's young, smart, and she trusts him implicitly. James Jarrett is back at Camp Grafton, overseeing the training of recruits. He has supplied Mary with a half dozen plainclothes bodyguards, the best of the best, all former marines who have volunteered to serve the Homeland as her protectors.

"Are we ready to go out and meet the citizens of the Homeland?" Mary asks. Everyone eagerly nods their assent. Her first stop today is going to be an elementary school. She's ordered new materials for all the schools that remove any mention of North Dakota as one of the United

States of America and detail the birth and growth of the Homeland. And of course she banned the reciting of the Pledge of Allegiance or the singing of any so-called patriotic songs. She'll commission a Homeland anthem soon. She's going to use today's school visit as the venue to announce a competition to design the Homeland's flag, open to every resident of the nascent nation.

As they leave her office and walk down the halls, the state employees they pass almost genuflect to their leader. She waves and smiles. It's all going so well. The general's assassination has generated a deluge of outrage, just as she knew it would. Homeland movements in other states are reporting a big surge in membership. And at the center of it all is . . . Mary. She's really on her way to becoming a deity, isn't she? To see the adoration on the faces of the masses is so affirming. They quite literally worship her. And they should. She's a goddess. Destined to build and lead an empire.

Mary and her entourage walk out of the capitol building and down the front steps. It's a lovely sunny day, what looks like a media helicopter hovers above the scene, and clutches of tourists and pioneers wave and shout at the sight of her, their faces exploding with excitement. She greets a group of about a dozen people, who squeal and jump up and down and turn bright red. And she's so gracious in response. Although she *loathes* it when they touch her. How dare they? Perhaps she'll issue a decree: anyone touching the premier will have their hands chopped off. Mary smiles at the thought, and the silly shriekers think she's smiling at them. More of her squealing subjects race over. Phones are held up, filming the scene—they'll brag about this moment for the rest of their lives. Mary points to her watch and gives a charming shrug. She and her entourage move toward the row of cars that will transport them to the school.

Suddenly eight Navy Seals emerge from around the side of the building and race toward Mary and her aides. In the sky the helicopter swoops down toward the lawn, ready to land. "RAISE YOUR HANDS AND STAND STILL!" one of the Seals screams.

Mary's bodyguards whip out their automatic weapons and start shooting. The firepower is returned. One of Mary's bodyguards throws her down to the ground and covers her body with his own. He's shot in the back and grunts in defeat and then he's shot in the head and now his blood, carrying bits of bone and hair, is pouring over Mary's face and scalp. She lies motionless until the shooting stops. Then she turns to see that all eight Seals are lying on the ground, dead. Two of her bodyguards are still standing. Dan Lundgren is lying nearby, clutching his stomach and moaning. The helicopter is about to land, and Mary's remaining bodyguards turn their fire on it, riddling it with bullets. The helicopter reverses and ascends about fifty feet, then lurches to the side and crashes back to earth, bursting into flames.

Mary struggles to get out from under the dead body. As she crawls away—and just before she goes into shock—she thinks, *Thank God it was all caught on camera.*

CHAPTER 79

ERICA IS IN THE CAR that's taking her out to Dedham to see Jenny. She's booked the jet to take her from Boston to Bismarck after the visit, giving her approximately two hours. Is that enough time to repair a mother/daughter relationship that seems rent at the seams?

As Erica looks out at the familiar New England landscape she feels a surge of nostalgia. This is where she got her start. This is where she became a star. Married a nice man. Had a beautiful daughter.

Beware of answered prayers.

This is where she started drinking at 9:00 a.m., this is where her marriage fell apart, this is where she appeared on air intoxicated, this is where she kidnapped and terrified her own daughter, driving her to a seedy motel and leaving her alone while she went on an "ice cream run" to the nearest liquor store.

Erica can feel her anxiety level spike as they approach Dirk and Linda's house. And, yes, Jenny's, it's Jenny's house, it's where she lives. Not in New York with her mother. That's where she *used* to live.

Beware of answered prayers.

She makes a pact with herself: today she will be absolutely honest with her daughter. Honesty is her North Star in her work—she must bring it to this table as well. She and Jenny have to understand and accept each other. It's the only way forward.

The car pulls up in front of the modest house—and Erica feels a stab of envy. Wouldn't it be nice to live in a small house and have small concerns and small pleasures?

So much for your pledge of honesty, Erica. You'd be bored out of your skull in twenty-four hours and you know it.

"I won't be too long," Erica tells her driver as she gets out.

Erica notices the car from Sentinel Security across the street. The detective is on his cell, but he duly notes Erica's arrival. It's reassuring. At least she can protect Jenny from *some* threats.

Dirk comes out of the house to greet her. He's a nice man, a good man, but it's hard to believe they were once married. They met so young, he was kind and smart and respectable and attractive, he represented what she longed for and had never had—a stable home life. They're different people today, and their only commonality is their daughter. For better or worse, Erica is having a big life, bigger than she could have ever imagined. And that's one genie you can never put back in the bottle.

"Thanks for coming," Dirk says.

"Of course. How's she doing?"

"She's very moody. I can't get her to say two words, and she rarely comes out of her room."

"Okay," Erica says as they step into the house. The staircase is right there, and Erica steels herself and climbs it. Jenny's door has a sign on it that reads *Entry by Permission Only.* Erica knocks. "Hi, honey, it's your mom. May I come in?"

"I'm busy," comes the heartbreaking answer from behind the door.

"Well, I'll just wait out here until your schedule frees up." Erica sits on the floor and leans against the wall. In the quiet she can feel the awareness, the connection between them, it's an invisible vein carrying . . . disappointment and anger and mistrust and hope and . . . *love.* "So . . . may I ask what you're busy with?"

"What difference does it make?"

"Just mom curiosity, no big whoop."

There's a pause and then, "I'm reading one of the books on the summer reading list."

"Cool. What is it?"

"*Their Eyes Were Watching God.*"

"I love that book."

"You read it?"

"Yes. When I was just about your age. I found it at the library and devoured it. What do you think of it?"

"It makes me sad. And happy. I love it." There's a pause and then, "Okay, you can come in now."

Erica stands up and opens the door. Jenny is on her bed, propped up on pillows. She's wearing jeans and a T-shirt and she looks older somehow. And she's so pretty, she's going to be a beautiful young woman in no time at all. Her little girl has rounded a corner and is heading into a whole new phase of her life. How desperately Erica wants to be part of it.

Erica sits on the side of the bed. She and Jenny look at each other for a tentative moment and then Erica gives Jenny a kiss and a hug. Jenny hesitates and then returns the hug. Erica cups Jenny's face in her hands. "You look very pretty."

"I wonder where I got that?"

"Don't say I never came through for you. So . . . how are you feeling about . . . ?"

"Being arrested?"

Erica nods.

"I feel rotten about it. I'm sorry to put you and Dad through this."

"Can I tell you what worries me the most about it? What scares me the most?"

It's Jenny's turn to nod.

"I'm an addict. Susan is an addict. The gene is in the family."

"I'm not an addict, Mom."

"It can start small, with a little pot."

"Yeah yeah yeah."

Erica decides not to go any further down that path right now. "Just keep it in mind." She takes one of Jenny's hands in her own. "I've been doing a lot of thinking . . . about *us*."

Jenny looks down, but Erica can see that she's listening carefully.

"I've put an awful lot of pressure on myself to be a good mom. So much pressure that it makes me insecure and bumbling, and then I do or say the wrong thing and make matters worse. Then I hate myself. You know I had a rotten, worse than rotten—I had a sick relationship with Susan, and I start to think there's this legacy in our family of terrible mothers . . . And, well, you know, Jenny, I just go down some very dark holes. It's painful. I love being your mom, and I love you more than I can say, but I think we both have to accept that I'm never going to be the mom you may want. Or even the mom that I may want to be. I have a lot of ambition and drive, my work is just terribly important to me, and I think the work itself is important. The truth is important. Justice and fairness are important."

"But see, Mom, that bothers me. You want to save the world, but you don't have time for your own kid."

"I don't have as much time as I wish. That's true. The fact is we're never going to have the kind of relationship a stay-at-home mom or a work-close-to-home mom and daughter have. Do you see what I mean?"

"Yes! We have a worse relationship."

"Does it have to be worse, or can it just be *different*?" Erica stands up and takes a few steps and then turns around. "Oh, honey, I'm asking you to accept me for who I am. Because part of who I am is a woman who loves you with all her heart and wants to be the best friend you'll ever have, who will stand with you and behind you as you grow into the amazing woman you're going to be."

Erica pauses and takes a deep breath.

"And part of me gets annoyed sometimes at the demands of being a mom, the emotional demands, the practical demands, who gets consumed by her work, who thrives on adrenaline and even danger, who is bored by domesticity. Who is neurotic and haunted and guilty. If you put it all together you have *me*. The one and only mom you'll ever have." Erica sits back down and takes Jenny's hand in her own again. "And you know what I think?"

Jenny shakes her head.

"I think we're pretty darn lucky to have each other. I think that we have a lot in common, that you're unmistakably *my* daughter, and that fills me with so much pride sometimes I think my heart is going to burst right out of my chest." She brings Jenny's hand to her face and kisses it, holds it against her cheek for a moment. "Know something else?"

". . . What?"

"I think there are a lot of moms and daughters out there who wish they could have what we have. Our connection, our commitment to each other, even at the low points. *Our love.* But we are kind of flying blind, there's no rulebook for moms and daughters like us. We're just two Sparks girls trying to do the best we can. And I think that's a pretty darn wonderful thing."

Jenny looks away and grits her teeth to try and stop it, but she can't—a single tear runs down her left cheek.

CHAPTER 80

ERICA IS WATCHING THE FOOTAGE on her laptop in a mixture of disbelief, horror, and journalistic excitement. The attempted abduction of Mary Bellamy by Navy Seals has the whole nation riveted. It all went so terribly wrong so quickly. Sixteen men and women are dead: four of Mary's bodyguards, eight Seals on the ground, four more in the helicopter.

Erica is on the private jet that's winging her back to Bismarck; right now they're over Illinois and she can barely contain her impatience. She owns this story, and if she doesn't get on the air soon, the fickle viewers will move to another network. Yes, their stringer is more than competent, but when something this big hits, viewers like to be guided through it by a familiar face. Broadcasting from New York is nowhere near as compelling as reporting from the place where the mission-gone-terribly-wrong actually happened.

The plane lands, and Eileen is waiting for her on the tarmac. As they drive straight to the studio, she fills Erica in on the latest developments. "Dan Lundgren, Bellamy's chief of staff, is out of surgery, in serious but stable condition. Bellamy is at home with her closest advisors, including Neal Clark and James Jarrett. She's expected to make a statement soon, and maybe take some questions."

"Is the Homeland a safe place for journalists? Could Bellamy issue a decree and have us all arrested?"

"As of now, we've gotten assurances that we're safe and welcome. After all, Bellamy has proven herself a master at manipulating the press. She needs us as much we need her."

"Of course all that could change on a dime," Erica says.

"What everyone is really waiting for is some kind of statement from the president. This is obviously an enormous blow to her administration."

"Success has a thousand parents, failure is an orphan. But I think she's got to own this or her credibility will take a big hit."

They arrive at the studio. Erica changes into a fresh outfit, grabs the copy that her head writer just handed her, and gets her game face on. Three minutes later she gets the go signal and the anchor in New York throws it to her.

"This is Erica Sparks, coming to you from Bismarck, North Dakota. Late this morning a mission to abduct Mary Bellamy, the newly elected governor—or premier, as she prefers to be called—of what she has renamed the Homeland of North Dakota, failed spectacularly."

In her earpiece Erica hears Eileen's taut voice: "The president is about to make a statement."

"I've just received word that the president will be making a statement from the White House about today's mission. She's expected in the pressroom within minutes. Let's go to the White House."

GNN cuts away to the White House pressroom. It's jammed with reporters and edgy with anticipation. The president appears, looking grim, and strides over to the podium. She has a briefing book with her; she opens it and reads:

"This morning at approximately 11:10 central time, a mission that I ordered to abduct Mary Bellamy, the newly elected governor of North Dakota, failed. I took this action because Mary Bellamy has taken illegal actions in unilaterally declaring North Dakota a sovereign governing entity not subject to the laws of the United States. By undermining the very foundation of our democracy, Bellamy has put personal gain and aggrandizement over the good of the country. She represents a threat to our nation and to every American citizen. I could not let her actions go unchallenged. Twelve brave Navy Seals died today. Our sympathies go out to their families. I would like to put Bellamy and her cohorts in the so-called 'Homeland movement' on notice that they are in our sights and that we will not rest until the threat they pose has been neutralized. Thank you."

The assembled reporters immediately start shouting questions. Press Secretary Josh Holden steps up to the podium as the president steps down. "The president will not be taking any questions."

GNN cuts back to Erica. "There you have it, the president's short and succinct statement regarding today's aborted attempt by the federal government to take Mary Bellamy into custody. The action had more than one goal. The Winters administration is eager to serve notice to the growing secession movements in other states that the federal government will not tolerate their actions. Will it succeed? Or will it backfire? So far, the condemnation from secessionists around the country has been swift and ferocious. The mood here in Bismarck and across the region can be likened to a tinderbox."

CHAPTER 81

MARY BELLAMY TURNS OFF THE television in disgust. "Who does Winters think she is? Who does she think she's dealing with? She'll find out soon enough."

She's in her library with Neal Clark and James Jarrett, who drove in from Camp Grafton as soon as he heard of this morning's ambush. The front hall, the parlor opposite, and the dining room are all wall-to-wall with flower arrangements from supporters in all forty-nine states, a dozen nations, and the Homeland, of course.

I'm so loved.

It's been an eventful day for Mary. She refused a trip to the hospital after the incident. She was in one piece, fine, thank you. Yes, she was in mild shock, but twenty minutes to regroup in her office was all she needed. Her doctor showed up and suggested a sedative, which she also refused. She did agree to take the rest of the day off. But the last thing she's going to do is cower. It's important for her subjects to see how indomitable she is. When she arrived home, covered in blood, she took a hot shower. Then her massage therapist arrived. That helped. Then Neal and James arrived. And now the president's pathetic statement.

Still, Mary can sense that Neal and James are nervous. They're both having a hard time sitting still; she senses uncertainty and fear. They're reaching a critical juncture in their mission, now is not the time to go weak-kneed. She simply won't stand for it.

"Are we still on track for Thursday?" she asks James.

"We are."

"All right. I want to make a short statement. I think the statehouse steps are the most appropriate place. Tell maintenance not to wash off the bloodstains. Then I'll visit Dan Lundgren at the hospital this evening. Alert Steve Wright, Judy Born, and Terri Bertolo. Get it out all over social and traditional media. We want massive coverage of my statement and my arrival at the hospital. We'll let a pool photographer into Dan's room with me."

"Should we clear that with him, or with his doctor?" Neal asks.

"No," Mary says simply. "Then I want to go visit the widow and children of one of my bodyguards. Have Steve look into which family is the most sympathetic. We want young kids and a distraught wife."

"I have that interview with Erica Sparks tomorrow morning," Neal says.

"She's too curious," James says. "I tried to take her out, but ended up with a near miss."

"By the end of the week she'll be irrelevant," Mary says. She feels just about back to 100 percent. Isn't that amazing? Mere hours after cheating death, she's running on all cylinders. The adrenaline is pumping. The world is waiting. Her mission is transcendent. She is going to end the United States as we know it. And build something far greater. Where the individual is paramount and sacrosanct. Where the cream will rise to the top. She makes a mental note to research sculptors. She wants to commission a statue of herself for the statehouse grounds. Nothing ostentatious, of course.

As she sits at the library desk and starts to make notes on her statement about the morning's failed ambush, she smiles and thinks, *Thank you, President Winters.*

CHAPTER 82

IT'S AN HOUR LATER AND Mary Bellamy—in a black dress—is on the steps of the state capitol, focused and forceful. In front of her is a vast crowd of supporters and media. The mood is somber, with an undercurrent of barely contained blood lust. These people want revenge.

"This morning, agents of the United States federal government undertook an illegal operation on Homeland soil. This reckless and failed endeavor resulted in the death of four Homelanders and twelve federal agents. In addition, my chief of staff, Dan Lundgren, sustained serious injuries. We are a nonviolent movement; however, we cannot and will not allow ourselves to be attacked without retribution. Our resolve has never been stronger. I am conferring with my closest aides, including James Jarrett, the head of Homeland Security, to determine the appropriate response. Thank you all for your kind wishes. God bless you, and may God bless the Homeland."

CHAPTER 83

IT'S THE NEXT MORNING AND Erica is in the offices of the Bellamy Foundation, about to start her interview with Neal Clark. He's put aside any testiness he might feel at being pressured into the interview and is subdued but gracious, even charming, as the two of them are lit and sound-checked.

Save the charm, buddy, I'm looking for some answers.

Eileen gives her the go. "I'm here with Neal Clark, the Canadian billionaire who raised eyebrows when it was announced that he and the so-called Homeland of North Dakota had signed an agreement to build a pipeline from the Homeland to Winnipeg, Manitoba, for the purpose of transporting oil from the Homeland's vast reserves to Canada. Can you tell us how this pipeline venture came to be?"

"Well, Erica, I've been a friend and admirer of Mary and Sturges Bellamy for a decade. We share a belief that private enterprise is the engine of economic growth and personal freedom. I support their movement, and this seemed like a natural, mutually beneficial project."

"Even though it's a violation of federal law to build it without going through the permitting process?"

"The Homeland doesn't recognize the authority of American laws. And neither do I."

"Some people would say that you're exploiting Mary Bellamy and the Homeland."

"Nobody exploits Mary Bellamy."

"You seem to know her very well."

Neal shoots her an icy glance. "When you do business with someone, you get to see their true character in action."

"So in effect you're acting as a character witness?"

"I thought we were here to discuss my business endeavors."

"Business and personal life often comingle, don't you find?"

"That depends entirely on the parties involved."

"Do you have any other joint ventures planned with the Homeland?"

"We're discussing a couple of possible projects. I can't say more than that."

"Why not?"

"Because the talks are preliminary."

"Did you know a Winnipeg businessman named Freddy McDougal?"

Neal flinches slightly but quickly recovers. "I know the name. Never met the man."

"He was implicated in the death of Joan Marcus."

"Joan Marcus?"

"The woman who was murdered in the ladies' room of the Staybridge Hotel."

"Terrible crime."

"Yes. And still unsolved. Were you aware that Ms. Marcus worked as a bookkeeper for one of your companies, Oil Field Solutions?"

Sweat breaks out on Neal's brow. Good. "I had no idea."

"Well, she did."

"Look, I have thousands of employees."

"Yes, but Joan Marcus is the only one who tried to reach me the night she was murdered. She told me she had some important information. I spoke with her just before she was murdered. She sounded frightened. Her daughter believed that she was murdered because she'd seen something troubling at your company."

"Look, this is ridiculous, I have no idea what you're talking about." He uncrosses and recrosses his legs, brushes at his pants leg.

"Can you access Ms. Marcus's employment history at Oil Field Solutions?"

Neal looks like he's about to storm off the set. Then Erica sees something remarkable. He reaches for his water glass and takes a long, slow sip. He nods his head in a little tic, sits up straight, and says, in a voice as smooth as satin, "I'd be happy to. I'm curious myself as to what poor Ms. Marcus was concerned about. You know, she may simply have been disgruntled. Something interpersonal. These things can escalate. But I'll look into it and get back to you as soon as possible."

"So you yourself weren't involved in her murder, or in Freddy McDougal's death?"

Neal Clark smiles indulgently. "Erica, I started working full-time when I was fourteen. I don't have a high school diploma. Everything I have, I've earned. I love what I do. I'm a happy man, a fortunate man, a *blessed* man. I pay my people fairly, provide benefits, and engender great loyalty. Now, what was your question again?"

Erica knows when she's been outmaneuvered. Besides, his loss of composure early in the interview told her what she most wants to know.

CHAPTER 84

AS SOON AT THAT UPPITY little nothing and her crew have packed up and left, Neal calls James and says, "She knows too much."

CHAPTER 85 ————————————————

ERICA HEADS BACK TO THE Holiday Inn. Feeling out of sorts and haunted by a sense of foreboding, she does a vigorous hour of Tae Kwon Do. Just as she's finishing up, her phone rings.

"Hello, Erica, it's Momar Neezan. I've been able to segregate Gloria Washburn's final words on your voicemail. Listen: 'I'm sorry, Erica, for being a bad girl. I did hire that man in Boston to kidnap you. I have to tell you something else though, they're bad people, worse than me even, and they're working with a Russian scientist up in Canada, they're close to developing a nuclear warhead—'" And then the phone hits the ground and goes blank.

Erica stands there as the blood drains from her head and a searing chill races down her spine. She manages a numb, "Thank you."

That's when there's a knock on her door.

CHAPTER 86

ERICA LOOKS THROUGH THE DOOR'S peephole. James Jarrett is standing there.

Erica feels her blood pressure spike as she opens the door. Jarrett favors her with his movie-star smile, which at this point just looks creepy to her.

"What do you want?"

"I'm hoping I can buy you lunch."

"I'm not hungry."

"Well then, I'm hoping we can have a little chat."

"What about?"

"I don't bite, Erica."

"Don't you?"

"Only if provoked."

Erica's wheels turn, race, spin. "You know, on second thought, I haven't eaten yet today. I'll meet you down in the restaurant in five minutes."

"Look forward."

Erica changes into a simple dress with open pockets. She runs a comb through her hair and puts on some lipstick. Then she slips her phone into one of the pockets and her backup phone into the other, grabs her bag, and heads down to the lobby.

The restaurant is buzzing, crowded with reporters, politicians, and hard-nosed businesspeople who look at Bellamy's ascension and see dollar signs. There's always a buck to be made. Jarrett is sitting at a table, reading something on his phone. He looks up and waves Erica over. As she crosses the restaurant she garners looks and smiles of recognition, and she returns them with polite nods. It's reassuring to be out in public, surrounded by witnesses. Still, her heart is pounding in her chest and she feels a light sweat breaking out over her body.

"The joint is jumping," Erica says as she sits. Jarrett puts his phone down on the table beside him. Erica stares at it for a moment. It's an iPhone 6, just like both of hers.

"Everyone wants to be part of history," Jarrett says smugly.

"You're coming off a rough day yesterday."

"It's going to get rougher."

"Say more."

"We'll surprise you."

"I'm already surprised—that you have time for me."

"Erica, we *always* have time for you. How did your interview with Neal Clark go?"

Erica pauses before asking, "How did *he* think it went?"

Now it's Jarrett's turn to pause. "He had some concerns."

"Did he?"

A waitress comes over, she's young and green and star-struck. Good.

"I'd like a large bowl of the minestrone and a grilled cheese on rye," Erica says.

"And a garden burger for me," Jarrett says. When the waitress leaves, there's a taut pause before he says, "Listen, Erica, as you know, I'm in charge of dealing with threats to the Homeland. I think we need to have a serious chat."

"I'm right here."

"You were very helpful in the lead-up to the election."

"Do you mean I gave you the kind of exposure no amount of money could buy?"

He smiles and nods. "Mary was very grateful."

"It's always nice to feel appreciated."

"However, you've gone from useful to nuisance."

"The truth can be so annoying."

Jarrett ignores this. "Now you seem to moving from nuisance to threat."

"Journalists are only a threat to people who are hiding something."

Again Jarrett ignores her words. "We're hoping we can get our relationship back on track."

"What are you offering?"

"The Homeland movement is spreading like wildfire. But its beating heart is right here in Bismarck. With Premier Bellamy. Her plans don't stop at our borders. No, the Homeland will eventually be the world's fifth largest nation. And we're not going to let anything or anyone impede us. Mary plans to expel all unsympathetic journalists this week."

"So you're shutting down the free press?"

"You make it sound so harsh. My point is Mary would like to offer you unprecedented access."

"You mean if I back off, you'll make me Mary's lapdog."

"Cynicism is a dead end."

"Sometimes it's just the beginning."

"And sometimes smart people outsmart themselves." Jarrett swipes his phone and then holds it up so Erica can see the screen. And there's a live shot of Greg jogging around the Central Park reservoir, shot from a few feet behind him. "All I have to do is say the word and your husband is a dead man." He taps a number and then says, jocular and arrogant, "Hey, Phil. Glad to see you're working off a few pounds. Stay tuned for updates." Then he hangs up.

Watching Greg on-screen, Erica feels a stab in her belly, her breath catches, her blood pulses, she feels icy, then red hot, sweat pours from her armpits, she's almost overcome with emotion—some crazy quilt of rage, fear, protectiveness, and . . . *love*.

Erica flashes back on that summer evening when, on the spur of the moment, she and Greg rode their bikes down Hudson River Park to the Battery, bought lobster rolls from a food truck, and sat on a bench feasting as the sun set behind the Statue of Liberty. They barely spoke, there was no need to, they understood each other, it was bliss and contentment, one of the happiest moments of Erica's life. And that time during her first week at GNN when she had a sudden panic attack about going on the air, and Greg sat her down in his office, talked her through deep-breathing exercises and assured her of her talent. He was gentle and considerate and wise. In so many ways he's what she's wanted all her life. And recently she's been sabotaging it all because . . . because on some level intimacy terrifies her. She's been short with Greg and distracted, taken him for granted. Seeing him on the screen, his loping stride, so vulnerable, one phone call away from dying . . . she knows with bone-deep certainty that this is the man she loves, forever and always . . .

"I've seen enough," Erica says. She has an urge to smash Jarrett across the face, to knock that self-satisfied look into next week. Thankfully the waitress is approaching with the tray holding their food. When she's just about to reach them, Erica stealthily slides her left foot into her path.

"Ahhh!" the waitress cries as she lurches forward and the tray slides from her grip. The food flies through the air, splattering Jarrett and Erica with minestrone and mustard and coleslaw.

"You idiot!" Jarrett barks, leaping up from his seat as Erica, in the commotion, slips Jarrett's phone into her pocket with one hand and replaces it with her backup phone with the other. Then she stands up.

"This dress is shot. I'm going to go upstairs and change."

Half the staff seems to be gathered around Jarrett, gushing apologies and dabbing at his suit with wet napkins. Jarrett shoots her a look of frustration but nods.

Erica fights not to break into a run as she crosses the lobby to the elevators. The elevator door opens and she steps on, pressing 2. As the elevator ascends she takes out Jarrett's phone and calls the last number dialed. When the doors open on the second floor, she cranes her head out—nobody in the hallway. As she bolts off the elevator and down the hall to the fire stairs, a male voice answers, "Yes, boss?"

"The mission has been aborted. Turn off the camera and go home."

"Who is this?"

"You're not being paid to ask questions, you're being paid to obey orders. The mission has been aborted."

Erica hangs up as she races one flight down the fire stairs. She reaches the exit door and stops. She goes to Contacts on Jarrett's phone and scrolls through—there's a Russian name: Anton Vershinin. There are two numbers, both with area code 204. Manitoba. She dials the first one. A woman's voice answers, "Prairie Health."

Prairie Health. One of Neal Clark's companies.

Erica hangs up, takes out her own phone, and calls Fred Gershon, her contact at the FBI.

"Fred, it's Erica Sparks. I have information that leads me to believe that Mary Bellamy has nuclear capability, missiles, and that they're in Manitoba."

"We don't have any jurisdiction in Canada."

"Did you hear what I just told you?"

"I did. I'll run it by the director, but our hands are tied."

Stupid bureaucrat. Stupid lousy bureaucrat.

Erica hangs up and calls the White House press office, the only number she has there.

"Press office. This is Frank Merlo."

"This is Erica Sparks and I need to talk to the president."

"You must know that I can't just put you through to the president."

"I need to talk to her!"

"What about?"

"The fact that Mary Bellamy has nuclear missiles. And that she may use one in retaliation for the Special Forces ambush on her."

There's a stunned pause and then Merlo says, "Hold on."

Erica waits, closes her eyes, and struggles to contain her fear. After what seems like an eternity she hears, "This is General Maria Sanchez. Please switch to FaceTime." Erica does. Sanchez is in her fifties, serious. "Okay, so you really are Erica Sparks. What's up?"

Erica spews out the short version of what she knows, closing with, "Don't underestimate Bellamy again."

"I'm going to run this by the president."

"I would do it immediately."

"The president's plate is very full, the failed ambush was a major blow. And I don't think Bellamy is a madwoman. Assuming she does have nuclear capability, which is hardly assured, she has to know that if she orders a preemptive strike, we could blow her so-called Homeland off the map in ten minutes. And of course, we need evidence. Hard, cold evidence. This is all obviously off the record."

"Of course. Please don't waste any time."

Erica hangs up and is hit by a wave of guilt. She's the one who gave Mary Bellamy her platform, who gave her national exposure, who aired a sympathetic interview with her. She let herself be used as a pawn. If the worst does happen, she'll be part of the story. And part of the reason.

And of course, we need evidence. Hard, cold evidence.

Erica pushes the exit door open. She's momentarily blinded by the blazing sun. And it's so hot. Stifling. Her rental car is parked in front of the hotel. She sucks down three deep breaths and as casually as possible walks over to it. She gets in, starts the car, and as she speeds out to Bismarck Municipal Airport, says into her phone, "Private or charter jet rental in Bismarck, North Dakota."

CHAPTER 87 ———————————————————

AS SHE DRIVES, ERICA CHECKS the rearview mirror—she doesn't see a
tail. And then comes the disembodied voice from her phone, "Up and
Away Charter Flights in Bismarck, North Dakota."

"Call."

The phone rings. And rings. Erica feels desperation rising in her
like floodwaters. And then a woman's voice: "This is Up and Away."

"This is Erica Sparks, and I need a plane to take me to Winnipeg,
leaving as soon as possible."

"We don't have any planes available. Since this Homeland business, we've been booking like crazy. I do have some freelance owners
who like to pick up a few bucks. Would you like me to call one?"

"Yes, please, it's *critical*."

"Hold on."

The phone goes blank and Erica wishes they had some mindless
elevator music on, anything to distract her racing brain. She grips the
wheel to stop her hands from shaking; her body is drenched in sweat.

"Miss Sparks?"

"Yes?"

"I've got you a plane, it's a turboprop but he says he can get you to Winnipeg in about an hour and a half."

"I'll take it."

"The pilot's name is Jake Risdal. He'll be waiting on the tarmac."

CHAPTER 88

ERICA TEARS INTO THE AIRPORT lot reserved for private plane passengers, jumps out of her car, and runs toward the turboprop. There's a middle-aged man standing in front of it.

"Jake Risdal?"

"That would be me."

Erica has a moment of panic: Can she trust this man? He looks trustworthy. Doesn't he? This couldn't possibly be a setup. Could it? There was no time to arrange a trap. Was there? Is she out of her mind to undertake this mission? But what if she *doesn't*? Her mind is racing into some dark places. "I'm in a hurry."

"I can see that. Come on."

She bolts up the steps and into the cabin. Risdal follows and heads into the cockpit. Within minutes they're cleared for takeoff and the plane lifts off.

On her phone, Erica searches for Prairie Health's headquarters and gets the location. Then she gets directions from the Winnipeg airport. Then she goes to a satellite map. The Prairie Health campus is surrounded by woods and consists of a large front building and a smaller one behind it.

"Call Avis at Manitoba airport," Erica says into her phone.

"Avis, how may I help you?"

"This is Erica Sparks. I need a car in about an hour. I'm arriving in a private plane. I need the car to be waiting for me on the tarmac."

"That's not standard procedure."

"I don't care what standard procedure is, or what it costs. Can you have a car waiting?"

There's a pause and then, "Certainly, Ms. Sparks."

Sometimes being a celebrity pays off.

Erica takes another look at the satellite map, zooming in as close as she can. Under the heavy forest canopy she can barely make out a dirt track that runs from the laboratory building for about a quarter mile before ending at a clearing. At first glance, and second glance, it looks like a field covered with tall grasses. But then Erica makes out a half dozen outlines, thin, dark seams surrounding circular areas, each about the size of a helicopter landing pad. Each circle is also bisected by another dark seam.

It's loud in the small plane, but Erica sticks her head into the cockpit. "Can you wait for me at the airport?"

Risdal nods his head. Erica returns to her seat and looks out the window, down at the endless expanse of flat prairie. It's too lonely out here. She's too lonely. And frightened. She's so frightened. If only Greg were here. Erica can't face her own thoughts. She pulls up GNN on her phone.

Anchor Carl Pomeroy says, "President Winters is expected in the East Room at any minute to comment on the latest developments in North Dakota. Aides have hinted that she will be announcing some sort of military response." The screen shows the East Room at the White House, it's jammed with journalists and presidential aides. The suspense and expectation are palpable. This is the biggest story in the world.

For a moment Erica wishes she was just reporting on it. Just sitting at a nice, safe desk, or even in the secure East Room, doing her job. But no, she's here in this tiny plane flying north in a desperate attempt to prove that Bellamy and her cabal have nuclear capability and the will to use it . . . Erica shudders, she can't follow the thought any further.

Then President Winters appears in the East Room, walks solemnly to the podium, and says, "I was elected to protect this nation and its citizens. As commander in chief I believe Mary Bellamy and her Homeland movement present a grave threat to our union. They have acted in direct violation of our laws and our Constitution. This has already led to bloodshed. I have met with the Joint Chiefs of Staff and have instructed them to draw up plans to use military force to stop the Homeland movement and remove Bellamy from office. Their orders include keeping civilian casualties to the minimum, but there may be some loss of life. I advise all and any trainees at Camp Grafton that they have been classified as enemy combatants."

CHAPTER 89

THE SIX FIGHTER JETS ARE flying in formation at thirty thousand feet, tearing through the sky on their way to North Dakota. To Camp Grafton on Devil's Lake, to be specific. The pilots have their orders from the commander in chief, and they're going to fulfill them.

CHAPTER 90 ——————————————————

MARY, IN HER OFFICE AT the Homeland Province House, clicks Mute on the television. So that fool Winters is going to take military action. *Go ahead, you'll live to regret it. Or maybe you'll die to regret it.* Mary hasn't decided yet.

She wants James by her side. Neal is fine as far as he goes, but James is her fixer, razor-sharp, he can handle anything. They're going to have to make some important decisions in the next couple of hours, and she needs his counsel.

"Where is James?" Mary asks of her assembled aides, keeping her voice calm and controlled. The muscles in the back of her neck start to twitch. Never mind. Her whole staff looks miserable. They are miserable. Spineless sheep. *This what you signed up for, kiddies. Man up.* Neal is here, but he's pacing and sweating. Is he choking in the clutch? You can't depend on *anybody* but yourself in this life. Well, in the end, she doesn't need any of them. She's done her planning. Still, *where is James?*

"No one has heard from him for over an hour. There's no answer on his phone," Judy Born, Mary's chief counsel, says.

"Can we track his phone?" Mary asks.

"I'm in the process of doing that right now," Steve Wright says.

"Well, hurry up."

There's a moment where the whole room feels suspended, no one is breathing, all eyes are on Wright.

"I've got it!" he exclaims. "The signal looks like . . . well, it looks like he's approaching the Canadian border, south of Winnipeg."

"What is he doing up there?" Mary asks, her voice suddenly raspy, her throat dry.

"The signal is moving very quickly, he must be on an airplane. An airplane approaching Winnipeg."

Mary feels her anxiety level ratchet up. This makes no sense. Why would James be flying to Winnipeg? When they last spoke, he was on his way to deal with that horrible Erica Sparks. What a troublemaker she is. And to think of everything Mary did for her. Giving her that exclusive interview about the Homeland that drove her ratings through the roof. Ungrateful little creep. No good deed goes unpunished. Mary takes Neal's arm and leads him into the office's reception room.

"We need reinforcements at the lab. *Now!*" she hisses.

Neal is already making the call, barking orders to his private security force. "Close the complex. Close the periphery. *NOW!* Nobody enters or leaves." Then he calls Anton Vershinin and says just two words: "High alert."

They walk back into Mary's office in time to see a shot of six fighter bombers piercing the sky as the newscaster says, "The White House has just confirmed that President Winters has ordered military action against the so-called Homeland of North Dakota."

Mary stands stock-still as she watches the jets. She pats her hair as a strange calm comes over her. Okay, it's official. It's started. Well, she's prepared for this moment. Yes, she has.

Mary turns to Judy Born and says softly, "Get me the president on the phone."

CHAPTER 91 ⎯⎯⎯⎯⎯⎯⎯⎯⎯⎯⎯⎯⎯⎯

RISDAL LANDS THE PLANE AND opens the door, and Erica barrels out and climbs into the waiting car. She looks around her. There's a black sedan parked about fifty yards away, a man wearing sunglasses is behind the wheel. Following the satellite map on the dashboard, she speeds out of the airport and gets on Route 7 north. The car follows her. She puts some muscle on the accelerator, pushing it up past sixty, seventy, eighty miles per hour. The black sedan stays right on her. She drives past the Winnipeg suburbs and the traffic thins. She switches lanes, back and forth, and the sedan switches with her. Erica is sweating and sucking air, her heart is thwacking in her chest.

"In three hundred feet, turn right," Siri intones.

Erica sees the exit ahead. It's level, with a grass strip between 74 and the exit lane. She drives past the exit—the sedan almost on top of her—and then she jerks the wheel to the right and peels over the grass to the exit road. The sedan tries to follow, but it's going too fast and cuts too hard and it goes up on its right wheels, then flips over and rolls three times before coming to a smoldering stop. Whoever was in there is no more.

At the end of the off-ramp Erica turns right onto Route 17 and continues for five minutes until Siri says, "In one mile, turn left onto Prairie Health access road."

Then Erica sees a roadblock up ahead, manned by about half a dozen armed and uniformed guards. They notice her and go on high alert. Two guards rush toward a squad car. Erica pulls a screeching U-turn and speeds away, her eyes darting from the road to the satellite map. There's what looks like an old logging road up ahead. She swipes to enlarge it—it looks like it loops around close to the clearing behind the Prairie Health lab. Behind her she hears a siren. She guns it, reaches the dirt track, and turns onto it.

When she's about a hundred yards up the road, she turns her car so that it's blocking the road. She leaps out and starts to run through the woods toward the clearing and the lab.

CHAPTER 92

"THIS IS PRESIDENT WINTERS."

Mary Bellamy is in her office. Alone. She wanted to do this mano a mano. She's standing in front of an ornate mirror—she's never looked more alive, flushed and fiery.

"This is Mary Bellamy."

"What do you want?"

"I want to establish communications."

"Consider them established. Now what do you want?"

"What do you think I want?"

"I'm not here to play twenty questions."

There's such an edge in the president's voice. She really should try and calm down—it's not good for her blood pressure, the poor dear. She's in over her head. Mary pats at her hair and turns to the left, admiring her best angle.

"First I want you to call off your dogs. The fighter jets."

"What's second?"

"I want you to recognize the Homeland."

"That's not going to happen."

"I think you might want to reconsider." Mary reaches into her purse and takes out her lipstick. She uncaps it and applies a fresh coat, leaning in toward the mirror. *Done.*

"I don't negotiate with criminals."

"That's an awfully strong word for a duly elected official."

"Elected, yes. Anointed, no."

"You see, Lucy—you don't mind if I call you Lucy, do you? I love Lucy." Mary titters at her witticism. Winters is such a stick-in-the-mud, Mary can practically smell her disapproval through the phone line. *Tsk-tsk.* "The thing is, dear, I have four missiles equipped with nuclear warheads that will fire at my command. One is aimed at Seattle, one at Chicago, one at New York, and one at Washington—that would be the one that would vaporize you. *Poof!*"

There's a pause and then, "I don't believe you."

But Mary can hear the uncertainty in her voice, and she flushes with triumph. But enough of these silly games. "So call my bluff. Either release a statement within a half hour stating that we have started negotiations on sovereignty for the Homeland or I'll nuke Seattle. Such a dreary, gray city, it could use a little pop and fizz." Mary laughs discreetly. She's on a roll.

"I don't negotiate with terrorists."

"Ta-ta then. The countdown begins." Mary hangs up and calls Anton. "Half hour till blastoff."

CHAPTER 93 ——————————————————

ERICA RACES THROUGH THE WOODS, sucking air, her heart pounding, temples throbbing, all fear and sweat. Praying her sense of direction is true, she cuts through the underbrush on a diagonal. Then suddenly, there in front of her, through the trees, she sees the grassy expanse. At this distance the launch portals are more obvious, the ghostly outlines of the doors visible through the grass. Past them, in the distance, she can see the back of the lab building. There's a guard posted at the rear door.

And then, with a loud grinding sound, the door on one of the pads slowly pulls apart. There's a gaping hole in the ground and then a missile slowly rises out of the earth, pointing west. It's black, terrifying, the size of a small submarine. Erica flashes on images of Hiroshima, the explosion, the mushroom cloud, the aftermath, when the living envied the dead . . .

Erica pulls out her pistol and races toward the lab.

CHAPTER 94 ———————————————

ANTON VERSHININ, IN HIS OFFICE at the lab, hangs up with Mary Bellamy and takes a moment to savor the exquisite feeling of power that's coursing through his veins. They're going to do it. With a bomb that's five times more powerful than the one dropped on Hiroshima, that will turn Seattle into a crater and vaporize its spoiled latte-slurping millennials. A bomb *he* built. Putin will curse the day he disrespected Anton Vershinin.

But as thrilling as the sensation is, he has no time to savor it. He gets up, walks out into the corridor, and heads to the stairs that will take him down into the bowels of the building, to the control room, where the buttons are. The little red buttons that will unleash a new chapter in human history.

CHAPTER 95

ERICA COMES OUT OF THE woods just fifty feet from the back entrance of the lab. The guard sees her.

"Who are you?!" he demands, raising his rifle. "Stop or I'll shoot!"

"Don't shoot! I'm with Vershinin!"

The guard's forehead knits in confusion.

Erica reaches him. "Let me show you my ID." Erica turns as if she's reaching for her pocket and then swings back lightning fast and kicks the guard in the stomach with every ounce of her strength. An explosive grunt comes out of him and he goes down. She brings the handle of her pistol down on his skull, hard, knocking him out.

Erica tries the door. Locked. She stands back and blasts it open with her gun.

She's in a long corridor. Up ahead, just disappearing into a doorway, she sees the back of a man, he looks older, has white hair. Erica races down to the doorway and pushes it open. She's in a stairwell. She sees the man rushing down the stairs a flight below. He turns and sees her. His face fills with alarm.

"*Stop!*" Erica cries.

He picks up his pace, racing down the stairs to a door and exiting.

Erica takes the steps two at a time, flying down. She reaches the door, pushes it open, and sees the man dart into a room across the hallway. He slams the door behind him and she can hear the lock turn but she throws her body against the door an instant before the lock clicks, and the door flies open. The man has been knocked to the floor but he turns and scrambles in the direction of a console covered with buttons with tiny lights beside them. One of the lights is red.

The man clambers to his feet and reaches out, his finger is six inches from the button. Erica throws herself across the room and slams into him. He cries out in pain, they both fall to the floor, and he folds himself into a small mass, sucking air and moaning.

Erica holds her gun to his temple. Then she thinks of Greg. And Jenny. Then she takes out her phone.

CHAPTER 96

MARY IS IN HER OFFICE at the Province House with Neal. They're waiting for *the call*, the one from Anton telling them the missile has been launched.

Mary is a little bit anxious, just a little, nothing she can't handle. She can handle anything. Neal is putting up a good show, but his eyes are darting and his collar is damp.

Then there's a *boom!*—a sudden loud boom that seems to shake the building.

"What was that?!" Neal asks.

Mary goes to the window and looks up. The sky is filled with fighter jets, a dozen of them.

Then her phone rings—*it's Anton!*—and she grabs it.

"Anton!"

"No, Mary, it's me, Erica Sparks. I just wanted to say hi. Oh yes, and to tell you that I'm here with Anton and that the launch has been aborted."

"You're lying!"

"Anton, say hi to Mary."

Anton comes on, he sounds like a broken man. "I am sorry, Mary, but I am going to tell everything."

"You are not! You cannot! You sniveling, pathetic little coward!"

Mary goes back to the window. A half dozen Black Hawk helicopters have landed on the Province House grounds, and troops are leaping off them and running toward the building. Up in the sky another squadron of fighter jets flies low, setting off more booms that shake the city.

"I think it's over for us," Neal says.

Mary whips around. "*Et tu*, Neal? After everything we did, all our work, you're ready to surrender? To betray me? You're a worm, a yellow-bellied traitor to the Homeland, you deserve to die." Mary runs over to the office door and locks it. Then she runs over to her desk and pulls a gun from a drawer. She starts to rush around the room like a caged animal, in a frenzy. Footfalls, running footfalls, echo in from the hallways.

"Open this door!" a man's voice shouts.

"Never!" Mary screams. "The Homeland will triumph! The Homeland forever!"

And now there's loud thumping against the door, they're using a battering ram. There's a splintering sound.

And then a strange and beautiful calm comes over Mary. Because she has courage. True grit. Right until the end. She is a god among men, a deity everlasting. Who needs this mortal coil?

As the door crashes open and the troops pour in, Mary smiles at them. A lovely, warm smile. A welcoming smile. Then she pats her hair, puts the gun in her mouth, and blows her brains out.

EPILOGUE ─────────────────────────────

ERICA STANDS ON THE PORCH looking out at the lovely sloping lawn, sloping down to the wide lovely Hudson on this balmy late-summer afternoon—September is the sweetest month. The lawn is full of people—laughing, chatting, eating, drinking. Erica's having a party in Moy's honor. Moy has just gotten engaged to television writer Jordan Monk and is visiting family in the East, showing off her fiancé. And no wonder, he's adorable and funny and smart, and Erica is swept up in her friend's happiness. In fact, some of it seems to be rubbing off on her.

Erica rented this beautiful old farmhouse on the river for the month. It's large and rambling and has a pool and sweeping views. She loves the Hudson Valley, filled with beauty and history and culture and fascinating people. Maybe she'll buy a place up here. Thanks to all the news she generated with the Homeland story, *The Erica Sparks Effect* is firmly on top in the ratings, and *Spotlight* has turned into a hit—and her stature and income have risen accordingly.

Down on the lawn, Greg is in some deep powwow with the good-looking young architect whom Leslie Burke Wilson brought along as her date. Greg looks so handsome and vital in cargo shorts and a blue oxford. Erica did something she long thought would be a bad idea: she hired Greg to executive produce *Spotlight*. She did it because (a) he's talented, and (b) she wanted to save her marriage. He was offered that two-year contract at a large Houston station, but they both knew the marriage wouldn't survive the separation. Because *Spotlight* demands less of her time than her nightly show, the arrangement is working out well. And Greg is thriving again, her equal, ally, and sounding board. And their marriage has never felt more solid. The old adage of what doesn't kill you makes you stronger is proving true.

There is one fly in the ointment. Erica has pulled away from Leslie and her glitterati crowd personally—keeping up was just too much work—but Leslie is still a consultant on *Spotlight*. She and Greg work together fine, but whatever chemistry there once was between them has played out. As to whether they ever slept together, Erica has been pretending, with limited success, that it doesn't really matter. But it does matter. Which is why she's afraid to find out.

As for James Jarrett and Neal Clark, they've both been charged with treason, conspiracy to commit murder, and a host of lesser crimes. They were denied bail and are languishing in a federal penitentiary. The case against them is ironclad, their trials will start in the spring, and both will spend the rest of their lives behind bars.

Erica watches as Jenny and three friends race across the lawn and leap into the pool. Jenny's lawyer was able to get the charges against her dropped. The amount of marijuana she sold was tiny, and her age, and the fact that marijuana possession has been decriminalized in Massachusetts all contributed to the judge's decision. The notes attesting to Jenny's sterling character from a half dozen famous journalists didn't hurt either. Procuring those took nothing more than a few phone calls. Yes, Erica lives in a world of privilege now, where doors magically open and favors are granted. And while she feels some guilt at her success and leverage, she will never hesitate to use it to help her daughter.

Their relationship has been flourishing since the day they had the serious talk back in August. Jenny is off to a good start at school, and while she still shows flashes of rebellion and anger, the decibel level is a quarter of what it was. And Erica's anxiety has decreased proportionally.

The farmhouse is an hour and change north of Manhattan, and most nights Erica makes it back up the river after her show (a feat made easier by the car and driver she negotiated from the network).

Out on the Hudson, the *Clearwater* sails by. A beautiful old wooden schooner, she was the life/love project of Pete Seeger, his clarion call back in the 1960s to clean up the filthy river. Today swimmers dot the glistening blue expanse. *Maybe we can save the planet*, Erica thinks in an uncharacteristic burst of optimism. One cut short by a wave of nausea. They've been coming with some regularity. She's about to head inside when Moy comes up on the porch.

"Okay, amigo, best party ever."

"Jordan is a *catch*. Now if only the two of you would move east."

"Stranger things have happened."

"Seriously?"

"An offer has been dangled. As to whether I accept or not, that's a different story."

"I'll be your best friend forever."

The old pals hug and it feels like home. "I'm going to go put on my bathing suit," Moy says, heading inside.

"Come on in, Mom!" Jenny calls from the pool.

"Your wish is my command," Erica calls back.

Erica goes inside and is crossing the living room on her way upstairs when Leslie Wilson comes out of the kitchen.

"I *had* to get that salmon mousse recipe from your caterer. Does that make me a poacher?"

"Only of salmon." There's a pause, and the two women look at each other before Erica takes the leap she's been resisting. "At least, I *hope* it's only salmon."

"Well, Mary Poppins I'm not. I may have *tried* to poach a certain two-legged mammal . . ."

"And?"

"To quote him, 'I have filet mignon at home.' Tired line, but message received."

Erica can't contain the big smile that spreads across her face.

"Now let me go find someone to flirt with. I'm bored with the architect already. For better or worse, but not for cornices." Leslie disappears, leaving a whiff of bergamot in her wake.

Erica heads up to her bathroom, which has a window looking down at the lawn. She takes another moment to savor the success of the party, Jenny splashing in the pool, Greg organizing a game of volleyball. Then she takes out the pregnancy test kit, sits on the toilet, and pees on the wand. She puts it on the side of the sink and stands up, feeling a mix of trepidation and . . . trepidation. Is she really ready to go through it again? Not just the inconvenience and discomfort of the pregnancy, but all the emotional ramifications with Greg and Jenny, and then there's her career, and her still dubious mothering skills, and when Jenny heads off to college the new baby would be just five years old . . . and . . . and the list never ends.

And then there it is—the plus sign.

Uh-oh.

DISCUSSION QUESTIONS ────────────

1. What is your opinion of American secessionist movements? Should a state be allowed to secede from the union? If so, why? If not, why not?

2. Given the polarized state of American politics, do you worry for our future ability to communicate and compromise? What steps would it take to increase our national unity?

3. In *The Separatists* Erica suspects her husband Greg of cheating on her, yet she doesn't confront him for some time, fearful that he'll confirm her fears. What do think about this? Would you confront your spouse if you suspected him or her of cheating?

4. Erica's daughter Jenny starts smoking pot. Erica decides not to make a big deal out of it. Do think this is the right way to handle it? How harmful is marijuana? Do you think it is worse, or better, than alcohol?

5. Do you think Erica is a good mother? If so, why? If not, why not? What positive mothering skills does she have? What does she lack?

6. Mary Bellamy will stop at nothing to get what she wants. Have you known women with this level of ambition? Do you think ambitious women are held to a different standard than ambitious men?

7. Erica still struggles with the trauma of her abusive childhood. How do you think she does handling it? Do you think it's ever possible to reach closure on trauma, or is it more realistic to accept that you will always be scarred, and move forward with this acceptance?

8. Do you think Erica should forgive her mother, or keep her at emotional arms length, or some combination of the two?

9. Erica thinks about Truman Capote's famous line "Beware of answered prayers." She certainly pays a high price for her success. Do you think it's possible to have enormous success without paying some kind of emotional price?

10. Do you think Erica would be fun to hang out with? Is her intensity balanced by her warmth, her humor, her intelligence, and her loyalty? Or is she just a little too intense to be friends with?

11. In many ways, Erica is a traditional journalist, with an abiding faith in the truth. Has the truth been devalued in our culture? Has it become difficult to determinate what is truth and what is a lie? If so, what are some ways in which we can expose lies and validate truths?

ACKNOWLEDGMENTS ————————————————

FIRST AND FOREMOST I ACKNOWLEDGE Sebastian Stuart, my "pardner" in crime in this wonderful series. Together we've made Erica Sparks come alive, and we've had fun every step of the way. Neither Seb nor I like perfect people because, frankly, they're boring. And so Erica is certainly not perfect. But boy is she interesting!

Special thanks to the amazing editor LB Norton, who edits all Erica's journeys. Thank you for your smart and witty pen!

This publishing team is amazing! They embraced "Erica" and all her journeys. And they, along with me, were so pleased at how closely her journeys foresaw national and even international news. Daisy Hutton, Publisher, has heart and vision. Thank you! Amanda Bostic, Associate Publisher, is a joy to work with. Her honesty and insight is invaluable! Thank you. Becky Monds. Hey lady, we go back a long time. You are simply the best! Karli Jackson, Associate Acquisitions Editor, such an invaluable member of the team with great ideas! Thank you! Kimberly Carlton, Associate Editor, I'm so happy to watch your journey. Thank you! Jodi Hughes, Associate Editor, you always go for it 110%. That does not go unnoticed. Thank you! Paul Fisher, Senior Marketing Director, you jumped in to this series with all your heart and have had a major part in its success. Thank you! Kristen Golden, Marketing Manager, I love your "we'll get it done" spirit. Thank you! Meghan O'Brien, Senior Marketing Associate, along with Kristen, you're getting it done, and it makes a world of difference! Thank you. And thank you all for embracing Erica and her journeys! Kristen Ingebretsen makes the book cover sing. Her artistic talent brings Erica's story, literally, to the cover. Thank you!

Thank you to my wonderful agent, Todd Shuster, who has been with me from the very beginning when he thought I might have a book in me. Now, our 17th book later, I trust his judgement 110%. I am blessed with Todd because he is more than an agent, he is my friend.

A special shout out to young Christian, from Auntie Lis.

Mom and Dad, Inga and Richard Wiehl, You told me that sometimes life wasn't fair, but you also told me to hold on to my moral compass and that would right everything. I have. Thank you ! Love, Lis

ABOUT THE AUTHOR

 LIS WIEHL is the New York Times bestselling author of over a dozen novels. She is a Harvard Law School graduate and has served as a federal prosecutor in the state of Washington and as a tenured faculty member at The University Washington School of Law. She is a former legal analyst and commentator for the Fox News Channel.

Visit her online at liswiehlbooks.com
Facebook: Lis Wiehl, Fox News Legal Analyst and Author
Twitter: @LisWiehl